FIRST CITIZEN

A THRILLER

RICK BOSWORTH

UPrising Publishing, LLC
Upper Peninsula, MI

FIRST CITIZEN

ISBN Number: 978-1-7341412-1-4 (Paperback)
ISBN Number: 978-1-7341412-0-7 (eBook)

Published by UPrising Publishing, LLC 2020
Upper Peninsula, Michigan

For Mary, forever.

If ever a time should come when vain and aspiring men shall possess the highest seats in government, our country will stand in need of experienced patriots to prevent its ruin.

— Samuel Adams

PART I

I hope I shall possess firmness and virtue enough to maintain what I consider the most enviable of all titles, the character of an honest man.

— George Washington

If you must break the law, do it to seize power: in all other cases observe it.

— Julius Caesar

CHAPTER 1

Josh Reid Allen stared at the puddle of blood on his plate.

He had never noticed how much ketchup looked like blood, but he was seeing many things differently now. The tepid red goop slid down the back of his throat, leaving a metallic taste in his mouth. He suppressed a gag reflex and swallowed hard.

"Daddy, what's the matter?"

Allen quickly gathered himself and looked across the booth at Nicholas, his only child. His perfect little six-year-old boy. The boy had his father's flaxen red hair and striking pale-blue eyes. His hair was short but unruly, just like his dad's, and his easy smile displayed the gap where his two front baby teeth had recently been. Allen envied his newness: smooth, unblemished skin; clear eyes; silky hair. All purity and innocence. He threw a pile of paper napkins over his ketchup puddle, no longer hungry for the few fries that remained on his plate.

"Nothing, buddy. Daddy's just thinking about something."

Allen was a man of average stature but owned the ground he stood on. He had a muscular build, and a quiet intensity that most men respected or learned to. He spoke infrequently and only when he had something worth saying. These days, he mostly kept to himself. He passed the hours reading books on a broad range of topics and playing war battle video games.

He checked his watch, and then shot a look out the window at his pickup truck. He had parked the truck in angled parking, directly across the street from their booth, with the truck bed fully visible. Allen had been keeping close watch on his truck since he and Nicholas had sat down to eat over an hour ago. On this Sunday afternoon, the good citizens of Adel, Iowa, were paying no attention to his old beat-up truck, or, more precisely, to what he had hidden in the bed under the tarp. It was a typical January day in the little town. The temperature was well below freezing, and the folks he saw bustling around the town square had their heads down and coat collars turned up as they battled the biting wind. No doubt most of its 4,000 residents were returning from church, as Adel had always been a good, God-fearing town. Allen himself had not seen the inside of a church in five years.

The diner had not changed much since Allen was a kid. Its big front windows looked out over the town square, and the prized seats were the weathered booths along these windows, where Allen and his son were now happily ensconced. There were many four-top tables aligned in rows in the big open room, and a sit-down counter near the kitchen. The place smelled of fried eggs and grilled burgers, specialties that were served all day. The waitresses were all born-and-raised locals who wore name tags with their real names, not ironic pseudonyms like Flo or Betty. Most were matronly and made you feel right at home.

Nicholas hummed softly as he colored his placemat with the crayons the waitress had provided. Allen had done the same thing in this same booth with his own father, and his father, in turn, had logged some time in this booth as a boy as well. Tradition still mattered in a town like Adel.

Allen glanced compulsively out the window again and looked past his truck to the Dallas County Courthouse, the jewel of the Adel town square. Built in 1902 and added to the National Register of Historic Places seventy-one years later, it was a four-story masterpiece that had been modeled on a French castle. It was constructed of flat gray Bedford stone and distinguished by its rounded turrets and 130-foot-high clock tower. The streets of the town square were red cobblestone and tree-lined, with nostalgic lampposts sporting banners that proudly welcomed visitors to Adel. Most times, its citizens greeted each other by first name. All others got a hello and a smile. It was a town where the locals left their front doors unlocked and their cars running as they ran into Hennessy News to grab the morning paper. Allen was certain that Washington politicians conjured up Adel when they spoke of the mythical "Main Street USA" in their patronizing sound bites; he had come to despise the treasonous bastards.

"Daddy, can I have your fries?"

Allen pushed his plate toward his son, who ate a few of the cold fries and then started to play with the ketchup-soaked napkin on the plate.

"Don't play with that," he said, more sharply than he'd intended. He winced as he saw Nicholas's face fall. His son was such a sweet and sensitive boy. Allen wondered where he'd got that from. Certainly not his mother.

He softened his tone. "Hey, buddy... Wanna play the thinking cap game?"

Nicholas pursed his lips, closed his eyes, and shook his head no in an exaggerated flurry.

"C'mon. It'll be fun. You like to play."

"I dunno."

"Well, I promise this will be the last time we play. Will you do it for me?"

"Okay," he sighed.

Allen clapped his hands together and then slid their plates to the front of the booth, away from the window. He winked at Nicholas, who was smiling in anticipation of what he knew would come next. With a theatrical flourish, Allen pantomimed withdrawing an imaginary hat from beneath the table. He shook it out and made a show of presenting it to the boy for inspection. Nicholas giggled and nodded his head vigorously in agreement. After gaining this acceptance, Allen slowly secured and adjusted the imaginary hat on his head and pronounced, "I now have on my thinking cap."

"My turn, Daddy. I put mine on now."

Nicholas then pantomimed securing his own imaginary hat on his head. His favorite part of the ritual was always when Allen closely examined his hat and offered his approval. It was Allen's favorite part, too. That done, Nicholas furrowed his brow and narrowed his eyes. He knew that when he had his thinking cap on, he and his father would talk about important things, and that he would have to think really hard.

Allen's heart ached as he watched his son; he had been dreading this moment for months. He had practiced in front of a mirror so he would be able to keep his emotions in check, but as he began to speak, his throat immediately closed up and he felt his lower lip quiver. *Shit.* He grabbed his glass of water with both hands and took a long sip. *C'mon, Marine... You can do this.*

"I gotta go somewhere," Allen began, "so I won't be able to see you next Saturday like I always do."

"Where are you goin', Daddy?"

"Oh, there's just something I gotta do, far away."

"Will you be back for the Saturday after the next?"

"We'll see, buddy. But first I have to tell you some important things. Things I want you to remember. Okay?"

Nicholas's face was etched with as much concentration as a six-year-old could muster.

Allen cleared his throat. "Be a good boy, son. Always be on time, and always do your best, okay? Treat others as you want to be treated. Be true to—"

He scanned the boy's face for any glimmer of understanding, but saw none; he knew Nicholas was too young to understand the significance of this moment. Allen desperately hoped that his son's little thinking cap would burn enough of this moment into his memory to provide him with some comfort in the difficult years that lay ahead.

"Remember I was telling you about a guy named Socrates last week?" Allen asked.

"Uh, I dunno," Nicholas said with a shrug of his small shoulders.

"Socrates was a Greek philosopher, a great thinker from a long time ago." Allen touched his own thinking cap for emphasis. "Socrates said all kinds of smart things. Like 'To find yourself, think for yourself,' and 'An unexamined life is not worth living.' When you get older, I want you to read some of the things this man said, okay?"

"I will, Daddy."

Allen had so much more he wanted to tell him. But a boy's thinking cap was only so big. This would have to do. He started to take off his own thinking cap, but stopped.

"One more thing," he said. He paused to look around, then leaned in. "Don't take shit from anyone."

Nicholas burst out laughing. "Daddy said a bad word."

"You're not gonna tell Mommy, are you?"

"No, Daddy. I won't tell."

"Good boy."

Allen looked at this watch. It was 3:00 p.m. Time to go. Allen motioned to the waitress for the check. She smiled and nodded. Her name tag was unnecessary; she had been at the diner for over forty years. Everyone in Adel knew Lucy. She had served Josh pancakes and burgers his entire life. Indeed, she had served three generations of Allen men at this booth.

Lucy approached the booth from behind and softly placed her hand on Allen's shoulder as she dropped the hand-scrawled check on the table.

"Well, Nicky, did you like your burger, sweetheart?" Lucy asked.

"I'm Nicholas. 'Cause I'm six now," he said, thrusting six fingers in her direction.

"A whole six, huh?" Lucy said. "You're a big boy now. Okay, Nicholas, how was your burger?"

"It was… good," the boy responded. "I like the cheese."

"Just like your daddy," she said as she squeezed Allen's shoulder. He rested his hand on top of hers and turned his head to look up at her. Her face was gaunt, lined by a two-pack-a-day habit she'd picked up in high school. Her stained teeth had been replaced with uniform white veneers, something Allen still had not gotten used to. Her voice was as sharp as chewed gravel. But her eyes still twinkled, her spirit untouched by age.

Lucy leaned over and whispered into Allen's ear. "So good to see you again, darlin'. Sorry to hear about you and Claire." She patted his shoulder. "See you soon, Nicholas." She gave him a wink, squeezed Allen's shoulder once more, and then returned to serving the good people of Adel.

Allen paid the bill at the counter, tipping Lucy generously, as he always did, and then helped Nicholas bundle up before they left the restaurant. Allen hated how his ex-wife dressed their son. He had synthetic snow pants and mittens, and a big, puffy down jacket and hood. He looked like an over-inflated balloon. The outfit made him move jerkily, like the Apollo astronauts in that grainy television footage of the moon landing. Allen preferred that his child support money be spent on more appropriate winter gear—Carhartt, maybe—but his ex-wife, as she had done in most matters since his divorce, took his money and spent it as she wished.

Allen opened the diner door, holding it securely against the wind, and stepped out into the cold. He held his son's hand as they crossed the street. Wispy snow fell from a pewter sky. The road surface was plowed down to a compacted sheet of ice. He walked to the passenger side of the truck and buckled his son into his seat. As he walked around the back of the vehicle, he traced his fingers along the tarp, felt the lines of the cargo underneath. The thought of his son sitting so near it gave him a chill.

He drove across town from the diner to his old house on Rapids Street in less than five minutes. Too short a trip to even bother with the truck's heater. Since his divorce three years ago, he had been to the house every Saturday for his court-ordered visitation. These Saturdays meant everything to Allen, and he never missed a visit. For the past two years he had been living on his younger brother's couch in an off-campus apartment at Iowa State, a hundred-mile round trip from Adel.

The judge had given the house to Claire, despite the fact that it was her infidelity that had ended the marriage. Then Claire had moved the guy into the house *he* was still paying for. Brad and Allen had worked together, and Brad and his then-wife had been over to the house several times for dinner and drinks. Allen ruminated on the injustice of it all, how the law turned a man into a cuckold.

Allen typically felt a surge of anger every time he pulled up to the house, but not today. Today was different.

Allen got his son out of the truck and suppressed his emotions as they walked toward the front porch. *I can't believe I am saying goodbye to him. Play it like every other Saturday. Nothing unusual.*

"You be a good boy," he said. "Remember what we talked about today."

"I will, Daddy. Love you."

"Love you too, buddy."

Allen kissed his son on the top of his head, then took a knee and wrapped him in a bear hug. The boy squeezed him back, laying his head on his father's shoulder, and Allen's dam broke, raw emotion flooding his body. He began to shake, hot tears ran down his cheeks. He clutched his son tighter and tried to steady himself.

The creaking of the front door interrupted their embrace. The boy wriggled free. Allen wiped his eyes dry, then rose to his feet. Claire stood in the doorway, her arms folded across her chest, lips pursed. She was a tall, sturdy Midwestern woman with shiny blond hair, pulled back to give her face a pinched look. She was still attractive, but she had aged since the divorce.

Nicholas trotted up the front steps, gave his mother a quick hug, and entered the house. And with that he was gone.

"I appreciate you letting me see him on Sunday," Allen said.

"Well… don't make it a habit. It messes up our weekend, you know."

"It won't be a problem," Allen said.

"I checked my account, and your check bounced this month. I—"

"That can't be. I mailed it last week. Tuesday the twelfth," Allen said.

"What year did you write?"

"This year—2021," he said.

"No, you didn't, dumbass. I talked to the bank. They won't cash it because you wrote last year's date, 2020. You need to write me a new check right now, or I'm gonna have to call the court."

"That won't be a problem, either. I'll get it in the mail tomorrow." He was lying. It would be the first check he'd miss in three years.

Brad came to the front door now. He put his arm around Claire and then leaned in and kissed her on the lips, one eye on Allen. He smirked, then retreated back into the safety of the living room, raising his middle finger in silent salute as he walked away. Allen noticed, with a small measure of satisfaction, that Brad had added an extra chin and a thirty-pound paunch to go along with his receding hairline.

"I cannot believe you're with that ass-clown," he said.

Claire closed the front door behind her to just a crack. "Brad makes good money, Josh. He's VP of sales at the company now. You know, the company you quit. The *fourth*-largest seed company in the United States."

"You know I never wanted to leave the Marine Corps to be a corporate chimp—like him."

"Yeah, you and your hell-raising Marine Forced Recognizance buddies—"

"It's Force Recon," Allen shouted. "How many times have I told you that?"

"Whatever," she said. "It's no life for a wife. Or a family. I needed a house and nice things. Brad remodeled our kitchen, and we got a second car—my car. We're even going to Hawaii in a couple of months. These things are important." She paused and pursed her lips again as though she'd smelled something unpleasant. "And look at you. Unemployed and sleeping on your brother's couch."

"I'm not willing to do what he does. Compromise. Lie and cheat. So, good for you, Claire. Congratulations on finding the man of your dreams."

"How do you think your son will see you, Josh? Especially when he gets older and understands what a loser you are?"

"I won't be around next Saturday," he said, not rising to the bait. "Take care of our son, will you?"

"Why? What? What do you mean?" she asked.

Allen reached into his jacket and pulled out a sealed envelope. His hand shook as he handed it to her.

"Give this to Nicholas. Make sure our son remembers who he is. Who his father was."

"What the hell is this?"

"Just give it to him."

Allen looked up and saw Nicholas watching him from the front window. He tried to smile but couldn't. He waved feebly, and the boy beamed and waved back. Allen's upper lip trembled. White noise filled his ears as the blood drained from his face. He grasped the porch railing for balance and closed his eyes to steady himself.

"Josh!" Claire shouted.

"Just give it to him." He turned and walked off the porch without looking back.

He got into the truck and sat for a moment, looking straight ahead. Finally, he turned the key in the ignition, gunned the engine and sped off, headed east on US-6 toward Des Moines. He had a long drive ahead of him.

CHAPTER 2

Vienna, Virginia, the gem of Fairfax County, consistently ranked in the top ten of every annual Best Places to Live list in every beautiful people magazine. Located about thirty miles west of Washington, DC, it had an upscale downtown, beautiful hiking and biking trails, and all the caramel macchiato and skinny cocktails one could drink.

Vienna was the type of place where the student parking lot at the local high school (James Madison High, ranked third nationally) was full of shiny BMWs and Audis, while the faculty lot looked like Saul's Used Car Emporium.

Ex-FBI agent and spy Robert Hanssen was a former resident of Vienna, thanks to the largesse of the Russian government. Vienna was also home to another FBI agent, George Nelson Moore, and his wife, Kacey Anne Moore.

It was Inauguration Day: Wednesday, January 20, 2021. George was shaving in the downstairs half-bath of his Vienna townhouse, preparing for another workday. He had commandeered this bathroom, having long ago abandoned the master bath to Kacey

Anne. It was just easier this way.

George stood square to the mirror. One hand gripped the sink while the other clenched his twin-blade razor. He pressed the razor to his neck and drove it downward, against the grain. He felt the pull of the razor against his coarse stubble. His father had taught him to shave with the flow, but George preferred going against the grain.

He leaned into the mirror and watched the blood spots emerge on his neck. He was a sturdy man with blunt features. Fair skinned, with a thick, flat nose that squared off at the bottom. He had a full head of reddish-brown hair, now streaked with gray. His deep-set pale gray eyes, once luminous, had grown dull with age.

George had just turned forty-nine a month ago and was at the end of his twenty-five-year career as an FBI Special Agent. He was not feeling particularly special these days. It had been a long twenty-five years, and he was ready to give back his gun and badge. He would be eligible to retire from the FBI on his fiftieth birthday, December 14, 2021. In Bureau culture you were anointed "KMA" on this glorious date, which meant everyone could "Kiss My Ass." But George would not stick around for any of his KMA time. He would leave the FBI when he became eligible.

George looked at the age lines etched in his forehead and around his eyes and mouth. He still maintained the muscular physique of a younger man, but his face carried all the stress and struggle of his life. He wondered, not for the first time, where all the years had gone. He and Kacey Anne had been in their townhouse for eighteen years. She had been born and raised in Vienna. In her day, Kacey Anne had been the "It" girl at Madison High, the most beautiful and powerful girl in school. She had had it all then: head cheerleader, homecoming queen, varsity quarterback play toy. She'd even bedded a few college frat boys, and a teacher or two.

Her enchanted life had begun to fade when she'd enrolled at George Madison University, where she'd quickly learned she was not the only "It" girl in Northern Virginia. She'd met George in the spring of 1993 at a GMU party (she a freshman on academic probation, he a senior), and locked on after she'd learned he was going to be an attorney.

She had closely monitored George's earning potential and committed herself only after he'd graduated from law school. She was sure that, as an attorney's wife, she would ascend to her rightful place at the apex of Vienna's nouveau riche. But then George had gone ahead and joined the FBI; his fixed government salary had afforded her none of the nice things she felt she richly deserved. Kacey Anne had seen this as a betrayal and reminded George of it often during their nineteen-year marriage.

George was not sure when he had emotionally withdrawn from the marriage, but he and Kacey Anne had been roommates for many years now. George buried himself in work, while Kacey Anne held court at the local bar. George had never cheated on his wife, though he struggled with the imposed celibacy. He suspected Kacey Anne had not extended him the same fidelity.

George came to understand that he had remained in his loveless marriage due to a toxic blend of loyalty, nobility, and inertia. But the past few years had seen him slowly awaken from his stupor. He now acknowledged he had to end it. Perhaps his impending retirement would finally spur him to action.

George finished shaving and splashed his face. The cold water stung the razor burn on his neck, causing the blood to flow once more. He had to stoop to see his reflection in the mirror. Kacey Anne had insisted that they build the half-bath to "normal" proportions, which left a large man like George (six feet tall and 215 pounds) constantly ducking and banging into things. He had long limbs and freakishly large hands. To a keen observer his shape was somewhat odd. He had a smallish head atop narrow shoulders, with wide hips and large thighs. This configuration centered his power at his core, which gave him prodigious strength. Not showy gym strength, but real power that allowed him to toss larger men around like rag dolls should the need arise.

George dabbed his bleeding neck with a swatch of toilet paper, then pressed it hard against his neck to stanch the flow of blood. Kacey Anne called out to him. Her voice effortlessly traveled from the kitchen, down the hall, and through his bathroom's hollow-core door. George's back muscles tensed, which raised his shoulders slightly. In his reflection he saw a slight grimace come over his face.

"George—don't forget, we're having dinner and drinks with the Thompsons tonight. You'd better be home on time. We had to reschedule last week because you worked late. I don't want to blow them off again."

No response from the bathroom.

"George! Did you hear—"

"Yeah. Got it. I should be home on time. Just doing crowd work at the inauguration today. No problem."

"You always say no problem, but then there's always a problem. How about for once you forget about your fucking job and make it home on time because I asked you to?"

More silence from the bathroom.

"Trent's an executive VP now, you know. He just bought a brand-new black BMW M5. It's beautiful. Fully loaded. Must've cost over a hundred grand, easy." Trent Thompson and his wife lived nearby, but in the neighborhood filled with McMansions, housekeepers, and nannies. Trent was some kind of corporate hotshot. Kacey Anne knew his company and title, George did not. She refused to host the Thompsons at their townhouse, which meant another night of inane conversation in a place he didn't belong.

"Trent's a tool," George said.

"No he's not. You think everyone's a tool."

No response.

"Trent promised to give me a ride in his new car. So you better be home on time."

George splashed his face again. His hands lingered over his eyes for a moment and he closed them, then withdrew his hands and opened them again. As he dried his face, he saw dots of red blood on the white towel and raised his eyes to the mirror to check his neck. Still bleeding. He pressed another square of toilet paper to his skin. He could faintly hear Kacey Anne going on about something, but he drifted away as he stared at his reflection.

George did not resemble anyone he knew, living or dead. Not even a slight coincidental likeness to his adoptive parents, Rose and Walt Moore. He knew nothing of his biological parents other than what he was told: that they were local high school sweethearts who died in a car accident before their twentieth birthdays. No other biological family was ever mentioned, and George knew that any questions would draw tears from Rose and the belt from Walt.

Though he knew better than to question it, the car accident story always felt a bit hollow to George. Sure it was *possible*, but as an FBI agent he knew that possible was for defense attorneys desperate to conjure up reasonable doubt in weak-minded jurors. George, like the rest of us, lived in the land of the probable, and as such knew there was probably more to his adoption story, and that he would probably would never know the truth.

George was unsure what good the truth would do him at this point. He had long since packed this stuff away, and only lamented over it at the end of one of his whiskey nights, which had become more frequent as the years passed in the townhouse with Kacey Anne.

The cut on his neck finally stopped bleeding. George buttoned up his shirt, ran his fingers through his hair, and walked toward the kitchen. He still moved with the grace of the athlete he had once been, and reached the kitchen in a few strides. It had a U-shaped configuration, and dark press-board cabinets and outdated appliances. The townhouse had been built in the early 1980s with construction-grade materials. George had never liked it, but Kacey Anne had to live in Vienna, and the townhouse was all they could afford on his FBI salary. As it was, George had had to borrow the down payment from Kacey Anne's father. He had never forgiven himself for having submitted to this indignity.

Kacey Anne stood at the kitchen sink with her back to George. She was wearing tight black yoga pants and a form-fitting purple top that hugged her ample curves. Her mane of highlighted blond hair fell down below her shoulders. Even at forty-five years old, she could still stop traffic. George slipped in behind her and lightly gripped her shoulders with his large hands. Kacey Anne jumped and let out a loud gasp. She whipped around to face him.

"Jesus, George! How many times have I told you not to sneak up on me like that?"

She fixed him with her piercing green eyes. George felt her gaze in the pit of his stomach. She had full lips, and her teeth had been whitened to the perfect shade, just short of reality show contestant. Her skin was baby smooth and bronzed by regular tanning booth visits.

"I'm heading out now. I'll see you tonight." George leaned in and gave Kacey Anne a peck on the cheek, the kind of kiss a man gave his grandmother, or the third-grade teacher he unexpectedly ran into at the supermarket.

"Remember, don't be late. We have—"

"Yup. Got it."

"And be nice to Trent tonight. Maybe he can help you get a good retirement job at his company. You know… finally be a *real* attorney and make some *real* attorney money."

George grabbed his jacket and turned to the door. As he opened it, Kacey Anne delivered her closing salvo.

"If you're late, I'm going to the Thompsons' without you. I'm gonna get my ride in that new Beemer."

"Got it," George said under his breath as he closed the door behind him.

CHAPTER 3

Allen drove straight from Iowa to Washington, DC, a caffeine-fueled trek that ended Monday morning when he collapsed on a hard bed at a Best Western one mile from the United States Marine Corps War Memorial. He secluded himself in his room for two days and nights. He ate out of the vending machines in the hallway. He left his room only once to walk one block to a local gas station to purchase a winter hat and healthier junk food. He kept his room shades pulled shut, his deadbolt locked, his .45 pistol within reach, and his television on CNN and Fox News. He scanned for any breaking news but saw none. All quiet. Allen knew this silence was deceptive, and that by now they most likely knew of the theft and had blacked out any media coverage.

Allen stood at the rear of the USMC War Memorial in Arlington, Virginia. He could see the Washington Monument in the distance, a white spike piercing the dark gray clouds. A few inches of snow and ice covered the ground. He checked the weather app on his iPhone: current temperature 27 degrees, 5 mph ESE wind, 20 percent chance of snow. He exhaled a sigh of relief and watched his frozen breath dissipate.

He had visited the memorial once before. It was a solemn place for him, and he was glad to be back. The memorial depicted the iconic 1945 photograph of six Marines raising a U.S. flag atop Mount Suribachi during the Battle of Iwo Jima in World War II. The bronze Marines stand thirty-two feet high, the raised Stars and Stripes a full sixty feet above the statue's black granite base. Today Allen would stand on the shoulders of these giants.

There was a hard case at his feet, dull green, about four feet long by two feet wide. It sat hidden under a tightly folded blue nylon tarp. Allen figured it weighed about fifty pounds. He nudged it with his right foot and felt its heft.

A few people stopped to say good morning and engage in banal conversation about the weather or the Washington Redskins' improbable deep playoff run; Allen had hastily purchased a Redskins winter hat at a gas station yesterday and was being mistaken for a die-hard fan. Allen smiled and nodded but did not allow any of these exchanges to linger. All these people would soon have microphones in their faces, basking in their fifteen minutes of fame. He was happy to see them go. He would have to set up soon, which would be the most dangerous part of his mission. He decided to avoid any further eye contact as he watched the live video stream on his iPhone.

Allen took several deep breaths to slow down his heart rate and counteract the adrenaline that had begun to ooze into his bloodstream. He fell back on his Marine Corps training. He had a mission to accomplish. He forced his racing mind to focus on the small incremental tasks at hand, tasks he had practiced until they were mastered. Allen was certain that what he was about to do was necessary. He forced himself not to think about the consequences, because that distraction might cause sloppiness and error. As he cleared his mind, a calm overtook him. *My time has come. I am doing this. I am good to go.*

Allen checked his watch: 11:40 a.m. (EST). He took one last look around and saw no one was in the area. He bent down, took the blue tarp off the case, and popped the big metal latches.

Inside the big green case sat an FGM-148F Javelin Missile System, the finest portable shoulder-launched fire-and-forget anti-tank missile system in the world. Made in the USA, it had wreaked havoc for the US Army and Marine Corps, as well as twenty other friendly countries, for the past twenty-five years. It consisted of two parts: the Command Launch Unit (CLU) and the launcher tube and missile. The operator simply attached the four-foot launch tube and missile to the CLU before each shot. The tube had built-in electronics and a locking hinge system that made it easy to assemble and fire. Allen had the whole thing put together, with target GPS coordinates entered, in under five minutes. All he had to do now was point and shoot. He carefully placed the assembled unit on the ground and covered it once again with the blue tarp.

Ten minutes to go. Allen felt a sharp acuity in all his senses. The air around him seemed electrically charged. He felt so... *alive.* Suddenly, in his peripheral vision, he saw movement off to his right. He turned to see a big dog pulling a young girl toward him. In an instant the dog and girl were upon him. The dog went for the tarp. Allen beat the dog to it and stood on the tarp's edge to hold it in place. Despite the cold, Allen felt beads of sweat begin to run down his spine.

"What's your doggie's name?" Allen asked the little girl as he bent at the waist to pet him.

The dog was a yellow Labrador that looked about three or four years old. The little girl was about seven or eight. Both were adorable. The dog wagged his tail and licked Allen's hand. The girl was out of breath and holding onto the leash with all her strength.

"Dougie! No!" she said. "Sorry, mister. He's friendly."

"Good boy, Dougie," Allen said as he petted the dog's head and slyly guided him further away from the tarp.

"Yeah. We named him Dougie. You know, after the president," she said.

"Douglas Turner."

"Yeah, that's the guy."

"Where are your parents?" Allen asked.

"My mom's in the car. Too cold for her. Dougie had to pee, so—"

"Well, you should probably be getting back—"

"What's under the thing, mister?" she asked. She pointed a mittened hand at the tarp.

"Uhm..." Allen's mind raced as he looked down at it. "My cat's sleeping under there. So you and Dougie better get going."

It was a pretty lame response, but it was all he had. Allen looked at his watch: 11:55 a.m. (EST). His stomach knotted.

"Ha!" The little girl rolled her eyes. "You're weird. C'mon, Dougie. Let's go."

The little girl pulled Dougie away from Allen and back toward her mother's car. Allen's thoughts flashed to his son.

"What's your name?" Allen shouted at the little girl, who was just about to round the memorial to his left.

"Emily."

"My name's Josh." Allen slowly waved goodbye to the girl. "Remember me, Emily."

The little girl waved back and smiled, a puzzled look on her face. Allen watched as she disappeared from view behind the memorial.

He looked at his watch, then at the video on his iPhone. Yes! It was starting, right on time.

Allen threw the tarp off the missile launcher, shouldered it, and sat down on the ground. He gave himself a nice stable platform— knees bent, feet flat on the ground, back upright with a slight forward lean. He looked through the CLU viewfinder, found his target, and checked the GPS coordinates. The missile had a solid lock on the target and would now be automatically guided.

Allen pulled his face from the viewfinder and checked his iPhone. He needed to hit his target at just the right time. These last few minutes were the most dangerous. He was sitting in a wide-open public area with a missile launcher on his shoulder. He felt naked. As his eyes remained fixed on his iPhone, time slowed to a crawl. His heart began to beat faster and faster. He took deep breaths in a futile attempt to calm himself, and then saw what he was looking for. *There it is! He's starting to talk!* Allen dropped his iPhone and pushed his face back into the viewfinder. His hands shook.

"Fire in the hole!" Allen whispered to himself. He took a deep breath and held it to prevent inhaling the toxins exhausted by the missile.

He fired the weapon, and the missile launched out of its tube. Allen felt the launcher kick against his shoulder, then saw the missile levitate in the air about sixty feet in front of him. The next second, Allen heard an explosion and saw the rear end of the missile dip as fire shot out of it. The missile then rapidly gained speed and height, about 500 feet, as it searched out its target. He smelled smoke and burned fuel as he reached into his pocket for his binoculars. While maintaining his view of the speeding missile, he raised the binoculars to his eyes. The missile was now closing in on the target three miles away. As it approached, it dove straight down and then dropped right on top of its GPS coordinates. Bull's-eye. Allen first saw the smoke cloud, then heard the explosion. It was louder than he expected. A huge fireball erupted, covering the entire targeted area. The thermobaric warhead had done its job. Allen pulled the binoculars from his eyes and tossed them away. He had seen enough.

He got to his feet, turned around, and mouthed the words of the monument inscription: *"In Honor and Memory of The Men of the United States Marine Corps Who Have Given Their Lives to Their Country Since 10 November 1775."* He said a silent prayer in honor of these men and hoped that one day he would rest among them. There would be no monument erected for him, not for what he had just done. He was no longer a father, friend, or neighbor. He would forever be "the man who did the deed." Allen was at peace with his decision. The rest he would leave to the historians and philosophers. He hoped his countrymen would not squander the opportunity he had just given them. *Sometimes bad things must be done for the greater good.*

He slumped down on the ground now, his back to the rear of the War Memorial as he faced east. The skies were clearing; a few sunbeams knifed through the receding clouds. Allen wished he could take this as some sort of divine omen, but he had lost his faith many years ago.

The smoke and the fire cloud above the target were more intense now. He saw a few helicopters circling the target, and heard the faint *whomp whomp* of their rotor blades in the distance. Allen turned away from the mayhem. *I did it. Holy shit. I really did it.*

He kicked away the spent missile tube and saw that his blue tarp was blowing around in the wind, about fifty feet from him. This ghostly apparition transfixed him, and he watched it float around for what felt like a long time. Then, blinking, he retrieved his iPhone from the ground and dialed 9-1-1. Allen told the operator that the guy they were looking for was at the USMC War Memorial, and that he was armed and extremely dangerous. He asked them to send the SWAT team immediately. He ended the call and threw his iPhone as far as he could. He no longer needed it.

He pulled out his .45 pistol and put it in his lap. He knew suicide would be cleaner, but he could not shake the notion that it was a coward's death. He could not sully the honorable ground on which he sat. No, this was better. He was ready to die, but only on his terms. He closed his eyes, took a deep breath, and waited for the cavalry to arrive.

But it wasn't the cavalry that arrived. Allen heard the wail of a police siren grow louder and more persistent, approaching from behind him. He then saw a single patrol car whiz by on the circular road that surrounded the memorial. The patrol car—lights and siren blaring—did not even slow down as it passed him. Allen saw only one cop in the car, driving haphazardly, tires screeching as he rounded the circle and disappeared out of sight. The officer didn't even look in his direction.

The cop then made a second pass around the circle, this time jamming on the brakes about 100 feet in front of Allen and then peeling out again for a third lap around the circle. Even at that distance, Allen was sure the cop had seen him. *They sent only one guy? This guy?*

The patrol car returned and finally came to an abrupt stop at a 45-degree angle in front of Allen. Allen looked calmly through the windshield into the face of a young officer. They locked gazes. The rookie's eyes were wide and frantic. He stared at the .45 pistol in Allen's lap, then flung open his door. The patrol car jumped forward. In his haste, he had not put it in park. He then attempted to jump out of the car but had forgotten to release his seat belt and was violently jerked backward. Red-faced and clearly flustered, the rookie finally escaped his vehicle and took a cover position behind his driver's door, kneeling with his weapon drawn. His mouth moved spastically as he began to scream commands to Allen.

Allen raised his left, non-shooting hand to his ear and mouthed "I can't hear you." The rookie had forgotten to turn off the siren. *You gotta be kidding me,* he thought, suppressing a smile. *This kid must be right out of the academy.* Concerned citizens must have flooded police dispatch with hundreds of calls about the explosion, and it was the boy cop's fate to be the closest unit to the only call that mattered.

The cop kept yelling. Allen again pantomimed the gesture, and this time the cop got it. Without taking his eyes off Allen, he reached into his car and slapped around until the siren finally went silent.

"Stop!" the cop croaked. "Sir, show me your hands! Drop the gun! Turn around slowly with your hands up!"

Allen was still seated on the ground, with his back to the monument and his gun in his lap. He could not possibly comply with this jumble of commands, even if he wanted to. He could see that the kid was no more than twenty-one years old. He had a textbook cop haircut, probably the one he'd got for his police academy graduation photo. Allen recalled how scared he had been when he'd first got off the bus at Parris Island and all those Marine DIs had crawled up his ass. Although Allen only had about ten years on this kid, he felt somehow paternalistic toward him. He was just doing his job, after all—albeit poorly. And Allen knew that soon enough a swarm of real cops would arrive. Allen decided in an instant to give the kid a break. He would end this now and make him famous.

"Officer, we both know you are well within your department's lethal force policy here," he said. "It's a good shoot. No one will fault you. Go on, now."

"Sir, I'm gonna ask you to—"

"Officer, I am a suspicious male with a gun pointed in your direction. I am ignoring your commands. Shoot."

"Sir... *Sir*... I'm gonna—"

Allen raised his gun from his lap and pointed it at the cop, who was still in his cover position behind the car door. Allen inhaled and held the breath as he watched the cop's gun barrel for muzzle flash. He exhaled. Nothing.

Allen then realized that, even though they were only about twenty-five feet apart, and even if he could entice him to shoot, the boy cop could never deliver a clean kill shot at this distance. Hell, he probably couldn't even hit him once. And this would not do for this young hero-to-be. No, much better for the report to read that the hero cop had coolly aimed and delivered multiple lethal shots as the evil terrorist had advanced on him. Allen knew what he had to do.

He rose to his feet and slowly began to walk toward the cop. He held his gun in one hand, outstretched in front of him. Poor tactics, but he had no intention of shooting, so no harm done.

"Officer, I am an armed assailant who is now advancing toward you. I unequivocally pose an imminent threat of serious bodily injury or death to you. Shoot."

Allen stopped walking to provide the cop with an easy stationary target. He moved his outstretched arm away from his body to expose his chest. Allen's body tightened as he anticipated the bullet's arrival. Nothing. The cop's eyes remained wide, his body rigid.

Allen sighed, raised his gun, and began again to close distance on the cop. As Allen slowly paced forward, he thought about how the truth of this moment would be lost to history. He was certain that the politicians and agency heads would spin this into yet another binary fable of good guy vanquishes bad guy. So much of our recorded history was built on a foundation of such lies, he thought ruefully.

And what of this hero-to-be? Allen liked to think that the boy cop would honor their shared truth, but he knew he wouldn't. No, the kid would go along with the fable, the first of many such lapses of integrity ahead of him in his career. It would forever be the first item in the boy cop's promotion packets, and, given the infamy of Allen's action, this boy would promote rapidly. Allen thought about the boy cop growing old as he advanced through the ranks of the police department. How many promotions would he earn on Allen's blood? How many niceties would these promotions provide? An attractive wife, and a couple of kids with straight white teeth? A nice suburban house in a top school district? Island vacations to break up the DC winters? What was about to happen next would join the two of them together, forever.

Allen had now closed the distance to about seven feet. He stopped, took a deep breath and held it. Allen looked directly into the boy cop's wide, dark eyes.

"Shoot straight. Don't make a mess of it."

Allen raised his gun and fired three rounds intentionally over the boy cop's head. He saw the cop's eyes regain focus as his brain registered the loud blasts of the .45 pistol. Allen wondered how many rounds it would take to put him on the ground. He braced himself, knowing the bullets would soon come.

The last thing Allen saw was sustained muzzle flash; the last sound he heard the staccato *pop-pop-pop* of the boy cop's gun. His vision quickly narrowed and then went black.

Eight. It took eight shots to put Josh Reid Allen on his back.

A hero was indeed born on that cold January day. But was it the boy cop, or the man from Adel, bleeding the snowy ground red as he lay dying?

The answer to this question would decide the fate of America.

CHAPTER 4

George swam through a sea of people as he advanced through the crowd of more than one million that stood shoulder to shoulder on the National Mall. They had all come to watch the 2021 Presidential inauguration, which was about to take place at the West Front of the U.S. Capitol.

He was among the plebeian class, the non-ticketed unwashed masses that could get no closer than one-third of a mile from their president on this day. The plebes were penned in like cattle by temporary chain-link fences and waist-high iron barriers. But they didn't seem to mind—or notice—this indignity. It was a cold and cloudy day, with temperatures in the mid-twenties. They were all bundled in winter attire, including hats and scarves that obscured their faces and made George's job all the harder.

Rows of large monitors and loudspeakers sat on elevated perches at intervals all along the mall. This gave the plebes the illusion that they were part of the spectacle, much like a video scoreboard did for football fans in the nosebleed seats. George looked up at the monitor and saw that the vice president was about to take his oath of office. It was time for George to find his place for the ceremony. He maneuvered himself to his chosen spot, elbowing his way through the onlookers to a patch of ground that paralleled Sixth Street, in the center of the mall between the Smithsonian National Air and Space Museum and the National Gallery of Art. He faced east and saw the

U.S. Capitol Dome directly in front of him, half a mile in the distance.

All of the people in front of George, on the opposite side of Fourth Street and continuing east all the way to the inaugural podium, were members of the patrician class; the anointed ones who would watch their president take his oath from the secured, segregated areas that grew higher in rent the closer they got to the president. Entry to this patrician area required a ticket and the ability to pass a security background check, but the real common denominator for admission was money. Lots and lots of money.

The only inauguration element mandated by the United States Constitution was that the president make an oath or affirmation before he executed the office. Over the years various pageantry had expanded the inauguration from a simple oath-taking ceremony to a day-long dog-and-pony show designed to demonstrate to the world that the Jeffersonian republican ideology of "one man, one vote" was still relevant and divine. It was democracy on parade. George recognized this charade for what it was but kept his thoughts to himself.

He looked up at the nearest monitor and began to watch the VP take his oath. His mind quickly wandered. This would be his last inauguration. His FBI career felt like a lifetime that had passed in an instant. He wondered how far he could have been promoted if he had just boot-licked like Kacey Anne had wanted him to. He'd earned a merit promotion to squad supervisor but had voluntarily stepped down fourteen years ago after repeated clashes with his office management over his part in the PENTTBOM case. Yet another truth-to-power martyr.

George had been the lead agent on the FBI Washington Field Office Joint Terrorism Task Force, the JTTF, for the past ten years, but for the past three he had worked exclusively on investigating and mitigating counterterrorism incidents—what the FBI called

Guardian leads. George didn't mind the work. It kept him out of the office, a welcomed rarity in an age where agents were increasingly tethered to their computers. It was a Guardian lead that had brought George to this year's inauguration.

President Douglas Joseph Turner was being inaugurated for his second term. He had first been elected as a polarizing outsider who had promised to shake Washington politics to its core. His fervent supporters had demanded fundamental pragmatic reforms, and candidate Turner had promised that, if elected, he would do just that. Early in his first term, however, it had become apparent that President Turner had no intention of making good on any of his promises. He was not the leader of a new populist revolution after all; rather, he was yet another charlatan politician beholden to the shadowy big-money interests that had controlled Washington for over 100 years.

The mood of the country had turned dark. Bipartisanism and compromise were long gone, a quaint notion of a bygone era. The voters had fractured into autonomous ideological blocs, and by the end of mid-term elections, the two political parties had coalesced along similar ideological lines. The only thing on which both parties agreed was that this was the historical nadir of political discourse.

The traditional Republican voters (who had put Turner in office and still maintained their slight 52 percent majority) had separated into three distinct blocs, colloquially called the Unplugs, the Agitators, and the Undecideds. The Unplugs (about 25 percent of Republican voters) had grown so disillusioned and hopeless that they'd disengaged from the political process entirely. The Agitators (also about 25 percent, but at the opposite end of the spectrum) had fused into a radical Sons of Liberty–type group so full of rage that any spark would bring them into the streets. The Undecideds (the remaining 50 percent of the party) were somewhere in between these two groups and vacillated between apathy and anger.

The traditional Democratic voters, almost half the country at 48 percent, despised Turner. They had not voted for him in 2016 and were apoplectic that he'd won a second term in 2020. They broke down roughly the same as the Republicans (Unplugs-Agitators-Undecideds), but lacked their raw anger or call-to-action grassroots network.

By the 2020 election, Turner had totally sold out to big-money interests, and it was big money that had put him back in the Oval Office for his second term. His strategy was as simple as it was effective, and his strategists called it BAM: *Buy* the Undecideds by giving them tax breaks and government benefits (with the promise of more to come in his second term); *Alienate* the Unplugs so they remained away from the polls; and *Marginalize* the Agitators with propaganda and targeted high-profile law enforcement actions.

The BAM Strategy was based on simple math and simpler minds. The Undecideds from both parties represented a full 50 percent of American voters and were also the most malleable voting bloc. Buy enough of these voters with shiny baubles, keep the Unplugs on their couches watching reality television, put enough Agitators in prison, and even a turd like Turner could be re-elected to a second term. Math never lies.

However, math is ever dispassionate, and the BAM Strategy was born of arrogance. It did not fully account for the pulsating rage of the Agitators, and the lengths to which some in this group were willing to go. Turner was dancing on a land mine.

The Guardian lead that had brought George to this year's inauguration involved reports of a threat regarding a man from Charleston, South Carolina, named Edward Rutledge. One of his ex-girlfriends had advised that Rutledge was a radicalized member of an underground Republican Agitator cell, and that he had been stockpiling firearms and ammunition for some time. Rutledge had recently been fired from his job at a local factory for his continued incendiary anti-Turner rhetoric in the workplace. He had been heard drunkenly proclaiming at several bars around town that he would "take care" of Turner at the inauguration.

Members of the WFO JTTF had had Rutledge under surveillance as soon as he'd arrived in the DC area the day before the inauguration. He had been out drinking all that night, and had staggered back to his seedy motel a little after 4:00 a.m. He had not emerged from his room all day. A ruse call by the hotel manager had confirmed this. George had concluded that Rutledge posed no direct threat to the president or the inauguration ceremony, but had deemed it prudent to mingle among the crowd, regardless, to take its temperature. Another day out of the office.

The rousing refrain of the United States Marine Corps Band stirred George from his thoughts. He refocused on the monitor and saw that the VP had finished his oath. It was now Turner's turn. Turner strode up to the Chief Justice of the Supreme Court, his wife and children by his side, and in that famous repeat-after-me cadence clearly stated,

"I, Douglas Joseph Turner, do solemnly swear that I will faithfully execute the office of President of the United States, and will to the best of my ability, preserve, protect and defend the Constitution of the United States."

And with that it was done. Cue the faint clinking of Waterford crystal champagne flutes as the Masters of the Universe sipped their vintage Dom Perignon and congratulated each other on their purchase of another election.

The band started playing "Hail to the Chief" as the twenty-one-gun salute began. George took another look around at the crowd. This group was subdued and morose, nothing like the celebratory cheering crowd at Turner's first inauguration. He looked into the faces that surrounded him and saw mostly anger and resignation. The country was in for another rough four-year stretch. He was glad he would not be in the FBI and on the front lines for the battles that lay ahead.

There was polite applause for the USMC band as they finished "Hail to the Chief" and the last of the twenty-one volleys ended, and then it abruptly stopped when Turner approached the microphone to deliver his final inaugural address. George hoped Turner would keep it short.

Everyone was facing east and watching in silence as Turner began to deliver his speech. As if on cue, the clouds parted just enough for the sun to light up the podium. George shielded his eyes and alternated glances between the U.S. Capitol Dome and the nearest monitor.

He heard it before he saw it. It was approaching fast, from behind, with a sound like distant military jets. He assumed the noise was a ceremonial fly-over and did not turn around until the noise was overhead. His jaw fell slack in disbelief as he saw what looked like a small rocket at an altitude of about 500 feet. It flew directly over his head and down the National Mall, toward the inauguration podium where President Turner now spoke. The missile was traveling at a high rate of speed and had a plume of smoke and fire coming out of its tail end. George heard a collective gasp from the crowd as they turned, expecting a fly-over, and spotted the missile instead. A sea of hands pointed toward the sky, frozen in place. Time seemed to stand still.

George stood dumbfounded as the missile approached the Capitol Dome, soared over the top of the inauguration podium, and then swiftly dropped straight down, head first, at a 90-degree angle. It hit the podium dead-center. George shielded his eyes as the entire West Front of the Capitol erupted into a huge fireball that looked like a second sun. This was instantly followed by a tremendous explosion, which produced a powerful shock wave that—even though George was standing a half-mile away from the blast—

staggered him back a couple of steps. He heard a persistent ringing in his ears; the crowd noise became distant and muted, as though he were hearing it underwater. He desperately gulped air to fill his lungs. A mere thirty seconds had passed since he had first seen the missile, but he knew what he had just witnessed would change everything.

George snapped into action as he took in the growing chaos around him. The crowd was in all stages of panic: some were frozen in shock; some were bent over, either vomiting or gasping for breath; some grimaced in pain with their hands clamped down hard over their ears. He knew it was only a matter of seconds before the spectators stampeded, like a herd of zebras at the scent of a lion. George was still right in the middle of the crowd. If he stayed put, he would have to run with the herd or be trampled to death. Neither option appealed to him. He saw a tree line about 100 feet to his left that ran parallel to the rectangular, grassy fields of the mall. If he could get there, he figured he would have a relatively safe passage down the mall toward the blast site.

He took off toward it, moving aggressively, knocking people to the ground as he went. He was about ten feet from the safety of the tree line when the crowd took flight. With a roar, everyone started to run west, away from the blast site and down the mall toward the Washington Monument. Elbows swinging, George fought hard to maintain his feet, and finally leapt out of the crowd and under the protective tree canopy.

The crowd continued its stampede; George watched helplessly as people were crushed underfoot. Chivalry and social graces were quickly abandoned; Darwin reigned supreme. George shuddered with the realization that surely one-tenth of the crowd would not survive this chaos—by day's end there would be over 100,000 trampled corpses on the National Mall.

He caught his breath, turned, and began to run again toward the blast site. His lungs ached as he struggled to maintain speed. His heart hammered in his chest, and his breath became more labored as he gained ground. The shock wave from the blast had toppled most of the temporary fences and barriers, so George ran unimpeded for the most part. He locked eyes with various people who had also taken refuge under the tree canopy. All had fear etched on their faces, and all shouted to George as he approached. George ran past them all without slowing down.

He crossed Fourth Street and entered the secured ticketed area. Without breaking stride, he glanced to his right at the last open field before the Capitol Reflecting Pool. Broken and dead bodies littered the ground. Some writhed and screamed, but most lay motionless. The few people who were on their feet shuffled around like zombies; witless, blind, and lost. It got worse the closer George got to the Capitol.

The fastest way to the blast site was across the Capitol Reflecting Pool, which was solid ice at this time of year. George hit it at full speed and instantly realized he had made an error. His boots had poor tread, and his feet whipped out from under him. As he went down, he instinctively shifted his center of gravity to his core, which prevented him from going over backward and cracking his head open. Instead, he hit the ice on his side, with his hip taking the brunt of the force. He gathered his balance as he glided on the ice, then pushed off hard with his right hand, using his forward momentum to pop back up onto his feet. It was a maneuver that would have made an Olympic gymnast proud, but George's athletic prowess went unnoticed. Everyone behind him was running in the opposite direction, and everyone in front of him was dead.

He regained his balance and crossed the rest of the Reflecting Pool at full speed. He passed the Grant Memorial and entered the West Capitol Grounds, where he halted as if struck by a blow. The scene before him reminded him of those famous photographs of the Battlefield at Antietam, only this was infinitely worse. The entire grounds were filled with corpses in all manner of grotesque poses. All appeared mummified, with flash burns blackening their skin and freezing their faces in monstrous expressions. The shock wave from the blast had been stronger here. Most of the bodies had limbs ripped off, heads blown apart, and internal organs protruding from gaping holes in their torsos. The acrid smell of chemicals and burned flesh filled George's nose.

George picked his way through the carnage toward the spot where, a few short moments ago, President Turner had begun his inaugural address. He slowed and came to a stop in front of where the inaugural podium once stood. He just stood there, slack jawed, too stunned to move. *They're dead... they're all dead.*

Through the ringing in his ears, he heard a sound like muffled screaming, and turned to see two Capitol Police officers, guns drawn and pointed directly at him. He raised his hands over his head and yelled "FBI! FBI! FBI!"

The officers approached cautiously and, after a few tense moments, identified him as friendly and lowered their weapons. The three men haphazardly traded information. George told the officers what he'd seen, and they in turn confirmed his fears: everyone on the east side of the Capitol Reflecting Pool was dead—including President Turner, the vice president, the entire Supreme Court and presidential cabinet, and most of the congressional leadership.

The command and control of all three branches of the federal government had been annihilated.

A crowd had begun to gather on the West Lawn near the Grant Memorial, 300 feet away; it appeared to be 100 strong and growing. As George and his new companions watched, a man in the crowd yelled something, and all heads turned toward him. Then, almost as one, the cluster of survivors began advancing on George and the officers. George heard intermittent shouting but could not make out the words. *So this is what a zombie apocalypse feels like.* George and the officers formed a tight perimeter, took combat firing positions, and prepared to face the mob and their fate. The mob grew more agitated and continued to advance.

"Hey," George said. "So… it was nice knowing you guys."

An awkward moment of silence passed between the three men.

One of the officers guffawed. "That's pretty fucked up," he said as his gaze remained fixed on the approaching mob. The other officer remained silent.

Suddenly the mob stopped moving, almost as one. A deafening roar filled the sky, and George saw two black military helicopters pass on each side of the Washington Monument obelisk. They were heading straight toward George and the two officers, and moving fast. They were the latest version of the U.S. Army Apache attack helicopter: 15,000 pounds of the most lethal bad-assery the United States could put in the skies.

Each was armed with Hellfire and Stinger missiles and a 30mm swiveling chain gun underneath the cockpit that automatically followed the eye movement of the pilot and fired up to 600 rounds a minute. Each round had the impact of a hand grenade.

The Apaches landed fifty feet in front of George and the officers, between them and the mob. The noise was deafening, and the wind from the rotor wash kicked up a swirling cloud of debris, snow, ice, and body parts. George and the officers stood their ground but bent their heads down and shielded their eyes with their hands.

A group of about twenty-five kitted-up SpecOp guys immediately jumped out of the choppers and formed a perimeter line in front of the Apaches, about 100 feet in front of the now frozen mob. No one moved or spoke. Then one last man jumped from the helicopter.

U.S. Army General Alexander Marius Taylor II's feet landed squarely on the ground. He stood just under six feet and ramrod straight. He looked resplendent in his army dress blue uniform, four stars gleaming on each shoulder.

General Taylor was the current chairman of the Joint Chiefs of Staff, or CJCS, which, by U.S. law, made him the highest-ranking military officer in the entire United States Armed Forces.

Taylor looked over his shoulder past his perimeter line to George and the two officers. The three immediately dropped their weapons to their sides. Taylor then gave a quick nod to his troops and held both his hands up in a halt sign. With the troops thus stationed, Taylor turned around and began to walk alone toward the mob. He walked with the military bearing of a man who had been in uniform since the Nixon administration. He looked straight ahead, paying no notice to all the dead bodies he stepped on or over as he moved. He quickly closed the 100 feet, drew himself up, and began to address the mob.

He spoke from a wide stance and moved his head from side to side to make eye contact with his entire audience. At times, he became animated and slammed his fist down into the palm of his hand. The mob appeared to hang on his every word and gesture. Taylor spoke for only a few minutes. When he finished, the mob erupted in cheers and applause. Taylor snapped them a quick salute and they quickly dispersed. It was one of the most amazing displays George had ever seen.

———————————

Taylor turned and made his way back through the debris field to George and the two officers. He was a fit man for his age, still taut and lean at seventy-two; he appeared to have been born in uniform. His face was weathered, and there was noticeable scarring on one side of his neck. His jet-black hair had been closely cropped and appeared to have been dyed. A perfectly cocked beret sat on his large, square head.

But it was Taylor's eyes that mesmerized George. They were

bright amber in color, with a russet, almost coppery tint. They were the eyes of an apex predator, the kind of eyes that looked right through you into your soul.

These remarkable eyes were now fixed on George, who took a deep breath and began his briefing. George had always been an excellent briefer, and he rose to the task once again, adeptly and concisely summarizing his observations and experiences since arriving at the inauguration site.

While Taylor had been addressing the mob, George had placed a quick call to his office using an emergency number that bypassed the jammed cellular grid, and he briefed Taylor on what he had learned during that exchange. The Washington Metro PD had reported the arrest of an individual named Josh Reid Allen as the prime suspect in this attack. He was currently in critical condition at a local hospital. Allen was a white male, thirty years of age, born and raised in Iowa. He was a retired USMC Force Reconnaissance Sergeant and had been an active USMC Reservist. No known connection to any terrorist groups at this time.

Taylor advised that the military would take custody of Allen, and he ordered that Allen be immediately transported under guard to Walter Reed.

George then told Taylor that the FBI was sending all its resources to the blast site—HRT and SWAT tactical teams, Evidence Response and Hazard Materials teams, bomb technicians, as well as all JTTF personnel. As George reported that FBIHQ was also sending an On-Scene Command component, Taylor interrupted him and said that Deputy Director Hale would be the FBI on-scene commander. George was taken aback by the certainty with which Taylor issued this edict: no one told the FBI what to do on U.S. soil. This was going to cause a major shit-storm on the seventh floor of FBIHQ, but Taylor appeared unconcerned.

George looked around and took measure of the apocalypse that surrounded him: the hundreds of thousands of dead bodies that littered the ground as far as the eye could see; the fireball that still burned in the smoking crater that had once been the U.S. Capitol; the acrid smell of burning chemicals mixed with the foul stench of burned human flesh; and the growing cacophony of sirens as additional waves of first responders arrived at the scene.

Taylor then declared that a National State of Emergency was now in effect, and that he was in command until further notice. He then ordered his troops to seize control of the U.S. Capitol Grounds.

He thanked George and the officers for their briefings, then turned on his heel and walked back to his troops. George and the officers looked at each other and shook their heads in disbelief as arriving armed military troops fanned out over the Capitol grounds.

CHAPTER 5

The din of wailing sirens and racing engines filled the streets around what was left of the U.S. Capitol. George stood on Third Street and looked west down Pennsylvania Avenue at the spire of the Old Post Office Pavilion jutting up above the surrounding buildings. This section of Penn Ave had become a parade route of first responder vehicles, all heading east toward the blast site. George recognized most of the traffic as FBI: armor-plated tactical assault vehicles; ERT and HazMat rigs; the ubiquitous tinted-out black Suburbans; and numerous BuCars—late-model American-made four-door sedans with their front grill lights flashing. The rest were DC Metro Police patrol cars. The responders had commandeered both sides of Penn Ave and flouted all traffic laws—not the first, or last, violation of law George would witness today in the name of emergency and expediency.

George leaned against a building and surveyed the mayhem that surrounded him. All these first responders gave him little sense of security; no one really knew much at this point about the bomber, his motive, or any accomplices he might have. For all they knew, there might be a second round of missiles en route, targeting the first responders and fleeing survivors, and if this were the case George knew he was dead. He looked up almost sheepishly. No missiles in sight, just numerous law enforcement helicopters buzzing around, jostling for airspace.

Or maybe the second wave would be armed terrorists firing indiscriminately at the citizens who now fled the city.

George wished he had his FBI raid jacket, with the big yellow FBI block letters across the front and back, but it was buried in the trunk of his BuCar. He chuckled at the irony of losing his life on this day not to a terrorist but to an amped-up cop in a friendly-fire incident.

George began to walk again. He took a right on Third Street and headed toward his office, about one mile away. He tried to run but found he did not have it in him. His adrenaline had dissipated, and his legs and lungs ached. He felt strangely detached, like he was dreaming. His mind was muddled and languid, refusing to process what he had just witnessed. No, he would walk the twenty minutes to his office. He needed the time to get his mind right, to get back into agent mode, before stepping into the controlled chaos that was surely waiting for him at FBI WFO right now.

All George knew was that the alleged bomber, one Josh Reid Allen, was a white male, born and raised in Iowa, with no known terrorist connections. He also knew that that missile he had seen today was not built in someone's garage. No, it was definitely a military-grade ordinance, and Allen was a U.S. Marine Reservist. That was probably how he'd got his hands on it.

Of course, George could not eliminate the possibility that this was an act of international terrorism, and that Allen had been either directed or inspired by an Islamic extremist group to commit this great act against the infidels. It might even be a state-sponsored attack, like Pearl Harbor, but George doubted any modern nation would plant its flag in the burning crater that once was the U.S. Capitol Building. No country on earth would risk incurring the full wrath of the United States military, and the extreme nature and scale of this attack was a red line even the most radical Islamic terrorist group would not cross. George dismissed international terrorism as the likely cause of the bombing.

George guessed he was looking at a domestic terrorism event. A cataclysmic event that dwarfed the Oklahoma City Bombing, or even the Battle of Fort Sumter that launched the Civil War.

And if it was domestic terrorism, it all came back to Allen. What was his plan? His motivation and objectives? Had he acted alone? According to the initial reports, Allen appeared to be the classic Midwest boy next door. So, what could have caused him to do something like this? Right now, the *what* mattered more than the *why* to George. The priority was to secure the country against any additional attacks, and then round up any of Allen's co-conspirators.

And what of all those innocent victims who had died today? People who had met their demise for nothing more than going to see their duly-elected president accept his second term in office. George himself had stood among these people a scant hour or two ago, and now hundreds of thousands were dead. He shuddered at the senseless loss of innocent lives.

He felt no such pity, however, for the government leadership that had been liquidated at the podium. Their corruption and treachery made them enemy combatants of the republic they claimed to serve, and George felt nothing for their loss. He believed most of his countrymen felt the same way—he was pretty sure Josh Allen did anyway.

But the terrorist attack itself was not George's biggest concern; the FBI would solve this crime, get its man, and see that justice was served. What worried George was the opportunistic political atmosphere that would be created by such an unprecedented disaster, and what the new president might do with this blank check. It was in such crises, he knew, that citizens must be most vigilant in the monitoring of their government.

Would the U.S. Constitution be twisted and bent until it was unrecognizable to the Founding Fathers? History said yes. There had been many instances where the Constitution and Bill of Rights had become unacceptable inconveniences to those who craved power. These documents sat proudly on display in the National Archives as quaint historical artifacts while the sun shone bright and tranquility reigned. It was only when darkness fell and the wet hour came that they were most needed—and it was also when they most often failed: the Alien and Sedition Acts under John Adams in 1798; Lincoln's suspension of habeas corpus in the first year of the Civil War; and FDR with the Japanese internment camps during WWII.

George considered himself mostly apolitical—an Unplug, in current parlance. He was too pragmatic to get tangled up in academic analysis or partisan political discourse. He had no patience with the hypocrisy of it all—politicians who waved the flag for the cameras while they wiped their asses with the Constitution in the shadowy back rooms of power. He found hypocrisy to be the height of cowardice, and it fundamentally offended him wherever he saw it. It was the coin of the realm inside the Beltway.

In times of crisis, however, the country was ruled by men, not laws. George wondered if Taylor was such a man. George did not know the exact presidential line of succession, but he was pretty sure it did not include an active-duty U.S. Army four-star general. Granted, Taylor had effectively filled the power vacuum during the post-blast chaos at the Capitol, but being in his presence had been unsettling somehow, like grinding fine sand with your back molars. Men such as Taylor needed to be watched in times like these.

His mind churning, George arrived at FBI WFO. He stood outside the building, closed his eyes and exhaled deeply. He would walk in and simply do his duty, he told himself. As the lead agent on the JTTF, he would be directly involved in the Capitol bombing case, and it was certain to be the biggest investigation in FBI history. Whatever role he was assigned, he would perform it to his usual high standard. He would work the case to its conclusion, even delay his retirement if necessary.

A shot of hot pain hit his back molar at the gum line. George instinctively grabbed his jaw and took a sharp whistling inhale through clenched teeth. He had stoically suffered through bad teeth his entire adult life. This molar was scheduled for a second root canal in two weeks. George would now have to cancel this dental appointment, reschedule it when the bombing case allowed. *Oh well, whiskey is good for dental pain, isn't it?*

George checked his watch. Shit. He was definitely not going to make it for dinner and drinks with the Thompsons tonight. Kacey Anne would be pissed, but what else was new? Even with this excuse of a lifetime, he knew she would cut him no slack.

Sighing heavily, he pulled out his phone. He dreaded calling Kacey Anne. It was as if they had signed a cease fire agreement, but no peace treaty. And like North & South Korea, both sides remained unsatisfied.

Better he should call her now, get it over with. Maybe her ride in douchebag Trent's new BMW would cheer her up.

CHAPTER 6

"Yeah?" Kacey Anne's voice rose as she answered her iPhone. The call was from George. Only his name appeared on her screen; she had deleted his contact photo years before.

"Hey… I'm at work. I'm not gonna make it tonight. Something happened, and—"

"Something always happens, doesn't it, George?" Kacey Anne spat out his name like used gum.

"There was a major terrorist bombing at the inauguration today. The entire office got called in. This is bad. Worse than 9/11, and—"

"Whatever, George. Do what you have to do," she said flatly.

"I'm gonna be here all night. The president's dead. Everybody's dead. The entire leadership got wiped out." He exhaled. "Damn, Kacey Anne—haven't you seen the news?"

"Gotta go," she said as she whipped the phone from her ear and disconnected the call. She dropped the phone on the nightstand, and then rolled over to lie flat on the bed. She was naked. Beads of sweat rolled down between her breasts and along her stomach, then gathered in her navel, like the infinity pools at those swank Caribbean resorts she looked at online while George slept beside her. She thought about those resorts now, as Trent's sweat cooled on her skin. She grimaced as its rank, musky odor reached her nostrils, then abruptly swiped the pungent liquid from her torso and wiped her hands dry on the sheet. Gravity pulled her large breasts downward to rest near her armpits. She watched until the flesh stopped jiggling and was still.

She flipped from her back to her side and looked into the face of Trent Thompson, the proud owner of the brand-new black BMW M5 parked outside their motel room window. He was still sweating profusely, a man unaccustomed to physical exertion. Trent's fine hair was thinning, a fact he attempted to hide with a stubble beard that only called attention to his fleshy face. Trent was young enough to still shine up nicely in a $5,000 custom suit, but that illusion had been shattered the first time Kacey Anne had seen him naked under the cheap lighting of a budget motel room. His skin was stark white, which accentuated the unfortunate wisps of long, straight chest hairs that surrounded his prominent, dark-red areolas. His chest was flat, unlike her husband's, which still looked like an anatomy chart. Kacey Anne bit back a sigh.

"That George?" Trent asked.

"Yeah," she said. "He won't be joining us this evening."

"Too bad. I like George."

"He would paint the walls with you if he ever found out about us." Kacey Anne knew George could easily do so, but wondered if he cared enough to bother at this point.

"Well, he's never going to find out… is he?" Trent said, his eyes widening.

Kacey Anne offered a weak smile but no response.

"Why? What did he say?" Trent raised himself to his elbows and stared at her.

"He said something about a terrorist bombing at the inauguration today. Bunch of people died. He's doing an all-nighter at the office."

"Who died? The crowd—" He sat up fully now.

"He said the president and a bunch of government people." Kacey Anne let out a low sigh. "I don't know."

"Holy shit!" Trent said. He ran his hands over his dripping face, then slicked his comb-over back in place. The hairs stuck haphazardly to his flushed, red forehead. Trent reached for the remote, then *poinged* the television to life. Fox News coverage of the inauguration bombing filled the room. They both watched in silence for a long moment.

Trent forcefully blew out enough air to puff his cheeks. "Damn. I can't believe it. That's crazy."

"I never liked that guy anyway. Wouldn't have voted for him even if I did vote," Kacey Anne said. "And who really cares? It won't change anything. Turner never did nothing for me. I still live in the same shitty townhouse and drive the same shitty Honda I did when he came into office four years ago. Take America Back, my ass. Fuck him. I've got my own problems to worry about."

Kacey Anne sprang off the bed, leaving a naked and prostrate Trent still engrossed in the television news coverage. In two small steps she was at the window of their $79-a-night room. Most guests used it for no more than an hour or two. A king-size bed dominated most of the floor space. The room had a stained white popcorn ceiling and beige striped wallpaper. One side of the room was dominated by a window that faced the parking lot; the other held a single sink and mirror. There was a tiny closet with several clothes hangers affixed to the rod to prevent their theft. The two pictures bolted to the wall were of bland pastel landscapes as soulless as the room.

She placed a hand over the cheap HVAC unit and felt the warm, humid air blowing against her palm. She flipped up the plastic cover and turned the dial to off. She then parted the heavy, lined beige curtains with a manicured finger and looked out through the slit at the parking lot. The curtains were moist and smelled of industrial cleaner. She and Trent had insisted on a room in the back of the motel, one that opened to the parking lot and was hidden from the street. Darkness was falling, and the security lighting gave the parking lot a muted fluorescent glow.

Kacey Anne admired the black BMW parked directly in front of the window. Trent normally never parked his vehicle anywhere near their room, but Kacey Anne supposed new-car ego had caused his security lapse. Or maybe they were both just getting indifferent as the years wore on. The security lights spotlit the beautiful machine, and Kacey Anne remembered how good the car smelled. Ooh, she thought, closing her eyes and smiling slightly. It was the car she should be driving, not the eight-year-old Honda Accord she slunk around in, desperately trying to avoid the wealthy Vienna trophy wives looking each other up and down at the red lights. She stared at the Beemer and knew it would never be hers.

"Beautiful," she said aloud.

"What's that, babe?" Trent asked, thumbing down the volume on the television remote.

Kacey Anne hated when Trent called her "babe," an expression that had appeared, along with the hipster beard, about a year ago when he'd got his big promotion to executive VP.

"Nothing," she said. "Just looking at the Beemer." Kacey Anne's shoulders slumped. "I'll never have one."

Trent gave her a short, empty chuckle. "Well… if you keep fucking me like that, maybe I'll buy you one."

Kacey Anne spun on him; her fiery green eyes found his.

"Just kiddin', babe… Jeez." He patted the sheet beside him. "Why don't you come back to bed? I think I might be good for another round."

The slice of illumination from the parking lot lights afforded Kacey Anne a good look at her paramour. He wore a satisfied smirk on his flushed face, a few long strands of misplaced comb-over hairs still plastered to his temples. He made no attempt at modesty, his body on full display in the harsh light of the room. He was soft and doughy, with irregular patches of dark body hair on his arms and legs. His flaccid penis had turtled back into the unkempt mound of coarse pubic hair that spread across his lap.

Kacey Anne knew there would be no second round. The longer she stared at Trent, the more she began to see herself. And she did not like what she saw.

In the beginning she had been the one who wielded all the power. Trent had been like an infatuated schoolboy, unrelenting with the compliments and playful innuendo; he'd showered her with thoughtful gifts. Kacey Anne, for her part, had enjoyed wielding power over a man again. Their affair began on an otherwise unremarkable night, three years ago, in his kitchen after a night of drinking. George was again working late, and Trent's wife and both kids were visiting his mother-in-law. The rest, as they say, was history.

But their market values were headed in opposite directions now. Kacey Anne was getting older, and Trent was getting richer. Kacey Anne figured she'd lost her power about a year ago, around the time when Trent had got his executive VP title and she'd turned forty-four. Trent had become less attentive, more callous and indifferent toward her. He had stopped buying her expensive gifts, and no longer jumped when she called. She was not his princess anymore.

Kacey Anne wondered what this now was. Who she was. She wasn't even a proper mistress. Trent no longer took her to nice places. No more expensive dinners, shows, or quick overnight getaways. Lately, the only places they went were sad, out-of-the-way motel rooms with parking lot views. Like this one.

Kacey Anne watched as Trent, his demeanor now aloof, scrolled through his phone. Her eyes then moved to the nightstand by his side of the bed, on which he had placed his billfold and the keys to the BMW. As her gaze lingered on the billfold, a sickening thought shot through her. Money. On the nightstand. Cheap motel. Oh my God… I'm a prostitute! Kacey Anne had no problem being a pampered mistress to some rich sugar daddy. That was a quid pro quo she could justify. But she was no street-walking whore, working the budget motels on the outskirts of Vienna. Kacey Anne shuddered as she remembered the girls in high school who had given hand-jobs under the bleachers just to get the boys to notice them.

A prostitute. Kacey Anne took a teetering half-step back from the bed as a wave of revulsion washed over her. The salty, warm taste of Trent's semen in the back of her throat made her stomach turn. A small amount of vomit lurched up into her mouth, and she forced herself to swallow it back down. Her eyes began to tear. She turned away to face the parking lot again.

"You okay, babe?" Trent asked.

"Yeah," Kacey Anne said as she swiped at her eyes. "Just tired. I need a minute... okay?" She stood still, staring out at the dark asphalt in search of her future.

"Okay, babe. But we need to get going soon. Told my wife we were going out for a test drive."

Kacey Anne felt lightheaded and gripped the curtain for balance. She exhaled and closed her eyes. What had happened to her? Someone had changed the rules of the game and neglected to tell her. When she was the "It" girl, everything had made sense. It wasn't her fault that she was born hotter and sexier than all the other girls. The world had always acceded to beautiful women. She had simply taken what was rightly hers. She'd deserved it then, just as she did now. If only George had been a good earner, everything would have worked out as she'd planned. How was she supposed to know that not all attorneys got paid? George had betrayed her. It was his fault, not hers. She was the victim here.

She turned and shuffled over to the single sink on the opposite side of the motel room. Trent said something to her as she passed, but she did not look at him. In a flat voice she told him to get dressed, that they were leaving, and to shut the damn television off. She did not listen to his response.

Kacey Anne studied her reflection in the mirror and knew her time was running out. She had to make her move—now. This might not be her rock bottom, but it would do. Kacey Anne had made up her mind, then and there, standing naked on sticky carpet in front of a cracked motel mirror. She silently proclaimed her future was no longer with George. And certainly not with Trent. No, she would now look for another way out.

She took a sink bath to wash Trent's stink off her. She gargled the tepid water and spat. Trent would never touch her again. She was now changing the rules of the game to suit herself. No man would enter her again without first paying full admission price. She was worth it. Kacey Anne knew she had one last score in her. She would get it right this time.

"C'mon," she said to Trent as he fumbled around getting dressed. "Your wife's making us a nice dinner tonight and I don't want to keep her waiting." She grabbed the keys to the BMW from the nightstand. "I'll be in the car."

CHAPTER 7

General Taylor strode into the temporary office of Congressman Jack Zackary Parker, giving him only a gratuitous knock as he entered. The entire Congress, those that had survived the bombing, had been relocated under intense security to an undisclosed location near Capitol Hill until construction of the new Capitol Building was completed.

Taylor looked resplendent in his fully adorned dress blue uniform. He had typically visited Capitol Hill with his chief of staff, Colonel Timothy Shelton, but today he would take this meeting with Parker alone. Parker was a well-liked member of the House of Representatives and had done well by the 4th Congressional District of Mississippi for over twenty-seven years. Taylor had groomed Parker to do his bidding on military budget matters on the Hill, and had successfully manipulated him for years.

Congressman Parker's office was small but ornate. Opposite the door was a large window with dark velvet curtains pulled back to let in a stripe of natural light. His large mahogany desk with two facing visitors' chairs was framed by the window. Parker seemed to disappear as he sat behind the big desk, like a child trying on his father's overcoat.

Parker smiled and rose to his feet when he saw Taylor. He greeted him and gestured for him to sit in one of the chairs in front of his desk. Taylor instead walked across the office and sat on the sofa, back straight, both feet planted on the floor. Parker scooted around his desk, moved one of the desk chairs to face him, and sat down.

Parker was a small, delicate man. He had an expressive, clown-like face, which often wore a big open smile that displayed his oversized, bright white porcelain veneers. His eyes were bluish-gray and bulged a bit, especially when he got excited. His thin gray hair was neatly trimmed twice a month at the Capitol basement barbershop. He had been born with one club foot, which gave his gait a comical little hop. He had been in politics for over half of his sixty-two years.

Parker had been raised dirt-poor in Biloxi, Mississippi, the misspelling of his middle name (Zackary—with a *k)* a lifelong testimony to the illiteracy of his parents. As a weak child, he had developed an uncanny ability to endear himself to the popular crowd, often by taking on the role of "mascot" or "clown" to amuse and entertain his audience. Parker had perfected this persona over the years, and it had served him well, although he privately abhorred it.

Most everyone liked Parker, but no one took him very seriously; like light beer at a Texas barbecue.

Like most of his Washington colleagues, Parker was duplicitous in his personal life. He was bisexual, with a strong preference for lithe black men, a proclivity Taylor exploited to his advantage. Parker's long-term marriage, to a heavy-set, bible-thumping wife from Biloxi, was strictly for political show. He had one adult daughter, a vocal lesbian activist, who was aware of his bisexuality and hated him for not publicly supporting the LGBTQ community.

His congressional colleagues respected Parker's political skills and enjoyed his homespun southern charm and non-threatening demeanor. Behind his back, however, they ridiculed him for his gimpy club foot, superficial intellect, and closeted sexual proclivities.

Taylor warmed Parker up with small chat about the fast pace of the repairs to the Capitol Building. It had been only twelve days since the terrorist bombing, and scaffolding masked the entire west side where the missile hit. Parker congratulated Taylor on being "The Toast of Washington" for the work he had done to stabilize the government immediately following the bombing. Taylor joked that his younger staff officers had informed him that he was "trending" on all the social media sites, whatever that meant.

Parker marveled at the fact that he himself would have been at the inauguration, and been killed like many of his colleagues, except for the fact that he had been at home passing a painful kidney stone. Fate is fickle, he said with a wry laugh.

Their meeting was ostensibly to discuss military budgets, but Taylor got right to the real reason he had scheduled this meeting with Parker. The week before, Taylor had gone to the Oval Office and met with the secretary of education, Jane Richardson, who was now the unlikely acting president due to a little-known government protocol called "Designated Survivor." The designated survivor was an individual in the presidential line of succession, usually a lesser cabinet member, who was segregated in a secure, undisclosed location when the president and the country's other top leaders were gathered at a single location—such as presidential inaugurations. The practice had originated during the Cold War amid fears of a nuclear attack and was intended to maintain continuity of government in the event of a catastrophic occurrence, such as the Capitol bombing.

Taylor explained to Parker that the White House was in chaos. The SecEd was weak, vulnerable, and in way over her head. Her appointed staff was young and inexperienced, and the holdovers from Turner's staff were disloyal. She was also unpopular with the public, who saw her as a usurper to the throne.

Furthermore, Taylor said, he had placed an ally, Deputy Director Hale, in charge of the FBI investigation into the Capitol bombing, and was using Hale to control the investigation. This terrorist bombing was an unprecedented political opportunity.

"Has a new speaker been nominated?" Taylor asked, once he'd concluded his summary.

"No," Parker responded. "The House is in shock. The speaker is still being mourned. He had many friends. No one dares make a move now, not until his seat gets cold. Couple of weeks at least."

Taylor leaned in toward Parker, invading his personal space. Parker pressed himself against the back of his chair.

"Jack, what would you say if I told you I could make you President of the United States—right now—without standing for election or violating the Constitution or any federal law?"

Parker's eyes bugged out, then blinked wildly. He flashed a nervous smile. Taylor let the silence simmer.

"What?" Parker squeaked as his smile folded. "General, you can't be serious."

"I am. You're president. Right now. All perfectly legal."

"Well, how in plumb hell could that happen?"

"It's quite simple, actually. There's a loophole, or let us say a way to the presidency our esteemed Founding Fathers could not have envisioned. The inauguration was attended by the entire government leadership, including all the individuals in the presidential line of succession, except one—the designated survivor, SecEd Jane Richardson. All of those people died in the bombing, which made Richardson the current acting president. However, she has made the mistake of not naming a vice president."

"I know all this, General," Parker said, frowning. "What are you—"

"The United States Constitution and the Presidential Succession Act of 1947 designated the Speaker of the House of Representatives as *second* in line to the presidency, behind only the vice president. SecEd is number fifteen. So you see, the Speaker of the House becomes a very interesting job at a time such as this."

Parker began to nod his head in agreement as realization dawned. He stroked his jowly neck.

"So, when the House elects the new speaker," Taylor continued, "the law allows him to assert his superior line of succession, remove the designated survivor, and assume the presidency for himself at any time."

"Holy cow!" Parker exclaimed.

"And, per Section Two of the Twenty-Fifth Amendment to the U.S. Constitution, this newly appointed president could nominate a vice president of his choosing, who would take office upon confirmation by a majority vote of both houses of Congress." Taylor paused to allow Parker to catch up. "Like I said. Simple. You get yourself elected Speaker of the House. I help you assert your constitutional right to the presidency. You take office and name me your vice president. All perfectly legal. The public will love it. The military will not interfere, nor will the FBI or the cops. Congress will be powerless. And no one will listen to any whining coming out of the courts."

"Oh, my lord," Parker said. He went silent for a moment. "Well, don't that just take the cake," he muttered, shaking his head slowly.

"This is a historic opportunity, Jack. A chance of a thousand lifetimes. The back door to the White House is unlocked and wide open. All you have to do is walk through it."

"I don't know," Parker said. "I may not be the right man for this."

"The right man is the man who seizes the moment. I've known you for many years, Jack. I wouldn't have brought this to you if I didn't think you could handle it. Trust me."

Parker squirmed in his chair, then stood up and started to pace around his office.

"You are secretly an ambitious and prideful man," Taylor said, changing tack. "I know you heard all the 'Jack Zak' taunts behind your back by your so-called friends. All the way back to grade school. You resent them—all of them—just like you resent playing the clown just to get your seat at the table. That is how the world now sees you. But it is not how you see yourself, is it, Jack? It is not how I see you. I see a cunning, angry man who has waited his whole life for this. *Respect!* That's what I'm offering you. Make them *all* pay, Jack. America will fall in love with you. All you have to do is say yes. I will take care of the rest."

Parker stopped pacing and stood with his back to Taylor, looking at his wall of framed photographs; he, wearing his clown smile, posing with various dignitaries and celebrities throughout his long congressional career. He stood there for a time, shoulders rolled forward, hands in his pockets.

"Could you win the speakership now?" Taylor asked.

"Yes," Parker said. He turned to face Taylor, his expression now sharp and resolute. "But I would need help. I have the support of most of my party, and even a few Democrats. But these radical agitating Democrats are fixin' to stir up a ruckus. They're ass-kissing Richardson right now, and she'll be in the bag soon. Then they'll use her to leverage the middle and regain control of the House. This is all going on in the shadows, mind you, but I've got my spies everywhere. I've been in this game long enough to spot a coup when I see one."

Taylor thought for a moment. "No problem. The FBI investigation will reveal that the Capitol bomber was acting as an agent of the Democratic Party Agitators. Supplied him with the missile and directed his actions. It will gut the Democratic Party and ruin Richardson as well. With your political rivals buried, you will waltz into the speakership."

"Can you do that?" Parker asked.

"Don't worry about that."

"Damn." Parker looked around his office, rubbing his chin. "I still don't know, General. This thing makes my ass itch. Fixin' an FBI case. Ain't that illegal? Aiding and abetting, or some such thing? Conspiracy? I don't want to go to jail over this."

"Nobody's going to jail. I'll take care of everything. Your fingerprints will not be on this."

Parker did not look convinced. "Let's call a spade a shovel, General. What you are proposing to do here is illegal."

"As Julius Caesar, a man I greatly admire, said, 'If you must break the law, do it to seize power: in all other cases observe it.' Caesar had the balls to march his legions into Rome and take the city." Taylor fixed Parker with a glare. "I've got the balls to do this, Jack. And I know you do, too."

After a long silence, Parker spoke again. "Well, General, we got a saying down in Biloxi—not as highfalutin as your man Caesar—that goes like this: If you can't run with the big dogs, stay under the porch." He walked back toward Taylor and sat next to him on the sofa.

"So, what do you say... Mr. President?" Taylor asked.

Parker fidgeted, then looked down at his shoes.

Taylor gave him a moment. "Mr. President...?"

Parker turned and was caught in those burning amber eyes. He gave a tentative smile, and then an almost imperceptible nod.

Taylor shot to his feet. He loomed over Parker, his hand extended. Parker's upper lip trembled as the color drained from his face. Taylor held his position with military precision. Silence filled the room. Moments passed.

Parker then slowly rose to his feet, steadying himself on the arm of the sofa. He straightened and faced Taylor, then tentatively reached out and placed his trembling hand in Taylor's.

It was a handshake that changed the world.

CHAPTER 8

TUESDAY, FEBRUARY 2, 2021; 2:25 P.M. (EST)
FBI HEADQUARTERS
WASHINGTON, DC

Three black Suburbans sped down Pennsylvania Avenue, lights on and sirens blaring. General Taylor saw the FBI Headquarters building come into view through his tinted back-seat window.

The only thing everyone in the Beltway agreed on was that FBIHQ was, without question, the ugliest building in Washington. It had no equal. The gray concrete monolith was literally falling apart. A large expanse of netting covered the upper levels of the Ninth Street side of the building, placed there to prevent crumbling pieces of concrete from falling to the sidewalk below. Three hundred planters had been placed on the sidewalk to secure the building's perimeter, all neglected and filled with weeds or lifeless dirt. Many of the entrance and exit points had been permanently closed, which gave the building the perplexing appearance of a carnival funhouse. The interior was worse, with its stained drop ceilings and threadbare carpet. A certain dispiritedness clung to the workers as they entered the building and trudged through the maze of barren hallways to their cubicle homes.

The building had originally been intended as a shrine to its namesake, J. Edgar Hoover, who ran the FBI as his private fiefdom for an unprecedented forty-eight years. It had taken twelve years to design and build, and at the time was the most expensive federal building ever constructed. President Ford christened it in 1975, three years after Hoover's death. Urban legend had it that upon his death, Congress had spitefully defunded the opulent marble siding that was to wrap the perimeter of Hoover's castle. The mounting depressions for these marble tiles, which look alarmingly like bullet holes, are still visible today on the concrete siding, a posthumous middle-finger salute to Mr. Hoover from the boys down at the other end of Pennsylvania Avenue.

Taylor straightened up in his seat as the vehicle barriers were lowered, the steel door raised, and all three Suburbans were whisked through the Tenth Street entrance into the FBIHQ courtyard. The three SUVs stacked up single file in front of the building entrance, facing forward to facilitate an easy exit onto Ninth Street. Taylor's security team dismounted from the lead and trail vehicles, quickly surveyed the area, and gave the all-clear. A team member approached the middle Suburban and opened the rear door.

Taylor emerged and saw Deputy Director Hale, hands in pockets, standing by the glass entrance doors. Hale was a cliché-spouting, FBI-mission-touting, flag-lapel-pin-shouting, first-class tool. A real company chimp. He was in his late forties, about the same size as Taylor, but not as well put together. His oversized head sat on a thin neck, which gave him a bobble-head look. His lopsided smile never seemed to reach his flat, serpentine eyes. He wore a prominent pinstripe suit with a bright red tie that failed to brighten his otherwise monochromatic appearance. Hale was a man who appeared to always be standing in the shade.

Taylor stepped smartly over to Hale and they shook hands. The two men then entered the building together and headed for Hale's office in Executive Row on the seventh floor. Their polished shoes clicked on the waxed linoleum floors as they walked briskly down the labyrinth of hallways to the elevator.

Taylor had visited FBIHQ several times, but today felt different. The FBI rank-and-file all parted as he approached, forming receiving lines on both sides of the hall. These people were actually gawking at him. At the Pentagon and White House, he was greeted with solemnity; people either saluted or averted their gaze. He was afforded no such decorum in the halls of FBIHQ today. The receiving lines burst into spontaneous applause as Taylor drew nearer. Several people wore fawning smiles; a few exclaimed his name, and a large African American woman shouted, "You go, General!", which caused the crowd to howl with laughter. Taylor thought of what his staff had said about him and social media, and realized they were right. He was now a bona-fide hero to a country that desperately needed one.

Taylor reached the elevator, which had been cleared and was being held for him and Hale. He turned and saluted the crowd, which erupted in loud cheers and began to chant *"USA! USA! USA!"* Taylor stood for a moment, his back to the elevator, facing his admirers. As he basked in the adulation, he glanced at Hale and noted he was not smiling. In fact, he looked very uncomfortable, so Taylor extended the awkward moment a little longer.

Finally, Taylor gave the crowd a nod, and he and Hale turned and stepped into the elevator. As soon as the doors closed, Hale started.

"Those bastards never even look at me in the halls. And I'm the number two man in the FBI! Just wait until I'm director. Things are going to change around here." He scowled and blew a breath out through his nose.

It was the jug ears. The image hit Taylor like a lightning bolt. Hale had the same jug ears as his father, Colonel Vernon Hale. Colonel Hale had been Taylor's commanding officer in 1971 and 1972, his first tour in Vietnam. Taylor, then a green first lieutenant fresh out of West Point, had idolized his bombastic colonel. Colonel Hale had likewise taken a shine to his dashing first lieutenant and had treated him like a son.

In April 1972, during the Easter Offensive, Colonel Hale had died heroically on a night combat mission in the Quang Tri River Valley. He was posthumously awarded the Congressional Medal of Honor. First Lieutenant Taylor had valiantly attempted to save Colonel Hale's life, for which he had earned the Distinguished Service Cross. As Colonel Hale had lain dying in Taylor's arms, he had extracted a promise from him that he would look after his newborn son, whom he would never see. Taylor had sworn this oath to Colonel Hale as he died, thereby committing himself to a lifelong relationship with the jug-eared man standing next to him in the elevator.

Taylor had loved Colonel Hale. Loved him as much as he hated his own father, Alexander Marius Taylor Sr. He visited Colonel Hale's grave at Arlington National Cemetery every year on the anniversary of his death. He always visited the gravesite at night, when he had the entire place to himself. He would kneel at the colonel's alabaster cross, click off his flashlight, and let the darkness envelop him. On clear nights, he gazed at the stars. The colonel had died on a clear night. The fates of war had taken the best man on the battlefield that night in the Quang Tri River Valley. Taylor was convinced that fate had spared him that night. He would be ready when the fates came calling again.

Hale was everything his father was not. He was a weak and wanting man, an exceedingly poor copy of the original. Taylor knew the colonel would be disappointed in his son. He sometimes wondered if the colonel would be disappointed in him as well. Had he fulfilled his battlefield promise? Sure, he had pulled strings to get Hale into West Point and had made the off-the-record telephone calls necessary to rocket Hale up the FBI executive ladder. But was that enough? He regretted not spending more time mentoring Hale as a child. Maybe he could have made him into the man he clearly was not now.

The two men entered Hale's office and took seats at the conference table across from each other. The room was suitably impressive for the number two man in the FBI. The walls were painted matte government gray and covered with framed plaques commemorating every one of Hale's FBI achievements, as well as photos of him shaking hands with all manner of important people—a display designed to impress the many supplicants and reprobates who came calling. It had the opposite effect on Taylor.

Taylor quickly summarized the results of his meeting the previous day with Congressman Parker. He told Hale how fate had spared Parker from perishing at the inauguration, and joked that Parker's kidney stone was about to become more famous than Plymouth Rock. He said Parker had committed to the plan, with one condition.

"I need you to link the bomber—this Allen kid—to the far-left Agitator faction of the Democratic Party. Make it look like they put him up to the whole thing," Taylor said.

"Why?"

"Parker needs to damage the Democrats to win speakership in the House, and we need Parker to be speaker before we launch our plan."

"When do I get named director?" Hale asked, like a petulant child.

"I told you, after we put Parker in the Oval Office. But I need you to fix this matter first."

"So… Parker's going to nominate me for FBI director? I thought—"

"Goddammit," Taylor shouted. "I will name you director when I am president, *after* you take care of this bomber case and I take care of Parker. Got it?"

Hale shrank back from Taylor and looked at the floor. "Are you sure you can get me through Congress?" he asked at last.

"Don't worry about that."

Hale pouted, then mumbled to himself, "Just asking."

Taylor steered the conversation back to the fixing of the bombing investigation. It had to appear perfect. The whole world would be watching, so it needed to be a model case from top to bottom that showcased the FBI at its best and left no lingering questions.

For starters, they had to replace the current case agent with someone who they could control. Someone who was highly skilled, had big case experience, was smart, organized, and highly respected by their peers. Most importantly, this new case agent must also be controllable, willing to follow orders without question. They needed someone who would play ball.

Hale struck the dullard's pose as he pondered this reassignment: tented fingers in front of the mouth, glazed eyes fixed on the ceiling. Taylor watched him and frowned. The thought of making Mr. Empty-Pants head of the FBI troubled him, but he would do it out of loyalty to the colonel. Were it not for the colonel, Taylor would have Hale killed the moment he no longer needed him. Killing Parker was strictly business. Hell, he even kind of liked the little gimp. But Hale he did not like, and worse, didn't respect.

"I got it!" Hale exclaimed. "George Moore."

Hale explained that he was a first office agent—FBI parlance for new agents right out of Quantico—on George's terrorism squad for his first five years in the bureau, and that they had worked the PENTTBOM case together. Hale said George was the best agent in the office, and the agents on his squad would have run through a brick wall for him. He was also guileless, often out-maneuvered in office politics. Incapable of deception or betrayal. Hale said he would be perfect for this assignment.

"Moore…" Taylor said. "Didn't I see this guy at the Capitol the day of the bombing?"

"Yes."

"I like the cut of his jib," Taylor said, considering. "But will he be with us? Will he pin this thing on the Democrats?"

"Don't worry," Hale said. "He does not suffer fools, and he has sharp elbows, but I can control George. He's due to retire soon, I think. I'll promise him a big SES promotion. That will put some good money in his retirement account."

"Are you sure about this guy?" Taylor asked, doubt filling his voice. "He does not strike me as a man who can be bought."

"I'm sure. George and I go way back. He was a good squad supervisor. Stepped down over some pissing match with the Assistant Director in Charge. I think George regretted it and always wondered how far he might have promoted. Especially as he watched me blue-flame to deputy director." Hale nodded. "Yeah, when push comes to shove, George will do what I tell him to do."

"Okay. Call him in and give him the job. Now, remember: this has to be done fast and done right. The kid's got to hang, and the Democrats have got to pay. Keep me informed."

Hale escorted Taylor out of his office and back to his awaiting Suburban. Hands in his pockets, he impassively watched the general's convoy roar out of the courtyard, his jug ears tuned to the fading wail of the sirens as the general sped down Ninth Street to the Pentagon.

———

Taylor gazed out the tinted side passenger window of the Suburban, deep in thought. He had not trusted Hale with the full extent of his plan. He had confided this to only one person—his chief of staff, Colonel Timothy Shelton. Taylor's real plan would begin only *after* President Parker sat in the Oval Office. William Henry Harrison Sr., the ninth president, had died thirty-one days into his term, the shortest tenure in United States presidential history. Parker would not even make it that long. Taylor would see to it that poor President Parker died in his sleep from a reported heart attack. Then, Taylor, as vice president, would address the nation in somber tones to offer comfort to the public and condolences to the Parker family.

After that, with a great show of humility, he would lawfully ascend to the presidency per his primacy position in the line of succession as delineated by the United States Constitution and the Presidential Succession Act of 1947.

As President Taylor, he would move quickly and decisively. He had never aspired to be a *mere* president—the history books were littered with mediocre men who had occupied that office. As for laws and rules, the Congress and the courts, Taylor had no interest in any of this. He believed this check-and-balance republic had run its course. The country needed a strong hand to face the challenges posed by the modern world, and Taylor believed fate had chosen him to be that strong hand. Fate had guided that missile and laid this historic opportunity at his feet. He was more than ready. The American people were ready. Everyone else had better step in line. There would be only friends and enemies, and he was equally adept at handling both.

Taylor was a proponent of the Great Man Theory, popularized in the 1840s by Scottish writer Thomas Carlyle. Like Carlyle, he believed that great leaders were born, not made, and that he had been imbued at birth with certain characteristics and traits that would allow him to rise and lead when his great moment arrived.

Taylor had become obsessed with great men from all walks of life while studying military history and American politics at West Point. He had primarily looked to Rome for his inspiration, particularly its great military dictators and emperors—Marius, Sulla, Julius Caesar (his personal favorite), and Augustus—and had striven to re-invent himself as a composite character of all of these great Roman men. He had begun to fantasize about possessing Caesar-like military powers in modern America, daydreaming his own "Rubicon" scenarios.

All these great Roman men had used the military to seize autocratic power, but only one of them had excelled at wielding it—Augustus. Augustus established The Principate, the initial 250-year period of the Roman Empire that was characterized by the reign of a single emperor who preserved the illusion of the republic. Like Augustus, Taylor understood that it was harder to effectively exert absolute power than it was to seize it. And harder still to preserve the illusion that one held no such power at all.

Military dictatorship had been his fantasy for decades, but thanks to the Capitol bombing, his fantasy was about to be realized. And once he was installed as president, Taylor would do as Augustus had done: end the American Republic and begin a new American Empire, with himself wielding autocratic power as America's first military dictator. He would also assume the title that Augustus had wisely taken, one that was intended to project humility and collaboration. He would simply be the first among equals. He would be Princeps Civitatis—*First Citizen.*

CHAPTER 9

The giant of a man seated facing George was the one and only Jude David Goldberg, known since the sixth grade as JD. He was an FBI Special Agent at WFO, and George's best friend.

Goldberg was six feet, five inches tall in stocking feet and carried 295 pounds of solid muscle. His blond hair was styled in a 1950s crew cut, and he was clean-shaven except for the neatly trimmed soul patch under his bottom lip. His deep blue eyes sparkled and danced whenever he laughed or smiled, which was often. Cauliflower ears and a gnarled, crooked nose bespoke his pugilist past.

George and JD sat at a table along the wall in the Great Hall of the National Building Museum, originally built in 1887 to administer Civil War pensions. The museum was only one block from the office, and one of George's favorite places in all of DC. It was a colossal brick barn of a building. Three stories of offices hugged the interior perimeter, which created a vast, open Great Hall fifteen stories high.

It was a brisk wintry day under a dull gray sky, a typical Friday afternoon in the District in early February. Both men soaked in the cavernous Great Hall view. The museum eatery served healthy fare, and they ate here together often. JD sipped his XL coffee. He consumed prodigious amounts of caffeine throughout the day without any discernible effect.

"It happened again," George said.

"What?"

"In line," George said. "That guy sitting behind us came up to me and said I looked like someone he knew, that I looked real familiar to him, but he couldn't place me."

"That happens to you all the time, dude. Just got one of those faces."

George found the entire ritual disconcerting. Inevitably the stranger approached him all happy, thinking him a long-lost friend, then George's denial followed by the stranger's confusion and ultimate surrender. George could practically hear the sad trombone song in his head—*womp womp womp*. The stranger then scurried away, spewing awkward apologies, and George was left feeling like he somehow let this person down, like he was not who he was supposed to be. This little failed social dance oddly contributed to George's sense of isolation from the world around him.

They finished their lunch in the kind of silence only good friends can enjoy together. George caught JD eyeballing a curvaceous mom, late thirties, bending over to seat her child at a nearby table. JD beamed a bawdy smile and slowly nodded his head up and down.

"Daddy likey," he said.

JD had taken a circuitous route to the FBI. At Purdue, he had been a second-team All-American defensive end. As an undrafted free agent with the Chicago Bears, he'd fought his way off the practice squad and spent two seasons as a special team star. When his third knee surgery forced him out of the league, he'd tried his hand at professional wrestling (he had been a three-time Nebraska heavyweight high school champ).

JD loved the WWE, but by 2010 more injuries had sent him back to Nebraska to regroup.

A family friend knew an FBI agent who had encouraged JD to apply. He'd struggled through the arduous application process, barely passing the written exam. But based on the strength of his oral panel interview, his quasi-celebrity background, and his physical presence, he beat the odds and was hired as an FBI Special Agent in 2011.

JD had breezed through the twenty-week New Agents Training at Quantico, after which he'd been assigned to the midsize Cleveland field office as a terrorism agent. He'd never stood a chance. Although he was hardworking and a good agent, his size and blunt honesty intimidated the office leadership, who had no idea what to do with him. JD had jumped at the first office transfer to come along: WFO, the second largest field office in the FBI.

He found WFO to be even more political than the Cleveland office, so he'd talked his way into the Computer Analysis Response Team's OJT program. Now, as a certified CART Agent Examiner, JD did forensic analysis on a variety of digital media—computers, CDs/DVDs, cell phones, digital cameras, flash media, etc.—that were lawfully seized on cases across all investigative programs in the office. He liked being a CART agent; he mostly worked on his own and kept his distance from all the office drama. JD had met George at a squad meeting during which George had told his boss—in so many words—to piss off. They had been fast friends ever since.

George took the last bite of his roasted chicken and feta sandwich, then checked his watch.

"Hustle up," he said. "We gotta get going soon."

"We got time, man," JD responded. He shook his head and shoveled a forkful of salad greens into his mouth. "Tell me about your meeting with that meat puppet Hale."

Hale had ordered George and his boss, WFO Assistant Director in

Charge Ben Jamison, to FBIHQ two days ago, and all the way over Jamison had badgered him with questions about what he could have done that was so bad to warrant such a summons. George had been unable to shake the feeling that he was being walked to the gallows.

Instead, Hale had informed George that he'd been selected as the new case agent on the Capitol bombing, now known as FBI Major Case CAPBOM. George's views on his selection were not solicited; another famous Bureau "volun-told" moment.

CAPBOM would most certainly be the biggest case in FBI history. But that was what the director told George almost ten years ago when his squad was designated as the lead in the WFO PENTTBOM case. This time, though, George vowed it would be different. He would be more circumspect, more diplomatic and flexible where possible. He had been an ideological martyr last time, and his principled stand had cost him his supervisor's desk. This time he would be better at avoiding the landmines CAPBOM was sure to present. He would see this case through to the end, with his integrity and reputation intact, and claim the redemption he secretly craved.

Still, he told JD, there were a couple of things about the meeting that continued to nag at him. Hale had been oddly animated, amped up with nervous energy. He'd emphasized that the case must be resolved immediately, and by whatever means necessary. Hale had also explained that General Taylor would be personally involved, and that the resources of the entire U.S. military were at George's disposal. Hale had repeated several times that he and Taylor were certain that the bomber had ties to the far-left wing of the Democratic Party.

George wanted this opportunity, but something just didn't feel right. Since when was an army general involved in directing FBI investigations? And what about Hale's clumsy attempt to rush this case to judgment before all of the evidence had been evaluated?

"That's a little jacked up," JD agreed. "How do you know Hale again?"

"He was an FOA on my squad. Useless." George's eyes narrowed. "His only talent was office politics. He kissed all the right rings until that big blue flame shot out of his ass. One promotion after another. He's stayed in touch, mostly making sure I was aware of his rise to the top."

"So... let me get this straight," JD said. "You were the hotshot PENTTBOM supervisor, and you get this little pissant FOA on your squad. Fast-forward twenty years: the boot-licker is now the deputy director, and you're a busted street agent counting down to retirement. That about right, buddy?"

"The irony is not lost on me," George said.

"More like tragedy, dude. Your parents must be so proud. Putting that fancy law school degree to work chasing around any imbecile or nut-job with opposable thumbs who can type a terrorist threat to the FBI. Well played, bro."

"Well, when you say it like that, it doesn't sound very sexy," George deadpanned.

The two friends shared a laugh.

"Anyone else would have punched that golden ticket," JD said. "Slapped on the kneepads and worked Hale until his eyes rolled to the back of his head. But not our good friend George here. No, he's a character man. Aren't you, George?"

"Remind me why we're friends?" George said with a smile.

"Hey—give me a color check, would ya? I look good, right?" JD asked.

George sighed and gave him a once-over. JD had genetic protanopia, a form of red-green color blindness that affects one percent of the male population. To him, red appeared as black, and certain shades of orange, yellow, and green all appeared as yellow. The condition had caused him to fail his Bureau physical examination and should have washed him out as a new agent applicant. But his doctor happened to be Jewish (like JD), and he'd resolved to address the paucity of Jewish special agents by making a few adjustments to JD's eye exam results. And that was how JD had passed his Bureau physical.

JD's biggest problem was buying clothes and matching colors. His prodigious proportions forced him to buy all custom-fitted clothing, and he still used the same tailor he had employed while he was a professional wrestler. JD's fashion sense was more flamboyant than the dark-suit-white-shirt look still favored in the FBI. He was obsessed with luxury fabrics and inordinately proud of his wardrobe. A 295-pound fashionista.

Although his tailor sewed numbers into all his clothes to allow him to color match his outfits, JD was still anxious about committing a fashion faux pas and forfeiting his best-dressed title. It was during these color checks that George caught fleeting glimpses of JD's vulnerability. They were shared moments of intimacy that endeared JD to him, like helping your elderly father read a menu in the dim light of a fancy restaurant.

"Looking good," George said, giving JD a thumbs-up.

"Dude, touch this shirt," JD said, as he extended his thick arm across the table. "One hundred percent hand-picked Barbados Sea Island cotton. Rarest cotton on earth. Only seventy bales of this shit are produced every year. And I'm wearing about half a bale of it on my back right now."

"I think I already felt this one—"

"Dude—just touch it! Melted butter! Over three hundred thread count. And the bright blue is poppin'!"

George reached out and lightly petted the arm of JD's bright blue dress shirt. He had to admit it felt wonderful. "Pretty sweet." George withdrew his arm and checked his watch. "C'mon, we gotta go."

JD reached over and grabbed George firmly by the wrist. "George, you sure you want to do this again?" he said, suddenly serious.

George paused, then nodded.

"All right, then. I'm in, too. I got you." JD released his grip and started to put on his suit jacket. George feared another round of dude-touch-my-suit was about to commence, and was relieved when it didn't.

"Just remember, buddy. Sometimes you take this shit way too seriously," JD said, rising to his feet. "It's all just a big game over there. Nothin' but bozos and ass clowns."

"Which one are you?" George asked.

The big man grinned.

CHAPTER 10

George searched for the building in the colossus known as Walter Reed National Military Medical Center. It was the world's largest military medical center, sprawling across 243 acres in Bethesda, Maryland. He hoped this trip would be worth it, that he could get Allen to talk. He also hoped the gathering winter storm would hold off until he got home. A few inches of blowing snow was forecasted for late this afternoon, which would gridlock DC.

It had only been five days since Hale had designated George as the CAPBOM case agent, but experience told him not to delay this subject interview. He was anxious to meet the world's most infamous terrorist and see if he could get him to talk, a feat the previous investigative team had failed to accomplish. George had pitched this initial meeting with Allen as strictly "rapport-building," not a formal interview, and thus convinced a reluctant Hale that he should do it alone. George worked better alone.

His gut churned as he entered the lobby and headed toward the bank of elevators. He presented himself at the nurses' station, flashed his creds, and asked for the head shift nurse and Allen's attending physician by name. The nurse behind the desk called both over the intercom. George looked around as he waited. White dropped ceilings, taupe linoleum tile floors with darker taupe walls. Some blue accent paint and faux cherrywood doors. The nurses' station was situated in the middle of the floor, flanked on all sides by patients' rooms. It was quieter than most civilian hospitals.

The head nurse arrived first. She wore a buttoned-up white lab coat with insignia on the right breast, and her name and title—Annie Williams, Head Nurse—embroidered in blue on the left. She appeared to be in her early forties, with the stern features of a bedside nurse who had seen it all. She told George that Allen was isolated in a room at the far end of the hall, guarded by armed military police. He had been admitted the day of the bombing, initially to the ICU, but later transferred to her floor when his condition had stabilized. She described him as a good patient, respectful to the nurses. She complained that Allen had been in full bed restraints since he'd arrived on the floor. It was unnecessary, she said, and made it much harder for the nurses to render treatment. Allen reminded her of her nephew, who was in the army and currently deployed in the Middle East. She sighed and shook her head. What a waste.

She then leaned in close to George, and in a low voice said that the cop guarding Allen's door was harassing her nurses. George asked for specifics. She motioned to the station nurse, who had just scurried past them down the hall. She returned a moment later with another nurse in tow. Williams introduced her as Allen's primary care nurse. She was young, with green camo scrubs and an open smile. She didn't hold back when George asked her about the cop. She said he was a total perv, badgering the nurses with lewd comments and propositions for quickies in the vacant rooms along the hallway. He creeped her out. George told both nurses he would see what he could do to get the cop reassigned. They thanked him.

The attending physician, Dr. Vincent Russo, then joined their group. He apologized for being late, said he had just gotten off the phone with his boss regarding the Allen case. Dr. Russo gave George a quick rundown on Allen's medical condition. He had been admitted to Walter Reed with eight gunshot wounds, three potentially fatal, and had been in full cardiac arrest. He had massive internal bleeding; his coronary artery had been nicked. He had a collapsed lung, and his liver had also taken a direct hit. Allen went from the ICU directly to the OR, where he underwent a five-hour operation to re-start his heart, stem the internal bleeding, and patch up all his holes. The doctor currently listed Allen in fair condition. His vital signs were stable, and he was conscious and on a fentanyl IV drip for pain. Dr. Russo warned George that Allen fatigued easily, and that he should keep his interview short.

George thanked the doctor and nurses. They exchanged handshakes, and all three hustled away down the hall.

George turned and walked toward Allen's room, passing through the military police checkpoint at the head of the hallway with his Bureau creds. Allen's room was lit up like a bright beacon at the end of the long, dark corridor. All the other rooms had been emptied. JTTF Officer Orlando Rodriguez slouched on a plastic chair outside Allen's door, spotlit in the bright light, his head tilted back against the wall.

As George approached, he could see that Allen's room was wide open to the hallway. A brown and gold striped shower curtain, which slid on a track in the ceiling, was tied off at the wall.

George greeted Rodriguez, who groaned as he pushed off the arms of the chair to his feet. His six-foot height matched George's, but he carried thirty extra pounds around his waist. His dark brown hair had receded on top, exposing a large, bulbous forehead. He wore an eighties-style cop mustache that masked a severe overbite.

George pulled Rodriguez aside and asked him about Allen. Rodriguez referred to Allen alternatively as 'the terrorist' or 'that fucking terrorist.' He reported that he was keeping Allen in line, and that the terrorist was not going to try anything on his watch. George asked Rodriguez if Allen had had any visitors. Rodriguez said no, then corrected himself and remembered that General Taylor and his colonel had visited Allen on Wednesday or Thursday of the previous week. The visit had lasted only fifteen minutes or so. Rodriguez did not know the reason for the visit or what was said. He had attempted to eavesdrop on the meeting, but through the curtain he'd heard only mumbled whispers, mostly from Taylor.

Rodriguez had been a Washington Metro PD officer for about ten years. He had a bad reputation and was regarded as badge-heavy by his peers. He was devious, always on the hustle. He'd got the coveted JTTF assignment solely because he was a drinking buddy of the lieutenant who made the department selection, and George had kept him on only to maintain the Bureau's relationship with DC Metro PD. He was scheduled to rotate off the task force soon, and George was counting the days.

Rodriguez wanted nothing more than to be an FBI Special Agent. He was in a panic because he had failed his agent applicant written exam, and would age out before he was allowed to take it again. Rodriguez had thus spent his time clumsily trying to curry favor with George, as he loathed the thought of going back to patrol for his old department.

George cut Rodriguez's posturing short and told him to leave the nurses alone. Rodriguez mumbled that he was just fooling around, and only promised to knock it off after George repeated himself more forcefully.

That done, George stepped past him and entered the room. The pungent odor of urine filled his nostrils and he choked back a cough. Allen was propped up at a 45-degree angle in a large mechanical bed that was centered in the room. The foot of the bed was only a few feet from the hallway. Allen lay on top of the sheet, in a thin hospital gown, with his arms and legs spread-eagled and shackled to the bed frame. His body shivered against the chill of the room. His head was turned to the wall, his eyes closed. The first thing George noticed was how young he looked. He had expected to feel a shot of rage or revulsion at the first sight of Allen, but realized with a start that he was just a kid.

The room was small and sparse. On Allen's right was a hanging IV bag. His urine bottle sat on his bedside table, just out of reach. A watercolor of an American eagle in flight hung ironically over his bed. The only window in the room had been boarded up.

George approached the bed and shook the side railing.

"Mr. Allen? My name is George Moore. I'm an FBI agent with the Washington Field Office, and I am here to ask you a few questions." No response. George repeated himself, shaking the bed a little harder.

Allen slowly turned his head to face George.

"I'm here to ask you a few questions about the missile attack on the Capitol last week."

The two men stared at one another. George allowed the silence to linger as he awaited his response.

Finally Allen spoke. His voice was gruff and raspy. "They got me in isolation. I haven't heard any news. What's going on out there? What are the people doing?"

George recognized this as his opportunity to take control of the interview. "I'll make you a deal. I ask my questions first. If you answer them all—truthfully—then I will answer your question. Deal?"

Allen pondered this for a moment, then nodded his assent. He then mouthed the word "private" and gave a sideways glance toward the open wall and Rodriguez. George got up and exchanged looks with Rodriguez as he closed the curtain. George then pulled the room's only chair up to Allen's bed and sat alongside him. George knew Rodriguez would be eavesdropping, so he leaned in to Allen, putting a finger to his lips.

"Whisper," George said in a hushed tone. "Is that cop at the door bothering you?"

"He likes to play his little games when no one is watching. He tightens the restraints to cut off my circulation, laughs when my feet and hands turn blue. He presses me into this bed until my bedsores bleed and ooze." Allen paused to cough and catch his breath. "When the nurses leave, he takes my blanket and cranks the thermostat down. Freezing in here."

"Where is it?" George asked. Allen nodded toward the corner of his room. George got up and found the blanket wadded up on the floor. He shook it out and placed it on top of Allen.

Allen looked George in the eye and said, "Thank you."

George stepped to the curtain, swung it open, and told Rodriguez to take a break, that he would call him when he was done. Rodriguez, startled, straightened up, grumbled and shuffled away down the hall and toward the break room vending machine.

George returned to Allen. "Why did General Taylor visit you last week?" he asked.

Allen's eyes flashed to the urinal container at his right, then back to George.

"You gotta go?" George asked. "Want me to get a nurse?"

Allen shook his head, then looked away. "They put me in a diaper. I'm sick of pissing on myself."

George looked at the urinal on the bedside table. Through the opaque plastic sides, he could see that the liquid had fermented to a dark amber. "You want a nurse?" he asked again.

Allen grimaced and shook his head no.

George then realized he couldn't get a nurse, as that would leave Allen unattended, and he did not want to summon Rodriguez back and risk breaking what little rapport he had built with Allen.

He shuddered with the realization of what he had to do. Then he did it. For the first time in his life, he helped another man relieve himself. He stripped off Allen's sodden diaper and tossed it in the room's waste container. He held the bottle in place, then turned his head while Allen let loose a long, steady stream. George quickly capped the bottle and set it back on the table, covered Allen, and returned to his bedside seat.

Allen sighed. Then a tight smile spread across his face. "Thanks, man."

George nodded and tried to continue the interview like nothing had happened. "Um…" He cleared his throat. "Did… has anyone visited you since you've been here?"

"I've been out of it most of the time. A couple of your people came to try to talk to me. Military intel tried too."

"Why did General Taylor visit you last week?" George asked.

"That jackass actually ordered me to confess that some left-wing agitators in the Democrat Party put me up to it. That I was their guy."

"Are you?"

"No!" He held George's eyes. "It's important that you believe me."

"Then tell me what happened, Josh."

Allen then told George what he had withheld from his other inquisitors. He admitted to committing the Capitol missile attack, and insisted he had acted alone. He said he had stolen the Javelin missile from the military base where he'd served as a USMC Reservist. The theft had been surprisingly easy, he said, with a small smile of satisfaction. He'd hidden the missile in his vehicle, then driven it right off the base at the end of shift. When George gave him an incredulous look, Allen reminded him that twenty-five years ago in San Diego, an unemployed plumber had stolen a Patton tank from a National Guard armory and taken it for a joyride.

George nodded and then asked him about accomplices at the base; he must have had help. Allen shook his head, refusing to give up any of his fellow Marines. George dropped it for now and shifted his approach.

"Why did you do it, Josh?"

"Have you read my declaration? It was in my pocket when they shot me."

"What declaration?" George asked. "According to the arrest report, your pockets were empty when you got to the hospital."

"I scheduled it to post on my Facebook page. At noon on Inauguration Day, the twentieth." His brow creased. "You mean it wasn't posted?"

"No. This is the first I've heard of it."

Allen turned his head away, visibly crestfallen.

"What did it say, Josh?"

A long silence. "Look," Allen said finally. "They're gonna call me a psychopathic terrorist, some crazy evil monster. They're gonna tie me to Timothy McVeigh, make me into some white-power Turner Diary whack-job. It's all nonsense. I'm just a guy from Iowa who got fed up and threw the tea back in the harbor."

"So you're a patriot, are you?" George asked.

"Our republic had been ruined by treasonous politicians. Centuries of corruption have broken the government beyond repair. The time for protest has long passed. Only a full revolution can save us now. So I started this Second American Revolution—alone—based on my own beliefs. I hope the American people have the stomach to finish it."

"So tell me, Josh—what kind of revolution did you hope to accomplish?"

"It's time to start over. This thing is almost two hundred and fifty years old. Take the spirit of the Founding Fathers, the experience of history, the wisdom of science and technology, and create a new form of government that addresses the realities and demands of the modern world. It needs to be done—now!"

His raised voice brought on a coughing fit. It took Allen a whole minute to catch his breath. "I hope someday my actions will be understood," he said. "I gave my life for my country. The rest is now out of my hands, and in the hands of the American people. I wish I could live long enough to see how it all turns out."

George leaned back in his chair and blew out a long breath through his nose. He had entered this room to help the government kill this man. But for what? Justice? To help the country heal? George lowered his gaze to the floor.

"Agent Moore?" Allen said. "Agent Moore?"

He raised his eyes and stared at the dead man in the bed. "Yes?"

"Any more questions for me?"

"No, Josh. You kept your word. Do you have any questions for me?"

"Tell me what happened after the bombing."

"Well, the secretary of education became acting president. Everything is slowly getting back to normal. Congress is—"

"The people—what are they doing?"

George was quiet for a moment, pondering his response. "The people aren't doing anything, really," he said slowly. "They're kind of in shock, waiting to see what happens next. What the government's going to do. They sure do love General Taylor. He's been all over the newspapers and TV. America's new hero—"

"No!" Allen shouted. "Don't you see? If the people allow this government to continue, it's going to come back—and it will come back *mean*. They're going to come down hard. Now's the time— don't you see? I got 'em all! I gave the American people a blank check—now's the time to cash it!"

Allen exhaled, exhausted, and dropped his head back to the bed. He motioned for George to come closer, then whispered in his ear, pleaded for him to go to Iowa, to speak to his mother and brother, and get his brother's laptop that he had hidden. Allen's declaration and all his other writings and work were on that laptop. It would explain everything.

"And please hurry," Allen said. "There's not much time. They'll kill me, you know."

"Who?" George asked.

"All of them," Allen said, and nodded toward the closed curtain.

George promised he would get the laptop and read the declaration. Allen relaxed, a small smile on his lips.

George got up from his chair and slid the curtain open. Allen said something that caused him to turn around.

"How's the boy cop doing?" Allen asked.

"What?"

"The cop who shot me."

"Oh. The arresting officer. The young cop. He's doing all right, I guess. He's been all over the media. PD gave him the Medal of Valor. I think he's posing for a statue right now."

"Good for him," Allen said. "Send him my regards."

———————

George stepped out of the elevator, found his car, and drove home. It had started to snow. Traffic was a mess. It would normally take him about forty minutes to cover the fifteen miles from Walter Reed to his Vienna townhouse. But tonight, in snowmageddon, he knew it would take him almost two hours. He thought about his interview with Allen the whole drive home.

George had conducted thousands of terrorism interviews over his career, including a few hard-core jihadists and serious domestic right-wing whack-jobs. He knew what a terrorist looked like. And based on his twenty-five years of training and experience, he had developed a finely calibrated bullshit detector. He pulled into the garage of his townhome, his slog of a commute mercifully at an end, and he knew one thing: *Josh Allen was telling the truth.*

CHAPTER 11

"How was Iowa?" JD Goldberg asked as he greeted George with a big bear hug in the entryway of his swank downtown DC condo. George had flown back into Dulles late last night and was working on four hours' sleep.

JD motioned George into the spacious living room.

"Quick trip. Got back late last night," George said.

"Get everything you needed?" JD asked.

"Yeah." George pulled out Josh Allen's laptop and gave it to JD.

"How'd it go?"

"Okay," George said as he plopped down on the sofa and rubbed his bloodshot eyes. "I took that simpleton Jenkins with me. Thought it would look suspicious if I went alone. I sent him upstairs to count socks and underwear while I interviewed Allen's mother and brother downstairs. Both born and raised in Adel. The mom was a sweet woman. Cried a lot. The brother's a senior at Iowa State. He and Allen were close."

George leaned back and jutted his legs out in a stretch.

"I did some neighborhood interviews, talked to his old minister, asked around at the town diner. Media's still sniffing around. The whole town's in shock. They've disowned Allen, that's for sure. His ex-wife is a piece of work. She asked me if she would be entitled to some kind of reward if she talked to me. I felt bad for Allen's little kid. It's gonna be tough sledding for him in that house... and that town."

"No problem getting the laptop, then?"

"No. It was right where Allen said it was. He buried it in an airtight bag in the woods behind his brother's apartment building. That's why we didn't find it at the search warrant. The brother gave up the password easy."

"So, what's up with this Allen dude?" JD asked.

"No surprises. Midwest Norman Rockwell childhood. Dad worked at Stine Seed for thirty-five years. Dropped dead at his desk about six years ago. Heart attack. Allen was an average student; played high school ball, popular kid. Went into the Marines after graduation, was a badass force recon guy. His wife gets pregnant and whines him out of his beloved corps. Allen does the right thing. His dad gets him an entry-level sales job at the seed company. Allen buys a tract home and becomes a good taxpayer."

"When did the wheels fall off his wagon?" JD asked.

"Hated being a cubicle monkey, his wife burning through his paychecks. She eventually divorced him for a more successful seed salesman. He quit his job and spent the last two years on his brother's couch. He stayed in the Marine Corps Reserve, faithfully visits his son. His ex-wife bled him for spousal and child support."

"Let me guess. It's been all cheap booze, cold pizza and porn for the last two years, right?" JD chuckled as he opened Allen's laptop and began to copy the hard drive.

"That's what I thought, too. But the brother says Allen went to the university library almost every day. Schooled himself on history, politics, anthropology, psychology, economics. Brother says he got dark, more introspective after their father died. And he got angry when he drank. Talked a lot of shit about politicians and the state of the country. Nothing about any terrorist groups or causes, though."

"Well, let's see what Mr. Allen's laptop looks like," JD said.

Soon the work copy of Allen's hard drive was complete. JD carefully wiped away his digital fingerprints and closed the laptop. No one would ever know he had accessed this original piece of evidence before it was properly entered into the chain of custody, a violation of Bureau policy that would get them both fired if ever it were discovered. George had done it because he had to corroborate what he already knew, that Allen was telling him the truth. JD had done it because George had asked him to.

JD now began his forensic examination of the work copy. He would search the entire hard drive for key terms and phrases, and attempt to locate Allen's declaration. He would also look for anything that would indicate a terrorism nexus, accomplices, or any previous or future planned attacks. He had stationed himself at the opposite end of the living room, at a small hutch that opened up to a standing desk, and settled into his task.

George knew better than to interrupt JD when he worked. He sank deeper into the sofa. Sleep deprivation had slowed his mind a beat or two, and he fought to keep his eyes open. JD'S condo décor was Scandinavian design, all crisp and clean. Hardwood ash floors, stained light gray, walls, ceilings, and trim all painted cream white. The one-bedroom unit had a well-designed floor plan that felt bigger than its 750 square feet. It had a shiny U-shaped island kitchen that opened into a large dining / living area. The place was sparsely furnished with modern pieces: one sofa, two chairs, a two-top round dining table, flat-screen television and stand, a coffee table, and a couple of area rugs. JD's bedroom was similarly decorated. He had hired an interior designer to decorate the entire condo, a concession to his color blindness.

JD continued to work in silence. The rhythmic click of the keyboard slowly lulled George's eyes shut and dropped his chin to his chest. He slid into a brief micro-sleep before his head violently bobbed up to snap him awake. He rubbed his eyes again.

"Got any coffee?" he asked.

"Yeah. Freshly made. Kitchen," JD said, without looking up from the laptop.

George walked across the room into the kitchen. JD had remodeled it with a full suite of stainless-steel Miele appliances, matched with dark walnut cabinets and black quartz countertops with contrasting white backsplash. George poured himself a cup and immediately felt better.

He returned to the open living area and stood in front of the floor-to-ceiling windows that covered the entire southwest wall. The helicopter view was spectacular. The 55th U.S. Congress had passed the Height of Buildings Act, which forever restricted the height of new structures in the District. JD lived in a corner unit on the penthouse floor of the highest residential building allowed in DC, sixteen stories above Mass Ave. NW. At this height he saw the entire National Mall, from the Lincoln Memorial in the west to the U.S. Capitol (what was left of it) in the east.

Seeing the Mall brought George right back to the missile attack three weeks ago. The magnitude of the tragedy struck him anew. The images of that day were seared into his memory: the countless dead bodies strewn all over the mall; the crowd stampeding away from the blast; the fear and shock on people's faces; the smell of burning flesh. He had tried to put all this aside to focus on his job, but it followed him like a dark shadow.

What next? he wondered. What lay ahead for this country? George was in the eye of the storm. Fate had cast him center stage. He was the case agent of the biggest case in FBI history. *Big cases, big problems.* He reminded himself it would be different this time, not like before with PENTTBOM. This time, he would be vigilant against the gathering storm.

George drained the last of his coffee as he stared at the Washington Monument, which, at fifty-five stories tall, dominated the skyline. It was less than one mile away from where he now stood. George always felt a strange kinship to this monument and sometimes walked there from the office on his lunch hour when he needed to clear his head. He wondered what the famously reserved General Washington would think of this obelisk, the world's tallest stone structure. Would he feel like the Father of *This* Country?

George walked back to the kitchen and poured himself a second cup of coffee, then opened JD's refrigerator, looking for milk. Its contents were perfectly organized: bottles and cans lined up like soldiers, airtight glass containers stacked at crisp right angles. The containers were labeled for each day of the week and grouped accordingly. Nina, JD's personal chef and nutritionist, had obviously been by to drop off his meals for the week. JD brought several of these containers to the office each day and ate every couple of hours.

George marveled at his friend. JD was king of the life hack. He had started his own private barter group on the Internet, and its members were rigorously selected for their professional skills and discretion. JD administered the group's private Internet site and secured all their encrypted communications. All members were free to barter as they wished. In this way, JD received personal chef services (Nina was great), dry cleaning and maid service (JD was very particular about this), and VIP treatment at the best cougar bars in DC. For his part, JD bartered his computer ability, was a personal trainer to several group members, taught basic MMA skills, and on occasion was a social escort for a few well-to-do women. No money changed hands, but the group maintained a prominent tax attorney as a member should the IRS make inquiries. This barter group, coupled with his NFL and WWE savings, allowed JD to enjoy a lifestyle beyond that of most government workers.

George returned to the sofa. He set his cup down on a coffee table coaster and checked his Bureau phone for any messages.

"Hey," JD said as he spun around to face George. "The exam's running now. It'll take a while. Come here. I want to show you something awesome." He got to his feet and walked toward his bedroom.

George got up and followed him. JD went to his walk-in closet and flipped on the light.

"In here," he said.

The space was immaculate, a curated museum for clothes. On one side was his professional wardrobe, each item custom made of the finest natural wool and cotton fabrics: five matching wool suits; silk patterned ties, cotton shirts; one black calfskin belt, one pair of black Berluti derby shoes; one cashmere black overcoat. On the opposite side of the closet was all his matching casual wear: five button-down Oxfords; three long-sleeve, two short; three pairs of pants—no pleats, no cuffs; one dark brown belt and matching pair of casual shoes; one cream-colored walking coat. All items hung equally spaced on matching polished beechwood hangers. A couple of large black gym bags rested on the floor in opposite corners of the closet. These contained all of JD's laundered workout gear. His minimal jewelry and electronics were lined up on the wraparound closet shelf, surrounded by several casual Henleys and V-neck t-shirts that had been folded and stacked with exacting care.

"Close your eyes," JD said.

"JD, c'mon. I—"

"Just close 'em."

George did as he was told and could hear JD rustling around for a moment.

"Okay... open up!" JD was smiling broadly as he held out a solid burgundy tie toward George, displaying it as a sommelier would a fine bottle of wine. "Check it out, dude!"

"It's a tie," George said.

"Damn, bro. It's not just a tie. It's Vicuna wool."

"Yeah?"

"Vicuna wool! The rarest, most expensive fabric on earth! This shit costs about two grand a yard. It comes from some kinda sheep in the mountains of Peru. They can only shear 'em once every three years. Their hair is four times finer than human hair. Touch it, dude. Makes cashmere feel like sandpaper." JD rubbed the tie against his cheek and cooed like a child. "I got this tie made with a matching pocket square. I'm gonna eventually get four more ties and squares— one for each workday."

He handed George the Vicuna tie with solemnity. George held it gingerly and lightly rubbed its surface. He had to admit, it did feel real good.

"That's pretty nice, JD."

"'Pretty nice'? Fiber of the gods, dude! Gimme that tie back!" JD said as he snatched it from George and carefully hung it back up. "I ain't showing you my matching pocket square," he said in mock indignation.

"I said it was nice."

"Too late," JD said as he clicked off the closet light. He gave George a playful smack on the shoulder and mumbled "dumbass" as he passed.

It took JD about thirty more minutes to finish his forensic exam, not counting the two times George interrupted him to ask how much longer it would take.

When he finished, JD summarized his findings to George: There was a large amount of data on the drive for Allen's two-year use period. Negative results regarding the keyword searches. No digital nexus between Allen and any terrorist groups or political parties. As his brother said, Allen had done significant target research on the U.S. Capitol, presidential inaugurations, military-grade ordnance, and the like. He had also done a vast amount of research on various academic disciplines and historical events. Allen had the usual amount of porn on his computer, but nothing deviant or unexpected.

"What's the usual amount of porn?" George deadpanned. "I mean, for you or the rest of us?"

"Oh, look—hey everyone, it's funny man George," JD said, then paused a beat. "Anyway—back to business. Allen's declaration didn't come up. I'm going to have to search for that myself."

He turned back to the laptop. George stared out the window again and let JD work in silence.

It took JD twenty minutes to find what he was looking for. "Got it!" he shouted, then leaned into the screen and began to read.

"What does it—" George began, but JD waved a hand to shush him. George watched his eyes widen as he scrolled.

When he'd finished, JD let out a low whistle and slowly shook his head. "Dude, you gotta read this." He motioned George over and moved away from the standing desk to give him a space in front of the laptop.

George skimmed through Allen's declaration, his stomach tightening as he read. When he reached the end, he scrolled back up to the top and read it again, more slowly this time. Finally, he turned away from the laptop and shuffled back to the window wall. He stared out again at the National Mall and the destroyed Capitol Building. The stage for Allen's martyrdom.

He turned to face JD, who had taken a seat on the sofa.

"Is it legit?" George asked.

"Yes," JD responded. "Forensically, there's no signs of fraud or manipulation, either in the document itself or anywhere on the hard drive."

"Allen told me he had a copy of the declaration in his pocket, but there's no record of it in his property inventory. And he said he tried to post it to Facebook—"

"He did," JD said. "But he screwed up the delayed posting feature. It never went out."

George paced the living room, thinking.

"All the hundreds of interviews we've done to date… All of them say Allen despised politicians and wouldn't have anything to do with them," George said, still pacing and rubbing his huge hands together. "And you didn't find any contact between Allen and any politicians on his hard drive, right?"

"Nope."

George sat down on one of the chairs, facing JD. "Come to think of it," he said, "We only interviewed a couple of people who said that Allen was politically motivated, and those were leads that came directly from Hale's office. And Hale rejected my request to polygraph them."

"Well, they buried that declaration, that's for sure," JD said.

"Yeah, and Hale's been acting different. He's been anxious, more involved than usual. I was his supervisor. Known him his whole career. Something's not right."

They sat in silence.

"I was with Allen for over two hours at Reed," George went on. "Face to face. He's not crazy. And he wasn't lying to me. And I spent an entire afternoon in his living room in Iowa, looking his mother and brother in the eye. They weren't lying, either."

Another long silence.

"He did this alone," George said in hushed tone. "Just him."

"Shit," JD said with a hard, protracted exhale. He slumped back into the sofa with his fingers laced behind his head. "This is not good."

CHAPTER 12

JD Goldberg filled the doorway as he entered the executive conference room. He wore a Carolina blue suit and mustard shirt, all perfectly tailored and pressed. He also debuted his new Vicuna wool burgundy tie with matching pocket square. As always, he was the best-dressed man in the room.

JD strode quickly over to George, who stood at the end of the long oval mahogany table. The room was packed, but everyone stepped aside to provide a clear path for the behemoth bearing down on them. His wide eyes and tense jaw told George that something was wrong.

"What's up?" George asked.

"Dude," JD whispered. "They deleted the declaration! I pulled Allen's laptop out of evidence this morning to do the official forensic review, and it was gone. Something's up, man."

"You got a copy of it, right?"

"Three different copies in three different places."

"Good. I was afraid this might happen," George said.

"Yeah, good call. Glad we did the exam before you booked that laptop into evidence. What's our move?" JD asked.

"I'm going to brief Allen as a lone wolf. I want you to keep a close eye on Taylor and Hale."

"Got it," JD said, as he turned to walk to his seat opposite George at the other end of the long table.

"JD," George said. JD spun around. "Nice tie."

"Giddy-up," JD said with a smile. He again parted the sea of people as he went to his seat.

George sat down and scanned the faces around the conference table. He was not like them: many had surrendered; others had always been drones; some thought only of their own advancement; most were just trying to get through their day. None of his colleagues (save JD) shared his fire or compass setting. George grimaced and tugged at his collar. He had never been completely comfortable in suit and tie, even the Brooks Brothers navy blue classic he now wore. But there was work to be done, so George exhaled and stepped into his role as FBI Special Agent.

As the senior FBI official present, Hale called the meeting to order. He was at the right hand of General Taylor, who sat ramrod straight with his hands folded in front of him on the table. George noted that although it was officially Hale's meeting, it was Taylor who occupied the power seat at the table. George's boss, Ben Jamison, sat to the left of Taylor.

The conference room was full; about thirty people ringed the table. Another twelve or so back-benchers filled the small chairs that lined the walls of the room, like children too young to sit at the grown-up table. Hale kicked the meeting off, but the gravitational pull of the table was at its center—with Taylor. He turned his head and locked onto George, his amber eyes on fire. George swallowed hard. Taylor flicked him a smirk.

After his brief introductory comments, Hale turned the meeting over to George for his case briefing. George's stomach clenched. He was grateful to be briefing from his seat. He quickly centered himself and gave a solid thirty-minute case summary from his bullet-point outline.

His pulse and breath quickened as he reached his final point. He looked to JD at the far end of the table; JD gave him a subtle nod. George swallowed and licked his lips.

"In conclusion, based on my interview of the subject Allen and all the evidence gathered to date, it appears that Allen was a lone wolf operator who was not directed or inspired by any terrorist group or other entity or individuals—foreign or domestic."

Taylor's eyes narrowed as he threw an elbow into Hale's rib cage. Hale popped up in his seat, his bulbous forehead flushing red.

"Agent Moore," Hale sputtered. "We have reliable witness and source reporting that Allen was an agent of the left-wing agitators in the Democratic Party. The evidence does not point to a lone wolf."

"I respectfully disagree, sir. The source is unreliable, a local low-level snitch with an extensive criminal record. He is money motivated, and I don't believe he had the proper placement or access to Allen. He has provided unreliable reporting in the past, and—"

"Agent Moore," Taylor said in a resounding voice that hit the room like a thunderclap. "Listen to your deputy director. Everyone at this table thinks the source reporting is accurate. The Democrats put Allen up to it." Taylor leaned toward George, his eyes glowing. "Now, look—the country needs to move on from this tragedy. We've solved this case, thanks to you and your team of agents. Good work. I'm proud of all of you. It's time to move ahead."

"Thank you, sir, but I—"

Hale abruptly cut George off and thanked him for his briefing. He then stammered the meeting to a close and clumsily gathered his papers into a pile. Taylor was the only one who was not in motion. He remained in his seat, hands folded.

George grabbed his briefing book. Everyone else was filing out of the conference room, and George joined the line. He wanted to get the hell out of there. He made it only a few steps.

"George," Hale said. "A word?" George turned to face him and watched JD file out of the conference room with the rest of the herd. He stood alone in the conference room with Hale and Taylor.

"George," Hale said, using his first name in a transparent attempt to draw on their shared history. "We need you to get on board with us on this one. The source is solid. His reporting is reliable and corroborated by witness statements. Allen acted as an agent for the radical left wing of the Democratic Party. Got it?"

"The source reporting isn't corroborated, and the witness statements won't hold up," George replied evenly. "When I spoke with Allen at the hospital, he denied any affiliations. Said he had written a manifesto—he called it a declaration—that would prove he acted alone."

"And where is this magic manifesto now?" Taylor asked. Each word cut the air like a knife.

"We haven't found it yet," George lied.

"Or it doesn't exist!" Hale shouted.

"Agent Moore, you seem to be enamored with this Allen kid," Taylor said. "Do you believe *everything* he told you? Why take the word of a murderous, treasonous coward over the evidence your own investigation has produced? Over the learned conclusions of your deputy director?"

"Sir, it's just that—"

"Agent Moore," Taylor shouted. "I am not here to parse words with you. I've got the weight of this country on my shoulders. The American people are looking to me to lead them out of this shit-storm, and that is what I intend to do. I will do it with you or without you. You need to pick a team, son. Understood?"

George held his ground. And his tongue.

"Yes, General," Hale finally stammered. "No problem. I'll take care of it."

"Good," Taylor said, then strode out of the conference room.

Hale turned to face George, his face redder than before. "Goddammit, George. You just embarrassed me in front of the general. Who the hell do you think you are?" Spittle flew out of Hale's mouth and landed on George's shirt, just below his collar. George felt it land, but remained motionless.

"I was just doing my job."

"Your job is to do what I tell you to do!" Hale screeched. George stood in silence as Hale's outburst hung in the air.

"Okay," Hale began again, calmer this time. "We go way back, George. I personally picked you to run this case because you are a good agent, and I knew you could handle it. We both know you stepped on your dick in the PENTTBOM case. I'm giving you a second chance here... don't you see?"

George ground his teeth and seethed.

"Look, George. The bottom line is, I am ordering you, as your deputy director, to go along with me and the general on this thing. Allen was an agent of the Democrats. Period. Got it? If you play ball here, I'll see to it that you get an SES promotion. I'll bump you from street agent all the way up to section chief. And who knows—six months at HQ and you could be a Special Agent in Charge." Hale paused and lowered his voice. "If you don't come my way on this, I'll reassign this case to someone else and transfer your ass to San Juan." Hale straightened up, hooked his thumbs on his belt. "So, what's it going to be, George?"

George had always wanted to lead an entire FBI field office. SAC was his dream job. It typically took a street agent about eighteen years and five difficult promotions to reach that level. Hale was now dangling that carrot right in front of him. All he had to do was grab it.

George cleared his throat. "Could I have some time to think about it?"

"I'll give you seventy-two hours," Hale said, then softened his voice to an almost friendly tone. "Take it, George. Don't sabotage your career again by doing the wrong thing for the right reasons. This is no time to be a hero."

Hale patted him awkwardly on the shoulder and then gathered his papers and departed, leaving George alone in the conference room.

George stared at his reflection in the shine of the mahogany conference table for a long time.

CHAPTER 13

"I hate the government!" George said as he took the first hit off his second scotch. He had just finished paying his income taxes, which put him in the same funk every year. George needed to blow off a little steam, and the scotch had begun to take his measure.

"George, you *are* the government. You know that, right?" JD asked as he motioned to the bartender for another Guinness black and tan.

JD had insisted George come out this Wednesday night for a drink. They usually did not drink during the week, but these were unusual times. The bar was one of JD's regular haunts, located less than a mile from his downtown condo. It had the requisite dim lighting, a long bar and a smattering of four-top tables in the darker shadows. Exposed beams and a stained concrete floor gave the place an edgy, industrial vibe. Its swank location and pretentious prices ensured the proper clientele: political mover-shakers, corporate executives, and well-preserved thirty-something women who knew what they liked and how to get it.

Tonight JD and George sat at the bar, at the end opposite the entrance. From their seats they could survey the entire crowd and keep an eye on the only door in the place. JD was a big tipper, and all the bartenders liked him.

"Just got back from my accountant," George said as he looked straight ahead at his reflection in the mirror behind the bar. "I'm going to owe money again this year. What the fuck? I'm only taking home about half what I make. The government's got its hands in my pockets, squeezing me dry every two weeks. I feel like burning something down every time I look at my paycheck."

JD knew what was coming—George's annual tax rant. He took a big hit off his black and tan, then sat back to enjoy the show. He didn't have to wait long.

"You know, wars and crisis have always led to tax abuses," George said, turning on his barstool to face JD. "Take 1862, for example. Lincoln started a temporary tax to finance the Civil War. Then World War One comes along—the war to end all wars. Congress passes the sixteenth Constitutional amendment, and—bam! Federal income tax is permanent."

JD rolled his eyes. "What's up with all you Boston guys and taxes?"

George took another hit off his scotch and kept going. "Do you know that Tax Freedom Day is May twentieth this year?"

"What?" JD asked.

"Tax Freedom Day. How long we have to work to pay our tax bill. Every penny you earn from January first until May twentieth— one hundred and forty days—goes directly to the government. You like that, buddy?"

"Okay—let it all out," JD said in his best therapist voice.

"This is why half my check is gone every two weeks!" George slapped the bar hard enough to cause a few people to turn and look in his direction. He didn't notice. "The government takes colossal amounts of our money—*my money*—and spends it on all kinds of shit I don't want. You know where your money's going?"

"No idea, bro."

"See? That's what I'm talking about." George threw back the last of his scotch and returned his glass to the bar with a *thwack*.

JD raised his eyebrows. "You're too uptight, man. Gotta loosen it up a bit," he said. "I may be color-blind, but you, my friend, are the one who only sees black and white. Don't take everything so seriously. You're like… a bull. Always ready to charge the red cape. That's how they trick you. You don't have to right every wrong, or settle everyone's hash. It's not worth it."

George groaned.

"You'd've been better off as one of those medieval knights. Rescuing princesses from towers and shit. Or running dudes through with those long poles… you know, those things…"

"Jousting," George said.

"Yeah, that's it. Jousting."

"Jester."

"What?" JD asked.

"That makes you the court jester, funnyman."

"That's okay, dude. Funnymen get all the pussy. Plus, look at me. I'm rocking that jester suit. That shit was real silk back then, I think."

"I think all those guys were eunuchs," George said with a grin.

JD puckered his lips and grimaced. "Nothing funny about losing your balls, dude. Tears of a clown."

George drained the last of his scotch, then rubbed his face with both hands. "So—I'm too serious. I should be more like you? That's what you're saying? You don't take anything seriously."

JD opened his eyes and mouth wide in feigned astonishment. "I'll have you know I take some things quite seriously."

"Like what?"

"Umm… high ponytails, for one thing," JD said, and then let out a visceral grunt. "Silky hair, cascading tail pulled up high on the head. Gotta be high on the head, bro." He grunted again. "Like a horse tail, you know? I could just grab that tail from behind—"

"What the hell?" George said with a chuckle.

"Dude—eighth grade gym class. Jenny Richardson's tits just came in—big time. So she comes out of the locker room wearing this tight little outfit, and she's got an awesome high ponytail tied up with a pink scrunchie. And we're playing co-ed volleyball that day. The *bouncing*, dude. *Both* my testicles dropped that day in the gym. I never looked back."

George smiled and shook his head. Raised his glass to the bartender and tapped the rim for a refill.

"I don't know, JD. Work. Cases. People. It doesn't have to be this way," George said, his voice trailing off.

"Dude, you spend too much time in Should-Be Land. You need to visit Planet Reality more."

"I prefer illusion to despair," George said as he looked at his empty glass.

"Well, George, my friend, when you're president, you can fix everything. But tonight, you're just another dude sitting on a barstool solving all the world's problems."

"That supposed to cheer me up?"

"You know I love you man," JD said.

The bartender arrived and delivered another round for both George and JD.

The two men sat in silence for several minutes as they looked at the television mounted up high in the corner of the bar. A panel of CNN talking heads were droning on about something, gesticulating wildly. Thankfully the sound was down.

"So—what are you gonna tell Hale?" JD asked.

George rolled the scotch around in his glass and sighed loudly. "I can't do it. I'm not getting into bed with Hale and Taylor. They're gonna pull me from the case. Transfer me to San Juan."

"You told Kacey Anne yet?"

"No. We don't talk much these days. Besides, she ain't going. Can you picture Kacey Anne in San Juan?" George chuckled and shook his head at the thought of it.

"Sorry, bro."

"So Hale's gonna end my career and my marriage. All because I'm not a 'team player,'" George said, using air quotes. He took a strong pull off his scotch. "Oh well. I've had a good run."

The two men sat in silence, studying their reflections in the mirror over the bar.

"Temptation resisted is the true test of character," JD blurted out after a time.

"What?"

"Heard it in a movie once," JD said. "Not many guys would stand their ground, facing what you're facing. I'm proud of you, bro."

"Well, I've got that going for me," George said with a weak smile. More silence.

"Dude, you know what you need? You need some passion in your life. When's the last time you had carnal relations with a woman?"

"Hmm. Let me think." George stroked his chin. "What year is it?"

"Daaamn, dude. How'd you even get out of bed in the morning? I'd have my head in an oven. How about I wing-man for you tonight? We'll find you a nice lady, and you can take her out back and bang it out. You could—"

Someone in the crowd yelled, "Turn it up!"

Both George and JD whipped around on their barstools and saw a guy pointing at the television. When they turned back around, the bartender had already turned the volume way up. A hush fell over the crowd.

George could not believe his eyes. CNN had broken to a live press conference. General Taylor stood at a podium in his dress blue uniform, the epitome of martial splendor. He was undeniably telegenic, completely at ease in front of the camera. The general's eyes looked through the camera and into George's soul. He shuddered.

It was a masterful speech. Taylor hit all the right patriotic notes. He took his audience on a brief history lesson of America's past wars and crises, and emphasized how "we Americans" always overcame adversity to grow stronger. He promised his audience that he would lead them through this current crisis and give them a stronger and safer America.

Taylor then dropped a bombshell. He looked right at the camera and said that the FBI CAPBOM investigation had revealed that the bomber, Josh Reid Allen, had acted as an agent of the radical left-wing agitators in the Democratic Party, and that these politicians would be held accountable for their treasonous acts. Taylor then promised that the government would vigorously pursue the death penalty against Allen, and that he would personally see Allen hanged from a gallows erected where his missile had struck—the West Lawn of the Capitol. Taylor banged his fist on the podium for emphasis.

He then thanked the FBI, the military, and various federal, state, and local agencies for their assistance in the CAPBOM investigation. And then he added, "And I want to issue a special thanks to Agent George Moore with the FBI for his tireless work in solving this case."

George felt all the air leave his lungs. *Did he just say what I thought he said?*

Taylor finished with the standard "and God Bless The United States of America" trope. The crowd paused a beat, then burst into thunderous applause. Someone in the back shadows of the bar started chanting "USA! USA! USA!" and it was immediately picked up by the rest of the patrons. JD and George just stared at each other until the chant finally died down and the high-fives began.

"Hale didn't even wait for my answer!" George exclaimed.

"And why is Taylor making the announcement?" JD asked, his voiced pitched higher than normal. "It should've been the AG, or the acting president... what's-her-name. He just bitched them both out on national television." JD shook his head. "Well—at least we know who's running the show now."

"They set me up!" George yelled.

The crowd was jubilant. A drunk guy in the far corner of the bar was trying to start a second round of the "USA!" chant. They didn't want the truth, George realized bitterly. They wanted the man with the chest full of shiny medals promising them everything would be all right. They wanted their 55-inch smart TVs and their 4WD SUVs. They didn't want a rogue FBI agent to pull back the curtain and show them their wizard was no wizard at all.

George dropped his head. *If I come forward now, they'll crucify me.*

He turned to study the exuberant faces of the bar patrons, aware that the scene before him was no doubt playing out all across the country tonight. He threw back the last of his scotch and slammed the glass on the bar.

"What're you gonna do?" JD asked.

"I'm fucked."

CHAPTER 14

I'm at a parade in a big city. The boisterous crowd lines the street ten deep all along the parade route. Kids sit on their parents' shoulders. Everyone is happy. The sun is shining, and the sky is cobalt blue. I stand deep in the crowd, enjoying the floats and marching bands that flow by. The crowd cheers. I eat popcorn from a large red-striped bag.

Suddenly, dark clouds obscure the sun. A blustery cold wind kicks up, causing discarded plastic grocery bags and other debris to blow around in the street, menacing the parade participants. Parents slap knitted hats onto their children's heads.

Then I see it. It's one of those VIP hero floats, and it carries the boy cop who shot me eight times. He is smiling and waving to the applauding crowd. His perky wife and two beautiful children—a boy and girl—join him on the float. The family dog is up there too. Wait. No, it couldn't be! I shield my eyes with my hands to get a better look. My stomach drops. The boy on the float is my son Nicholas. The girl is Emily, whom I saw the day I blew the Capitol all to hell. The dog is her yellow Lab, the one she named Dougie, after President Douglas Turner—one of the thousands of people I killed that day. They are all waving to the cheering crowd.

I drop my bag, and popcorn scatters to the wind. I desperately push through the crowd as the float passes by. I finally reach the curb, hurdle the barricade, and stand in the middle of the street. The float is about thirty feet in front of me, moving away down the parade route. I scream *my son's name several times. He turns around. He is the only one who can hear my voice. His face has aged since I hugged him goodbye. Nicholas just stares at me, melancholy. He slowly waves goodbye. I scream his name again. He nudges the girl, Emily, who turns and gives me the same cheery see-you-later wave she gave me at the memorial. Dougie the dog barks his adieu. All three then turn away from me.*

The float begins to pick up speed. I run to catch it, dodging people and screaming my son's name as I go. But the float is going too fast, and it pulls away from me and goes off into the distance. I stop running, bent over, hands on knees, gasping for breath. The parade continues around me. The marchers pay no notice, bumping me as they pass.

I catch my breath and stand up. I turn around and start slowly walking down the middle of the parade route, in the opposite direction of the marchers. I walk with purpose, chin up and shoulders squared. The crowd now sees me for the first time and they begin to boo and jeer. The parade marchers still pay me no heed as they pass by. I walk this way in silence for over a mile.

A light, fluffy snow begins to fall. I finally reach a large gap in the parade procession where the crowd on either side has gone silent. In the distance I can see Santa. He's at the end of the parade, slowly walking down the center of the street, his long beard and unruly mop of white hair blowing in the wind. But Santa is not dressed in his red outfit. He's wearing my Marine Corps dress uniform. Marine Santa has a single-harness snare drum slung over his shoulder, resting slightly askew on his left hip. He is playing the iconic military drumbeat, a scowl etched on his face.

As the gap between us closes to about fifty feet, Santa turns into a young drummer boy in the Continental Army of the American Revolution. He is no more than fourteen years old, with a dirty face and a tattered, mismatched uniform. He has no shoes, only rags wrapped around his feet that leave a bloody trail behind him. Yet he marches erect and proud, his drumbeat cracking the still, cold air.

As the drummer boy approaches, I see he now wears my son's face, the same aged face I saw on the float. I quicken my step as the drumbeat gets louder and louder. I reach out to the drummer boy, and as I am about to touch him everything begins to fade. I flail about, to no avail. I begin to rise, floating to the surface of consciousness.

Josh Allen opened his eyes to the sight of Officer Orlando Rodriguez standing at his bedside, his fingers drumming on the plastic side rail of the hospital bed. Rodriguez was unshaven, his tie and top two buttons undone to reveal his second chin. It looked like he had slept in his police uniform. An arrogant grin had replaced the mad-dog stare that Rodriguez usually wore when he greeted Allen. Rodriguez's musky body odor caused Allen to tilt his head away. Rodriguez kept one hand on the side rail of Allen's bed, while the other remained behind his back.

It was the middle of the night and the floor was quiet. Allen's door curtain was closed, his room lights off; both things were highly unusual. The room was dark, except for the slivers of dim hall lighting that danced around the corners of the curtain. Rodriguez hovered over Allen, backlit in the faint light. The only sound was the hum of Allen's life support machine.

"I never thought it would be you," Allen said.

"General Taylor spoke on national television tonight. It's all over for you. Case closed. Even called you 'the new Benedict Arnold.' Whaddaya think of that?"

Rodriguez leaned over the bed as he spoke. His teeth were yellow and stained. His breath reeked of cigarettes and cheap whiskey.

"It was the money, right?" Rodriguez asked. "I mean, that's why you did it."

Allen kept his silence.

"How much? Must've been some serious bank, huh? Am I right?"

Silence.

"How about you tell me where all that money is, huh? I'll split it with your wife and kid. Fifty-fifty. Ain't gonna do you no good no more. Whaddaya say?"

Allen again kept his silence.

"Okay," Rodriguez said as he slapped his hand on the bed side rail. "Have it your way. Tonight the general told the country he was gonna hang your ass on the Capitol steps. But you're gonna die tonight—right here, right now, strapped down in this hospital bed," he said with a sneer. "They called me in. They said they couldn't wait no more. Said there were timelines to keep and lessons to be taught. Whatever the hell that means. All I know is that they offered me FBI creds to kill you. And you know what? I jumped at the chance."

Allen thought of the boy cop and wished the kid had finished the job. Or maybe he should have just done it himself at the memorial. He did not fear death, had already accepted it as his fate for what he'd done. But he did not want to die at the hand of this man.

"I just wish I didn't have to do you in the dark like this. Shit. If everyone knew what I was about to do, I'd be a hero—like that cop that shot you. I'd be drowning in pussy." Rodriguez laughed, which caused him to cough, washing his fetid breath over Allen.

"So, Mr. Allen. I'm gonna kill you, and they're gonna make me an FBI Special Agent. What do you think of that?"

"Why don't you loosen these straps, and I'll show you what I think."

That wiped the smile off Rodriguez's face. He brought the big hospital bed pillow out from behind his back.

"Any last words, shit-stain?" Rodriguez asked as he grabbed the pillow in both hands and raised it to his chest.

The bombing flashed through Allen's mind. He saw the missile leave the tube and fly toward its target. He saw himself slumped at the base of the monument, awaiting the arrival of the boy cop. He saw the barrel of the boy cop's gun, big as a sewer pipe, spit fire and smoke. Felt the punch of the first bullets hit his body before everything went dark. He regretted nothing, other than leaving his son without a father. He would carry that sin into the afterworld. All he could do now was hope his message reached his countrymen, and that they would answer the call.

Allen took his final breath, then slowly exhaled. A lightness filled his body. He felt he could float to the ceiling but for his bed restraints. He felt free. His spirit soared. He found the serenity and clarity that had eluded him throughout his short life. The best part of him would survive. A man such as Rodriguez could never take this from him.

"I resign my spirit to God, my son, and my country," Allen said in a soft voice. He then turned his head away from Rodriguez. Allen would die well. He would not struggle or yell out. He would not give Rodriguez the satisfaction.

The pillow covered his face. He held his breath as Rodriguez applied force.

Josh Allen embraced the approaching darkness.

CHAPTER 15

Asphyxia was the official cause of death. Josh Allen's autopsy was done at Walter Reed within two hours of his death. The military forensic pathologist's findings were that Allen had died of natural causes, and that the asphyxia was most likely caused by a pulmonary embolism.

George was awakened by a call from Allen's attending physician at about five a.m. He jumped in the shower and rushed down to Walter Reed. He arrived just before sunrise. The darkness reflected his mood.

George rushed through reception and up the stairs, and found the doctor at the nurses' station. He explained that Allen had died in his bed at approximately 1:40 a.m. The doctor said that Allen had likely developed a blood clot in his leg, probably the result of him being strapped immobile to his bed for an extended period of time. He'd thrown the clot, and it had blocked the pulmonary artery, which deprived his organs and tissues of oxygen. The doctor explained that pulmonary embolisms were common in bedridden patients.

The nursing staff had seen nothing unusual or suspicious on the floor that night.

George asked why Allen's autopsy had been conducted so fast. The doctor replied that there were standing orders to autopsy Allen immediately should he die at Walter Reed. Allen was to be cremated immediately following his autopsy, which was unusual as well. When asked what he made of these policy deviations, the doctor shrugged and said he was just following orders. These matters were decided well above his pay grade.

George asked to see Allen's body before cremation. The doctor made a couple of calls, then escorted George to the basement. There were two military guards posted at the door to the autopsy room. They glared at George as he and the doctor entered the room. The autopsy had been completed, and Allen's body was in a refrigerated chamber awaiting transport to the crematorium. The morgue attendant slid open the chamber and unzipped the body bag.

George felt an unexpected jolt of emotion as he looked down at Allen. His body had long lines of metal sutures, like zippers, that crisscrossed his torso. His skull cap had been hastily stuck back atop his head, askew like a jack-o-lantern. He had just interviewed this boy two weeks ago, found and read his declaration only last week. And now he was dead. What a waste. George took one last look at the terrorist America did not know, and motioned to the attendant that he had seen enough.

It took George most of the day to finish his investigation and interviews at Walter Reed. He summoned Officer Rodriguez and interviewed him about his last night with Allen. Rodriguez was now animated and buoyant, not the same sullen guy George had seen sitting outside Allen's hospital room the past two weeks. He said nothing unusual had happened during his shift, that he was as surprised as anyone when the nurse had found Allen dead in his bed. The world was better off, he said with a sneer. He was sick of pulling security duty and tired of having to wear his police uniform every day.

Rodriguez then requested that George assign him to the CAPBOM command post so he could get caught up on all the action. When George demurred, Rodriguez began to pepper him with questions about Quantico and new agents' training. George cut their conversation short and told Rodriguez to go home.

George did the same, and arrived back at his Vienna townhouse a little after three p.m. With traffic, he knew he wouldn't have made it to the office until after four p.m. It was a waste of time to drive all the way into the office, just to turn around and drive back home. He owed the government two more hours of work today, but there was no need to spend it in traffic. He poured himself two fingers of scotch and sat at his kitchen table to review his notes from all the interviews he had done today.

In the silence of his kitchen, his mind drifted to the chilling thought he had tried to dismiss all day: Were General Taylor and Hale involved in Allen's death? The medical evidence that Allen had died of natural causes was plausible enough, but George's gut told him otherwise. Why the rush to autopsy and cremation? Based on all he knew, he doubted Allen would have consented to such a thing.

And Rodriguez was acting peculiar; the guy clearly knew more than he was saying.

But more to the point, would a chairman of the Joint Chiefs of Staff and a deputy director of the FBI really be involved in murder? It sounded preposterous to George as he phrased the question to himself. Why would Taylor and Hale want to kill Allen? And why now? George knew Allen's conviction had been assured, his date with the hangman's noose a certainty. The public had clamored for it, and the government had been all too eager to oblige. Why not let the investigation play out?

An insider had stolen Allen's declaration; that much he knew. He also knew that both Taylor and Hale were pushing Allen as an agent of the Democratic Party, which George knew was a lie. George was sure Taylor and Hale were up to something big. But what? Why had they gone to such great lengths to silence Allen and hide the truth?

George had a life-changing decision to make in less than twenty-four hours. Tomorrow he would report to Hale's office and provide his answer. Would he "play ball" and collect his big promotion at the end of the case? Or would he tell the truth and go down in flames—just like he had in the PENTTBOM case?

He sipped his scotch, considering. What would his big promotion really get him? Entry into the boys' club—the Senior Executive Service. George had known many good "SESers," but most were risk-averse, career-first office politicians who had sold their souls for the brass ring. This was Hale's Club, filled with his people. George had seen it before, a phenomenon known as the Dunning-Kruger Effect: incompetent people failing to recognize their own lack of skill, grossly overestimating their abilities, all the while unable to recognize talent in other people who were actually competent. Did he really want to join such a club?

He really had no stomach for office politics, nor had he ever respected anyone who did. He was a good agent who had earned the respect of his peers in the trenches. A real call-it-like-I-see-it guy. And as such, he would always be an outlier in the SES club.

And what to make of Hale's promise? Even if he did give George his SES promotion at the end of the CAPBOM case, George would promote no further. Hale and Dunning-Kruger would see to that. So, in the end, George would likely never obtain the position he coveted most—Special Agent in Charge of an FBI field office.

George could not be like Hale or any of his SES buddies. He would not lie or "play ball" to get ahead. His soul was not for sale, and that was what differentiated him from Hale and his ilk. As always, he would stand his ground and let the chips fall as they may.

But standing up to Taylor and Hale was not without risk. He thought of Josh Allen. George did not fear Hale, but Taylor was another animal altogether. He was much more dangerous. Taylor was cunning, decisive. He would take extraordinary risks to get what he wanted. The general was also a psychopathic megalomaniac. George had a healthy fear of Taylor and would try to avoid direct conflict with him if possible.

Heroes are often born in the dark shadows, fated to be martyred at the bar of injustice. George shot back his last slug of scotch. So be it.

He got to his feet and walked his glass to the kitchen sink, decision made. In twenty-four hours, he would meet with Hale to inform him that, effective immediately, he was stepping down as the CAPBOM case agent. Fourteen years earlier, George had withdrawn as the PENTTBOM squad supervisor for similar reasons. He wondered if Hale was serious about transferring him to San Juan.

He would also leak Allen's declaration to the media. He had never leaked anything before, never even considered such a thing, but he felt strongly that the American people should know the truth. History should judge Allen on his merits. George owed him that much.

George marveled on his failures as a husband and an agent. He was a good man. How could it all have gone so wrong? *Good lenses, bad frames.*

George had faced into the wind all his life, had never been afforded the shelter of fraternity. He felt exhausted and alone.

He then saw the headlights of Kacey Anne's car filter through the sheer drapes in the living room. George looked at this watch—4:35 p.m. The fireworks were about to start. Tonight he would tell her about his lost promotion, and their prospects for San Juan.

No bueno.

CHAPTER 16

The old woman matter-of-factly explained that the CIA was spying on her through the microwave oven in her kitchen. She said she'd visited WFO last month and the man had told her to wrap her head in tinfoil to keep the CIA from intercepting her thoughts. She had been dutifully wearing her tinfoil hat all month, but complained that it was no longer working. She was desperate.

This was George's life now. It had been two weeks since he'd met with Hale and stepped down as case agent of the CAPBOM investigation. The retribution had been swift. George had received a call over that weekend that he had been relieved of his duties as the JTTF Coordinator, and reassigned as the full-time complaint duty agent, a position created especially for him. Complaint duty was the bane of every street agent. It required them to suit up and interview "walk-in" complainants, who were mostly mentally unbalanced. Few matters they raised warranted further FBI inquiry. It was a bad used car lot, cold black coffee in a Styrofoam cup. Nine hours a day, five days a week. It was hell.

George dispatched the old woman adroitly. First, he got her to focus by telling her that this was a serious matter, and that she had to listen to him very carefully. Then, in his most authoritative FBI voice, he instructed the woman to go into a dark closet and remove her tinfoil hat, because everyone knew the CIA could not penetrate hollow-core doors. Next, she must roll that hat up into a tight little ball, to trap all the spy rays, and leave it in the back of her closet. Finally, and most importantly, George told the woman she had to cover her microwave oven in tinfoil, as this was the only way to thwart the CIA villainy. She thanked George repeatedly as he shuffled her out of the WFO reception area.

All field offices rotate complaint duty, so a given agent only has to do it a couple of times a year. George's reassignment to permanent complaint duty agent had been designed not only to grind him down but also to humiliate him, as the entire office was made aware of his demotion. Throughout the day, agents would come by to thank him for covering their complaint shift. George responded with good humor, but he was a fiercely prideful man and the jabs stung. *The Bureau sometimes eats its own.*

Between walk-ins, George's mind wandered. Hale had not taken his decision well, and he had been looking over his shoulder for the past two weeks. Hale had first tried to talk him out of it, then rebuked him with spittle-spewing vitriol. He had accused George of leaking Allen's declaration to the media, then said he would see him prosecuted for it. George had feigned ignorance and reminded Hale that no declaration had been received into FBI evidence. This sent Hale into a rage, and the encounter had ended with Hale dismissing George with the warning that things were about to get difficult for him.

It was 4:05 p.m., March 15, 2021. The Ides of March. George had noted the portentous date when he'd first arrived for work this morning, but just as he was breathing a sigh of relief that the endless shift was almost over, the security officer appeared at George's desk, accompanied by a young SWAT agent he did not know.

"Mr. Moore, please come with us," the officer said in a neutral voice.

"What's this all about?" George asked.

"Sir, please come with us. ADIC Jamison wants to see you."

George rose to his feet and followed the pair to Jamison's office. George figured he was probably about to receive his transfer orders to San Juan, but the two-person escort seemed incongruous. His suspicions were heightened when they brought him not to the boss's office but to his private conference room.

His heart sank as he entered the room. It felt cold, and his mind involuntarily flashed back to the morgue that held Josh Allen's corpse. A dark-haired woman in an expensive-looking suit sat at the head of the conference table, and she motioned for George to sit down. He took a seat on one side of the large conference table; ten grim-faced FBI executives sat lined up across from him. Taylor and Hale sat in the center of the group, and both men smirked as George settled into his seat. Hale avoided eye contact with him, as juries did when they were about to return a guilty verdict.

So this was going to be worse than San Juan.

The woman introduced herself as Elizabeth Bennett, the FBI Assistant Director for the Office of Professional Responsibility. George felt his blood run cold. OPR investigated agent misconduct and levied heavy-handed punishments. Bennett got right to business. After she notified George that this meeting was being recorded, she read the charges: insubordination; lying under oath (false certification of time and attendance records); time and attendance fraud; misuse of a Bureau car; and drinking on duty.

The insubordination charge was based on George's refusal to follow one or more of Hale's direct orders. The remainder of the charges stemmed from the day George had gone to Walter Reed to investigate Allen's death, to wit: George had signed out his time card (under penalty of perjury) at 5:00 p.m. that day, when in fact he had ceased work at 4:35 p.m. He was not approved to work from home, so operating a Bureau car to his home was an unauthorized deviation that constituted misuse. Additionally, he had consumed alcohol while still on duty, a violation of the FBI's so-called bright-line prohibition.

George's throat tightened; his breathing became labored. Each charge hit him like the lash of a whip. The jackals seated across the table—their nostrils filled with the scent of blood and distress—leaned forward in their chairs, watching him closely, creeping in for the kill.

Everything in the room slowed down. George felt like he was falling. The woman kept talking. George's vision narrowed as her voice grew distant. His heartbeat, ever quickening, echoed in his ears. George saw his right hand begin to shake. He grabbed it with his left and put it under the table on his lap.

The woman explained that this meeting constituted official notice, and as it was not a hearing on the merits, she would not allow George to comment on the charges leveled at him. George looked at Taylor and Hale. *They were enjoying this.* His anxiety evaporated, replaced by raw aggression. These two men were trying to destroy him. This was war.

He took both hands out of his lap and placed them solidly on the table in front of him, fingers laced together. If it was war they wanted, war they would get. He was not going down without a fight.

"Special Agent Moore?" she asked a second time, her tone agitated now.

George focused his thoughts and looked directly at her.

"I asked if you understood and acknowledged the charges filed against you, and that these charges may result in you being dismissed from the rolls of the FBI?"

"Yes."

"For the record, the agent has acknowledged the charges and potential outcome he now faces," she said, reading from a form in front of her. She pushed the form across the table to George. He read and signed it, and pushed it back toward her. She placed the form in her folder, closed it, then lifted an expensive leather briefcase from the floor and placed the folder in that, leaving the tabletop in front of her empty. She snapped the briefcase shut, sat up straight, and fixed George with a look of disgust.

"Agent Moore, after much deliberation, and based on the severity of the charges against you, I have decided that it is in the best interest of the FBI that I place you on paid administrative leave—effective immediately."

She motioned to someone behind George. "Agent Ross, please assist Agent Moore in surrendering his weapon and credentials to ADIC Jamison." Ross, the young SWAT agent, stepped forward as George rose to his feet. Ross reached for George's arm, a soft control technique used to escort compliant prisoners. George froze him with a hard look, and the young agent dropped his hands to his side.

With every eye in the room on him, George walked the length of the table to where ADIC Jamison was seated. Both men fought to keep their emotions in check. Jamison knew George to be a good agent, and that he was witnessing a good man getting screwed. George removed the folding leather case containing his FBI credentials and gold badge from the left breast pocket of his suit coat. He reached across the table and offered it to Jamison, who winced as he took it from George's hand. George then reached for his weapon, which he carried in a leather holster clipped to his belt.

"I'll take that. Leave the gun in the holster," Ross said from a respectable distance to his left.

Jamison nodded, and George walked slowly back to Ross, removed his holster, and handed it to the young agent. Jamison's eyes narrowed; his lips pressed into a thin line. He then turned to face Hale, who ignored him.

The phalanx of executives now rose to their feet and stood behind their chairs on the opposite side of the table. They all wore the same smug expression. Ross and the security officer flanked George and walked him out of the conference room.

The defrocking of George Nelson Moore was complete.

They were in the lobby area outside the conference room, headed toward the elevator, when George heard a familiar voice at his back.

"May I have a word, Agent Moore?"

George and the two officers turned and saw Taylor walking double time toward them. He wore his ASU Class B uniform: blue pants with yellow stripe, pressed long-sleeve white shirt with a chest full of medals, and four-star shoulder bars. Taylor smiled as he approached, but his eyes were having none of it.

Ross, clearly just out of the military, straightened up and said, "Yes sir, General," as he stood aside.

Taylor made a grand gesture of shaking George's hand and thanking him for his contribution to the CAPBOM case. Ross took another step away from them. Taylor grabbed George by the elbow and forcefully pulled him close. George was taken aback by the old man's strength.

Taylor put his lips to George's ear and whispered in a guttural tone, "You're finished. You know that, don't you? And I'm the one who put you down." He exhaled in George's ear. His breath smelled like burned coffee. "I just wanted you to know that." His irregular, jagged teeth were inches from George's jugular. His razor stubble scratched against George's face.

"It was your wife who betrayed you," Taylor went on. "She gave us everything. And she was easy. We offered her a hundred grand and she jumped at it. I would've paid double to put the noose around your neck." He grunted. "I just wanted you to know that too."

George shoved Taylor with enough force to separate the two men. The SWAT agent jumped in between them.

"You mess with the bull, you get the horns," Taylor gloated.

Ross guided George toward the elevator. George spun around, taking the SWAT agent with him.

"General," he called across the lobby. "I look forward to seeing you again."

"Until then," Taylor said, standing at attention.

George shook Ross off his elbow as they waited for the elevator. The car was packed when it arrived. On the way down to the first floor no one would look at him. Finally, the elevator door pinged open and everyone piled out.

George turned to Ross and said, "I got it from here."

The agent shook his head and said, "They told me to escort you off the property."

Ross walked one step behind George as they crossed the field office main lobby past the metal detectors. George felt the eyes of the security cameras watching him. He paused in front of the big, heavy glass doors that swung out to the stone courtyard in front of the building.

"Sorry about all this," Ross said as he pointed toward the courtyard. "I'm just doing my job."

George stepped out into a horde of media, which sprang to life when they saw him, encircling him like hyenas. Television cameras flicked on; microphones were shoved in his face. It was Taylor and Hale's last humiliation: former agent George Moore would lead the evening news with footage of his "perp walk" out of the FBI office that he had faithfully served for over two decades.

George stood erect in the eye of the media storm. He ignored the questions shouted at him, and instead found a television camera and glowered into the living rooms of America.

CHAPTER 17

WEDNESDAY, MARCH 31, 2021; 10:52 P.M. (EDT)
THE GARDENS; WASHINGTON HIGHLANDS
SOUTHEAST WASHINGTON, DC

George came to sprawled out on the stained stall floor in a puddle of urine. His neck hurt, and a coppery taste filled his mouth. His rolled his parched tongue around in his mouth. His lip was split and bleeding, but at least all his teeth were there, as best he could tell. He struggled to his knees. The rancid frothy water in the toilet bowl made him retch. The bowl had a brown slime ring at waterline. Several curly black pubic hairs glowed against the filthy white porcelain. The sight of those pubic hairs is what started his retching—or maybe it was all the cheap whiskey he had slammed into his body the past seven hours. He spewed several more times, chunks of partially digested fast food floated on top of the green stew in the bowl. Bile and stomach acid stung his throat and filled his nostrils.

At last, spent, George pushed against the wall to steady himself as he rose to his feet and stumbled out of the bathroom. He looked both ways down the long, dark hallway. He had only been here two weeks and was still unsure which room was his; all the doors looked the same. He turned right and hugged the wall, shouldering his way down the hall, peering at each door in turn. Finally he saw one that looked familiar. He tested the doorknob, then stumbled in and passed out on the air mattress on the floor.

———————————

Thursday, April 1, 2021; 8:20 a.m. (EDT)
The Gardens; Washington Highlands
Southeast Washington, DC

He was awakened by a pounding on his door, the first time anyone in this place had acknowledged his existence. Angry male voices growled for the white boy to get his ass out in the hall—now. George opened the door to see four large black men staring him down. The biggest one grunted that Nesha wanted to see him, and told George to follow him. So, with two in front and two in back, George was escorted back down the long, dark hallway. He noticed several doors crack open as he approached, and heard the soft jeers and snickers as he passed.

They walked toward a beacon of light at the end of the hallway, which turned out to be a solitary room, set apart from the others. The four angry men posted up outside it, and the big guy leaned into George, warned him to be cool, then pushed him over the threshold and into the bright light of the room.

George squinted and held onto the back of a chair to steady himself. A king-size bed took up most of the space in the room. The woman in it took up *all* of the space in the bed. She was enormous, easily over 600 pounds, and appeared bedridden. She sat upright, her back braced against the wall. The large window behind her was open slightly; a set of mini-blinds tinkled like wind chimes in the cold early morning air. The room was clean and tidy but smelled of cigarettes and fried chicken.

Her huge legs were spread-eagled around an overturned plastic bucket tucked tightly into her crotch. Her feet looked small and dainty against her gargantuan legs. Her manicured toes were painted rose pink. A new MacBook Pro sat on a large tray that rested on top of the bucket. George could not tell if she had anything on below the waist. He sure hoped so. Thankfully, a short-sleeve fuchsia t-shirt, with the armholes slit open, covered her enormous breasts.

"Well, good morning," the woman said in a soft voice that belied her size. "Name's Tre'Nesha. Everyone round here calls me Nesha." She looked George up and down. "I've been wonderin' when you gonna stop by to visit. PM done told me he be puttin' someone in that broke-ass room, but I never figured it'd be a white boy."

George swayed as he fought to keep his balance. He clutched the chair back with a death grip.

"You know what day it is?" Nesha asked.

George shook his head.

"It be April Fool's Day—fool! And child, you be actin' the fool since your ass be on my floor!" Nesha laughed, which prompted a hacking cough that made her fat rolls undulate like a lava lamp. "I figured you to be the po-lice. So I told my people to leave you be. We all been watchin' you, though." She grinned. Her teeth were straight and brilliant white. "And child... whooo... you ain't no cop no more. No cop be drinkin' and pukin' like that! No Feds neither. Sheeeeit. You be vomiting up my hall every night for the past two weeks. You just a broke-down, drunk-ass white boy."

"What do you want?" George asked.

"Let's be real. I can smell your drunk ass from here. Go sober up and come back to see me tomorrow mornin'. Get you some soap and water, and wash your damn self. A man needs to be proper clean before he sits to visit with a lady." Nesha paused to catch her breath. "Mmmm-hhhhmmm."

George just stared at her, dumbfounded.

"Go on, now. I got business to do." She waved her hand, and the four angry men suddenly reappeared and escorted George out of the room. They walked him out a few steps, then pushed him firmly in the back. By the time George regained his balance and turned around, the men were back at their sentry posts.

"Go on now, white boy," the big guy said. "You heard her. Bounce."

George stumbled down the dark hallway back toward his room. Graffiti and peeling paint covered the walls. His shoes made a tacky, crunching sound on the sticky linoleum floor tiles, which were littered with broken shards of fluorescent bulbs that had fallen from the dropped ceiling.

He came to the hallway bathroom he had defiled last night, and went in to check the damage. He flicked the light on and paused while his eyes adjusted. The squalid little room still reeked of vomit. He flushed the toilet a few times, using his shoe on the handle.

George grabbed the sides of the sink and looked into the cracked mirror. He gasped at the man staring back at him. Dried vomit crusted the corners of his mouth. His split lip still oozed blood. This man had hollow, yellowed eyes, sunken and devoid of expression. His hair was unkempt. His sweatshirt had dried vomit down the front of it, mixed with the blood from his split lip. His jeans had a circle stain at the crotch. He had pissed himself when he passed out on the air mattress.

He stared hard at the stranger in the mirror, into the distant, dead eyes of his reflection. What had this man done with George Moore? He leaned forward, brow furrowed, searching for the shadowy remnant of himself that had not yet surrendered. George thought of all the other people who had lost their shadows in this mirror over the years. He knew his own was growing fainter every day.

It wasn't supposed to be like this. But everything had changed, a mere two and a half weeks ago, when he was perp-walked out of FBIHQ. It felt like a lifetime ago.

George had taken the Metro home that day; he'd asked Kacey Anne to pick him up at the Vienna station. Once in the car, he'd told her what had happened; she'd lost it completely. What had he expected? She'd screamed and fumed for hours back at their townhouse. Things were said that could not be taken back. George had said nothing. No point to it really.

When she'd finished, George had walked silently upstairs to their bedroom and packed two gym bags full of clothes and toiletries, knowing that he would never return to this place. He'd checked into a cheap hotel that night and was not surprised when, a week later, he was served with divorce papers. He'd walked away from his nineteen-year marriage with a twelve-year-old Jeep Wrangler and whatever fit in his two gym bags. He was entitled to half of the townhouse, but Kacey Anne was contesting this, and the court-ordered spousal support ensured Kacey Anne would get most of his future earnings.

The FBI, for its part, saw to it that those earnings would be miniscule. In the same week he had received the divorce papers, a certified letter had arrived informing him that he was dismissed, and that, effective immediately, he was no longer an FBI Special Agent. The Department of Justice had declared him guilty on all charges. As a terminated-for-cause employee, George forfeited his entire pension and all government benefits. After twenty-four years of toil and sacrifice, he was leaving the FBI with nothing.

George went from respected FBI agent to homeless drunk in less than a month. The speed of his descent gave him vertigo. Sheer happenstance had placed him here. George was friends with the court-appointed property manager for the public housing unit called North Garden Estates—or the Gardens as it was known to its residents. It was a forsaken 400-unit low-income apartment building that the District had seized for bank and tax fraud violations. The PM called George when he heard of his fall from grace, and offered him a free off-the-books room. The PM sheepishly explained that the room had no electricity or bathroom, but the price was right, and George moved in three nights after leaving Kacey Anne and their Vienna townhouse. George thought the place good enough for his rock bottom.

The Gardens was a Great Society debacle located in Washington Highlands, the poorest, most violent and crime-ridden section of the District, ranked one of the top ten most dangerous neighborhoods in America. It was twenty-four miles and a galaxy away from Vienna, Virginia.

And now it was home.

THURSDAY, APRIL 1, 2021; 11:42 P.M. (EDT)
THE GARDENS; WASHINGTON HIGHLANDS
SOUTHEAST WASHINGTON, DC

George rinsed and spat, splashed his face and neck, then left the hall bathroom and stumbled back to his room. He went inside and pushed in the lock on the doorknob, which rattled loose in his hand. His room was at the back of the building and faced the rear parking lot. Most of the security lights in the lot had been shot out, but the few that remained cast a ghostly light through the room's only window, which was sealed shut.

The room looked better in the dark. The District had condemned it as unfit for human habitation. A major water leak upstairs had flooded the unit, leaving pipes and wire mesh exposed through a large hole in the ceiling. Damp mold spotted the walls; the thick, stale air catalogued the past odors of its dispirited inhabitants.

George's only possessions were an air mattress, one brown plastic patio chair, which he'd found discarded in the dumpster behind the building, and his two large black gym bags. He kept the bags zipped tight to deny access to the cockroaches, who came down through the hole in the ceiling and crawled over everything in the room—including him.

He fell heavily onto the mattress and heard a *whoosh* of air escape as he sank to the floor. He lay still and looked up at the hole in the ceiling. The room started to spin, so he rolled off the mattress and sat in his dumpster chair, facing the muted light of his only window.

When he finally gained his equilibrium, he staggered to his feet and crossed the room to one of his gym bags. He unzipped it and rummaged around until he found his Sig Sauer P227 .45-caliber pistol. He brought it back with him to the chair. It felt good in his hands. Seated, he took a two-handed combat pistol grip, arms straight out, elbows not quite locked. He looked through the glowing night sights at a spot on the middle of the window. He chuckled, then brought the pistol down to rest in his lap. He sat motionless for a long time.

A door slam down the hall snapped George out of his trance. He studied the pistol, then raised it, turned it on himself and looked down the barrel. In the dim light he could see the faint glint of the Federal .45 ACP 230-grain Hydra-Shok hollow-point round that had his name on it. He slowly placed the gun against his temple and slid his finger from the stainless-steel frame onto the trigger. One ten-pound trigger pull away from eternity.

He held this pose as he reviewed his life, particularly the events that had brought him to this dark, squalid room. George was not a religious man, and so considered suicide more of a pragmatic option than a mortal sin.

Do it?

The world would not miss him, nor he it. He had no blood family, and never did. His adoptive mother Rose was dead, his adoptive father estranged. George had never been part of any group, always the perennial outsider. The FBI turned out to be just a job;

Kacey Anne, the wife that never was. George would miss JD, of course, and his uncle, Henry Cabot. That was about it. He could only hope they would understand.

Do it!

What a waste of a life, he thought. George had spent his entire adult life committed to the FBI and Kacey Anne, and both had betrayed him in the end. For twenty-four years he had routinely worked ten- to twelve-hour days, then had dutifully returned home to Kacey Anne for weekends filled with chores and trivial social interactions. All that wasted time and effort. None of it mattered now. Maybe it never had.

Do it!

George's strict personal discipline had been the gatekeeper of his demons and darker self his entire life. But he had now released this gatekeeper, had stripped himself bare and vulnerable to the dark virus attacking his soul. His immune system had been compromised. George realized the danger he was in. He had never before been suicidal, but for most of his life it mattered little to him whether he lived or died. This had been an asset as an FBI agent, manifesting itself as coolness under fire, but in truth he just didn't value his life as much as the others valued theirs.

Do it?

There was only one thing standing in the way of that final ten-pound trigger pull. George could not shake the feeling that suicide felt like quitting; at least it did to him on this night, drunk and sitting in the dumpster chair in his condemned room. George was not a quitter, never had been. He would not quit tonight.

George lowered the pistol from his temple and placed it on the floor at his feet. His hands shook as he realized how close he had come to doing it. He had granted himself a twenty-four-hour reprieve. He would try again tomorrow night, see if he felt like quitting then.

He spent the rest of the night sitting in the dumpster chair, looking out his small window, awaiting the sunrise. George Moore would live to see another day. A day that included a date with a 600-pound regal woman named Nesha.

CHAPTER 18

"**C**ome on in and sit, child. Nesha ain't gonna bite ya," she said to George as he stood in the doorway of her room. He sat down on a chair beside her bed.

"That's better, baby. You cleaned yoself up. Don't smell like no liquor bottle no more," she said with a smile. "How you doin', baby?"

"Okay. I'm fine," George said. But really he felt like shit. He had slouched in his dumpster chair, drunk, most of the night, and was still shaken by his close call.

"The PM told me a little somethin' 'bout you. Said you were cool. You're George… uhm… Mason, or—"

"You can just call me George."

"Okay, then. Mr. George it is. Now, we gonna set some rules, Mr. George, 'cause I can't be havin' you puking up my bathroom and actin' the fool on my floor. You feelin' me?"

George nodded. Nesha's mocha skin was smooth and unblemished. And she smelled good too, like the lotions Kacey Anne spent a fortune on.

"So tell me. Why you be drinkin' yoself to death, child? Ain't none of my business, but I can't have you staggering round my halls all liquored up. We got kids on this floor, and they don't need to be seeing that."

George felt his face flush. He looked at his lap and nodded.

"Good. You and me gonna be friends, Mr. George." Nesha

shifted her enormous torso and leaned toward him; less than one foot now separated the two of them. Her expression darkened. "Just one thing. Don't cross me. This is my building. I run things around here in the Garden. Plenty of scandalous motherfuckers tried to beat me, and I buried all their asses. You cross me, I'll bury your ass, too. You got that, Mr. George?"

"Fair enough."

She smiled and the darkness left her face as suddenly as it had appeared. "You hungry, baby? Stay and have lunch with Nesha."

"Thanks, but I—"

"C'mon, Mr. George. You ain't gonna turn down a proper lady for lunch, now, are ya?" Nesha said, grinning coyly. George found himself smiling back at her. "Good. Dwayne'll put our plates out and we'll get acquainted."

Nesha picked up a small handbell from atop her tray and rang it daintily several times. A moment later, a diminutive black man rushed into Nesha's room. He was in his mid-thirties and tiny, under five feet. He had sharp features, and, as George would come to appreciate, a sharper tongue.

"Okay. I heard ya the first time," Dwayne said as he looked George up and down. "The usual, Nesha?"

"Yeah, baby. And Mr. George will have some green tea and a muffin."

"What? I ain't bringing this white boy no tea and muffin!" Dwayne said as he shot George a surly look.

"Mr. George is my guest for lunch, and your ass be bringing him whatever I tell you to, Lil' D," Nesha said.

Dwayne shook his head. "Shit. Now I gotta feed the white boys round here too?" He pointed a little finger at George. "And don't you be callin' me Lil' D. Or any of that other dwarf shit neither. I'm four foot eleven—got it? I ain't no motherfucking dwarf." George opened his mouth to reply and then thought better of it. Dwayne turned and stomped out of the room. George couldn't help but smile.

"Dwayne's my play cousin," Nesha explained. "He do a lot of things for me now that I be in this bed. He be with me for years. Loyal. I protect him 'round here, give him what he needs, and he takes care of me. I only called him Lil' D to get a rise out of him."

George sat back in his chair and looked around. Nesha's room was immaculate. The walls had been painted a soft green, and the warm natural light from the window bathed everything in a soft glow. There was a white stained maple dresser, on which sat a matching set of bronze modern statuary, and several bookshelf units filled with hardcover books of commercial fiction and non-fiction, mostly history and politics. On the walls hung framed photographs of scenic landscapes from around the world. Her room was an oasis amid the squalor that surrounded it. George felt more human here. He began to relax.

A few minutes later Dwayne stepped back into the room pushing a small trolley. He replaced Nesha's desktop with a bigger tabletop, covered in fine linen, then set a heaping plate of fried chicken and an oversized bowl of sweet potatoes in front of her, along with silverware rolled up in a white linen napkin.

Dwayne then pushed a small tray at George, which he balanced on his lap. It contained his cup of tea, an oversized bran muffin, and a stirring teaspoon.

Nesha thanked Dwayne and dismissed him. She ate delicately, her table manners refined. The chicken pieces looked small in her chubby hands. George picked at his muffin. Dwayne returned several times during the meal to clear plates and bring Nesha a big salad, which, like her fried chicken, she doused in ranch dressing. He muttered something under his breath as he passed George.

After their meal, Nesha lit up a cigarette. George hated the habit but remained silent.

"I be down to two packs a day," Nesha said with pride as she turned her head and exhaled the smoke away from George. "You probably be wonderin' how Nesha got stuck in this bed, and how much my fat ass weighs. That what you be thinking, huh?" She gave a booming laugh. Her enormous bosom bounced and stretched against her t-shirt.

"Well, I was born and raised in the Highlands, right here in the Gardens. My mama had five kids before she died. Never knew my daddy. My G-Mama raised me. We lived in unit 206, down on the second floor. G-Mama gone now too, rest in peace. I ran the streets as a girl, had a couple of babies, got into some things I shouldn't, did some time in jail. Stupid young bullshit." Nesha paused to catch her breath. "Oooh, child… I was sexy back then. All the boys be chasin' my hot black ass."

Nesha shifted her weight. The bed groaned in protest.

"Shit changed when my G-Mama passed. I promised her I'd get right, no creepin' round the hood tradin' babies for gov'ment checks. So I got me this place up here on the ninth floor, got me a little crew, and started hustlin'. Never hurt nobody, you know, just takin' what's mine. I made good money, and got my respect 'round here. Then I got me a bigger crew, some straight G security, and ran it all outta this room. I worked and ate, worked and ate, and twelve years later my fat ass is stuck in this bed. But I ain't complainin'. Dwayne helps me with my personal stuff, and I got people out there get me anything I want."

George remained silent. Nesha's mouth-breathing was raspy, and she often had to pause to catch her breath.

"I kept my promise now. Never took a penny from the gov'ment. I *earn* my money. You just shame poor people by givin' 'em free shit. People gotta earn it. These people in the Highlands all be on government money. Ain't doin' 'em no damn good."

Nesha lit another cigarette, took a deep drag, then flicked something off her tongue with a long, manicured fingernail.

"Been 'bout ten years now. You hear 'bout that hoe that done killed all four of her babies? She lived with those dead babies—rest in peace—for six months, right there in her little Section Eight. Bitch looked at those dead babies every day, paid them no mind. That hoe lived half a mile from here." Nesha shook her head. "Sheeeeit. It be a jungle out here, Mr. George."

"Darwin's dustbin," George mumbled.

"What's that now?"

George shook his head. "Nothing."

"I quit the eighth grade," Nesha continued, "but I got a curious mind. The Internet has changed my life. Even though I be stuck in this bed, my mind can go anywhere, learn anything. I study all kinds of shit, even taken some online classes."

They talked about a surprising number of topics, and George found that Nesha did indeed have a curious mind. She smoked cigarettes and held court, often punctuating her points with hand and body gestures. Time flew by. George forgot about his hangover. Forgot about everything for a while. Various members of her crew appeared at the door. Nesha dismissed them with a flick of her hand, never interrupting their conversation.

Finally one exasperated crew member returned for a third time and would not leave, wriggling around like a child trying to hold his pee. Nesha fixed him with a stare and held up five fingers.

"Nesha's gotta talk to this fool," she said, turning back to George. "Like this all day every day. But I really like talkin' to you, Mr. George. Finally some intelligent conversation 'round here! Lord knows I get nothin' from these dopes I be dealin' with every day."

"I enjoyed it as well," George said, and meant it.

"Good. We gonna do this again. I make you a deal, Mr. George. You can stay on my floor long as you want. And I'll protect you. Nobody gonna mess with you. For that, you come by here every day and have lunch with Nesha. Be good for my brain. Deal?"

George raised his eyebrows in surprise, unexpectedly touched by Nesha's sweetness and vulnerability. She had just asked him out on a date.

"Okay, Nesha. It's a deal."

"And no drinkin' before lunch, Mr. George. I ain't fittin' to talk to no drunk-ass fool now," she said with a smile.

George nodded, which was as good as his word. He thanked her and got up to leave. She called out to him before he reached the door.

"Mr. George, when you come to lunch tomorrow, can you bring Nesha her cigarettes, baby? Two packs Newport Menthol Gold 100s, in the soft pack? Go to Gene's Liquor Store, 'bout a mile from here. Tell 'em I sent you. Got me a little account there. Be good for you to get outta the Gardens and that nasty room of yours once in a while. Get you some air, you know?"

George smiled and nodded again, then took his leave of Queen Nesha, she who reigned with a fair but firm hand.

George was true to his word. The next day, he brought Nesha her Newport soft packs from Gene's Liquor Store, and every day after that for the next four weeks.

Nesha and George's friendship grew closer and more intimate as the weeks unfolded. He confided to her that he was an ex-FBI agent, wrongfully dismissed and stripped bare. Nesha received this information with grace. She listened as he spoke of his anger and shame. They discussed George's marriage, and Nesha's own regrets over her two children. They talked about their friends and families.

Nesha encouraged George to call JD. He had been exchanging text messages with JD since his arrival at the Gardens. JD repeatedly pleaded with George to come live with him at his condo, but George refused this kindness, not wanting JD to see his rock bottom. George never told JD where he was but tried to assure his friend that he was all right, even when he was not. George was a proud man. He would face this on his own.

But mostly they just talked about things—history, politics, science and technology, philosophy. Nesha held her own in these discussions, which surprised and delighted George.

Nesha was running some kind of identity theft ring, in addition to Internet-based fraud and no doubt other criminal enterprises. She and George did not directly discuss her criminality, but she took no steps to hide it from him. George saw Nesha's reach in the Gardens and all throughout the Highlands. Since their lunches had begun, the local gangsters had started giving him begrudging nods when he passed. In the hallways, the "white boy" catcalls were replaced by half smiles, and even an occasional hello. Dwayne had even started calling him Mr. George, and they now exchanged playful barbs whenever they saw one another.

And so George settled into a rhythm as the days and weeks passed. He now set his phone alarm to ensure he got out to the liquor store for Nesha's cigarettes and then back in time for lunch. And she was right. Getting outdoors every day had begun to lift George's spirits. Their lunch date usually ended around two p.m., which left George on his own for the rest of the day.

At first, the hard drinking started as soon as he returned to his room after lunch. George bought his liquor on his daily cigarette run to Gene's. He would slug down a few quick shots, shuffle the playlists on his phone, plop onto his air mattress, and wait for the music and cheap whiskey to take him away from his life in the Gardens.

Those first few weeks he drank every day, but not to black out like before. His pistol stayed secured in the gym bag. But he still chewed on the shame and humiliation he could not drink away, vacillating between self-pity and bitterness. He had bad days and worse days, days where he simmered with rage at the injustice of it all.

At first he turned this rage inward on himself. But a few weeks after his lunch dates began he pivoted this rage outward toward its source—General Taylor. It was he who had orchestrated George's downfall. He was the one who pulled all the strings. George lay in the dark at night, looking up at the huge hole in the ceiling, with its rotted pipes and hanging wires, and brooded over Taylor. What he had done gnawed at George, ate away his pride and sense of justice. George was still a fighter, always had been. Taylor had punched him in the face. He had to fight back, knock the bastard out. George couldn't live with himself if he didn't. Besides, he really had nothing to live for anyway. Better to go out on your own terms, honor intact.

George's epiphany came to him after a month at the Gardens. It arrived on one of those dark nights on his air mattress. He chose to destroy not himself, but Taylor. George would kill him.

The darkness lifted after his silent vow of vengeance against Taylor. George no longer rushed back to his room to start drinking after his lunch dates with Nesha. Many times he went out for an afternoon walk. His drinking moderated. Some days he didn't even drink at all. He paid more attention to his health and started to gain back the weight he had lost. He washed himself and his clothes regularly.

It had been his daily lunch dates with Nesha that had saved George from the abyss. Their lunch dates prevented him from morning drinking, and he realized his cigarette runs were her ploy to get him out of the Gardens and his depressing room. At first George kept his lunch dates with Nesha because he gave his word. He kept going because he saw how much she enjoyed them. Gradually, though, he realized he went because he wanted to. Nesha accepted him as he was, not what she wanted him to be, or thought he should be. He was not the adopted kid, the would-be attorney, the failed husband, or the fallen FBI agent. He had always been simply George to her.

George's time at the Gardens was his baptism; it had stripped him bare and purged all the falsity from his life. The Gardens saw him for who he really was; first a drunk; then a white man; then just a man. The Gardens was an odd place for his rebirth. But he *belonged* while he was there. It felt good. It felt like home.

And so it was, slowly but surely, George Moore rejoined the human race.

April 29, 2021 was a particularly frantic day in Nesha's room. George had been at the Gardens for six weeks now. Her crew members buzzed around her and George all through lunch. Nesha was their sun, her money the gravitational pull that kept her crew in orbit around her.

Toward the end of their meal, George received a text from JD. He glanced down at the screen and read the message, in all caps:

CALL ME ASAP.

George excused himself and stepped into the hallway and pressed call. The conversation lasted less than two minutes.

"What's wrong, baby? What happened?" Nesha asked when he came back into the room.

"My father died," George said. "I have to go to Boston for the funeral."

CHAPTER 19

JD felt her eyes on him. He turned his head toward the big woman in the bed to his left. They exchanged nervous smiles.

"He'll be here," Nesha said.

Minutes passed in silence. JD picked at his fingernails and squirmed in his chair, which was too small for his large frame. His gaze floated around Nesha's room, taking in the spectacle.

He finally arrived. The blood drained from JD's face when he saw George in the doorway. He looked smaller and had aged considerably. His reddish-brown hair was now awash in gray. His pale face was gaunt and wore a two-day stubble. A black t-shirt and blue jeans hung off him.

JD rose from his chair, hurried to George and gave him a tight embrace; George returned it weakly. JD held him at arm's length and probed George's blue-gray eyes. He hoped his best friend was still in there somewhere.

"Hey, buddy. How you doin'?" JD asked.

George remained in the doorway, his eyes darting between Nesha and JD. He swallowed hard. "What… what are you doing here, JD?"

"Well, I came here to—"

"I called him, baby," Nesha told George. "Got his number from your phone the other day. We had ourselves a nice little talk."

"Nesha, you shouldn't have—" George said.

"Don't be mad at Nesha, now, child. C'mon in here and shut that door. Too many hall rats out here be tryin' to hear my business. Sit down here next to me." Nesha patted her mattress.

George sat next to Nesha, in a chair tucked up tight against her bed. JD sat back down in his seat on the opposite side of the room. JD had been uncharacteristically quiet since Dwayne had escorted him into this room and introduced him to this enormous woman. He had envisioned something quite different based on his long telephone conversation with the funny lady with the lilting sweet voice.

Nesha offered her hand to George. He wrapped both his hands around it, dwarfing hers. She pulled him closer to her.

"Now child, you know I love our lunch dates and all… and I gonna be missin' all our good talks… But you don't need Nesha no more. You don't belong here, child… The Gardens ain't no place for you. Me and JD had a long talk, baby. He's gonna take you home now."

George gave JD a blank look. JD smiled back weakly. This was going to be harder than he'd thought.

"Gene at the liquor store be sayin' you ain't been buyin' near as much of that cheap whiskey as before, and you ain't puked up my bathroom in weeks. Y'all cleaned up now. Your mind right, too. You ready. It's your time, child."

JD heard Nesha's voice catch and saw her lower lip quiver for a second. He watched as she and George looked at each other in silence.

"Darryl done packed up your mattress and broke-ass chair," Nesha continued. "It'll be here for you. Now grab your bags and go with JD, okay, baby?" Nesha asked in a soft voice. Her eyes welled up and a single tear ran down her cheek.

George nodded.

"Come on in here and give Nesha a goodbye hug."

George stood at the side of her bed and leaned in. His head came to rest on her left breast, over her heart. He wrapped his arms around her shoulders.

"I'm gonna miss you, baby," Nesha said. She placed her hand on George's head, gently stroking his hair. He nuzzled into her. A muffled sob escaped his lips. Then another. JD saw George's shoulders shudder and then shake.

"It's all right, baby," she said in a hushed voice. "I see you. Nesha sees you. Let it out, child. Let it all go."

George moaned and then began to weep, openly and without shame—the tears of an innocent man. Tears streamed from Nesha's eyes, but her face held firm. She pressed George's head tightly against her breast as she continued to stroke his hair.

JD had never seen his friend like this. George was a stoic man. He now realized how much his friend had suffered since being paraded out of FBIHQ. JD would never know what George and Nesha had shared, but he would remain forever grateful to her for all she had done for him. She had saved George's life. JD wiped the tears from his own eyes as he watched the redemption of George Nelson Moore play out in this most improbable setting.

At last, George eased his head from Nesha's chest and collapsed back into his chair. He rubbed his eyes with both palms and exhaled loudly. George shot a nervous glance at JD, which JD returned with a big open smile. *No problem, buddy. I got you.*

Nesha gathered herself up. "Mr. JD, you take this boy up outta here now," she said, her voice again firm. "Go on."

"Yes, ma'am," JD said. He got to his feet, walked around the bed and wrapped a huge arm tightly around George's shoulder.

Nesha looked JD up and down, and then smiled and winked at George. "You never told me yo friend be such a big 'un," she said to him, wagging a finger. "That's a whole lotta man right there." Nesha turned to address JD. "And you, sweet child—you treat Nesha right and you can come back and see me *anytime*. Mmmm-hhhhmmm."

All three shared a laugh.

Nesha rang her hand bell and Dwayne appeared. He dragged both of George's gym bags into the room—one at a time and with difficulty.

"Damn, what you got in here? Fuckin' rocks or some shit?" he grumbled. He straightened up and rubbed his lower back.

"Mr. George be leavin' us now," Nesha said.

George extended his hand to Dwayne. "Goodbye, Dwayne. It was nice meeting you. You take care."

Dwayne shook George's hand, then jumped in for a quick hug. The little man's head reached George's belt line.

"Come on through and see a g-ballin' dwarf sometime," Dwayne said as he released him and headed toward the door. Then he stopped and turned around to face George.

"You know, I don't be messin' with too many white people," Dwayne said. "But you remind me of someone, you know. Like I seen you before or some shit."

"Yeah, I get that a lot," George responded.

Dwayne stood deep in thought for a moment, then shook it off.

"You be cool, Mr. George," he said. Dwayne smiled, his gold teeth glistening, then turned and left the room.

JD looked at his watch. "We should get going, George. I told your uncle I would call him."

George looked to Nesha.

"Go ahead, baby," she told him. "And make peace with your daddy in Boston, you hear?" Nesha looked down at the MacBook on her desktop. "Go on, now."

JD and George each grabbed a bag and headed for the door.

"And Mr. George," Nesha said. "You take care of yoself out there. Nesha's always here for you if you need her, baby. And remember—everyone needs a good friend now and again."

PART II

---

*Truth will ultimately prevail where pains is taken to bring it
to light.*
— George Washington

Arms and laws do not flourish together.
— Julius Caesar

CHAPTER 20

George stood facing the gravesite in a cold drizzle. His last trip home had been ten years ago to bury his mother. Today it was his father's turn.

Woodbrook, a typical old New England cemetery, had accepted residents since 1845. A maze of narrow serpentine roads, lined with old-growth maples and oaks, led to pre–Civil War headstones, all blackened and rubbed smooth with age, as well as twenty-first century polished granite monoliths.

George checked his watch and frowned. The funeral service had started late, and the small procession to the cemetery had hit midday traffic. His father remained unreliable, even in death. George toed the spongy ground. The yellowed grass was beginning to shake off its winter slumber. George's beloved mother, Rose Moore, was also buried here at Woodbrook, in a family plot with her parents and siblings. George's father Walt would be buried alone, as his wife's family had forbidden him from their burial plot. George enjoyed the thought of Rose and Walt being separated for eternity.

George had been adopted at age five and raised in the blue-collar town of Woburn, Massachusetts, nine miles north of Boston, just south of the intersection of I-93 and I-95. Woburn was infamous for its contaminated groundwater, which had caused unusually high incidences of leukemia and other cancers in the 1980s. They'd made a movie about it in 1998 called *A Civil Action*, starring John Travolta and Robert Duvall.

Rose and Walt Moore had spent their entire lives in Woburn. They had been high school sweethearts and married young. Walt had worked for thirty-two years at the local semiconductor factory, while Rose worked part-time as a department store cashier.

Rose had doted on George, her only child. Walt had been a good enough man when he was not drunk; but, alas, he had often been drunk. And Walt was an angry drunk. There had been verbal and physical abuse in the home, as the social workers liked to say. George had put an end to this when he'd grown tall enough to look his father in the eye.

George had learned of his adoption, and much else, from the elderly man standing to his left at the gravesite—Henry Codman Cabot, a small but sturdy man of seventy-six years, with bright alert eyes that twinkled when he smiled. His thinning white hair was just long enough to wave and curl, a subtle act of non-conformity for a Cabot man. He wore a woolen flat cap and an overcoat buttoned high against the cold. His rimless eyeglasses were speckled with raindrops.

Just after his twelfth birthday, Cabot had taken George to the Boston Public Garden and told him everything as they sat on a park bench and watched the pedal-powered swan boats glide across the pond. George always felt calm in Cabot's presence, in stark contrast to the chaos he often endured at home.

On the park bench that day, Cabot told George that he had spent his first five years in Northern Virginia—George remembered none of this. It had been Cabot, not Rose or Walt, that told George of his biological parents and their young demise behind the wheel of that

'64 gray and rust Chevy Chevelle Sport Coupe.

Later, when George was in high school, he told him the rest of his story. Cabot explained that Rose was actually his illegitimate half-sister, the result of a one-night tryst between Cabot's philandering father and Rose's mother, a cocktail waitress at one of the private clubs to which his father belonged. Upon learning of her pregnancy, the Cabot family had gone into full damage control mode and paid off Rose's mother and her family. Rose was born in secrecy at a Protestant group home in Upstate New York, and had been adopted to a solid working-class family. Cabot only learned of his half-sister Rose as a young adult, and later found her living in Woburn. He had maintained a close sibling relationship with her throughout his life, albeit in secrecy, as the Cabots neither acknowledged Rose's existence nor condescended to her lower-middle-class milieu.

As an adult, Rose desperately wanted her own family, but medical tests proved Walt sterile. She pushed for adoption, which Walt resisted. Cabot stepped up, handled all the adoption details, and delivered five-year-old George to Rose in 1975.

Cabot had embraced his role as uncle and godfather to young George, and became the most prominent male figure in his life. He'd exposed George to a world outside of Woburn, and had given him the courage to compete in that world. If not for Cabot's influence, George would never have made it to college or law school, or become an FBI Special Agent.

George had been fascinated to learn that his mentor, Henry Codman Cabot, was directly descended from John Cabot, who immigrated to Massachusetts in 1700 and promptly established a merchant shipping empire. The Cabot family were prominent founding members of the Boston Brahmin—Boston's traditional elite upper class, as memorialized in the famous 1910 toast:

"And this is good old Boston,
The home of the bean and the cod,

Where the Lowells talk only to Cabots,
And the Cabots talk only to God."

Yes, Henry Codman Cabot was a member of *that* Cabot family. He had been raised in the affluent enclave of Weston, Massachusetts. He had realized his birthright in 1966 when he'd graduated from Harvard, cum laude, with a history degree, then earned his PhD in Colonial American History three years later. In 1970, Cabot had expanded his doctoral thesis into a published book that was nominated for a Pulitzer Prize.

Cabot became a tenured history professor at Harvard, one of the world's top experts on the American Revolution. For forty-eight years he had been happily married to his college sweetheart, Helen, a fiery 1960s civil rights advocate who had graduated from Radcliffe as Cabot was completing his Harvard PhD. They'd met during a student protest against the Vietnam War, the day that marked the beginning of Cabot's slow drift toward the liberal left and away from his Brahmin pedigree.

Cabot removed his eyeglasses, swabbed off the drizzle with a cloth he withdrew from the inside pocket of his overcoat, then set them back, somewhat askew, on his face.

"Walt was... he... well..." Cabot's voice trailed off to poignant silence. "He did not always do right, but he did his best," he said, finishing his eulogy.

"Maybe we should've put that on his gravestone," George responded.

Henry fought back a smile. "Now, George. One ought not speak of the dead like that. It's not nice."

"Nice and that man were unacquainted," George said.

They were the only two people left at the gravesite; the few other people who had bothered to show up had long since scurried back to their cars to beat the traffic. George was strangely empty; like reaching the end of a disappointing movie you wished you'd never watched.

George felt Cabot's stare and turned to face him.

"Yes?"

Henry held his gaze, unblinking, head tilted to one side. "You have aged just as I thought you would."

"Oh, thanks a lot Henry."

"No, nothing like that. I mean your appearance. I see him in you." Cabot raised his hand to his mouth, his eyes widened. "Incredible."

"Walt? I look nothing like him."

Cabot shuddered, then quickly changed the subject. "It's good to have you home, George. Helen is anxious to see you. It's been too long."

George looked away. "Sorry I haven't come up more often, Henry. After Mom died, I—"

"No need for apologies. We are just glad you are here now, albeit it under these difficult circumstances." Cabot gently grasped George at the elbow. "How are you doing, George? You look like you've lost some weight."

"It's been a rough couple of months."

Cabot nodded. "Your friend JD called me recently. He said something about you living with an African American woman in some underserved neighborhood in DC?"

George laughed. "I wasn't living with her Henry. She is just a friend I met in my apartment building is all. You heard about what happened... with Kacey Anne, and my job and everything?"

"Tell me," Cabot said.

And so George told Cabot everything. Well, almost everything. He told him about how he'd lost his job and marriage, and how General Taylor had orchestrated his demise. He told him about being financially destitute, and about his life at the Gardens. He did not, however, tell Cabot about his near suicide, or about his plan to assassinate Taylor. George kept these details to himself.

Cabot silently absorbed the news. His face dropped, and his grip on George's elbow tightened.

"Oh, George," he said softly when George finished speaking. "You should have contacted me. Helen and I would have—"

"I know you would've. And I appreciate that. I really do. I just had to be alone for a while. Get my head right."

"What will you do now?" Cabot asked.

"I don't know. Stay with JD for a while, maybe."

"Well, I insist you stay with Helen and me, here in Boston. We have plenty of room at the townhouse. You remember the townhouse?"

George remembered. The Cabots' Back Bay townhouse had been a sanctuary to George as a child. It stood on the corner of Arlington Street and Commonwealth Avenue, directly across from the Boston Public Garden and the Equestrian Statue of George Washington. It was a stately three-story residence that dominated this golden corner of the city.

"I don't know. I don't want to be a bother. I'll just—"

"Nonsense. You will be our guest until you are back on your feet. You look as though you could use a square meal and a good night's sleep. Yes?"

Henry paused; George offered no further resistance.

"Wonderful!" Cabot exclaimed. "It's settled, then. You'll stay with us."

George and Cabot then walked a distance to George's mother's gravesite to pay their respects. George clasped Cabot's arm to steady him on the slick road. They arrived at Rose's plot and stood in silence. Cabot sniffled and wiped at his nose with a white handkerchief.

"She loved you, Henry," George said, still looking at the headstone.

"Rose was a lovely woman," Cabot said. "I miss her."

"Me too," George said, jamming his oversized hands into his front pants pockets. "Me too."

The drizzle had stopped by the time they got back to Cabot's old Subaru for the drive to the Back Bay.

CHAPTER 21

"Wake up, dear," Aunt Helen said as she gently nudged George awake.

George had slept hard last night, his third night in the townhouse. He rolled onto his back, disoriented. Helen's sweet face and the aroma of strong coffee brought him out of his stupor. He rubbed the sleep out of his eyes and sat up in bed.

"Henry would like to see you in the study," Helen said. "Pancakes and scrambled eggs okay?"

George nodded. Helen bent down and kissed him on his wide forehead, then softly closed the door as she left.

He got up, made his bed, and opened the oak shutters wide to look outside. His second-floor room faced the Public Garden and the Washington statue. Spring had arrived and everything was in bloom on this blue-sky morning. For the first time in months, the world appeared agreeable—welcoming, even.

George dressed quickly and hurried downstairs to join his uncle in the first-floor study. He checked his watch as he hit the bottom of the stairs: 8:35 a.m. He hadn't slept that late in years.

The study was grand. Floor-to-ceiling mahogany bookshelves covered the walls; a sliding cast iron ladder granted access to the upper shelves. Sunshine streamed through the magnificent palladium windows. Cabot sat at his desk, opposite the separate informal seating area that fronted an oversized brick fireplace. He was engrossed in something on his computer monitor. George sat in one of the office chairs in front of the desk. He called out to Cabot twice before he got his attention.

Cabot looked up at him, his face ashen, eyes wide. He motioned for George to come around the desk, then pointed at a video paused on his computer, a headline link on the *New York Times* website.

"Look at this," he said as he maximized the view window and clicked play.

It was a live press conference. The video crawl identified the man at the podium as Speaker of the House Jack Parker. To his right stood a familiar figure. George felt a jolt as though he'd been caught hard by a seat belt after a sudden stop. General Taylor stood at attention, wearing his war face. George swallowed hard.

The press announcement was terse. Parker appeared nervous, and barely lifted his head as he read from a written speech on the podium in front of him. In a matter-of-fact tone, he stated that, by law, his House speakership now positioned him first in line for presidential succession, and that he was now exercising this primacy to take his constitutional place as the new president of the United States. Parker thanked the secretary of education for her service as acting president and assured the American people that his transition of power would be seamless. Parker finished his speech by announcing that, pursuant to the 25th Amendment of the Constitution, he was appointing Taylor as his vice president.

Parker then looked up from the podium and stared blankly into the cameras. He looked queasy, his hands visibly shaking as he clutched his speech with a death grip.

The pool of reporters gasped audibly and then began shouting questions at Parker, who stood frozen in place. Taylor stepped forward, nudged Parker away from the podium, and began to take questions, pointing at one reporter after another, answering each man and woman with skill and aplomb.

Cabot clicked out of the video when the press conference ended and the Beltway political analysts began their histrionics.

George stood motionless, his thoughts racing. *Of course. That's why they were so adamant about Allen being an agent of the Democratic Party—so Parker could whip his Republican Party to House majority, take the speakership, and then take the presidency. This proves they killed Allen to maintain their cover story. Hale was in on it the whole time. And it was clear that Taylor was now running the show.*

Cabot stepped around his desk to the informal seating area. George followed him, and the two men sat opposite one another in front of the fireplace, where a low fire crackled and snapped. They sat for a few silent moments, each man lost in his own thoughts. There was a light tap at the door, and Helen stepped in carrying a pot of strong black coffee. She kissed the top of her husband's head before she left, closing the door softly behind her.

Cabot's hand shook as he raised his cup to his lips. The color had not returned to his face.

George sipped at his own coffee, then set it on the low table between them and cleared his throat.

"Henry, this may sound a little crazy, but hear me out."

Cabot nodded, and over the next half hour, George confided all of his suspicions to Cabot: the Taylor/Parker scheme, Hale's complicity, Allen's murder, all of it. Cabot leaned forward as he listened, nodding attentively. Both men readily agreed that Taylor was behind the whole scheme, and that it was he who now posed the real threat to the country. Cabot explained that one of the Founding Fathers' greatest fears was that of a standing army, and the abuses attendant to it. He viewed Taylor as the realization of this fear and knew that the republic would end if this man ever seized power.

Both men agreed on the problem, but differed dramatically on the solution.

"The country must oppose this man with vigorous public

protest," Cabot said. "Mobilize all the institutions of government to stop him. Court injunctions, congressional inquiries, a mass media campaign, picketing—"

"No," George said urgently. "It's too late for words. Taylor has everyone in his pocket. He cannot be stopped using the tools of government. He *is* the government."

"I have very influential friends," Cabot reminded him. "I will call them and—"

"It's no use," George said. "I know Taylor. He's cunning, ruthless. And the public loves him. No, it's too late for words or political maneuvering. He's gotta be taken out."

Cabot drew in a sharp breath and looked at George as if seeing him for the first time. "George, you're not thinking of doing anything rash, are you? Revenge is never the answer."

"Revenge is vastly underestimated."

"It's also immoral," Cabot reminded him sharply. "That is not how a civilized society solves its problems. Enlightened people rationally negotiate to compromised solutions. It is not a simple zero-sum proposition. I'd like to think we have evolved past that."

George started to reply but thought better of it. His uncle clearly did not understand what was at stake here. This was personal, between him and Taylor, and Taylor would die at his hand.

"George," Cabot said, almost as if he'd read his mind. "Promise me you will not resort to vigilantism. Do not martyr yourself over this. Promise me." His eyes narrowed. "Give me your word."

George maintained his silence, then looked away into the fire. When he returned to Cabot, he saw that the old man was trembling. George was a man of his word, and both men had understood the meaning of his silence.

Cabot rose and sat down next to George on the sofa. He wrapped his frail arm around George's broad shoulders and squeezed tight. Cabot was not a demonstrative man, and this display of emotion took

George aback. They maintained this embrace while Cabot fought to regain his composure.

Cabot then straightened, took off his eyeglasses, and wiped his eyes with a white handkerchief. George turned to face Cabot, whose staid countenance had returned.

"George," he said evenly, "I have something to tell you."

CHAPTER 22

General Taylor sped down Pennsylvania Avenue in a three-armored-vehicle motorcade, lights flashing and sirens blaring. He had just finished his morning press conference with (now) President Parker. He would press his advantage and take bold action while his enemies were back on their heels. On the battlefield as in life—always on the attack.

Eight Delta Force Operators accompanied Taylor. They had voiced strong concerns about plying their trade on U.S. soil, but were assured by Parker and Taylor that this mission was legal and vital for national security. Besides, they had all been ordered to do so by their new commander-in-chief and the highest-ranking man in the U.S. military. And so, like all good soldiers, they had saluted and reported for duty.

Taylor was now the vice president, the first active duty military officer to hold this, or any other, political office. His first act as vice president would be a felony: using military personnel to enforce domestic policies within the United States—an express violation of the Posse Comitatus Act.

Rolling down Pennsylvania Avenue, Taylor thought of U.S. Air Force General Curtis LeMay, "Old Iron Pants," who had orchestrated the fire-bombing campaign of Japan during the last six months of World War II that resulted in the deaths of half a million Japanese civilians. LeMay had been unapologetic but had fully acknowledged that, had the U.S. lost the war, he would have been hanged for war crimes. History was written by the victors. Taylor smiled as he imagined what future grade-school history books would say about what he was about to do.

The motorcade arrived at the White House and bluffed its way through the vehicle checkpoints and barricades. They went unchallenged by the Secret Service uniformed officers that patrolled the exterior of the White House. Taylor, encircled by the Delta Operators, moved briskly into the White House, where they were stopped by two Secret Service agents. The agents timidly informed Taylor that he was not on the official visitors list and could not be permitted entry. Taylor curtly informed the agents that the FBI had called their director, who had approved his visit. The wobbly agents held their posts and mumbled something about checking with their headquarters. Taylor brushed past them, with the operators regrouping around him. The rear-guard operators spun and walked backward, weapons at shoulder ready. The two agents stood frozen in place as the scrum moved unchallenged into the White House.

The armed team double-timed through the historic halls, their boots clicking on the polished floors as they passed the shocked faces of White House staffers. They met no further resistance and reached the Oval Office in minutes.

Taylor opened the door and entered without breaking stride. Two of his operators posted up in the hallway by the door, while the remaining six fanned out around the general. The secretary of education was seated at the president's desk, talking on the telephone. Her eyes grew wide at the sight of the intruders.

"Madame Secretary, hang up the phone," Taylor ordered her.

She took the telephone from her ear and placed a hand over the mouthpiece. "I saw your little presser this morning, General. You'll never get away with this. *I* am the president of this country. I'm on the phone with congressional leaders right now, and they—"

Taylor approached the secretary from her left side. The operators moved with him. He reached out and pressed the cradle of the telephone, disconnecting her call.

"Who the hell do you think you are? Get out of my office right now!" the secretary shouted.

"Madame Secretary, just a few moments ago, in accordance with the twenty-fifth amendment to the Constitution, I was duly appointed vice president of the United States," Taylor said. "In this capacity, and on behalf of President Parker, I have come to remove you as acting president. This action comports with the Constitution and the Presidential Succession Act of 1947."

"You bastard! I will—"

"You will go with these men right now. I will not ask you a second time."

"I will do no such thing!" she shouted.

Taylor gave the team leader a nod, and the six operators instantly surrounded the secretary as she sat at her desk. Fear washed over her face.

"Ma'am, please get up and come with me," the team leader said.

The secretary froze for a moment as she looked up at the six operators. She then frantically grabbed for the telephone on her desk. Two operators scooped her up, one holding her under each arm, and easily lifted her from her seat. She struggled and kicked as they held her aloft, and then began to shriek, a high-pitched wail that filled the Oval Office.

They planted her standing in front of her desk, arms and legs still flailing. In one fluid motion, they zip-tied her arms behind her back, then bound her ankles together. The secretary went silent as she snapped her head side to side to stare at her assailants, blinking as if coming out of a bad dream. Then her eyes flashed anger, her face a grotesque mask of panic and fear. Impassively, the operators lifted her once more and started to carry her toward the door. The secretary let out a low growl, then turned to the man on her right and spit in his face. Then did it again. The man wiped his face clean with his spare hand. Another operator stepped swiftly up and placed a piece of duct tape over her mouth, then slipped a spit hood over her head, closing it snugly around her neck.

Properly hooded and zip-tied, the secretary was then dragged, still writhing and twitching, through the halls of the White House to a waiting armored vehicle. Two operators sat in front, two sat at her side, and two were stationed in the back. The duct tape and hood reduced the secretary's screams to the guttural moans of a wounded animal. A knot of terrified White House personnel crowded around and watched as the vehicle sped off.

Back inside the White House, the halls were lined with dumbfounded staffers, rendered mute with terror. They would all soon flee the White House and try to explain to a disbelieving world what they had just witnessed: the president of the United States, gagged and bound, being dragged through the halls of the White House like a hooded terrorist at Abu Ghraib.

Taylor remained in the Oval Office. He stood at the French glass door and looked upon the Rose Garden for a long time. Then, he turned and ordered the two operators left behind to give him a minute. They nodded and shut the door on their way out.

He felt a surge of supernatural energy within him. This office would be his soon enough. There was already a team of military officers en route to secure the rest of the White House. Tomorrow he and Parker would have a media photo op right where he now stood. They would smile and let the American public know that the transfer of power had been amicable and without incident. The smear campaign against the secretary would launch within the hour. Taylor was not worried about her; the American people saw her as their imposter president. The secretary could scream all she wanted. No one was listening.

Taylor approached the desk. Behind it was a table that contained framed photographs of the secretary with her family and various dignitaries. He studied the smiling, confident faces. With one swipe of his arm he cleared the table; the glass picture frames smashed as they hit the floor. He then turned and sat at the president's desk. He made eye contact with the portrait of George Washington, centered over the fireplace across the room. If Washington were alive today to see what had become of his country, Taylor thought, he might not have relinquished absolute power so readily. Taylor would not make the same mistake.

He put his feet up on the desk and smiled. He could get used to this. He lingered a full five minutes before he left the Oval Office. He knew he would be back soon.

For good.

CHAPTER 23

The late afternoon sun had warmed the park bench; its heat radiated up from the wooden slats and warmed George and Cabot as they sat side by side enjoying the fresh air. George stretched his legs out and tilted his head back toward the sky. A perfect spring day in the Boston Public Garden. Suited office workers walked briskly about, poking at their smartphones. Gaggles of well-kept wives, gourmet coffees in hand, strolled by at a more leisurely pace.

The bench was aside a paved circular walking path, partly shaded by a large beech tree that was leafing out. They sat directly south of the George Washington Equestrian Statue. The great man sat confidently astride his beloved horse Nelson, his bronze face canted toward them, as if they had called out to him and he had turned to reply. The Cabots' townhouse was easily visible from the bench, as it occupied most of the block directly across Arlington Street.

Beside him, his uncle shifted uneasily. He had waited for Helen to run her errands before he and George had walked across the street to the Garden to talk.

Any spring cheer this afternoon provided quickly drained away as

George turned to look at Cabot. His face was grief-stricken; his hands fidgeted in his lap.

"What did you want to tell me, Henry?"

Cabot kept his eyes down. "I am violating the law by telling you this. I never imagined I would have to share this secret with you, George, but General Taylor's actions this morning have left me no choice." He cleared his throat. "Please forgive me for what you are about to hear."

Cabot turned toward George, their eyes met. "Have you ever heard of a government agency named DARPA?"

George nodded. Cabot was referring to the Defense Advanced Research Projects Agency, the Department of Defense agency responsible for the development of emerging military technologies. Eisenhower had established it in 1958 in response to the Soviets launching Sputnik.

Headquartered in Arlington, Virginia, DARPA's reported funding was about $3 billion, but in truth it was practically unlimited. It was unlike any other government agency. It had only 250 or so employees, of which half are program managers, who run short-deadline projects at breakneck pace. DARPA's successes are legendary: the Internet, stealth technology, GPS, and automated voice recognition, among many others. DARPA secretly develops technology that is twenty years ahead of the rest of the world.

George looked at his uncle quizzically. "Yeah, so what's up with DARPA?"

Cabot cleared his throat and appeared uncertain where to begin.

"DARPA has created a few truly extraordinary technologies, projects that have fundamentally and forever altered our world," Cabot said, then paused. "Such a project was initiated in 1970."

"What'd they do?" George asked.

"Now, before I continue, you must remember that the America of 1970 was a very unsettling place. Nixon had ordered an invasion of

Cambodia, widening the war in Vietnam. Nationwide student protests. Kent State. The Beatles even broke up in 1970." Cabot shook his head. "It got worse in '71. The Pentagon Papers proved the Johnson Administration had systematically lied to everyone about the Vietnam War. Nixon took the U.S. currency off the gold standard. The U.S. Supreme Court instituted forced busing of school children—"

"I know all this, Henry." George sighed.

"Okay," Cabot said. "The early '70s were an especially bad time for the Pentagon. The country had turned against not only the war but the military itself. Morale hit an all-time low, drug use and desertion were common. The generals realized they were about to lose the first war in U.S. history. The Pentagon saw the Vietnam War as a failure of leadership, and they were prepared to do anything to remedy this failure."

Cabot leaned into George and lowered his voice to a whisper.

"In 1970, my book on the American Revolution and Continental Army was nominated for a Pulitzer Prize. I was a young history professor at Harvard at the time. These DARPA men came to me one day after class and pitched me on an extraordinary project. Breathtaking, really. I agreed to join them. I could not resist. I joined because I thought I could help preserve the founding principles of our republic—liberty, democracy, individual rights, equality." Cabot exhaled. "I was young and naive. I regret this decision every day."

Cabot looked out into the distance at the duck pond, then cleared his throat again. "I'm so sorry, George."

George's mouth went dry. He had never had a conversation like this with Cabot.

"Best to just come out with it," Cabot said. He took a deep breath. "In early 1970, I partnered with a brilliant scientist on a top-secret DARPA project to… uh… to… create… the… first human clone."

George sat frozen, stunned into silence. "What?" he said at last. His voice sounded hollow in his ears.

"The Pentagon wanted to engineer a super-general who would successfully lead our military, and nation, out of its current dire situation," Cabot said.

"You can't clone people. The technology doesn't exist today, never mind in 1970," George said. "Can't be done."

"That's what I thought as well. I'm a historian, not a scientist, but my DARPA colleague was an expert in bioengineering, biotechnology, genetics, and several other related fields. He explained the science to me. Cloning is not very complicated scientifically, just very difficult to execute," Cabot said.

Cabot then gave George a quick layman's version of the science behind human cloning, which to George's surprise was remarkably straightforward. Cabot explained that cloning was simply asexual reproduction. Single donor DNA is joined with a female egg from which the DNA has been removed. This reconstructed embryo is then tricked into developing like any other fertilized egg. At the appropriate time the cloned embryo is transferred into the womb of a surrogate mother and developed normally to birth.

If successful, the human clone will be genetically identical to the single DNA donor, like identical twins but whose births were separated by years, not minutes. Environment would ensure that the clone would not be an exact human photocopy of the DNA donor, as it is impossible to precisely re-create for the clone every life condition and experience encountered by the DNA donor. Most cloned embryos fail to develop, and when they do a wide variety of abnormalities occur. Dolly, the sheep cloned in 1996, was the only success in 277 failed attempts.

"No. No way," George said, shaking his head. "There is no way our country has cloned a person."

But the look on Cabot's face said otherwise.

"In 1970 we were losing the Vietnam War, both at home and abroad. The Pentagon was panicked, desperate," Cabot said. "Crisis begets the impossible. Human history is rife with examples of the impossible happening when unlimited resources and resolute will collide: the pyramids of Egypt, the Great Wall of China, Roman roads and aqueducts, the Manhattan Project—"

"Our government wouldn't do this… would they?" George asked. "Unleash this technology on the world? The atomic bomb was one thing… but this?" He then thought about what the government had done to him and fell silent.

"Like I said, Nixon and the military were desperate, and capable of extreme acts when threatened. These are the same folks that brought us Project MKUltra," said Cabot. "They experimented on U.S. citizens like lab rats, without their knowledge or consent."

George harrumphed and shook his head at the mention of this dirty little secret.

The CIA had initiated Project MKUltra in April 1953, with an aim to develop mind-controlling drugs for use against the Soviet bloc. Experiments on humans were intended to develop drugs and procedures to be used in interrogations and torture, in order to weaken the individual to force confessions through mind control.

The researchers had used numerous methodologies to manipulate people's mental states and alter brain functions, including the surreptitious administration of drugs (particularly LSD) and other chemicals to unwitting government employees and private U.S. citizens. Other MKUltra techniques had included hypnosis, sensory deprivation, isolation, verbal and sexual abuse, as well as various forms of torture.

The scope of Project MKUltra had been broad, with research undertaken at eighty institutions, including forty-four colleges and universities, as well as hospitals, prisons, and pharmaceutical companies. The CIA had partnered with these institutions through fictitious front organizations.

In 1973, the CIA had destroyed all Project MKUltra files amidst the government-wide Watergate panic. All that is known of it now is based on sketchy witness testimony and 20,000 project documents that were accidentally found in 1977; these escaped the CIA shredder only because they were misfiled.

George closed his eyes and blew out a long breath. In his heart, he knew Cabot was right. The government could and would do anything to ensure its own survival when threatened. It had unlimited resources and power. And power never surrenders without a fight.

"Well? Was your project successful?" George asked, half dreading the answer. He looked around and lowered his voice. "Did you create a human clone?"

The question hung in the air for a long time.

Cabot finally spoke. "Yes, we did," he said in a subdued voice that trailed off. "God help us, we did."

George's eyes widened as he fought for breath. He now knew the most closely held and highly classified secret of the U.S. government. A secret that only a handful of people on the planet knew. Man had begat man. Pandora had opened her box. The enormity of it all began to sink in. George felt the weight of it. His bones began to ache.

"Who?" he blurted out. "Who'd you clone?"

Cabot slowly turned his head away from George to look straight ahead at the statue in front of them. George followed his gaze, and the two men silently regarded the twenty-two-foot bronze man looking back at them from astride his horse. The truth hit George like a thunderclap.

"Him?" George pointed at the statue. "You cloned George Washington?" He stole stealthy glances over each shoulder to ensure no one had heard, then asked again, this time in a hoarse whisper, "*You cloned George Washington?*"

Cabot's eyes welled up with tears. His lower lip trembled. He removed his glasses and covered his face with his hands. George stared at Washington's stoic bronze face as Cabot wept softly. Finally, he straightened up and wiped his face with a handkerchief.

"Give me your hands, George," Cabot said. His voice now strong and clear.

George joined hands with Cabot; his large hands swallowed the older man's up to the wrist. Cabot latched onto George with an iron grip.

"Look at the statue again," Cabot said. "Take a good look."

George felt Cabot's eyes burning into him as he turned back to the bronze man. His neck and jaw tightened as Washington's familiar face looked impassively back at him.

"It's you, George," Cabot said in a resolute voice. "You're him."

George reflexively jolted backward, but the old man's grip was like steel.

"Are you telling me I'm the clone?" George's heart was racing now. "That I'm… *George Washington*?"

He stared at Cabot, a man he had known for almost his whole life, a man without deceit or guile. Cabot was telling the truth. Somehow, this was the truth. George's new truth.

George's stomach tightened and convulsed with fear. Cabot said something that he did not hear. It was as if George was submerged underwater. What he did hear, loud and clear, was the voice in his head shouting "No! No! No!" over and over.

"I'm so sorry, George."

Cabot released his grip now, and George stood on rickety legs, fighting to steady himself. Cabot had never lied to him before. Now his entire life was a lie. He had lost his career, reputation, and marriage at the hands of General Taylor. He had nearly lost his life by his own hand at the Gardens. And now he had lost his identity, his essence—himself. An electrical storm raged within him and he heard the thundering of his own pulse in his ears.

"George—" Cabot said plaintively.

George turned and walked off toward the darkening skyline of Boston.

CHAPTER 24

The heat of the tavern was a welcome relief from the chill night air. George plopped down at the bar and draped his light jacket over the back of the weathered stool. It felt good to be off his feet; he had been walking around Boston for hours. The tavern had dark wood and dim lighting, which suited his mood. He caught the bartender's eye and ordered a scotch, neat.

He had walked aimlessly all evening, first through the Commons and then down Tremont Street. Finally, he'd come to the Old Granary Burial Ground, Boston's third-oldest cemetery and the final resting place for many notable Revolutionary War–era patriots, the five victims of the Boston Massacre, and three signers of the Declaration of Independence.

Touring the old cemetery had calmed him a bit, so he'd set off to look at some other historical sites, which in Boston lurked around every corner. From the cemetery, he'd walked to the nearby Old South Meeting House, the church building where the Boston Tea Party was planned, and then down the street to the Old State House, where the Boston Massacre had taken place and six years later the Declaration of Independence had been proclaimed to jubilant crowds.

On a whim, he'd taken the fifteen-minute subway ride (the Red Line "T" to Bostonians) to Harvard Square and walked to Cambridge Commons, where George Washington had formally taken command of the Continental Army. He'd loitered at the spot where the Washington Elm once stood, a tree under which legend claims Washington stood as he first assumed command. George had hoped for an epiphany as he stood on the same ground as the great man; or lacking that, some inspiration or clarity. He'd got neither. On this day it turned out to be just another tree in modern, bustling Harvard Square. George grew morose and took the T back to downtown.

Darkness was falling as he got off the subway. He'd walked around Faneuil Hall, then had a nice meal at Durgin Park, which had cheered him up slightly. His waitress, a sweet older woman with a delightful Irish brogue, had recommended the Green Dragon Tavern as a good local watering hole. A four-minute walk along the cobblestones of the Freedom Trail had put George on his barstool enjoying his first scotch of the night.

He held the first sip on his tongue for a good three count and then swallowed. That soothing bite hit the back of his throat. George had not touched a drop since he'd left the Gardens, but tonight he needed a partner to figure this all out.

To his dismay, he had felt nothing—no kinship, no spark of déjà vu—at any of the historical American Revolution sites he had visited. He took another sip of scotch and shook his head. He couldn't possibly be George Washington. No one could. It was impossible. Preposterous. He was George Nelson Moore, the adopted kid from Woburn who had reached the heights of the FBI, only to crash and burn less than a year before his pension kicked in. The past two months of his life had been one long bad dream. Perhaps today's events would mark the end of the nightmare, and at any moment he would be jolted awake and back to reality. Maybe another sip of scotch would help. George closed his eyes as his lips touched the glass.

He opened his eyes. Nothing had changed. *Dorothy was still in Oz.* Damn it. *Why me? Why did this have to happen to me? Why am I the universe's urinal?* This was so unfair. He didn't deserve this. But as William Munny had said in his favorite movie, *Unforgiven*, "Deserve's got nothin' to do with it."

Deserve means nothing in this modern world. George knew that much. Nesha too. There was no benevolent ethereal hand to level the scales of Lady Justice. She was a concubine of the rich and powerful. She would not unsheathe her mighty sword for George. He would have to fight his way out of this somehow.

But maybe there was a way. George could just move on with his life as if he had never had the discussion with Cabot. With the proper blend of willpower, alcohol, and hypnosis maybe he could drive this clone nonsense from his mind. Cabot was the only person alive, to his knowledge, who knew this secret. George could swear him to silence and try to put his life back together. It might work.

George waved the bartender over. He was a middle-aged, stocky Irish guy with a white bar towel draped over one shoulder. Best of all he poured scotch with a heavy hand. Everything you could hope for in a neighborhood bartender.

"I'll take another scotch. And could you hold my stool for me while I hit the john?" George asked.

"Sure thing, buddy."

George returned from the bathroom to a second scotch and an empty stool. Good man. George put a twenty-dollar bill in the bar well in front of him. The bartender returned and scooped it up. The two men exchanged respectful nods.

"Hey," George said to the bartender as he began to turn away. "I saw a plaque on the wall on my way to the bathroom. It said this place was the 'headquarters of the revolution.' What's up with that?"

"Yeah. This place used to be in the North End. Long time ago. They say the Sons of Liberty used it. Tea Party was planned here too," the bartender said.

"Well, to the Sons of Liberty, then," George said as he raised his glass and took a full swig.

"Fuckin' A," the bartender said with a smile.

The second scotch brought melancholy. George felt a dull, aching fatigue in the marrow of his bones. His shoulders slumped. *Do I have the energy for this? Is it worth it? Why bother?* Self-pity is the spoiled little dog that incessantly snaps at your heels when your back is turned. George drained his glass; he had never felt so alone.

With the third scotch, George pantomimed a silent toast to the great man—General George Washington. Then he smiled at the absurdity of it all. Was he actually toasting himself? He stared at his reflection in the mirror behind the bar. Who was he looking at? In the dim light, George thought he saw a fleeting resemblance. He only knew Washington's appearance from the dollar bill and the few portraits he had casually seen over the years. And the statue, of course. But still, he thought he saw something. Maybe.

George wondered if General Washington had ever sat in this bar when he liberated Boston. He had certainly walked the streets George himself had walked today. What if Cabot was right? *What would all these people think if I stood up on my stool and told them I was Washington?* They'd laugh their asses off, of course. *But what if I could prove it?*

This was mind-bending stuff. George fantasized several sci-fi scenarios where he returned to 2021 America as the Great Washington. Ludicrous comic-book superhero delusions that made him chuckle despite himself.

Okay, time to focus, George. What do you know to be true... right now, sitting on this barstool? George inventoried his thoughts. He knew what Cabot had told him, and that Cabot was an honest man who George believed would never betray him. But what if this was somehow an elaborate ruse Cabot had concocted? To what end? It made no sense to George.

The bartender arrived with another scotch. George had been absentmindedly rolling his empty glass in his hands while he brainstormed, and the bartender had interpreted this as a refill signal. George checked his watch: 12:05 a.m. Friday morning. One more for the road wouldn't hurt. It was still about two hours until closing time.

George nursed his final drink as the clock moved forward and the bar began to empty. He realized that he would be unable to completely wrap his mind around all this tonight. No matter. The more important question was what he was going to do about it.

It came down to a binary decision, as most things ultimately do: A/B, yes/no, go/no-go. George framed his decision as last call was served and the bar lights went up. Historically, closing time was when fantasy met reality. And so it was for George on this night.

He had two choices: one, he could return to Cabot and face his past. Two, he could escape his past and flee abroad to start a new life.

George got off his stool, buzzed but steady on his feet. He shielded his eyes from the bright lights. The bathroom had a line, which he decided to skip. He caught the eye of the bartender, who strolled over. They shook hands, and George palmed him another twenty. The bartender smiled and told George to take care. George left the tavern and stood outside on the cobblestone street. The cool air braced him. It was a clear night, under a full moon.

He walked a few blocks and found a dark alley to relieve himself. In mid-stream he made his decision.

It would be a decision that changed human history.

CHAPTER 25

George found himself in the exact same spot he had been twenty-four hours earlier. A lifetime ago. He sat across from Cabot, chasing the chill from his bones by the fire in the townhouse study. George's hands enveloped his coffee mug. His head throbbed. Scotch and sleep deprivation were not a good look for any man north of fifty.

"I'm sorry about yesterday. A lot to take in, I guess," George said.

"I was worried sick about you. Where were you last night?" Henry asked.

"I wandered around the city a bit, got a bite to eat, had a drink or two," George said. He waved away Cabot's look of concern. "I ended up back on our bench. It was freezing. I spent the night talking to the big bronze man on the horse. He and I had a lot to talk about."

"They close the Garden at night. How did you get in there?"

George shrugged and took another long sip of coffee. Cabot shook his head. George loved this man, and that was why he had returned to him instead of launching out of Logan Airport this morning.

"I'm not sure who I am anymore."

"I know this must be very hard for you."

"Who are my real parents?"

"Everything I told you when you were a child was true. But it was not the whole truth." Cabot put down his coffee cup and folded his hands in his lap. "You were born and raised in Northern Virginia, by people who cared for you. At age five you were adopted by Rose and Walt and raised in Woburn. I really am your uncle and godfather."

"Was I born, or…?" George trailed off.

"Yes, of course. You were birthed by a surrogate as part of TRENTON. She—"

"Trenton?" George asked.

"Project TRENTON was the code name for the DARPA cloning project. I selected the name myself to commemorate the Battle of Trenton, General Washington's crossing of the Delaware River to attack the Hessians. His victory greatly raised the morale of the troops and saved the Continental Army from collapse. The battle occurred in 1776, the day after Christmas, in terrible winter weather, and—"

"Henry, you were saying?"

"Oh, yes. Of course," Cabot said, with a brisk nod of his head, then continued. "Your surrogate mother was a beautiful young woman. A CIA case officer. She carried you to term and raised you in TRENTON. But all your DNA is from a single donor—General George Washington."

"So, who's my mother?"

Cabot sighed. "It is complicated, George. You have no biological mother, per se. But I can say both your TRENTON mother and Rose were wonderful women. And they both loved you."

"Was I the only one?" George asked. "Clone, I mean."

"Just you," Henry replied. "Rose and Walt knew nothing. Neither does Helen. Only a handful of people know. You are the first person I've ever told."

"What happened to the project surrogate?" George asked. "Is she still alive?"

"I have had sporadic contact with her over the years. I have not spoken with her recently. I believe she is still alive."

George's mind raced. He was the only person in human history not to have a biological mother. *He came from... no one.* It all felt so cold and scientific, as if he was examining another person's life and not his own. He was unmoored, adrift in uncharted waters.

"Here, let me show you something." Cabot got up and retrieved a leather-bound book from the mahogany bookshelf behind George. He returned and sat down on the sofa, the book open on his lap, and began to page through it, his brow furrowed. At last he seemed to find what he was looking for. "Look at this," he said, as he turned the book around and presented it to George. "This is what Washington looked like at your age. You are fifty, correct?"

"Yeah. But I've aged a bit of late," George said.

"This is General Washington after his Victory at Yorktown. He was one year younger than you are now in this painting. The artist is Charles Willson Peale, my favorite of the period. To Washington's immediate left is the Marquis de Lafayette, his young French protege. The second man is Lieutenant Colonel Tench Tilghman, Washington's military secretary and aide-de-camp."

George closely examined the painting. General Washington was a large man, a full head above the other two men in the painting. He wore a blue wool coat with matching pale-yellow waistcoat, and breeches with gold buttons. He took an open stance, his left hand tucked in his waistcoat, his right hand on his hip. He looked straight ahead, directly into the eyes of the world. This was a confident man, a man other men wanted to follow.

At first George felt no connection, but the longer he looked at Peale's painting the more he registered the resemblance. It was the subtle things: the peculiar shape of the body—big hips and thighs, small head, narrow shoulders; the thickness of the nose bridge; the same hairline and shape of the lips. George's eyes widened; his breathing quickened. *Oh my God. I am him.*

Cabot then showed George another painting, this one of General Washington at age fifty-one, at the time of the Newburgh

Conspiracy of 1783. George studied this image as acutely as the other, with the same result. He was aware of Cabot's eyes on him.

"As a historian," Cabot said, "I cannot express to you how surreal this moment is for me. These history books are your scrapbooks George. It's time travel. It is… sublime."

"I don't know if I'm up to this," George said. "I'm a fifty-year-old disgraced FBI agent. I've spent the last two months inside a bottle." He shook his head. "I'm also a bit hungover right now. So I'm sorry if I don't feel like the Father of Our Country."

"General Washington had struggles and doubts at your age, too," Cabot said. "But he endured, and it was his steadfastness to the cause and his principles that made him a great man." He pointed at the book. "Take Newburgh, for example. In March 1783, a mere six months before the end of the war, officers in General Washington's Continental Army—aggrieved that they had not been paid the back salary and pension payments they were owed—plotted to supplant Congress by force of arms and establish a military government. General Washington learned of the coup and called the mutinous officers to a meeting. At this meeting, he gave a short but impassioned speech in which he urged his officers to be patriotic and patient, but his rhetoric had no effect on the men. General Washington then produced a letter from a member of Congress to read to the officers. He then took a pair of reading glasses from his pocket, which few of the men had seen him wear, and said offhandedly, *'Gentlemen, you will permit me to put on my spectacles, for I have not only grown gray but almost blind in the service of my country.'*

"This simple remark moved many of the men to tears, as they realized how much their leader had sacrificed for them and for their country. The conspiracy collapsed, and the republic was saved."

"I get it, Henry," George said. "Some things are bigger than one's self. But Washington didn't have to deal with being a human clone. I do. And these are different times."

"Different times, yes," Cabot said, striking fist to palm for emphasis. "But the *ideas*, the *principles*, are the same. And this is what matters most."

George sprang from the sofa and walked to the window. General Washington, immortalized in bronze, stared back at him from across Arlington Street. George felt claustrophobic.

"So you see, George," Cabot went on, "General Washington faced crisis and self-doubt at age fifty, as you do now. He rose to the challenge when the bells of history tolled for him. So can you. Look to General Washington for your strength. You are both the indispensable men of your time."

"This is different," George muttered, still contemplating the larger-than-life bronze man in the Garden.

"Do you think if General Washington were alive today, he would be making excuses and feeling sorry for himself?" Cabot said sharply.

George spun from the window and glared at him.

Cabot looked away. "I'm sorry, George. That was insensitive of me." He slowly rose from the sofa and walked gingerly across the study to George. They stood together, looking out over the garden. At length, Cabot spoke again. "Your cloning was a combination of nature and nurture. The nature component, the DNA science, was a complete success. You are an *exact* biological copy of General Washington. The nurture component, however—exposing you to the same environmental and personal experiences as young Washington—proved difficult. As project historian, that was my responsibility: to re-create eighteenth-century colonial America in the twentieth-century modern world."

"How'd you do that?" George asked.

"It was challenging. Since we could not time travel," he turned and gave George a small smile, "we placed you, as best we could, in the modern version of General Washington's childhood home. You lived in the same area—Westmoreland County, Virginia—and in a home with the same floor plan. Your TRENTON parents were well trained in their roles as Washington's biological parents—Augustine and Mary Ball Washington. We were even going to remove your TRENTON father when you turned eleven, as that was when Augustine Washington died. But we never got that far."

"So what happened with TRENTON?"

"Early on, everything went well," Cabot said. "You can imagine our excitement when the TRENTON surrogate gave birth to you. I monitored you and your TRENTON parents very closely. Did my best to replicate all aspects of Washington's childhood for you. It was the most challenging and rewarding work I have ever done."

"Like a lab rat," George said. "You watched me like a lab rat."

"No. It was nothing of the sort. We all cared deeply for you, George, particularly Virginia, your TRENTON mother. She cared too much, I think."

"What do you mean?" George asked.

Cabot explained the demise of TRENTON to George. Despite early success, Virginia began to experience difficulties maintaining her role. Mary Ball had been a hard woman who showed scant affection to her young son. But as Virginia's personal feelings toward baby George grew, she began to feel uneasy in her rigid role as the aloof and demanding Mary Ball. At first, she had objected, and when TRENTON leadership had insisted that she strictly maintain her role, she'd secretly gone "off-script." The clash between Virginia's assigned role and her tender feelings toward her baby George became almost intolerable, and she'd ultimately confided in Cabot, who had quietly supported her as her struggles worsened.

The project took a major hit on Thanksgiving Day 1974 when its lead scientist, Arthur Bailey, was killed in a car accident. Though brilliant, Bailey had been scatterbrained and a poor record keeper. Worst of all, he'd kept key components of TRENTON's proprietary science in his head, and that knowledge had died with him in the accident. DARPA was unsuccessful in replacing him, and the project had floundered.

Turbulent 1975 brought post-Watergate repercussions, to include a witch hunt on Capitol Hill. The Church Committee had revealed many secretive and illegal acts committed by the U.S. government. The CIA was reeling from its MKUltra fiasco. DOD was terrified that its darkest secret—TRENTON—would be exposed. And TRENTON was now failing with the death of Bailey and Virginia's recalcitrance. TRENTON was officially terminated in late 1975. All project records were destroyed, and all participants were silenced with money and threats.

"The end of the project was very chaotic," Cabot said. "I fought to ensure your adoption details, and got you placed with Rose and Walt in Woburn. I secured visitation rights for myself as your uncle. You were five years old when TRENTON ended."

"I don't have much memory before Woburn," George said.

"The TRENTON psychiatrists pumped you full of drugs to wipe your mind of any memories. I vigorously fought them on this too, but lost."

They fell silent again as both men looked out the window at normal people going about their normal lives.

"It was a difficult time… after the project ended," Cabot said. "I was worried the government would kill you—and me—to cover its tracks. I lived with this fear for years. Waiting for the telephone to ring, Rose wailing about the death of her only child. Or imagining the sound of footsteps coming down the hall late at night, hoping they would kill only me and leave Helen alive." Cabot took a deep breath. "But as the years passed and my fear subsided, I went about my life as best I could."

"Why are you telling me all of this now, Henry?"

"I swore I would never tell you. But General Taylor is a very dangerous man who poses a grave threat to the survival of our republic.

The republic created by General Washington and the founders." Cabot turned to face George. "I fear General Taylor is scheming to establish himself as a military dictator."

"I don't think he can get away with it," George said. "The American people won't stand for it."

"Don't be so sure. People can easily be swayed by authority figures, particularly when they're under stress. The Milgram and Stanford Prison experiments taught us that."

"Henry, please, I'm not in the mood for another lecture. My head is throbbing."

"You need to hear this, George," Cabot said, waggling his finger in the air.

Professor Cabot then began his lecture:

In 1961, Yale University psychologist Stanley Milgram conducted a social science experiment to determine the willingness of people to obey authority. In the experiment, the test subjects were encouraged by an authority figure to administer an escalating series of electrical shocks to another person every time that person provided a wrong answer to a series of simple questions. In reality there were no shocks, and the shock recipient (whom the test subject could hear but not see) was in fact an actor who was in on the experiment.

At around 135 volts, the actor started to bang on the wall and complain about his heart condition. At around 300 volts, the actor became unresponsive. At this point, many test subjects indicated their desire to stop the experiment, but at the insistence of the test authority figure, a significant majority kept administering multiple shocks, up to the experiment maximum of 450 volts, despite the actor screaming in pain.

Before his experiment, Milgram polled forty top medical school psychiatrists; they confidently predicted that only one-tenth of one percent of the test subjects would administer the highest shock (450 volts). The experiment results were that a full 65 percent of test subjects administered the highest shock. Milgram concluded "*The extreme willingness of adults to go to almost any lengths on the command of an authority figure constitutes the chief finding of the study.*"

In August 1971, about a decade after Milgram, a Stanford University psychology professor named Philip Zimbardo conducted an experiment regarding the psychological relationship between prison guards and prisoners. In the study, Zimbardo assumed the role of the authoritative prison warden. Readily accepting the roles assigned to them by the authority figure, the guards quickly became brutal and oppressive, while the prisoners became meek. The experiment got out of hand and had to be abruptly stopped after only six days.

Like Milgram, the Stanford Prison Experiment demonstrated the susceptibility of ordinary citizens to authority figures. When it counts, most people can be influenced by authority to commit acts very much against their individual morals and ethics.

"Don't you see, George?" Cabot said, locking eyes with George as he stepped toward him. "As in Milgram, General Taylor will convince the public to follow his dictates, against their better judgment. Our country will become one big Stanford Orwellian Prison, with Taylor as warden and we his prisoners."

It was all too much to process. How could this be real? George felt like he was sliding out on thin ice, tentatively testing it to determine if it would hold his weight. He felt a sudden need to move, escape. He strode across the room and then dropped onto the sofa. He lost himself in the flames of the fireplace. *How could this be real?*

He and his uncle sat quietly once more, each man alone with his thoughts. The crackle of the fire filled the protracted silence.

"George," Cabot finally said. "How would you like to meet Virginia?"

CHAPTER 26

General Taylor sat smugly under the auditorium lights. He had last stepped on campus seventeen years ago, when he'd earned a master's degree in psychology while serving as the West Point Commandant. He was a rising one-star Brigadier General then, not the four-star cock of the walk that strutted on stage tonight. Taylor sat across from a professor whom he'd met backstage but whose name he had already forgotten. No matter. He was there for a softball debate on the role of the military in a modern democracy. Piece of cake.

It had been only one week since he and Parker had ascended to the Oval Office. An adoring public had anointed Taylor their true red-white-and-blue American hero. His popularity and polling numbers were the highest ever recorded for any vice president. President Parker lacked Taylor's charisma and telegenic presence, however, and his polling numbers reflected this. Soon enough it would not matter, of course. Taylor planned on giving the public what they wanted.

The student moderator kicked off the show. Taylor gritted his teeth and pasted on his public smile; he was resplendent in his dress uniform, four stars agleam under the bright lights. He resented being here, a dancing bear for public titillation, but his staff had convinced him that he must get out and do some public appearances, to "assuage fears" and "solidify his brand," they said. They'd suggested he reach out to young voters and visit a college campus. Taylor had selected Columbia; as a major contributor and prestigious alum, he expected this would be a lay-up. Plus, he could find a great meal and discreet entertainment in Manhattan.

Colonel Timothy Raymond Shelton, Taylor's ruthlessly efficient chief of staff, had accompanied him on this trip, as per usual. Colonel Shelton was a man to be reckoned with. In his late thirties, he was a shade under six feet and two hundred solid pounds. He wore his sandy blond hair in the standard military cut that somehow looked fashionable on him. His piercing dark blue eyes were known to make knees wobble—those of both his subordinates and a profusion of admiring women. Like JD, he had cauliflower ears and a busted-up nose. The scars of a pride lion.

Shelton had briefed Taylor on the ride from the airport to the auditorium, but this was largely pro forma, as Taylor could speak on the topic of military and democracy in his sleep. Shelton had warned him that the audience might not be one hundred percent supportive of his message, and that college campuses had changed in the past two decades. Taylor had dismissed Shelton's concerns with a wave of his hand, said he could handle a bunch of snot-nosed kids.

Taylor's introduction was greeted with tepid applause. He sensed a little haughtiness in the student moderator, a willowy metro-sexual sporting a crisp white V-neck t-shirt and a perfectly knotted neck scarf. As the debate progressed, Taylor noted that he was getting attitude from his opponent as well, a professor of social justice studies who refused to stay on topic and lobbed provocative statements filled with implied connections between Taylor's military and totalitarianism.

These comments solicited hoots and jeers from the audience.

A flash of anger ignited within him, but Taylor controlled himself with practiced aplomb. He easily parried the professor's biased opinions and specious logic. The little man's officious bleating neither surprised nor concerned Taylor. No, what concerned him sat out in the audience. He had seen it all before with the Vietnam War student protesters—the ignorance and arrogance only entitled youth can shamelessly wear. But the kids in this audience looked and acted different. They appeared soft and sanctimonious, writing checks on empty accounts. The "Snowflake Generation," Shelton had called them, a generation of children raised by over-protective parents with a misplaced emphasis on manufactured self-esteem. They were the least resilient and self-reliant generation American had ever produced. *How am I supposed to fight a war with this lot of bullet-catchers?*

The debate segment finally ended. Taylor sneaked a look at his watch and silently groaned. He had no desire to endure thirty minutes of Q&A with this audience. He attempted to signal the student moderator to wrap it up, but the kid would not make eye contact.

The first question came from a female student who rose to speak before she was called upon; there was a round of applause before she even spoke. Taylor could spot an ambush when he saw one. He cursed his staff for putting him on this stage and braced himself for what came next.

She struck an indignant pose, hands on hips, her chin slightly elevated. She was a plump girl with a round face set off by square green-framed eyeglasses she wore far down the bridge of her perky nose. She had dirty brown dreadlocks past her shoulders, and the straight white teeth her parents had paid for.

"Mr. Taylor, on behalf of all the underserved people of color in this country, and those oppressed by white privilege, we welcome you to Columbia," she said to deafening applause. Taylor immediately recognized her omission of his honorary titles (*Mr.* Taylor, not General or Mr. Vice President), and he seethed at the intentional slight.

"And let me say that as a woman and a feminist I am deeply offended by your decision to wear a military uniform on stage here tonight," she said in a sing-song cadence. "And I intend to file a grievance with the Dean of Students for this fascist right-wing publicity stunt!"

Taylor felt his anger rise, envisioned the look on this young woman's face as he put a bullet deep in her forehead.

He looked in the wings for his chief of staff, but Shelton was not there. He had warned Taylor that Columbia was one of the most progressive universities in the country, and had suggested he go to another campus—perhaps in Texas somewhere.

Taylor kept his rage on a leash and allowed the young woman to continue her virtue signaling. He could wait her out. He was certain his chief of staff would return any moment to end this charade.

And that's the way it should have ended. But then she overplayed her hand. Taylor was barely listening, but he distinctly heard her disparage his beloved troops—the brave men and women who voluntarily placed themselves in harm's way so that pissants like her could sleep safely each night.

Taylor shot to his feet and walked to the edge of the stage. His amber eyes bored into her. She stopped in mid-sentence as if choked.

"Young lady," he began, his voice cold and even. He couldn't hold back. He unleashed his temper, and methodically tore the young woman to pieces as the audience gasped. As his tirade ended, she trembled, blinked, then clamped her hands over her mouth and fell into a fit of uncontrollable sobbing.

Friends gathered around her to offer comfort and hugs. The audience began to grumble and hiss. Then the iPhones came out. The video hit the Internet in minutes.

The student moderator and the professor stood mute and frozen. Shelton emerged from the wings and strode across the stage to Taylor.

"Sir, you're losing them," he whispered, biting off each word. "Tell them they're good. For God's sake, tell them they're good and let's get the hell out of here."

Taylor strode back to the podium, cleared his throat and pasted on a smile. He could be quite charming when needed, and he proceeded to charm the hell out of his audience. Told them all the things they needed to hear: how they were the future of this country; how each one of them could make a difference, make the world a better place; how he would reach out and include young people such as them in his administration. He even saluted them—certain in the fact that none of them noticed only his middle finger extended as he did so.

And that was all it took to turn them around. He silently mocked them as they applauded at the conclusion of his patronizing soliloquy. Taylor had given them their participation trophies, and they loved him for it. He smiled through gritted teeth, and took deep pleasure in knowing their days were numbered.

"Did you see that?" Taylor shouted at his chief of staff. Shelton braced for the tirade that was coming, and hoped the general would get it all out of his system by the time they reached LaGuardia. When he got like this, he was much easier to handle in the back of a Suburban, away from the public.

"Yes, sir. The students were out of line, sir."

"Did you hear that little bitch? Addressing me as *mister*? Disrespecting the uniform I have worn with honor for over forty years? Who the hell does that little shit think she is?"

"The American public respects your long and exemplary service to this country, sir. The polls reflect that. Forget this one, sir. We should have gone to Texas."

"'Thin the herd' is what they say in Texas, right? What we need is a good war in a bad place to thin the ranks of these pampered little snots." Taylor snickered at the thought.

Shelton remained silent and let the general enjoy his happy place.

"I'm the sitting vice president, for Christ's sake. The highest-ranking military officer in the country. That's my goddamn alma mater. And that's the reception I get? To hell with Columbia. Stop all my money to them, you understand? Nothing. Not a goddamn cent."

"Yes, sir."

The Suburban went silent, except for the barely audible growling noise General Taylor made when he was really angry. It was as if he actually chewed his anger, masticated it with his molars. The anger nourished him, as essential to his survival as oxygen.

"What the hell did that bitch call me... a *micro-aggression?*" Taylor asked after a few moments, putting sarcastic emphasis on the last word. "What the hell is that? She wants aggression? I'll show her and her little play-dates what real aggression looks like. Our time is coming. Am I right, Colonel?"

"Yes, sir."

"Our country is really in the shitter. This democratic nonsense has got to end. You mean to tell me my vote counts the same as the votes of those idiots in that audience? Ridiculous. We cater to the least of us—the weak, the stupid, the infirm. We reward them, give them hand-outs. Time for Darwin to take out the trash. Am I right?"

"Yes, sir."

"Even our Founding Fathers knew this wouldn't last. They said as much. To survive, our republic requires an educated and engaged citizenry. Look around. Look what we just saw—at one of our finest universities!"

Shelton discreetly looked up at the dashboard clock. Despite traffic, their motorcade was making good time. They would be wheels up soon enough. He looked out the tinted window and wondered what the people he saw on the street would think about their hero general if they could hear him right now.

"Well, I'll tell you one thing, sure as shit," Taylor went on. "You and I are going to save this country from itself, aren't we, Colonel?"

"Yes, sir."

Shelton turned to the tinted window and the gathering darkness outside.

CHAPTER 27

Shelton pulled the nondescript Ford sedan head first into a guest parking spot in the underground garage. He cut the headlights and ordered his passenger to remain quiet. Shelton moved the rear-view mirror all around to check for surveillance. Nothing. He got out of the vehicle, shielded himself behind a pillar, and took a good look around the dimly lit garage. All clear. Only then did he lope around the vehicle and take his passenger out. The woman was blindfolded. She wore a long stylish coat that covered most of her body. Shelton, head down, walked the woman to a nearby elevator. He repeatedly pounded the elevator call button, while maintaining a firm grip on the woman's arm. She did not resist.

The elevator arrived and Shelton hurried them inside. He hit the eleventh-floor button and sighed in relief when the door closed. He turned to the woman and removed the blindfold. She was a beautiful African American woman, dark-skinned with fine features and large bright eyes. A tall woman, almost eye level to Shelton. She wore expensive perfume.

"So I'm a nasty street-walking hoe, correct?" the escort asked in a soft voice.

Shelton nodded; his skin crawled.

"What kinds of things does the client prefer?" she asked. "I'm new to this account, and I want this to be a good date."

"What you and the client do is none of my business. I'm just the driver." Shelton could not look this woman in the eye. He knew her fate. *Why did she have to be so perky and enthusiastic?* She was just trying to make a good first impression. This was a first date, after all, and for the $10,000 payday they all wanted to please. There would be no second date; there never was with Taylor.

The elevator door opened at the eleventh floor. The escort took a step forward. Shelton placed an outstretched arm in front of her, and she abruptly stopped. He checked both sides of the hallway, found them empty, and walked her to condo unit 1101. Shelton initiated the knock code, then the occupant knocked the second half. Shelton unlocked the door, then leaned in and whispered "Good luck" in the escort's ear. She gave him a wide, bright smile that made his heart sink.

Shelton locked the door behind her and walked briskly, head bowed, back to the elevator. Thankfully, it arrived quickly. He stepped in, pushed the lobby button and leaned against the back wall. He observed his disguised appearance, reflected in the shine of the stainless-steel doors: baseball cap pulled down low over his face, dark tinted eyeglasses, and an authentic bushy mustache expertly dyed to match his sandy blond hair. Taylor, the client in unit 1101, wore an even better disguise. Shelton could not bear to look at himself. He turned away from his reflection before the elevator reached the lobby.

He strode through the lobby, flung the glass doors open and walked out into the streets of the nation's capital, zipping his coat against the cold wind. Heavy clouds filtered the moonlight to an eerie glow. Shelton was grateful for the weather. It numbed him, and emptied the sidewalks of potential witnesses. His pace quickened. He wanted to run.

He knew it would be about an hour and a half before Taylor would contact him to return to the condo to retrieve the escort. Shelton had an ominous feeling about tonight, a sense of foreboding he could not shake. He typically waited in his vehicle, lying down in the back seat, in the dark and out of sight. But tonight he was restless and had decided to walk the neighborhood in an attempt to silence the pounding in his ears.

And so he walked and thought, head down to avoid eye contact with the few passersby he encountered on the street.

How did I get here?

Shelton had always stood out among his peers. He had been a three-time All-State high school wrestler in Ohio, then on to West Point, where in 2003 he'd graduated in the top 10 percent of his class. He had insisted on an infantry billet so he would be in the middle of the action.

Shelton had done two tours in Iraq and one in Afghanistan. He had performed bravely (some said recklessly) in combat and had received commendations, two purple hearts, and fast-track promotions. His troops feared more than respected him, and saw him as another by-the-book careerist from the Point.

Shelton had selected Taylor as his patron and curried his favor. As a full bird colonel, he had eventually maneuvered his way into the prestigious chief of staff position. Shelton had hitched his wagon to Taylor, and he expected to ride him to the top echelon of the U.S. Army. His blind loyalty to Taylor was the price he paid for his fast-tracked military career.

He had been with the general for almost three years now, and had seen and done things he had never imagined. Bad things he had to swallow and try to forget. He did not know how to get out, or if he would even get out alive. Some days he did not care.

Tonight Shelton was doing a bad thing. He hated himself for it. And he hated Taylor even more.

It had begun last night when Shelton had accompanied Taylor home from their debacle at Columbia. Shelton had watched him fume on Air Force Two and brood in silence on the half-hour motorcade from Andrews AFB to Taylor's residence.

Shelton had been to the Taylor residence several times. It was a tidy two-story colonial in the affluent Woodmont neighborhood in Arlington County, Virginia, about five miles north of the Pentagon, up the Potomac River. Taylor's long-suffering wife Patricia maintained the family home, which they had purchased in 1974 upon his return from Vietnam. The couple had marked their fiftieth wedding anniversary last year, but the marriage had long ago become one of convenience. The couple had two grown daughters; both knew of Taylor's adultery and were estranged from him.

General Taylor was dismissive with his wife, which was difficult to watch because Shelton liked Patricia Taylor. When they arrived at the residence, Patricia greeted Shelton as she always did, with a warm embrace and a peck on the cheek. She was a gaunt woman with sunken, sad eyes. She maintained a meticulous home, as antiseptic as a hospital. The house gave Shelton the creeps, and he tried to spend as little time there as possible.

It was in the foyer of the house, as Shelton was rushing to leave, that Taylor caught up with him and told him he required an escort for the following evening. He had begun using escorts in 1998, when he was a fifty-year-old two-star assigned to the White House as a Security Advisor.

Shelton had assumed command of this escort operation soon after he had become Taylor's chief of staff. It made him feel like a pimp, and he despised it. He had gone along the first time, but afterwards he had meekly approached Taylor to state his objections. Taylor had dressed him down, and Shelton, now fully compromised, had been forced to continue. The encounters happened about every other month, and Shelton's hatred of Taylor and himself grew with each incident.

The escort operation presented nothing but problems for Shelton. To preserve secrecy, Taylor always dismissed his military protection detail on escort nights. This meant that Shelton alone—one man— was solely responsible for the physical security of the number one man in the U.S. military, a man who had made many enemies over the decades.

And there was a new problem. Taylor had been vice president for nine days now, and that job came with a large 24/7 Secret Service protection detail. Taylor had bullied the director into allowing him small blocks of privacy without his detail, but this concession could end at any moment.

But by far the biggest problem Shelton had with the escort operation was with the general himself. Taylor was a sexual sadist. He only became sexually aroused in response to the extreme pain, suffering or humiliation of others. On several occasions the service had charged General Taylor an extra $5,000 fee for "excessive wear and tear." This fee was simply added to the general's account and paid without protest by his lobbyist benefactor.

Shelton was lying under a blanket in the back seat of his vehicle when he got the coded text message that the date was over. He was relieved. It had run forty-five minutes longer than most of the other dates. Shelton's stomach churned as he jumped out of the back seat and headed toward the elevator.

Up on the eleventh floor, he unlocked the door and entered the condo. He sensed something was wrong before he saw it. A chilled tension, a kind of malevolent odor, hung in the air, like the sudden silence that falls when you walk in on your parents fighting, or the charged atmosphere a severe thunderstorm leaves in its wake.

It was a small studio condo, with the open kitchen and dining area closest to the door. General Taylor sat at a small circular dining table, sipping tea and reading the *Washington Post*. He was serene, his demeanor totally incongruous to his surroundings.

In his disguise General Taylor was a sight to behold. Shelton had never got used to it. He wore a thin, short-sleeved white t-shirt hoodie and white boxer shorts. On his feet were dark knee-high socks and house slippers. His legs were crossed elegantly at the knee. A full black domino mask concealed the entire upper half of his face. The rest was covered by the hoodie, which he had cinched loosely around his face.

But it was his eyes that chilled Shelton's blood. Taylor wore oversized black contact lenses to hide his telltale amber eyes. They covered most of Taylor's eyes, leaving only a little white sclera showing on each side. The black demon eyes, coupled with the black domino mask, gave Taylor a ghoulish look, like a slasher film killer.

Without looking up from his newspaper, General Taylor pointed to the queen-sized sofa bed on the other side of the room.

Shelton followed the general's finger. The escort lay on her side, in the fetal position, facing Shelton and the door. A blood-stained sheet covered her nude body to the waist. Her eyes were swollen shut; blood from her split lip trickled down her chin. Shelton saw the bite marks on her breasts, around the nipples.

"What the fuck!" Shelton said under his breath. The escort heard his voice and began to whimper.

He raced around to the other side of the sofa bed, softly put his hand on her shoulder and eased her over on her stomach. The bedsheet tented high over her midsection. He pulled it aside and gasped. A wooden broomstick had been rammed in her anus, then snapped off with extreme force. The jagged end protruded eighteen inches in the air. There was blood on the stick, on the sheet, everywhere.

Shelton glared at Taylor, still coolly reading his newspaper. From this angle, he now noticed the blood on Taylor's white hoodie. A white light flashed in front of his eyes. He began to shake. It took every ounce of self-discipline he possessed not to lunge at the general. Shelton forced a few deep breaths.

"What do you expect me to do with this?" Shelton said in a tone he had never dared use with Taylor before.

"Do as you will, Colonel," Taylor said as he sipped his tea, his eyes fixed on the newspaper. "The young woman now has a handle. I suggest you use it to escort her back from whence she came."

Fuck you, General.

Shelton turned back to the young woman and leaned down to whisper in her ear.

"I have to remove this. Sorry."

Shelton covered her mouth with one hand, then grabbed the base of the broomstick with the other. He placed his knee on her buttocks for leverage and gave one strong pull. Blood spurted like a geyser; the sucking sound the broomstick made as it came out would haunt Shelton for the remainder of his life. The woman shrieked in pain and began to sob convulsively against the palm of his hand.

"Shhh… I know, I know," Shelton said in a soothing voice. "I gonna get you outta here, and I can't do it if you're making noise. Okay?"

She continued to wail.

"Please, be quiet. Can you do that for me?"

She fell silent and nodded her head.

"I'm going to take my hand off your mouth, and you will not scream, okay?"

She nodded again. Shelton slowly released his hand from her mouth.

She choked, then coughed. Her wide eyes pleaded with his.

"Help me… God, please help me," she rasped.

Shelton covered her in her long coat, then scooped her up off the bed. She did not resist him. Taylor did not look up as they passed.

In the parking garage, he bundled her into the back of his vehicle and then rushed her to the Virginia Hospital Center. He caught most of the stoplights, ran the rest, and got her there in fifteen minutes.

He listened in stricken silence to her soft moans and whimpered prayers, then suddenly he retched and lowered the window to spit the bile out of his mouth.

Fuck you, General.

He pulled into the hospital's outdoor parking lot and stopped in a dark area at the edge of the lot. He opened the rear door, cradled the woman in his arms again, told himself not to panic. *I'm simply bringing someone in who needs medical assistance.* He looked for security cameras and kept his head down.

He saw a sign in big red letters—URGENT CARE—and walked toward it. He entered through the automatic door and strode to the admittance desk. He told the bespectacled white-haired woman that he had found this woman collapsed outside his front door. No, he did not know her. He was just a Good Samaritan. She started to pepper Shelton with questions. He apologized, said he had to go, and gently laid the woman on the floor.

"I'm sorry," he whispered, then turned and ran out of the lobby. He hugged the dark edge of the parking lot all the way back to his vehicle, jumped in, and sped off into the night.

———

Shelton pulled his car into his driveway and killed the engine. He could not recall any details of the drive home. He stepped out, stood in his driveway and looked up at the stars. His suburban neighborhood. So peaceful. So normal. He felt numb.

The house was silent and dark when he entered. He locked the deadbolt, then crept upstairs to where his family slept. He went directly to his small daughters' bedroom, cracking open their door enough to let the hallway light fall on his two sleeping beauties. They clutched stuffed animals as they slept. He slipped into the room and gently kissed them both. Tears sprang to his eyes.

Shelton went down the hall and entered the master bedroom. His wife Rachel stirred. He whispered that he was going to take a shower. He rolled his clothes up in the hamper, thought of burning them. He stood facing the water, head bowed, until the shower ran cold.

He threw on a clean pair of black cotton boxers and slipped into bed. Rachel cuddled up to him.

"How'd it go tonight?" she asked.

Silence.

"Sweetheart, how'd it go?"

"All right," Shelton said after a long pause. He lay flat on his back, staring up at the ceiling. "Am I a good man?" he asked her in a hushed voice. "Tell me I'm a good man… please."

"You are a great man," she said softly. "And a wonderful father."

Shelton was bound by the Uniform Code of Military Justice to disobey unlawful orders. His ultimate moral and legal obligation was to the Constitution, not silver stars on shoulder boards. But what if Taylor's commands were not orders, exactly? What if they were more like rhetorical requests and implied threats from the highest-ranking officer in the entire U.S. Military? What did the Uniform Code of Military Justice say about that? Shelton swallowed. He knew the answer; he had always known.

"What is it, honey?" Rachel leaned up on one elbow. "What's wrong?"

Shelton responded with another long silence. He squeezed her hand.

"This is not what I signed up for," he said at last. He turned and kissed her. Her hair smelled wonderful. There was still beauty in this world.

She told him she loved him, then cuddled close, her head on his chest. She fell asleep quickly. He listened to the sweet cadence of her breathing.

Shelton went back to staring up at the ceiling. Sleep would not come to him tonight.

CHAPTER 28

"Take this left—here!" Cabot exclaimed, pointing at a gravel driveway that was hidden among the mature oak, maple, and hickory trees lining Highway 11.

"Thanks, Henry. Maybe a little more notice next time?" George slowed the rental car, made a tight U-turn, and inched back toward the missed driveway.

"Okay, take this driveway, up here on your right," Cabot said as he read the hand-written directions mailed to him. "I'm accustomed to driving in Cambridge and the Back Bay. This place is not even in GPS."

George eased the sedan off the highway and onto the gravel driveway, which quickly became a two-track with tall weeds growing down the center. He centered the hood on the overgrown vegetation, which scraped the undercarriage as the vehicle crept forward. He and Cabot bounced in their seats as the sedan dipped in and out of the deep ruts. George regretted that he had let Cabot talk him out of renting an SUV and hoped they would reach the trailer before they snapped an axle.

The five-hour flight from Boston to Lexington had been

uneventful. Cabot had booked them both first-class tickets. George always flew coach, and marveled at how much more civilized life was at the front of the plane.

From Lexington Blue Grass Airport, they headed southeast on Combs Mountain Parkway, through Daniel Boone National Forest, and then south on Highway 11. It was an invigorating spring day, bright and warm with a slight breeze. Driving through the hills and hollows (*hollers* to locals), George was awestruck by the beauty of the Kentucky countryside. It was a verdant paradise, and a pleasant surprise to both George and Cabot as they negotiated the narrow mountain roads. The two-hour drive passed quickly.

George tottered down the two-track for about half a mile before it ended in a clearing about the size and shape of a football field, surrounded on three sides by wooded hills. A mongrel dog was chained to one of the rusted yard cars at the edge of the open space. It went berserk as their car approached, snarling and showing its teeth. It pulled at the chain with such force that the rusted car lurched forward. Its deep, incessant howling echoed in the bowl of the clearing.

A dilapidated mobile home sat on cinder blocks, perpendicular to the two-track driveway. It was a twelve- by sixty-foot single-wide, typical of the mobile homes from the late 1960s and early 1970s, and was rusted through and tilted to one side. Its lack of skirting displayed the original tires, long since flattened. The rusted front hitch was driven into the ground, topped with two large propane tanks. Corroded metal steps, like the type wheeled up to small airplanes, led up to the front door.

George parked in front of the ramshackle box, as far away from the howling dog as possible, and sat with his hands on the wheel, his heart sinking. Could this possibly be where Virginia lived? *How* she lived? George dreaded going inside this aluminum can. He imagined it smelled worse than it looked.

"You sure this is the place?" he asked, hopefully.

"Yes. I think so. We followed the directions," Cabot responded. He frowned and re-examined the directions on the folded-up printout on his lap.

They got out of the car and approached the front steps. The dog intensified the cadence and ferocity of its howling. The flimsy front door flew open, clanging against the railing of the metal steps. A scraggly old man emerged on the top step, the barrel of a shotgun trained on both of them. George and Cabot froze. George casually raised his hands to chest level. Cabot's arms shot straight up over his head, like he was signaling the winning touchdown at the Super Bowl.

"What in hell you jaspers doin' on my land?" the old-timer said in a high-pitched voice. "I don't know either of ya from Adam." The dog was going completely crazy now at the sight of the old man. "Quiet, ya old hound, 'fore I come over there and put a right whuppin' on ya," the old man shouted without taking his eyes off George and Cabot. This admonition muted the dog, which stopped pulling on its chain and lay down.

"Is this the Virginia Dare residence?" Cabot asked, his voice cracking like an adolescent boy.

"That name don't mean diddly squat to me," the old man said, and spit a jet of tobacco juice out one side of his snaggle-toothed mouth. He wore filthy overalls over a stained white shirt. He was short and wiry, and mostly bald but for the snow-white shocks of hair sprouting from each side of his head. His beady eyes squinted from behind cheap eyeglass frames, which were askew on his face.

"Sorry," George said. "We must have the wrong address. We were—"

"You city fellas must be dumber than a coal bucket." The old man spit some more tobacco juice; this time he turned his head and shot for distance. "Comin' up a man's road in this holler will get ya killed."

"We'll be on our way, then," George said. He shot Cabot a look, and they both began to slowly walk backward toward the car. Cabot's face was ashen; his arms remained locked over his head. *Touchdown Harvard Crimson!* George almost laughed.

"Wait. I plumb forgot." The old man was fishing around in the bib pocket of his overalls with one hand while he held his shotgun steady with the other. "Both you fellas hold yer ground." The old man pulled out his phone, then fumbled and almost dropped it. He squared it up in front of his face and took two quick photos of George and Cabot. George wanted to ask the old man what the hell he was doing, but looking at those double barrels, he chose prudence.

"Now git, 'fore I get mad and forget my manners." The old man waved his shotgun barrel at them. "Git!"

They climbed back in the car, and George turned the key in the ignition. The old man hobbled over to the mongrel and unclipped its chain. The dog rushed the car and lunged at the passenger side window, bellowing and snapping, smearing the glass with frothy saliva. Cabot yelped and reared away from the window toward George, his arms across his face. George hit the gas and roared out of the clearing, churning up gravel in his wake. The dog chased them halfway back down the two-track driveway.

"It's okay, Henry," George said as they approached the main road. "You can put your arms down now."

CHAPTER 29

George found his way back to Highway 11 and pulled off onto the shoulder. It was a miracle they hadn't snapped an axle.

"What the hell was that, Henry?"

"I followed the directions!" Cabot exclaimed. "Holy cow." He patted his heart. "I've never had a gun pointed at me before. Do you think that old man would have shot us?"

"Call her. See what the problem is."

Cabot pulled out his phone and looked at the screen. "I can't. I have no bars here."

"Great," George said.

"I think I had reception in the last town we passed, about twenty miles up the road."

George sighed heavily.

"You have a better idea?"

George jerked the rental car back onto the road and sped north, doubling back over the section of Highway 11 they had just traveled. He pegged the speedometer at eighty, passing every vehicle in his way. They drove in silence and reached their destination in less than twenty minutes.

Booneville, Kentucky, population eighty-one, was the Owsley county seat, set in the heart of Appalachia. Owsley and Clay Counties (home of Old Man Shotgun) were two of the top five poorest counties in the United States, 24 percent poorer than Nesha's neighbors at the Gardens.

George pulled into the only gas station in town, a worn three-pump next to the bus stop diner. Cabot hurried inside to use the restroom, while George approached the pump. "Pay Inside" was scribbled on a piece of paper taped above the nozzle. George topped off and headed inside.

The guy behind the register was pale white, mid-twenties, with a dark patchy neck beard. He wore a sweat-stained ball cap pulled down low over his sunken eyes, sunglasses balanced backward on it, resting at the base of his skull. He was about George's height, but half his weight. His camo t-shirt hung on his skeletal frame; both arms were littered with cheap tattoos. He greeted George with a smile of neglected dentition.

"Gas on two," George said as he reached into his wallet and pulled out his credit card.

"Reader's broke," the guy said.

A gaggle of unemployeds to the guy's left guffawed. These 'left-behinds' had made the station their clubhouse. Besotted by cheap liquor and home-grown marijuana, they filled their days scratching losing lottery tickets, discussing which local pillbilly would be doing the Oxy Express to Daytona, and which local hoe was giving it up for a case of Pepsi, the going rate of exchange. George looked at these young men and again thought of the Gardens.

He paid the guy cash just as Cabot exited the bathroom.

"Hey, Henry, wait in the car. I'll be right out." George got his change and some directions from Neck Beard, then left the store. He got to the car just as Cabot was ending a phone call.

"Okay, I reached her," Cabot said. "I got good directions this time. She's waiting for us. Let's go."

It turned out they had just missed the driveway. It was only a mile or so north of Old Man Shotgun on Highway 11. This driveway was much better maintained, smooth and level all the way. Virginia's residence was deep in the woods, more than a mile off the highway. George parked next to a clean Ford F-250.

The home was another single-wide trailer, sitting high on a bluff. It overlooked a large field through a curtain of hardwood trees in spring bloom. The site was tidy, a hidden oasis in the forest. The trailer was modern and clean, about sixteen by eighty feet, and was wrapped in a vinyl skirt, with a freshly painted cedar deck that extended its entire length. Red Adirondack chairs, lined up razor straight, faced the field and rolling hills beyond.

George and Cabot walked up the steps to the front door, and Cabot knocked. No answer. George saw the curtain flutter in the window closest to the front door. Cabot knocked several more times. Again no answer. They waited in silence. George wiped his sweaty palms dry, then laced his fingers in front of him to avoid fidgeting. *What will she be like? Will I remember her? Will she remember me?*

The front door creaked open, and Virginia Dare stepped out into the sunlight. She froze as she saw George and took a small backward stutter-step away from him, as if she'd seen a ghost. She was a petite woman, all sinew and bone, a couple months shy of her seventieth birthday. Her shoulder-length gray hair, center-parted, was tucked behind her ears. She wore faded jeans and a white-patterned long-sleeve cotton shirt, left untucked at the waist. Her dark eyes were bright and alert. The sun on her face showed the deep lines and leathery pallor of a smoker.

"Virginia!" Cabot exclaimed.

The woman snapped out of her trance, turned to Cabot and buried her head in his shoulder. Her spare frame trembled and George heard a few muffled sobs escape her. Cabot whispered something to her, to which she nodded. At length, she broke their embrace and wiped at her eyes with the back of her hand.

Cabot put his arm around her and they both turned to George.

"Virginia—you remember George. George—this is Virginia Dare, the woman I told you about."

Virginia extended her hand. George shook it. Her hand was small, her grip firm.

"Pleased to meet you, Virginia," George said, surprised by the flatness of his voice.

Virginia placed her other hand on top of George's. It looked like a child's in comparison. She gawked at him in silence, and then finally spoke again.

"Oh! Where are my manners?" Virginia released her grip and fanned her hand over her chest like a southern belle. "Welcome to my home. Please come in."

They followed Virginia into her trailer. The front door opened into the living room, which was about fifteen feet square. It had beige walls and carpet, with a three-foot section of dark brown wainscoting that matched the drapes. Timeworn furniture was arranged around the room. The cushions on the sofa across from the forty-three-inch flat-screen TV were threadbare.

"Let me give you the grand tour." Virginia stood in the middle of the room and pointed to her left. "Two bedrooms and a full bath." She dropped her arm and raised the other. "Kitchen and master bed and bath," she said as she pointed to her right. "That's about it." They all shared an awkward laugh. Virginia led them to the kitchen and pointed to a round table in a small nook next to the refrigerator. George and Cabot pulled out chairs and sat down.

"Get you guys anything?" Virginia asked. "I have soda, iced tea, water... more soda..." The two men opted for the iced tea. George lost himself in the hum of the refrigerator as Virginia busied herself at the counter. She returned to the table with a pitcher of tea and filled three glasses.

"Here's to new beginnings and old friends," Cabot said as he raised his glass.

They clinked a toast. The tea was cold, with a touch of lemon and real sugar. George hadn't realized how dry his mouth was. He took a deep gulp.

"Nice place, Virginia," Cabot said, breaking the silence.

"Thank you, Henry." She dabbed her mouth with a napkin. "Had this one going on ten years now. About twelve hundred square feet. It's only me, so it's plenty big. I'll be trading it in for a new one in another five years or so."

Another silence as they all smiled politely and sipped their tea. George could feel Virginia's eyes on him.

"So, I understand you met my neighbor Percy earlier today?" Virginia smiled as she pulled out her phone and scrolled through it. She held it up, and George and Cabot were shocked to see the photo taken by Old Man Shotgun. The photo was slightly out of focus, and the top of George's head was cropped out, but it was them sure enough.

"You know that crazy old man?" Cabot asked.

"Old Percy's all right, long as you don't cross him." Virginia dropped her chin slightly and looked at both of them through her eyebrows. "Full disclosure—I sent you both over there on purpose. Had Percy take your picture. I had to be sure it was you. I'm real careful 'bout who comes my way. You know what they say—just 'cause you're paranoid don't mean they ain't out to get you."

"Virginia, that old coot could have killed us!" Cabot said, flustered. "He had a shotgun pointed at us and—"

"You were never in danger. Percy promised me the gun was unloaded." Virginia shrugged her shoulders. "Still a CIA girl after all these years, I guess."

George picked up Virginia's phone and laughed out loud as he looked at the photo again. "Looking good, Henry." He passed the phone back to Virginia.

"Well, I am glad you both find this so amusing," Henry said with feigned indignation. "Unlike both of you, I am not accustomed to having weapons pointed at me."

More nervous laughter, which Virginia ended with an audible *whew* and deep exhale.

"Well, let's get down to it," Cabot said as he looked at George. "Virginia has some things to share with you about her role in TRENTON. This is difficult for her, so please hear her out, okay?"

George nodded. This was it.

"Go ahead, dear," Cabot said as he gently touched Virginia's hand.

Virginia locked eyes with George. She tucked strands of hair behind both ears and licked her thin lips. "First of all, I want to apologize to you…" Her voice wavered, and she took a moment to gather herself. Cabot squeezed her hand. "This is the biggest regret of my life," she said. "I have thought of you every day. I did my best, George, I really did." Her lower lip began to tremble. She covered her mouth with her hand.

"It's true, George," Cabot said. "Virginia always stood up for you, always fought on your behalf. She really tried to shield you as best she could. It was a long, hard five years for her… for all of us."

"Henry too," Virginia said. "They tried to bully me, but Henry always stepped in. Even threatened to quit a few times." She reached out and squeezed Cabot's hand. "I was twenty-one and straight out of college when TRENTON started. Henry was only five years older, but much more accomplished than me. They listened to him."

Cabot placed his hand on top of hers. They exchanged a knowing glance.

Virginia turned to George and smiled weakly. Her eyes searched his.

"I remember the last time I saw you. My little boy." Virginia sniffed and wiped her nose with her napkin. "Henry arranged for me to see you and your new mom in Woburn. I watched you and her play in the park. You looked happy. And she obviously adored you. I told myself I had done all I could, that you would be better off not knowing anything about me. So I said goodbye to you that day. It broke my heart."

A heavy silence fell over the table.

"Henry asked me to tell you everything," she continued. "And you deserve the truth—the whole truth. I think the best place to start is at the beginning."

And with that, Virginia bared her soul to the little boy she had raised and then given away.

The year was 1951. America had just discovered *I Love Lucy*, rock and roll, and thermonuclear bombs. Truman was keeping the Oval Office warm for Ike. In this same year, Virginia Dare was born into poverty in Manchester, Kentucky, to a hard-drinking coal miner father and a teenage mother. Her mother ran off when Virginia was just six years old. This sobered her father up enough to raise Virginia with a firm but loving hand. He had worked in the mines until black lung took him. He had never remarried.

Virginia had enrolled at Eastern Kentucky University on a full academic scholarship, the first of her kin to make it past high school. She had graduated from EKU in 1970 with a mathematics degree and a 4.0 GPA. Just before graduation, Virginia had become a local celebrity when she was featured in the *Lexington Herald-Leader* for leading a conservative demonstration at EKU that grew violent. The article was picked up by several national newspapers, and that was how the CIA had found her.

They had been aggressively recruiting surrogate candidates for TRENTON, and believed that Virginia matched their requirements for the role of "Mary Ball." The CIA contacted her, ran her through a battery of tests, and offered her the job. They told her that her country needed her, and that she would be richly rewarded for her sacrifice. Virginia, never having been outside of Eastern Kentucky, believed what she was told and accepted the job. What the CIA had failed to tell her was that they had hired over one thousand other Mary Balls. But as it turned out, Virginia was the only surrogate who was able to bring the cloned embryo to term.

After Virginia gave birth to George, her job became that of a full-time actress. She would be Mary Ball, 24/7/365. The project became a Hollywood production: Virginia the ingénue, an eager-to-please starlet in her first role, struggling to learn her lines and hit her marks; Cabot the beleaguered director, trying to coax the best performance out of his star. Both would grow to resent, then loathe, their roles.

From the very beginning, Virginia struggled to live her life as Mary Ball. In life Ball was a querulous and selfish woman who provided little praise or love to her son George Washington. An incessant complainer, this stubborn woman ran her household as an unbending task master, which resulted in Washington maintaining an antagonism toward her in his adult life.

At first, Virginia's ad-libs were simply spontaneous acts of affection toward baby George: a kiss on the forehead; a playful hair tousle; kind words of encouragement. But TRENTON leadership had sharply chastised both Cabot and Virginia for these script deviations. Her TRENTON husband, a CIA case officer who sought the patronage of his superiors, had offered Virginia no support.

By the third year, Virginia and TRENTON leadership were clashing regularly. As the middleman, Cabot tried to maintain the peace. Virginia started to drink more than she should.

By the fourth year of the project, no amount of alcohol could keep the ghosts of her past at bay. Virginia began to lose her grip on the project and herself.

The fifth and final year of TRENTON saw a series of setbacks, beginning with the death of Virginia's father from black lung disease. Due to the secrecy of the project, Virginia had not seen much of him in the last five years of his life. And she never grew accustomed to all the lying and deception that was necessary when he asked her simple questions about her life. She was guilt-ridden over her father's death, and her resentment toward the CIA grew. Only Cabot continued to support her, and Virginia grew surly and defiant. She felt trapped, and wanted out. Only her love for young George kept her in the project.

In late April 1975, as America watched the Fall of Saigon on television, a small group of men, meeting in total secrecy in the bowels of the Pentagon, signed the agreement that ended TRENTON.

The CIA implemented a scorched-earth retreat from TRENTON. All records of TRENTON were destroyed, and all project personnel made to swear an oath of silence under threat of death. A significant lifetime monthly stipend was paid to each TRENTON member as long as they stayed quiet. Carrot and stick.

As Cabot handled all the details of George's anonymous adoption, Virginia resigned from the CIA and fled back to Eastern Kentucky. She used her hush money to buy a used single-wide trailer and her forty wooded acres in Oneida, Kentucky, a mere sixteen miles north of her birthplace. She had been here ever since.

The first decade following TRENTON was a dark period for Virginia. She lived in seclusion, her only company the ghosts and regrets that continually haunted her. She smoked too many cigarettes, drank too much cheap liquor. She thought a lot about her life, and about young George. She kept in sporadic contact with Cabot, who provided her with updates on George and his new life in Woburn. She aged hard.

By the mid-eighties, Virginia was thirty-five and empty, utterly hollow inside. She woke up one morning and decided she had had enough, and toughed her way out of the hole she had crawled into. She took a job as a school bus driver for Owsley County Elementary in nearby Booneville, a few blocks from where George and Henry had gassed up earlier that day. Virginia cherished her time with the kids, and they adored her in return. She'd been doing the job ever since.

When she finished her story, Virginia excused herself to the bathroom. She was gone for a long time. George's mind raced as he tried to sort out all he had heard. Cabot left him to his thoughts. The hum of the refrigerator was all that broke the silence, until the bathroom door opened and Virginia rejoined the table. Her eyes were red and puffy. She gave them both a quick, nervous smile, then began to pick at the wet napkin on the table in from of her.

George," Virginia said. "I promised Henry I would tell you everything... the whole truth." She raised her eyes to meet his. "So I reckon I will."

She took a gulp of tea and looked to Cabot. He nodded, and she again began to speak.

"When I was eighteen, I met a boy at EKU. We fell in love. He was my first. He died in the Quang Tri Province during Operation Hastings. July 1966. He'd been in Vietnam for less than thirty days. I learned I was pregnant one month after his death. I couldn't bear to raise our child without him."

Tears began to roll down Virginia's cheeks. She made no effort to stop them. The tears fell from her chin to the table in front of her. She swiped them off the table with the tattered paper napkin.

"I took the bus to Louisville and had an illegal abortion in some after-hours clinic. The doctor was drunk. I still remember his odor, his rough hands. I cried all the way home in the back of that bus, with cold packs and bloody towels under my coat."

Cabot was crying now, too.

"It was a boy," she whispered. "A baby boy... just like you."

Virginia began to sob, then dropped her head. Cabot stood and went to her side. Minutes passed. Virginia's moaning turned to sniffles. Finally, she blew her nose and rubbed her face with both hands. Cabot whispered something into her ear and then took his seat again.

The refrigerator continued to hum.

Virginia laced her thin fingers together, placed her hands on the table in front of her. She regained eye contact with George.

"Don't you see, George?" she said. "You were *my* baby boy, the boy I couldn't have in 1966. I thought I'd put it all behind me, but when you were born, and I looked at your face, I knew I hadn't. And I tried, but I just couldn't be mean to you like they wanted me to. I deeply regret my decision to take part in TRENTON. I thought I was doing the right thing—"

"We all did," Cabot said. "We all did."

Virginia reached across the table for George's hand. He gave it to her.

"Do you forgive me, George?" Her voice softened. "Please forgive me for what I've done."

George's insides churned. This woman had bared her soul, had stirred something deep within him. Not memories, but feelings. Feelings of safety. Of belonging. Feelings of love. Being with her felt right. The scientists would say he had no biological mother. But George now had two mothers; one adoptive, one surrogate.

Virginia's dark eyes bored into him. Now it was George's turn to tear up. He fought for control. This woman, a stranger to him a few hours ago, now sought his absolution. He knew in his heart she spoke the truth. His truth. *I am George Washington. This is my mother.*

George stood and walked around the table to Virginia. She rose to meet him. They embraced, and she buried her head in the middle of his chest. George felt her thin body tremble as she sobbed. They began to sway. George held out his hand to Cabot, who stood and joined their embrace.

They cried together, then dried their tears and laughed as they clung to each other in the small kitchen of that mobile home in the heart of Appalachia. There was no other place on earth any one of them would rather be.

CHAPTER 30

George was trying hard to believe the unbelievable.

Not that he was Washington's clone, or that he had lost his career and all his money, or even that he just found a second mother. No. What he couldn't believe was that Henry Cabot, of the blue-blooded Boston Brahmin Cabots, was drinking Bud Light—from a can!

He and Cabot were at a hillbilly bar, rubbing elbows with the locals and enjoying the country folk singer on a stage made of discarded wooden pallets. Cabot had a wide smile on his face as he lurched to the beat. This Yankee was a long way from home.

The singer was Virginia Dare. She was dressed in jeans and boots, with a three-quarter-length pale violet cotton jacket, open in the front and covered with embroidered flowers. Her gray hair shimmered in the bar lights. The packed crowd sang along and danced in the sawdust at the front of the stage. She had performed here for years; the crowd was filled with her people. On occasion while playing she gave someone a subtle nod as they passed her on the way to the bathroom.

Virginia began her fifty-minute set with a beautifully melancholy cover of "Both Sides Now" by Joni Mitchell. She sang the song to George, didn't take her eyes off him as her sonorous voice reached its apogee. George was grateful the bar was dark enough to hide his emotion.

"She's pretty great, isn't she?" Cabot asked.

George's eyes remained fixed on the stage. Anger and self-pity traded blows within him, each fighting for supremacy. He gripped the tabletop with both hands.

"Should've told me," George mumbled.

"What?" Cabot raised his voice over the music.

George knocked back his bourbon, then turned to face Cabot. "You should have told me, Henry."

"I didn't know how." Cabot leaned over the table. "How do you tell someone they are George Washington?"

Turning back to the stage, George thought of all the memories he and Virginia had missed, how his life would have been different if this remarkable woman had been part of it. As was his nature, his anger had triumphed over self-pity; it rose within him.

"Should've told me," he repeated.

They watched the rest of the set in silence. George put his anger on slow boil. The bourbon helped.

When she finished her set, Virginia left the stage to foot-stomping applause and joined George and Cabot at their table against the wall in the back of the bar. She took a seat next to George and signaled the bartender. A tray of drinks arrived less than a minute later: three Bud Lights and three bourbons. Maker's 46, top shelf at the Road Kill Bar.

"Your money's no good here tonight," Virginia told them over the noise of the crowd. "Randy'll keep these coming regular until we say otherwise." She raised her bourbon. "A toast. Here's to... old times." She turned to Henry with a puzzled look. "What was that toast, Henry?"

"To new beginnings and old friends."

"Yeah, that's it!" Virginia said. "To new beginnings and old friends."

They clinked glasses. George and Virginia took long pulls off their bourbons, then slapped their glasses down on the graffiti-scarred wooden tabletop with satisfying thuds. Cabot took a less enthusiastic sip and winced as the firewater shot down the back of his throat. He coughed a few times.

"Smooth," Cabot croaked.

As they settled into their drinks, locals approached the table to pay their respects to Virginia; tattoos and unkept beards on the men, outdated hair on the women. All were deferential to her, and by extension to George and Cabot as well.

After the second round, Virginia pulled out a small round tin of chewing tobacco from her bag, pinched off a wad, and tucked it between her cheek and gum.

"You chew tobacco?" George asked, his eyes widening.

"Yeah," Virginia replied. "But only when I drink. I kicked a three-pack-a-day habit a long time ago. I missed smoking when I drank, so I switched to dip. Figured I'd keep the cancer guessing, you know?"

"So… you spit in a cup, or what?" George asked with a chuckle.

"Don't you sass me, young man. Of course I don't spit in a cup. That's disgusting. I gut it, like a proper lady."

George and Cabot looked blankly at Virginia.

"Gut it. You know, swallow it. The tobacco juice."

"Ow!" George blurted out. Cabot brought his hand to his mouth.

"Beats smoking. It's part of my commitment to a healthy lifestyle," Virginia said with a wink.

The third round arrived right on time. Cabot looked at this round of drinks with foreboding.

"Henry, why don't you nurse this round," Virginia said as she placed her hand gently on his. "No use tryin' to keep up with me. And George here… Well, looks like this ain't his first rodeo." She raised her glass to George. They clinked and gulped. Both glasses hit the table at the same time.

"So, George." Virginia lowered her voice and shot a glance over her shoulder. "How are you doin' with all this? It must be a lot to process." She palmed her beer can and took a delicate sip. "I remember when they first told me about you. It was only after I brought you to term that I got the whole story. Fifty years ago. I remember like it was yesterday." She gave a low whistle and shook her head.

A silence fell over the table.

"Didn't sleep much last night," George admitted. "Like I'm walking a tightrope without a net. I've gotta figure this all out. Gonna take a while." He looked down at his bourbon, swished the remainder around in his glass. "What I do know is that I believe you both. Trust you both. I know I'm... *him*."

"We will help you through this," Cabot said.

"Henry tells me you've had a rough couple of months." Virginia canted her rickety wooden chair to face George. It scraped loudly on the plywood floor. "Some problems at work and home?" She looked George in the eye. "You can tell me."

And to George's surprise, he realized he wanted Virginia to know everything. To see him as Nesha did. So he told her his whole truth, from start to finish, as she had done yesterday. But it was only when he spoke of General Taylor that his anger resurfaced. The pitch of his voice lowered and his speech became clipped. It was Taylor who had orchestrated George's demise. It was he who had secured Kacey Anne's betrayal, coached Parker's and Hale's duplicity, and created false evidence. It was he who had killed Josh Allen to cover his tracks.

"Henry," Virginia said, when George had finished speaking. "Could you go to the bar and tell Randy to set us up with another round?"

Cabot excused himself from the table.

Virginia watched Cabot go, and then turned back to George. "George, look at me." George did. Her eyes were filled with warmth and wisdom. "I know what you're thinking. I thought that way too after TRENTON ended. But you gotta let this guy go. You carry this hate around in your belly, it will eat you like cancer. The bastard ain't worth it. Let it go."

George shook his head stubbornly. "I couldn't live with myself if I don't do it. Besides, I don't have much to lose at this point."

"No!" Virginia exclaimed. "I don't give a shit if that bastard dies. Probably has it coming for what he did to you. And of course Henry's all fired up about his big picture stuff—Taylor's threat to the country, his precious Constitution. Now don't get me wrong, George. That stuff's important. But what he did to you is *personal*. And my hillbilly blood knows how to settle a score, believe me. I—"

Virginia abruptly stopped talking as a peroxide-blond waitress in a tight rebel flag t-shirt approached to drop off the last round of drinks. When she'd left, Virginia leaned in to George and continued.

"The problem is, you won't be able to get to him. Not alone. He's the vice president now. He's got a 24/7 Secret Service detail. You bum-rush him and they're gonna light you up like a Christmas tree. Then they'll spin it like you were some crazed lunatic. Booth and Oswald type shit. They'll have future generations of American school kids spittin' on your grave."

George nodded forlornly.

"I know you better than you think," she said gently, "and I know you ain't gonna stop until you get this bastard. Just promise you won't do anything rash. No lone wolf stuff, okay?"

George nodded again.

"Say it, George. Promise me!"

"Okay. I won't do anything stupid."

"Good." Virginia grabbed his big hands and gave him a peck on his cheek. "Thank you, George."

Cabot rejoined the table. "I hate to be a killjoy, but it's close to midnight and we have an early flight tomorrow. We should probably get going."

"Yeah. Guess so," George said. He finished his bourbon in two gulps. No self-respecting man lets bourbon go to waste.

"Wait," Virginia said. "Before you go, I got something for you."

She riffled around in her big bag, found what she was looking for, and plopped it down on the table. It was a 1970s Knickerbocker-version Curious George stuffed monkey. It was about fourteen inches tall, wearing a faded yellow shirt with *Curious George* emblazoned across the front. He had small round eyes, a black button nose, and a big red felt smile. He smelled musky and of cigarette smoke, but otherwise was well preserved.

George studied the doll. This monkey was familiar to him. *I've seen that face before.* George reached out and touched the doll. He was soft. He picked it up, held it up to his face for closer examination.

"Do you remember?" Virginia asked. "I snuck him into the house for you. When you were about three years old. We hid in the bathroom and played with him together. You really loved that little guy."

George looked up at her. So she did love him during TRENTON, as she said. Still did. He was not just some scientific experiment. Virginia had raised him as her own and had given him away because she had to.

"You take him with you," Virginia said, and flicked at the corner of her eye. "Something to remember me by."

They all stood. Virginia wrapped both her arms around George. He held her tight. She patted George's chest as they separated.

"Go on now. You both got a plane to catch."

"It was so nice to see you again, Virginia," Cabot said. They embraced and Virginia gave him a kiss on the cheek. She whispered something to him and Cabot's face grew serious.

"So you two come back and see and me some time," Virginia said.

"Thanks… for everything," George said.

"You know—I caught a young fella giving me the eye on stage earlier. Think I'm gonna find him and see what that's all about."

They all laughed, and then George and Cabot turned and walked toward the door.

"And George," Virginia said in a firm voice. Both men turned. "Don't forget your promise. In the holler it's a sin to lie to your mama."

CHAPTER 31

"How is DC?" Cabot asked.

"Okay," George replied in a hushed tone. He adjusted his smartphone closer to his mouth. "I forgot how humid it is here. It's weird being back. Doesn't feel like home anymore."

"You have been through so much recently."

George sighed.

"How is JD?" Cabot asked.

"Good. He's in the shower now, so we can talk."

It had been ten days since they'd left Virginia and flown back to Boston. Cabot and George had had the entire first-class row to themselves and were able to talk privately. They'd talked through the entire five-hour flight. George had asked Cabot a flurry of questions about TRENTON, which he'd answered with candor. Most of the conversation had centered on a plan that Cabot had devised.

"Did you find a place for the meeting, like we talked about?" Cabot asked.

"Yeah, Henry... About that. I don't know. I don't think it's gonna work. I know Taylor. Know what he's capable of. He ain't gonna go for it. I still like my plan better."

George got up off the sofa and walked to the bathroom door. The shower was still running, and he could hear JD singing, or rapping, or whatever it was he was doing. He would be in there for a while.

"It will work, George. General Taylor is a villainous megalomaniac, but he will listen to reason. He is not stupid."

"He's untethered," George said. "Through the looking glass. He's making his own rules now. He won't listen."

When it came to Taylor, George and Cabot agreed on one thing: that he was plotting to overthrow the government and establish himself as a military dictator. Where they differed was a reflection of their contrasting personalities. George was pragmatic, a man of action who viewed the world as black and white. Cabot was theoretical, an idea man who viewed the world in infinite shades of gray. George the realist, Cabot the idealist.

Occam's Razor. The simplest solution is best. For George, it was that straightforward. He had a personal score to settle with Taylor, and he would do it with a sniper rifle. How history, or his country, viewed his actions was of little consequence to him.

Cabot, by contrast, embraced the complexities of life. The endless variables, hypotheses, and but/for causations of the learned mind. A man of staunch logic and reason.

Cabot's plan reflected his sensibilities. He believed they now had the leverage needed to present Taylor with an ultimatum: He and President Parker must resign immediately, reinstate the secretary of education as head of government, and schedule a new populist presidential election. If not, they would expose him for the military dictator he was and force a recall presidential vote, where he would face an unbeatable candidate: the Father of the Country—George Washington himself!

"I don't like it," George said. "And I'm sure as hell not running for president. I don't want anyone to know about me. My past, who I am. It's nobody's business."

"It's a bluff, George. It will never get that far. All we have to do is convince Taylor that you are Washington, and he will fold."

"This is insane, Henry. How do you—"

"I cannot condone murder," Cabot said. "Besides, Taylor is surrounded by security at all times. You will not be able to get close to him."

"His weaknesses are arrogance and ambition. He's in the middle of a thirty-day PR campaign. Traveling the country and mixing with the masses. He's exposed. I'll make the shot."

"Even if you do…" Cabot trailed off. "They'll kill you. You know that."

"Yeah, but I—"

"I will be an accomplice in your death, George. I can't."

"It's the only way."

"No! The solution must be a nonviolent one," Cabot exclaimed. "Please. Let's do this my way."

"Taylor will never believe I'm George Washington. He'll think we're bat-shit crazy."

"We will make him believe. I will bring copies of some TRENTON documents I still have in my possession. And Virginia said she will come with us. She has documents also."

"She said that?" George asked incredulously. "She wants to do this?"

"She does not want anything to happen to you, George."

"I don't want her involved in this," George said.

"It is the only way," Cabot said. "Taylor is already making his move. In the past two weeks his speeches have been laced with ominous innuendo. Remember the Milgram and Stanford Prison experiments? It's happening again, right before our eyes."

George took a long breath. He was standing at the floor-to-ceiling window that offered a bird's-eye view of the White House. He wondered if Taylor was in the White House now, and what he might do to stop the two men plotting his demise less than a mile away.

"George? You still there, George?"

"Yeah."

JD emerged from his bedroom. He wore knee-length cotton shorts and nothing else. He finished toweling off and hung the plush towel around his neck.

"That Henry?" JD asked.

George nodded.

"Tell him I said hello."

George held up a finger. "Gotta go, Henry. JD's out of the shower and we're gonna grab a bite. He says hello, by the way."

"Let's do this my way, George. Promise me you won't do anything on your own. Give me your word."

Cabot had forced his hand. *Damn it.* "Okay," George said, still not convinced. "We play it your way."

"Good! It is for the best, George. Trust me."

"Hope so," George said with resignation. "I'll get to work on it down here. Talk soon." He disconnected the call and stuffed his phone in his left front jeans pocket. He took one last look at the Washington Monument and turned to face JD.

"What was that all about?" JD asked.

"Nothing. Henry wants me to check on something for him at the Library of Congress while I'm here in DC."

"Well, that's a good time right there," JD deadpanned. "Can I come?"

George wanted to tell his friend everything, but of course he could not.

Hey, JD. I'm really George Washington. Yeah, really. And I'm gonna assassinate the vice president too—because he deserves it, and, like Josh Allen, I just don't give a shit anymore. And last week in Kentucky, I met my mother for the first time. My surrogate mother, I mean, the one that carried my cloned embryo. Yeah, that's right, buddy. I have two mothers, but no biological parents.

It all still sounded so preposterous. How could he possibly share this with anyone?

"You know what you need?" JD said with an ever-widening grin. "You need to get your drink on with your pal JD."

This put a smile on George's face.

"Yeaaah. See that? That's what I'm talkin' about!" JD gave George the double-gun salute. "It's on, Bubba!"

CHAPTER 32

"Wow," George muttered under his breath. He sat down on an overpriced patio chair, and right in front of him, less than half a mile away and larger than life, was the Washington Monument. Its marble and granite glowed a ghostly blue-gray against the clear night sky. The two red lights at the top seemed to stare back at him, unblinking.

He's watching me now. He knows. Waiting to see what I will do. What would he do? What would he have me do?

"I feel like that monument is staring at me," George said.

"Best view in the place," JD said. "I'm tight with the GM; he's in my group. Hooks me up every time I come here."

JD had it all worked out. They had used plastic key cards at the guest entrance on F Street, then were escorted past the long lines to their reserved table.

George and JD's drinks arrived within minutes.

"How'd they know our drink order?" George asked.

"I texted the bartender from the condo," JD replied. "Walker Green for you and Guinness Black and Tan for me. They'll keep our glasses filled until I say otherwise."

"Thanks," George said. "I'm drinking bourbon these days."

"When'd you start that? You've been a scotch man since I've known you."

"Down in Kentucky. It's the state drink down there."

"Well, all right, then." JD pulled out his iPhone and tapped out a quick text. He looked at the bartender until he nodded back. "Next round you go to bourbon. House best. Neat with a cube, just like the scotch, yes?"

George gave him the thumbs-up.

JD wore a sharply pressed suit jacket and slacks, with a white oxford buttoned shirt open at the neck. The jacket and slacks were a matching dark violet color, two hundred count sheep's wool. It draped perfectly.

He scanned the room.

"Major eye play. Smokin' hot blonde at two o'clock." JD motioned with his head. "White cocktail dress, bare shoulders, big curves."

"Oh yeah?" George said. "That gonna be the one?"

"Could be. Don't know if she had a second, but there was an empty barstool next to her. Her girl could've been in the bathroom." JD swigged his Black and Tan. "Now we just sit back and wait, bro."

It didn't take long for the blonde to appear. She was in her late thirties, right in JD's wheelhouse. She had a perky sculpted nose and large breasts that strained against her sheer dress. She struck an alluring pose in front of their table, a Hermes clutch in one hand and a glass of Pinot Gris in the other.

"Great view, huh?" she said, gushing at JD and ignoring George. "Mind if I sit down?"

JD gave her a nod, and she joined their table sitting next to JD and across the table from George.

"I'm Paige," the blond said, leaning into JD as she extended her hand, displaying her bountiful cleavage.

"I'm JD, this here's my buddy George." JD shook her hand. It was warm and soft. "Giddy up."

It was always that easy for JD. George was grateful that at least Paige now blocked his view of the two glowing red eyes that had been boring into him all night.

JD got the waiter's attention, and a fresh round of drinks quickly appeared. The three bantered a while. Then Paige started rubbing on JD. First the bicep, then the chest, and then her hand slipped under the table. George excused himself. JD protested, but not much.

George took an aimless stroll around the room. It felt good to be up on his feet and moving. The place was packed with shiny young faces, untouched by the world. He took a stool at the end of the bar. He would hang here a while, give JD and Paige a little time to get better acquainted. Not the first time he'd played third wheel to JD.

A commotion behind him caused George to spin around. A stunning woman was walking toward him. The crowd parted in her path.

She was perfection. Tall and lean; looked to have some Jamaican or Caribbean blood in her. Her skin was luminous, the color of caramel cappuccino. Dazzling hazel-green eyes offset full red lips. She moved with the silky confidence of a big cat. She locked onto George as she approached. A jolt of electricity ran through him, and he fought the urge to turn around to see who she was really looking at. He felt every man's stare on him as she approached.

"Hello, my name is Grace," she said in a velvety voice. She extended a manicured hand. George stared blankly and gripped it. She smelled delicious. "And your name is?" she prompted him.

George noticed he was still shaking her hand. He released his grip awkwardly. "George," he croaked.

"Nice to meet you, George. I noticed you walking through the bar and I said to myself, 'Now there's an interesting man, not like the rest of the boys in this place.' And I thought, 'I bet that man has an interesting story to tell.' She took a half-step closer to George. "Well, do you, George?"

"Do I what?" George stammered.

"Have a story to tell," she replied.

"Uhm..." he stalled. "We all have stories. You too, I bet."

"What brings you to this place? A little vapid for the likes of you, I think."

"I came with a friend of mine." George turned and pointed at JD and Paige.

"Well, why don't you introduce me?" she said as she locked her arm in his and began to walk him back toward the table.

As they approached, JD had the same slack-jawed reaction to Grace that all men did. George had never before seen JD stunned silent by a woman's beauty.

"Grace, this is my friend—" he began.

JD rose to his feet and extended his hand. "JD."

They all took their seats, Grace now next to George.

Paige regarded Grace warily. "JD's a big lobbyist." She drew closer to him, now practically sitting on his lap. "What do you do?" she asked Grace, her words laced with sarcasm.

"International finance, mostly," Grace said. "I do a little modeling on the side. Mostly fashion runway stuff—Paris and Milan—and some magazine covers."

"What magazines?" Paige asked, not knowing when to quit. "Have I seen you in anything?"

"Depends. What's on your reading list?"

"Well, let's see…" She twirled her hair. "I like *U.S. Weekly* and *People*, of course. Uhm… *Woman's Health* is good. *In Style*. Sometimes I read *Real Simple*—"

"Perhaps not, then," Grace said. "I do most of my covers for *Elle*, *Vogue*, and the like."

"Oh," Paige said with resignation. She took a gulp of Pinot white and twisted her table napkin into a knot.

JD was still staring at Grace. George knew why, and mouthed "No."

"Love that ponytail," JD said, apropos of nothing.

Okay. Here it comes.

"Yeah." JD grinned. "Full and thick. High on the head. Waterfall spread. Hair knot. Smooth taper at the bottom. Nice work."

"JD—" George started.

"So you're a ponytail guy, are ya?" Grace asked in a lighthearted cadence.

"Oh, you don't know the half of it," JD said.

"Check this out!" Paige took another quick gulp of wine and then fidgeted with the back of her head until her hair fell to her shoulders, then flipped it around until it was tied off in a ponytail. "Ta-da!" she exclaimed, then turned her head toward JD for his approval.

"Sweet," he said.

Paige turned back around, blond ponytail flying, and gave him another kiss. She didn't know it, but that ponytail had just sealed her fate.

JD ordered the group a fresh round of drinks and the group settled into conversation. Paige relaxed when she realized that Grace had no interest in JD. For the next two hours, they swapped anecdotes and snippets of their life histories.

Grace appeared particularly interested in George's past. She asked him probing questions that he either half-answered or evaded. Despite his wariness, George really enjoyed Grace. They had a comfortable rhythm and banter together. At one point, Grace even leaned across George to sample his bourbon, a playful gesture that he welcomed. George had not been this happy in years.

"If you'll excuse me, gentlemen," Grace said after a time. "I need to go to the ladies' room."

"Me too!" Paige said.

The two women left together, Grace leading the way.

JD waited until they were out of earshot, then leaned in.

"Damn, George. Grace is... ridiculous. Cartoonishly hot. Damn."

"I know. Haven't felt like this since Kacey Anne and college."

"Oh, yeah," JD said. "Kacey Anne came by the office the other day to see me. We went out for coffee and talked."

"What?" George felt himself go pale.

"Yeah. I wasn't sure if I should mention it, but decided you should know."

"When did you decide that?"

JD took a big gulp of beer. Then another. "Right now, I guess."

George had made his peace with his ex-wife, but her name hit him like a gut punch. Nineteen years was hard to ignore, especially the early ones, which had been good.

"What'd she want?"

"She was pissed."

"What'd I do?"

"No, not you. Pissed at life… herself maybe," JD said. "She looked like shit, George. You know I haven't been her biggest fan over the years, but I kinda felt sorry for her. She seemed different, actually showed some humility. She asked how you were, by the way. I think she meant it. She's got regrets."

"So do I."

"She said she wants to move to LA, start over. She's gone through a lot of money though. She wants to sell the townhouse, but that ain't gonna get her to LA."

George thought for a moment.

"Give her my half."

"What?"

"She can have my half of the townhouse; go to LA and have her new life. Tell her I wish her luck."

"You sure about this, George? You could use that money right now."

"I never wanted that townhouse anyway. Give it all to her. I'll survive."

Grace and Paige approached the table. Both men cut off their conversation and smiled.

They picked up right where they left off. Grace questioned George about his childhood, which he glossed over. What could he possibly say? Grace, for her part, was adroit at appearing to fully answer questions about herself without actually providing any substantive details, like some of George's more skilled interrogation subjects. She often touched him as she spoke; a soft hand on his, a playful swipe to the shoulder. Time passed quickly.

Grace said her goodbyes a little after midnight. She had an early morning flight to catch. She gave JD a hug; Paige got air kisses.

Then it was George's turn. He got to his feet. "Nice to meet you, Grace," George said. "I had a great time."

"Me too."

George leaned in to kiss her on the cheek. She turned toward him at the last moment, and their lips met. She had the softest lips, like moist cashmere. She pressed as he tried to pull away, and the kiss lingered a moment longer.

"I'll see you again, George Moore," Grace said with a smile, then turned and left.

George watched her go, knowing he would probably never see her again. Time to return to his reality.

George said goodnight to JD and Paige. They were calling it a night as well. Paige headed off for a final visit to the ladies' room. JD watched her walk away, then turned back to George.

"Dude, what the hell was *that*?" he said incredulously. "Jesus! That was the most beautiful woman I have *ever* seen. Period. Epic pull."

"I know. Weird, huh?" George said. "Way outta my league. Wonder why she zeroed in on me?"

"First of all, she's outta everyone's league. Second, who cares? And third, don't sell yourself short, my friend. You're a beautiful man."

"I'm really more striking than beautiful."

JD laughed that childish, unrestrained laugh of his.

"So, what's up with Paige?" George asked. "Am I going home alone tonight?"

"Yeah, she's good to go. I texted my guy about an hour ago. He put us in room 916, a nice corner room at the end of the hall."

"I'm gonna take off, then," George said, then gave JD a hug that ended with a sharp back-slap. George hoped he could tell his friend everything someday. He passed Paige on his way out. She still had her ponytail up. George thought of little Jenny Richardson bouncing around the volleyball court, and the 295 pounds of coiled testosterone waiting for her back at the table. There was going to be a party in room 916 tonight.

George walked north along Fifteenth Street, his head down, hands jammed deep in his pockets. It was a crisp, cloudless night. He impulsively turned left onto Pennsylvania Avenue and found himself standing in front of the North Lawn of the White House. The grounds were well lit. George stared at the upper windows, wondered if President Parker was asleep. Or maybe Taylor had already moved in. George knew who wore the pants in that administration.

Sleep tight, General. See you soon.

CHAPTER 33

George had been picking at his chocolate chip and pecan cookie for over thirty minutes. It was the size of a small salad plate. He broke off a piece and popped it in his mouth. The cookie was a prop, meant to camouflage him among the other governmental office workers at the busy food court.

He didn't belong here, a stranger to a city he lived in most of his adult life. Being here now made George appreciate what a lie his life had been. The Gardens taught him that. He pushed his cookie aside and incessantly scratched at the top of his hand, fighting the itch to get up and leave this place forever. He held no kinship for the city that bore his name.

George's chosen meeting location—the Reagan Building Food Court—provided many advantages: it was a secure building, with identification and scanning at all entrances, multiple egress points, and easy counter-surveillance opportunities. It was also a crowded public area filled with distracted people, and conveniently located to the guest. George had selected a spot in the northwest corner of the food court, behind a large pillar, and pushed three small tables together to create a private seating area. Cabot sat at a table across the room near the large rotunda. Virginia Dare was outside at the main entrance. She would follow the guest into the building and to the food court.

All good agents know that Murphy's Law lives between the lines of even the best operational plans. George relied on two tactical assumptions: first, the guest would attend the meeting clandestinely; and second, the guest would arrive alone, without his security detail or any law enforcement in tow. Anything that happened after that he would have to address on the fly.

The food court began to fill up with the early lunch crowd. Customers had seventeen eateries to choose from, all serving a light fare designed around the forty-five-minute federal lunch break. The food court was about the size of a football field, with a large rotunda at midfield and the eateries lined up along the sidelines. It was modern and gleaming, with happy yellow seats and light cherrywood accents. No one noticed the fifty-year-old man who sat alone in the far corner picking at a cookie.

George checked his watch. The guest was late. The bastard was not going to show. He glanced over to Cabot, who appeared to be engrossed in his newspaper, as instructed.

George slumped down in his chair, suddenly overcome by remorse. How had Cabot talked him into this? And Virginia? She should not be here. He should've stuck to his own plan. Maybe it was not too late. Maybe when the guest arrived, he could just—

The sight of Virginia silenced his thoughts. She walked into the food court with a rushed gait. She gave George a quick glance, then sat down opposite Cabot. She ran her fingers through her hair, then again, a second time. Their guest had arrived and was on his way to the food court. And he was not alone. Two hair combs meant he had brought someone with him.

George shot up straight in his chair. He pushed his half-eaten cookie aside and took a few deep breaths in a futile effort to slow his racing heart. He locked his eyes on the grand staircase that led down to the food court.

It didn't take long. Taylor's martial bearing gave him away. He was casually dressed, with a new navy Washington Capitals ball cap pulled down low over his face. Tinted glasses finished the look. The disguise was surprisingly effective. The sitting vice president walked through the crowd unnoticed. A similarly disguised man, more stocky and sans glasses, walked two paces behind.

They saw George at a distance and began to walk toward him. George watched the two men close on him. His vision tunneled. Crowd noise disappeared. His rage rose as they approached the table. Predator and prey.

Taylor sat across from George, and he felt his adrenaline spike at his proximity to this man. His jaw clenched; his fists tightened. He almost lurched out of his chair. He saw his hands wrapped around the man's throat. Squeezing, crushing. If he'd had a gun or knife, he would have used it—to hell with Cabot's plan.

"Agent Moore," Taylor said, not offering his hand. "We meet again. This is my chief of staff, Colonel Shelton." Shelton nodded curtly.

"I am a very busy man, Agent Moore. Tell me what this is all about."

"Well, like I told you. My network at the Bureau is still intact, and I have some important information you'll want to hear."

"Such as?"

"Deputy Director Hale is going to betray you to the Democrats. He wants to be director, and they promised it to him as soon as they're back in the White House."

"And why in hell should I believe you?" Taylor asked.

"I have it on tape," George lied. "I can get you a copy."

Taylor studied him coolly. "What do you want in return?"

"I want my job back," George lied again. "Or at least my pension and benefits reinstated."

Taylor sat back and sneered. "You see, Colonel," he said to Shelton, without averting his eyes from George, "what we have here is a cautionary tale. Agent Moore was a proud man, a walk-the-line man. I offered him everything, and he defied me. Pride goeth before a fall." He chuckled. "Look at him now, tail between his legs. Know thyself, Colonel. Know thyself."

"I just thought—" George said.

"Lost it all, didn't you, Agent Moore? Not only your career and pension, but that wife of yours too. Kacey Anne, isn't it? She turned so easy. Sold you out like that."

Taylor snapped his finger for emphasis. The loud pop made George jump.

George locked eyes with Taylor. His arrogance spoke ignorance of their plan. George had waited long enough. If Taylor had anything planned for George, say arrest or abduction, he would have done it by now.

Time to spring the trap. George signaled Virginia, then leaned back and folded his arms across his chest. She and Cabot arrived and took their seats on either side of George.

Taylor considered Cabot and Virginia, then turned, agitated, back to George. Shelton sprang to his feet. His chair screeched on the tile floor, which caused a few lunch-goers to turn and look in their direction. Shelton noticed the stares and sat back down.

"You—" Taylor said to George in a low, guttural voice, stabbing a forefinger at him.

"General—listen to me very carefully," George said, snapping each word. "I lied to you about Hale. I don't want a goddamn thing from you. But my colleague here has something very important to tell you, and you'd better listen. Got it?"

Taylor remained silent, incredulous.

Cabot launched into his pitch, just like they had rehearsed, presenting his talking points in the esoteric style one would expect of a long-tenured Harvard professor. He dryly explained the history of TRENTON, pushing documents across the table to Taylor, who lowered his gaze to look at them and then looked right back up again. His head never moved, and he never touched the documents. His face was a mask of contempt.

George shifted uneasily in his chair: Cabot was losing his audience.

When the moment of truth arrived, Cabot matter-of-factly told Taylor that the TRENTON clone was George Washington, and then pointed to George and pronounced him the new Father of Our Country.

Shelton, who had sat silent during Cabot's speech, let out a loud snort. He and Taylor exchanged dubious looks. Both men grinned.

Shelton shook his head vigorously from side to side. "Are you shittin' me?" he said in a sharp tone. He faced George. "You brought the general here for *this*?" Shelton's face flushed red. "I ought to—"

"It's okay, Tim," Taylor said with a wave of his hand. "I'm sure the professor has a point to make with all of this." He turned to Cabot. "You do, don't you, Professor? Surely you didn't come all the way from Cambridge just to tell me Agent Moore here is really *George Washington*—did you?"

George gave Cabot the abort sign, but it was too late. His uncle was on a roll. Undeterred, he stammered out his ultimatum: Taylor and Parker must resign immediately, or be exposed and defeated by the undefeatable George Washington.

"Ahhh," Taylor said. "There it is." He paused. "Extortion? Is that it, Professor? You're trying to extort me—the vice president of the United States of America—with this nonsense?" His voice began to rise. He turned and wagged his finger at George. "I don't care who you think you are—George Washington, George Bush, or George Fucking Patton. Have you seen my poll numbers? The American people love me. I would beat God himself in a popular election right now!"

He refocused on Cabot. "And you, Professor. Do you have any idea whose leg you're pissing on?" Taylor shook his head. "You just opened the wrong door, my friend."

Taylor looked around the table. Virginia met and held Taylor's stare.

"And who the hell are you again?' he asked Virginia.

"I'm his mother," she said, jerking her thumb toward George. "That's who in hell I am."

General Taylor adjusted his ball cap lower on his head. He leaned back from the table.

"Well, General," Cabot finally sputtered, breaking the awkward silence. "What is your response?"

Taylor smiled at Cabot, baring his teeth, then finally turned to Shelton and spoke again. "What do men covet, Colonel?" he asked rhetorically. "What do they most desire? For most men, it is ultimately love and family, yes? Other men—men of passion, learning, or commerce—seek more perfunctory pursuits, pleasures of the flesh, mind, or purse. I believe Agent Moore and the professor are such men."

Taylor gestured toward Shelton, then turned his attention back to the trio across from him. "But the colonel and I, we are men of a different stripe. We seek not love or money, nor sins of the flesh, nor absolute truth. No, these things mean little to us. What we seek is to conquer, to stand over our vanquished foes, our boots to their necks. We live to kill the strong and subjugate the weak. Mercy, forgiveness, and compassion have no place in our world. They are but the empty platitudes of cowards and fools. I live to gut my enemy, to slake my thirst with his blood. And you are all my enemy now."

Cabot's eyes narrowed, and his posture stiffened.

"I should thank you, Agent Moore. My plan had succeeded too easily, and frankly I had found myself growing bored. I had forgotten all about you until you called last week. What had passed between us earlier was business. But what you have done today is personal. You and your little friends now have my full attention. From this day forward, your anguish is my oxygen. I will sharpen my fangs on your carcass until a more worthy adversary presents itself."

"Let's do this," George growled. He rose to his feet, as did Shelton. George felt a tug on his arm, and looked down at Cabot's pleading face. He allowed Cabot to pull him back down to his seat. Shelton also sat but remained locked onto George.

"Now, I don't know these two," Taylor said, sweeping his hand dismissively at Cabot and Virginia. "But it's obvious to me that you care for them deeply." Taylor showed his yellowed teeth. "Thank you for sharing this vulnerability with me, Agent Moore. I will put it to good use, I assure you."

"No!" Cabot exclaimed. "You must listen to me. Walk away from this, General, while you still can. There are forces at play that you do not understand. This is our last chance to avoid bloodshed."

Taylor snorted. "Are you threatening me, Professor?"

"Sir," Shelton interrupted. "We should be going, sir."

Taylor ignored him. "I will attend to you last," he said to George, "so you may witness the demise of your two friends. It will be my final gift to you."

"You bastard!" Virginia shouted. A couple at a nearby table turned and looked.

"Sir—" Shelton said again.

"When I am through with you, Agent Moore," Taylor continued, "you will welcome the last day of your life. And you know what day that will be? Tuesday. Just another Tuesday for me."

"I'm gonna kill you!" George said through clenched teeth.

"We shall see, Agent Moore. We shall see."

Taylor rose from the table and marched off without a backward glance, Shelton following one step behind.

George, Cabot, and Virginia watched in silence as they left the food court.

"Fuck that guy," Virginia said. "Excuse my French, but nobody threatens me and my kin and gets away with it. I'm a Kentucky girl. I know a thing or two about feuding." She raked her hair behind both ears. "Count me in on this thing, George. Whatever you need."

George put his hand on hers and squeezed, and Virginia squeezed him back.

They both turned to Cabot. He looked despondent, like a kid who just had his lunch money stolen.

"I did all I could," he mumbled. "I had to try. This is out of my hands now. God help us." Cabot looked away, off in the distance.

George never said 'I told you so.'

Sometimes silence speaks loudest.

CHAPTER 34

"He'll have a pale ale, and I'll take the IPA," George said to the indifferent twenty-something college waiter, who gave a perfunctory nod and left the two men sitting at their corner table, facing the front door.

"Any problems getting here?" George asked.

Cabot shook his head. "I did just like you said. Two taxis to the T, got off at Kendall, and walked here. Got a little wet in the rain; that's about it." Cabot gulped his glass of water. "Do you really think—"

"Did anyone follow you here?"

"No," Cabot responded. "I didn't see anyone."

"They're on us, Henry," George said. "I had the binocs up on the top floor. They had two agents on benches in the Public Garden all day. Benches with a perfect view of the front of your townhouse."

"Well, that doesn't mean—"

"Both of these guys left their benches between three thirty and four p.m., and were immediately replaced by two other guys. The FBI daytime surveillance shift is eight to four. I saw the shift change, Henry."

George looked past Cabot out to the street. "We've definitely got a tail."

"Taylor?" Cabot asked.

"Gotta be." George's eyes darted to the front door and tracked a group of college kids as they sauntered to their seats. The Kendall Square bar was semi-industrial chic, with stained concrete floors, a light red oak bar and stools, and a large hanging blackboard with the night's beer and ale offerings written in a youthful hand. George and Cabot sat at one of the small tables scattered around the perimeter of the bar by the windows. The smaller upstairs loft area was closed, giving the place a more intimate vibe.

"Well, it's been about a week," George said. "Taylor must've gone to Hale, and Hale most likely opened a case on me. It'll be off-the-books. They couldn't predicate me legally." He checked his new burner phone to make sure it was powered off. "Taylor doesn't want me in jail. He wants me dead."

"You don't know that."

"You remember Josh Allen?" George asked.

"Of course."

"Taylor had him killed," George whispered. "And I'm in his crosshairs now. It's personal. You heard him."

"I am so sorry, George. I should never have got you and Virginia involved in this like I did. I never thought he would—"

George hissed "*Shhhh*," and slapped the table, which silenced Cabot just as the waiter returned with their ales. They clinked glasses and silently drank.

"How could this country produce someone like Taylor?" Cabot asked after he had drained half his glass. "He's a monster."

"I'm surprised it's taken this long," George said. His eyes drifted to the front door and then back to Cabot.

"Didn't this almost happen before, during the Depression? FDR came in with his New Deal, and the New York bankers went apeshit. Didn't they start a plot to overthrow the government?"

"The Wall Street Putsch," Cabot said. "That's what it was called."

"Yeah," George said. "That's it. They tried to recruit a retired Marine Corps general to lead the coup, but he blew the whistle." George took another draw off his IPA. "We'll have no such luck with our friend General Taylor."

George caught the eye of their feckless waiter, who was tapping on his phone. George held up two fingers, and a second round belatedly appeared.

"Henry," George began as soon as the waiter cleared out. "I'm gonna have to go underground. Taylor will stop at nothing. It's him or me now. And I won't endanger your life. Or Aunt Helen's."

"George, no—"

"It's the only way. I've got my bug-out bag right here." George patted the large canvas messenger bag on the seat next to him. "Packed it as soon as we got back from DC. Got everything I need. Thanks for the cash, by the way."

"I don't know," Cabot stammered. "I wish you had told me about this sooner. Let's talk about this."

"No, it's—"

"I know you were right about Taylor," Cabot said. "But what you are doing is suicide, George." He repeated the word, drawn out for effect. "*Suicide.*"

"I gotta do it, Henry."

Cabot shook his head. "Think, George!" He thumped his index finger against his temple. "You're not going to get close to Taylor now, not after our meeting."

"Don't need to get close. All I need is for Taylor to stick his head up in public somewhere. I was a SWAT team sniper. I can make the shot."

"They'll kill you," Cabot said softly, with resignation. "And even if you are successful, history will mark you a political assassin, and Taylor a national martyr. They'll praise him in song and build statues in his honor. Is that what you want?"

George shrugged.

"And it won't change anything. Parker will just be taken advantage of by some other general or politician, and our country will continue on the road to ruin. I can't let that happen."

"Well, I never claimed to be a savior," George said. "One of us is going to die, and this country is gonna have to be satisfied with that. That's the best I can do." He scanned the bar again.

Cabot retreated into himself, sitting back in his chair and ignoring his ale. "Are you leaving tonight?"

George nodded.

"So…" Cabot's voice cracked. "This is it? I may never see you again after tonight?"

"I'm sorry, Henry." George gently patted Cabot's forearm. "There's no other way."

The two men sat in silence. George scanning the room, Cabot's eyes on the table, deep in thought.

After a time, Cabot lunged for his ale and took a big swig, then set it back down abruptly.

"I know a man," he said. "I think he may be able to help us." He sat up straighter in his chair, his eyes burning intently now behind his spectacles.

"It's too late, Henry. There's no one who can help me now. Taylor has the whole government at his disposal."

"You don't understand," Cabot said. "This is no ordinary man."

George sighed in exasperation, but motioned for Cabot to continue.

Cabot looked around, then leaned in and whispered. "Before I say anything further, let's switch tables. There's an empty table across the bar, in that corner." He signaled with his eyes. "What I am about to share with you must be held in strict confidence."

It was unlike Cabot to be so melodramatic. They walked their ales across the bar and sat down. Their new table provided no view of the front door, which made George anxious, but it was dimly lit and abandoned. No one within thirty feet of them. George took the seat against the wall.

"His name is… Daniel Flanagan," Cabot said. He fell silent and his breathing became more rapid. He took a long gulp of ale, then deliberately set his glass in front of him. He let out a long sigh followed by silence, which George waited out.

"Daniel Flanagan," Cabot repeated at last. "Or at least that is the name by which I know him. He has many names, I suspect. I met him at MIT in 1966 when he was a freshman and I was auditing some economics classes there. Daniel was a fourteen-year-old math prodigy who began to torment professors as soon as he stepped on campus."

George rubbed his eyes. "Look, Henry, I don't have time for—"

"Daniel was amazing," Cabot continued. "Our professor was a Nobel laureate, and Daniel just *toyed* with this poor man in class. Actually brought him to tears once. They tested his IQ in elementary school, and he scored 245—the highest ever recorded. And this was really just an estimate, as the test was not calibrated to address someone like Daniel. He and I sparred in class, but all in good fun. He the cat and I the mouse. I liked him instantly. We have been friends for over fifty years."

"Okay, Henry, I get it. He's a really smart guy. You have lots of really smart friends."

Cabot smiled. "No. You don't understand, George." He took another sip of his beer and grew more animated now. "Daniel graduated early from MIT; 1970, I believe. I suspect the administration was happy to see him go. He went to Wall Street and was the first to apply game theory to the oil and gas markets. He made his first billion by correctly predicting the behavior of OPEC, which allowed him to control millions of barrels of oil at low pre-boycott prices. He later sold this oil at peak market prices and made a tidy four-hundred-percent profit."

"Sounds like white collar crime to me," George said skeptically.

"Daniel was just getting started," Cabot continued. "The 1973 oil crisis created an urgent demand for smaller, fuel-efficient vehicles. Detroit's Big Three automakers could not deliver these cars to market, but Japan's emerging auto industry could. He invested billions in Toyota and Honda, becoming the anonymous majority shareholder of both companies. By the early eighties he had become the world's first trillionaire." He paused for effect and looked at George, eyes wide. "That's a one with twelve zeros!"

George cocked his head to one side. "How come I've never heard of this guy? He's not on any of those 'Richest Men on Earth' lists."

"He went off the grid in 1984. He did all his business in secret, an indecipherable web of corporations and financial accounts. His anonymity was his greatest feat. Helped quite a bit come tax time, I know that."

George gave Cabot a dubious look.

"How much money did you earn as a brand-new FBI agent, George?"

"About forty grand, I'd say."

"At that salary it would take you about…" Cabot looked up as he computed, "…one hundred and fifty million years to earn what Daniel has in his pockets right now. His net worth is a little over six trillion dollars. That's more than the GDP of Africa and South America—*combined.*"

George's mouth hung open.

"This man lives in anonymity, beyond the reach of laws or politics. Don't you see, George? He could help us with Taylor. I'm sure of it."

"What the hell, Henry? Why didn't you ever mention this guy to me before?"

"That's not how it works."

"What is he—an evil Bond villain or something? Some creepy bald dude stroking a white cat?"

"Not exactly," Cabot said with a chuckle.

"Why would he help us?"

"I can't tell you that."

"What could he do?"

"Anything. Everything. I am not prepared to say goodbye to you tonight, George. Give me one more chance. If this doesn't work, I will stand aside and let you do what you feel you must do. I promise." Cabot clamped his small hand on to George's forearm with surprising strength. "Please."

"How long are we talking here?"

"I will send an urgent message to Daniel tonight. It's a rather complicated process, but he will respond to me quickly. Three or four days."

"Okay," George said. "Set the meeting."

Cabot smiled. "You don't meet with Daniel. He meets with you. If he agrees, he will provide instructions."

George pressed his lips together, thinking. "All right," he said at last. "I can wait a few more days. I'll be holed up in a hotel, somewhere close but out of the city." He reached into his bag and retrieved a cellphone. "Take this." He pushed an encrypted phone across the table to Cabot. "This is safe. I have one too. From now on, use this to contact me and no one else, okay?"

"Can I use it to contact Daniel?"

George thought for a moment. "I guess so. But just him and me. I suppose anyone who can disappear for thirty years with over six trillion dollars knows what they're doing."

"I'll call you as soon as I hear from him." Cabot put the phone in his pocket. "What about Virginia?"

"I'll contact Virginia." George said. "I'm sure they're watching her too. She gave me her neighbor Percy's number. He'll relay messages to her for now."

"Here's to Percy, that crazy old coot." Cabot raised his glass and drained the last of his ale.

George raised his own glass and drank. "And don't worry about the surveillance. Just act natural, go about your daily routine. All your phones are tapped. Internet too. Home and work. But don't stop using them. Just don't say anything. Got it?"

Cabot nodded.

"Three or four days," George said, standing.

The two men embraced, each grateful they were able to avoid their final good-bye. At least for now.

George turned and walked out into the wet, dark night.

CHAPTER 35

George zipped up his jacket and pulled his hat down against the steady, driving rain. He had just finished ninety minutes of surveillance detection routes, or SDRs in FBI parlance, and was certain no one was following him. He imagined frantic FBI surveillance agents running around trying to find him on this cold and windswept night. Radios crackling, the cursing and complaining, irritable supervisors awoken by bad news. George had been on both sides of this now, and he had to admit it was liberating to be the criminal for a change.

Fugitives and bad guys seek the familiar when they are on the run, and that is how they are usually caught. A call to a loved one, hiding out with a family member or friend for a few days. All rookie mistakes that result in handcuffs. George knew better. They would expect him to contact Cabot and Helen, JD, or maybe even Kacey Anne. His familiar Boston haunts were all in downtown Boston and north of the city. George would go south.

He circled back to Kendall Square, found the subway station, and walked down the rain-slicked steps to the platform. He was unfamiliar with the Red Line, so he studied the transit map outside the turnstile. The southern terminus of the Red Line was a station in the town of Braintree, located about fifteen miles south of Boston. George had never been there before, had visited the entire South Shore of Boston only a couple of times as a kid. Perfect. Braintree it would be.

He purchased his tokens with cash, pushed through the turnstile, and took his place on the far end of the platform. The air was thick and humid; the acrid stink of urine clung to the dirty floor tiles and stained white walls. George avoided eye contact, and tried to blend in with his fellow travelers. They were a motley group. Each one of them had made a series of bad, or sad, decisions that had put them on the midnight train to Braintree this Thursday evening—although none of them could come close to the story George had to tell. He shifted his feet and stared into the black void of the train tunnel.

Would the FBI ever trace him back to this platform, or to his upcoming Braintree sojourn? George visualized the nationwide investigation that would inevitably follow his death after he assassinated Taylor. He was creating history in real time, as a stage actor in a parallel dimension. At first George had found this realization disturbing, but he was growing accustomed to it.

George boarded the almost empty train and got off in Braintree forty minutes later. The station was well lit and cleaner than Kendall. The rain and wind had stopped, and the clouds had cleared to reveal the few stars whose wattage could penetrate the garish artificial light of the modern night sky. A Motel 6 sign blazed from across the street.

He crossed the large parking lot that fronted the motel. Shards of broken glass crunched under his feet. The motel consisted of two identical rectangular buildings, each two stories high and its rooms aligned directly on top of each other. The rooms on both floors opened directly to the outside, the bottom floor to the parking lot and the top floor to an outdoor walkway.

The motel lobby was dimly lit, the front desk unattended except for the lingering stale cigarette smoke. George waited a moment before he pinged the bell on the counter. It took a second ping to bring the night clerk out from the back room. He was a young skinny guy with a patchy goatee. He stole glances over his shoulder at the back room as he checked George in. Probably had someone tied up back there, but George had his own problems.

George booked room 231, located on the second floor opposite the staircase. The most difficult room to access via forced entry, to George's trained eye. He paid for seven days, in cash, and checked in under an alias. The clerk smirked as he took the cash. He didn't bother to ask George for any identification. The no-tell motel.

George climbed up the interior staircase and went through the door to the second-story outdoor hallway. He looked over the railing to the parking lot and the freeway beyond. He could hear the low rumble of the eighteen-wheelers going in and out of the city.

Room 231 was at the far west end of the motel. George passed a handful of rooms before he got to his. Most had their front window shades pulled closed. One did not, and George saw two little kids, a dirty-blond girl and a bare-chested mixed-race boy, in mismatched pajamas running and shrieking around the room. He did not see any adults.

He kept walking. One door down from his was a gray plastic barrel, its cover pushed out of place by the overflowing trash within. It smelled of stale beer and decaying fast food. As he put his key card in his door, George noted the room on the other side of his was occupied, apparently by someone with a hearing impairment, judging by the volume of the television.

The locked clicked open and he stepped inside room 231. It was not bad. Light laminate wood flooring and prison-white walls made it feel bigger than it was. Two single beds faced the television, which was built into the wall. The only furniture was a half-moon two-seat table under the television, and a small open cubby storage unit near the bathroom sink. Both were bolted to the floor. George double-locked the door and closed the window shade. He then wedged one of the two chairs under the door handle. He took both comforters off the beds and folded them neatly in the corner. His motel rule was that he only touched things that were regularly laundered. He shut off his room lights, inched back the window shade with a finger, and peered down the long outside walkway. For fifteen minutes he crouched there, gun drawn, waiting, but saw nothing out of the ordinary. All quiet except the occasional screech of the kids, and the incessant blare of the television next door. Satisfied, George holstered up, placed his weapon within easy reach on top of the toilet tank cover, and jumped in the shower.

He finished his warm shower with a blast of icy cold water, then dried himself with a thin scrap of towel. He pulled on a t-shirt and cotton boxers from his bug-out bag and lay down on top of the sheet on the bed closest to the door. His mind wandered. He tried to conjure up images of the mysterious Mr. Flanagan. He must exist, for the same reason George was the Washington clone: because Henry Cabot would not lie to him about things such as these.

George fantasized about what he would do with six trillion dollars. It was an absurd amount of money. Impossible to spend in a lifetime—or a hundred lifetimes. Nice problem to have though, he supposed.

He got up to pee, and then caught sight of himself in the mirror on his way back to the bed. He stared at his reflection in the muted light. *Am I an assassin? Can I do it?*

He killed the lights and plopped back down on the bed, between the fitted and top sheets, and closed his eyes. His mind raced. After thirty minutes of tossing and turning, George got up and sat at the table. He took out his encrypted phone, which he would swap out in the morning, and pecked out a text message:

Hey JD –
Thanks for putting me up for the past couple of weeks. I have a lot on my plate right now, most of which I cannot tell you for your own good. Thanks for understanding.
I decided to go on a little vacation. Sorry I didn't get a

*chance to see you before I left. Give your new number to my
new bourbon friend, and I will keep in touch.*
   Take good care of yourself, my friend.
   *And as always: if I don't come back—remember me as a
hero and avenge my death!*
   G –

The message was coded. Easy for JD to understand, but just vague
enough should it reach the wrong hands. JD would know to get a new
encrypted phone and pass the number to his bartender friend, the one
who'd served them the night they were out with Paige and Grace.
George would contact the bartender to obtain the number. It was
important that he establish secure communications with JD as soon as
possible. George would need him when he went underground.

It was just past three o'clock in the morning. George sat at the
small table in the dim light, rolling the last line of his message over
and over in his head like a mantra. It had been a running joke
between George and JD for the entire time they'd worked together
at WFO. JD had come up with it, of course.

If I don't come back—remember me as a hero and avenge my death!
Now, for the first time, George meant every word.

CHAPTER 36

Taylor's eyes fluttered open after a fitful sleep. He lay on his back, rigid and at attention on the twin bed. He had not shared a bed with his wife for many years now. She slept in her own bedroom at the opposite end of the hall. Two nightlights lit the general's room. He did not like to sleep in darkness. His wife had always objected to this, but that was not the reason they slept apart.

Today was the birthday of the U.S. Army, 246 years old and going strong by Taylor's hand. This had been the biggest day of the year in Taylor's childhood home, more revered than either Christmas or Thanksgiving. In fact, it had been the only birthday celebrated there, the primary way that the Taylor family had chronicled the passage of time. Taylor's father and namesake, Alexander Marius Taylor Sr., had allowed individual birthdays to be acknowledged but not celebrated. No, sir: inside the Taylor household, birthday celebrations were reserved for his father's beloved army.

Taylor checked the digital alarm clock on his nightstand. The bright red display blazed 4:35 a.m. Next to the clock sat the framed photo of a woman. It was a studio portrait, with an aged patina that made it look more like a painting than a photograph. The woman depicted was young and beautiful. She wore a pageboy haircut that stopped at her sharp jawline. Her straw-blond hair had a slight wave at the sides like Grace Kelly, whom she resembled. Her shoulders were squared, her face turned three-quarters toward the camera, as if she had just skipped past the photographer and turned when he called her name. She wore a string of white pearls around her neck and an open, lighthearted smile.

Taylor brought the framed portrait to his chest. He softly traced the woman's face with his gnarled finger. It was his favorite photograph of his mother, Katharine—or Kate as she preferred to be called. His mother was the only woman he had ever loved. It was sixty-five years ago today—Army Birthday 1956—that Kate had committed suicide. He had never recovered.

Taylor's second most memorable Army Birthday was nine years ago, in 2012. The army was then 237 years old, his father a cantankerous eighty-eight. It had been the last time Taylor had seen or spoken to the old bastard.

Earlier that year, Taylor Sr. had slipped getting out of the shower and broken his hip. Surgery had been successful, but he had developed a life-threatening post-operative infection. The bug had been no match for his orneriness, however, and he'd rallied.

And so it was that Taylor had found himself dutifully going to his father's bedside at Walter Reed on Army Birthday 2012. He'd heard him bellowing all the way down the hall.

"Get your hand off my pecker! I can take a piss all by myself, Nancy boy."

Taylor walked through the door in time to see his father swatting a male nurse's hands away, causing him to stagger-step back from the hospital bed.

"And why in hell do I have a boy nurse anyhow?" the old man shouted. "Go fetch me that cute little blonde that was in here yesterday."

"Sir, I am perfectly qualified to—"

"That's an order! Dismissed." The nurse stood his ground, more dumbfounded than defiant. "I said go!" Taylor Sr. fixed him with a fiery stare; the young man turned and left the hospital room, head bowed.

Taylor turned his back to the bed to allow his father to drain his bladder in privacy. He heard the old man rustling and cursing, then the flow of urine hitting the plastic container. Taylor took a step toward the window. His mind wandered as he looked out over the acres of cars in the parking lot.

Father and son had a standing lunch date every year on Army Birthday. It was the only time they could stand each other's company. The tradition had started in 1984, after Taylor, then a Pentagon colonel, had returned from Grenada and Operation Urgent Fury. They had done lunch every year since, except when Taylor was overseas, in which case they exchanged cards. It was their only interaction all year, other than when Taylor earned another promotion or commendation. He made sure his father received notice of every one of these via official embossed U.S. Army stationery.

Taylor had eagerly anticipated Army Birthday 2012. He had four stars now, the highest rank in a peacetime military, and was coming off a universally lauded stint as CENTCOM Commander, where he ran all U.S. military operations in the Middle East, North Africa, and Central Asia.

But most importantly, he had just been promoted to Army Chief of Staff: he was now the highest-ranked man in the entire U.S. Army. Taylor was now the top dog of his father's beloved army; he could not wait to rub it in his face.

And this last promotion was no small feat. Taylor had turned sixty-four in 2012, the mandatory retirement age for military officers. To become Army Chief of Staff, he had had to convince the secretary of defense to grant him a two-year extension. General officers typically retire well in advance of their statutory age and service limits, so as not to impede the career paths of more junior general officers. Taylor had ignored this tradition, however, and was secretly resented for his selfishness.

"Well, did you come here to see your father, or to look out the window?" Taylor Sr. barked. Taylor turned and looked at the man he had once idolized but now despised.

Taylor Sr. graduated from West Point in 1947, fourteenth in a class of three hundred ten. He was a bright and ambitious cadet, with a touch of arrogance that transcended self-confidence. He competed in football and boxing, and was known for his fiery temper when provoked. He and Kate married six weeks after his West Point graduation; she was nineteen years old and pregnant with Taylor on their wedding day.

The marriage was doomed from the start. Taylor Sr. resented the pregnancy and felt forced into the marriage to save his army career. He was a domineering and brutish husband; Kate, in contrast, was submissive and warm-hearted. From the start he was jealous and possessive of Kate, and was physically and emotionally abusive to her—and anyone who got in his path—when drunk. Kate patiently endured his dark moods, always hoping it would get better. The marriage aged her, stealing first her innocence, then her spirit. She suffered in silence, because that was what was expected of a good army wife in the 1950s.

Kate had been an attentive and loving mother, and young Alexander had adored her. He grew up a sensitive and bookish child. Taylor Sr. was often deployed and had little to do with raising his son. Alexander clung to his mother in those early years.

The toxic marriage finally got the best of her. By the time

Alexander was seven, she was chain-smoking and fighting a losing battle with alcohol. Her once porcelain skin had aged to a sunken yellow pallor. She was rail thin, which sharpened her features to severity, and her lilting voice was now more gravel than birdsong. Taylor Sr. mocked her for her fading beauty, which made her descent all the more rapid.

It happened on Army birthday 1956. Taylor Sr. celebrated this birthday in the arms of another woman, while Kate stewed at home with Lucy and Ricky and a cheap bottle of wine. Kate's spirit, like that bottle of wine, was empty when the front door flew open sometime after eleven that night. The shouting started almost immediately. Alexander was in bed, wide awake and trembling, the covers pulled tight to his chin. He heard it all that night, things a seven-year-old boy should never hear. Things that would haunt him for the remainder of his life.

The argument continued in his parents' bedroom, a mere twenty feet down a common hall from Alexander's room in their modest ranch home. The fighting escalated; his father's voice hard and sharp, his mother's plaintive and wailing. She began to sob. Taylor Sr. slammed the door and pounded down the hall. Then a long silence. Alexander lay rigid in his bed, straining to hear. Then a single piercing gunshot. In a fit of despair, Kate had put her husband's Colt 45 service weapon in her mouth and pulled the trigger. It had conveniently been left loaded and unattended on the nightstand.

Taylor had always held his father responsible for Kate's suicide. Through sheer will he forged his childhood rage into revenge. He would dedicate his life to beating his father at the only thing that mattered to the man—the U.S. Army.

Taylor had waited fifty-seven years for his moment. The moment when he would avenge his mother's death. As Chief of Staff, Taylor now owned the U.S. Army. And he was ready to finally own his old man too.

"Did you hear the news?" Taylor asked.

"Yeah," Taylor Sr. spat. "Got some calls about it. Surprised you didn't send me one of your little notices in the mail."

"I wanted to tell you this one in person."

"Well, goodie for you," Taylor Sr. said sharply. "It's not like they gave you another star."

"Army Chief of Staff," Taylor said. "I own the entire U.S. Army. Your beloved army. What do you think of that?"

Taylor Sr. grimaced. "Bah! Not like it used to be in my day. Marshall, Eisenhower, Bradley, Ridgway. Now those were real chiefs. Real men. Army's gone down the shitter since I got out. Damn straight." He crossed his arms and jutted his chin out.

Taylor felt his rage rising. The skin on the back of his neck began to tingle.

"So, how far did you get in your army, Dad?" Taylor asked. "You were a one-star riding a desk at the Pentagon when they pushed you out, isn't that right?" Taylor leaned over the bed, catching and holding his father's eyes. "And it took you—what—forty years to get that single star?"

"Don't smart me, boy," Taylor Sr. shouted, with a shake of his finger. "Goddamn stars meant something in my day! Not like today's army. Giving 'em out like lollipops nowadays. Even giving 'em to women." He shook his head. "Lady generals. What's this world coming to?"

The nurse supervisor stuck her head around the door at the sound of shouting, then withdrew again and closed the door with a thud.

"So what're you saying, boy?" Taylor Sr. roared. "You got your four stars, so that means you're four times better than your old man?" He coughed and hacked something up. He turned his head, spat on the floor, and continued. "I'll tell you one thing, you ain't four times the man I am. That's for damn straight."

"I scrape one-stars off my boots every day," Taylor growled.

"You're a paper general! Never fronted an army on the battlefield.

266   RICK BOSWORTH

All you're good for is hand-jobbing your little political friends. That's how you got all four of those goddamn stars!"

Both men knew this was a lie. Taylor had fought bravely in every American war and armed skirmish since Vietnam, and had earned many valorous commendations—the Distinguished Service Cross (twice), Silver and Bronze Stars, numerous Purple Hearts, among others. No one in the U.S. military, and certainly not any enemy he faced on the battlefield, could say any different. But the old man was stubborn and prideful, and he had nothing else.

The lie still stung Taylor to his core. The old man would not allow his son his moment. Taylor would not have his revenge. Not this day. It would take more to break the old bastard. He wished the infection had taken him.

"You know, if your mother had lived, she would've never allowed you to enlist in my army," Taylor Sr. said. "She would've pushed you to be a schoolteacher, or some other lady job. And you would have done as she said. You were always a momma's boy, hiding behind her skirt."

Taylor erupted with fifty-seven years of suppressed fury.

"You killed her!" he screamed. Taylor stepped toward the head of the bed and grabbed the bed rail in a death grip. "You killed her! You made her do it. It's all your fault, you fucking bastard!" He glared at his father, who lay frozen in the bed, his mouth open, eyes wide.

He was right over him now. Taylor grabbed the extra pillow from under his father's head, watched the old man's head buck forward then drop. He squeezed the pillow hard in his hands, felt his power well up within him. He raised the pillow to chest height, stared into his father's eyes until he saw that flash of fear, then—three sharp knocks at the door. The nurse supervisor burst into the room.

"General Taylor, sir. I'm going to have to ask you to please lower your voice. We have many sick patients on this floor in need of rest. Sir."

Both men remained transfixed.

"Sir?"

Taylor looked down and saw the pillow compressed in his hands. He dropped it on the bed and looked up at the nurse.

"Sir? Did you hear me, sir? I'm going to have to ask you to please lower your voice."

"Yes, of course." Taylor said. "I was just leaving." He smiled thinly at the nurse, then strode past her and out the door without looking back at his father.

———————

General Taylor's gnarled fingers still held tight the framed portrait of his mother Kate. The soft glow of the rising sun illuminated his bedroom. His cheeks were wet, his throat dry. A few teardrops had pooled at the bottom of the photo, where the glass met the frame. He gingerly dried them with his nightshirt. Then he did something he had not done in many years: he kissed his mother's picture. He mouthed the words 'I love you,' then returned the photograph to its rightful place on the nightstand.

It had been seven years since he had almost killed his father in that hospital bed at Walter Reed. The old bastard was still alive today, his ninety-five-year-old heart kept beating by bitterness and hate.

He would show the old man, but good. He would show them all.

CHAPTER 37

THURSDAY, JUNE 17, 2021; 8:15 A.M. (EDT)
LOGAN AIRPORT
BOSTON, MASSACHUSETTS

"Your boarding pass." The TSA security officer looked down at the valid Massachusetts driver's license of a Charles D. Fisk from Wakefield. "Mr. Fisk."

Henry Cabot stood silent.

"Mr. Fisk?"

George nudged Cabot in the back.

"Oh, yes, of course," Cabot said, and produced a first-class ticket from Logan to LAX. The TSA officer examined the ticket and driver's license, then handed both back to Cabot with a smile and wished him a good flight. Cabot robotically walked through the rest of his TSA screening and waited for George on the other side with the rest of the harried travelers belting their pants and tying their shoes.

George breezed through TSA as Robert I. Gedman of Rockland, Massachusetts. He and Cabot were both traveling on false identification provided by Flanagan. He rejoined Cabot, who was straining to look natural.

"Relax, Henry. We're bulletproof."

"Phrasing."

"Your man Flanagan has a sense of humor. Our aliases were both catchers for the Red Sox in the seventies and eighties—Carlton Fisk and Rich Gedman."

"The man is full of surprises," Cabot replied. At George's instruction, he was dressed in a ball cap and big-framed eyeglasses— "Less Harvard and more Arizona State," George had told him. He squirmed in his new look, like a small child who wished to shed his Sunday church clothes.

"I see you made it to Walmart," George quipped as they walked to their gate.

"What?" Cabot followed George's eyes to his outfit. "Oh. Ha ha. Very funny." Cabot dropped his voice. "First time I have ever been in disguise. I don't even like Halloween."

"Well, you nailed it. Lookin' good Mr. Fisk."

The two men had an uneventful non-stop flight from Boston to Los Angeles; the first-class accommodations helped. They rented a nondescript sedan at LAX, and George spent the next several hours driving SDRs all over LA until he was convinced no one was following them. It was only then that he turned the car north and headed toward their true destination: San Francisco, where Cabot had arranged a meeting with Flanagan. Given their long and trusted relationship, it had not taken much salesmanship from Cabot. All Flanagan needed to hear was that he was desperate and needed his help. Securing an invitation for George was a much harder sell. Flanagan was loath to meet strangers, even ones who came with a personal validation from Cabot. It took four full days for Flanagan to complete his background check of George, followed by another hour of selling by Cabot to get George on the plane.

George settled into the far-left passing lane of the I-5 freeway for the six-hour drive to San Francisco. They were to meet Flanagan's head of security, Vitor Luiz Oliveira Lima, at the InterContinental Mark Hopkins hotel at 8:30 p.m. sharp. Lima had emphasized the "sharp" part of that arrangement.

"What's up with this guy Lima?" George asked. "What do you know about him?"

"I know all about him," Cabot responded. "But I can't tell you much at this point."

"Well, what *can* you tell me, Henry?"

"I have known Luiz for thirty years, about as long as he has been with Daniel. He's Brazilian, a couple of years younger than you, about your size. He grew up in the favelas outside Rio de Janeiro. Hellish places. Urban slums full of poverty and violence. Have you heard of these places?"

"No," George said. "I mean, I've heard of 'em, but I don't really know anything about 'em."

"In a 1964 coup d'état the Brazilian military overthrew the president, then quickly crushed all political opposition. The economy crashed. By the early seventies, many rural people had moved to the cities for work. But most were unable to find employment or a place to live, and they ended up in the favelas. This military dictatorship lasted almost twenty-one years in Brazil."

The car fell silent. The idea of a free democracy falling to a tyrannical military dictator seemed so far-fetched, until one looked around the globe and realized this was the rule, and the United States the exception.

"In the seventies," Cabot went on, "Brazil's military dictatorship started a favela eradication policy. They bulldozed the slums and forcibly displaced hundreds of thousands of residents to squalid public housing projects. One such place was the famous City of God outside Rio de Janeiro, where Luiz grew up. By the early eighties, these housing projects grew extremely violent due to the rise of organized gangs and drugs. The government responded by sending in paramilitary troops. Later, merchants hired these troops as death squads to hunt down and kill the thieving street kids."

George gave a low whistle. "Wow. Makes DC look like Disneyland."

"Indeed."

They were just approaching Bakersfield. The sprawl of the Los Angeles metro area was thankfully behind them, and traffic had begun to thin. No one was following them. George began to relax.

"How did Flanagan and Lima meet?"

"Daniel was on a business trip to Rio in 1989 when he heard about the legendary slum-boy assassin. They called him 'Assassino de Deus'—God's Assassin. The death squads tried to kill him when he was just eleven years old. By the time Daniel found him, Luiz was fifteen and had killed over twenty highly trained paramilitary troops. Imagine that."

"Impressive piece of work," George said.

"Daniel hired a local to find this boy, and he eventually did— sitting cross-legged on a big mound of garbage, reading a book. Daniel enjoys telling this story. He finds it poetic, or even Delphic, I suppose. Anyway, they met, and young Luiz made quite an impression. Daniel took him back to the States. Educated and trained him. Five years later, Luiz became Daniel's head of security, a position he has now held for thirty years."

George checked the rear-view mirror and moved to the middle lane to allow a speeding pickup truck to pass. He was being careful not to speed.

"Sounds like a bad guy."

"No, not at all. Luiz is a good man," Cabot explained. "He's very capable. At times I have entrusted my life to this man. He's soft-spoken. But don't let that fool you. There is not a man on earth that Daniel respects more than Luiz. We're in excellent hands."

"Very good, then," George said. He looked at the dashboard clock. They were making good time. "As long as we aren't late, we should be good, then."

"Just one thing about Lima…"

"Yes?" George asked.

"Do not stare at him when you meet him. You're going to want to, but don't."

"Why would I stare at him?"

"Just don't. I am serious, George. He doesn't like it."

Cabot changed the subject, and he and George chatted some more, mostly small talk to break up the long bouts of silence. Finally, both men fell silent and retreated into their own thoughts. George was anxious to learn more about Lima and Flanagan. His imagination began to wander, conjuring up all sorts of wild what-ifs to fill in the missing details surrounding these two men.

As they approached the city, the traffic began to get worse. They arrived in the Bay Area behind schedule. George slotted into the post–rush hour flow over the Oakland Bay Bridge and into the city. He raced up California Street toward the crest of Nob Hill and its grand, elevated views of the business and shopping districts of downtown San Francisco. He reached the apex of the hill at Mason Street, where he hit a red light. The InterContinental Mark Hopkins was directly to his left. He had to circle the block a few times to find the entrance to the hotel's underground parking garage. Once inside, he searched the garage for an open spot, but found none. He looked at the dashboard—8:14 p.m. *Shit!* George frantically circled the levels of the parking garage, tires screeching. He finally found a spot by creeping behind an elderly man who was walking to his car. *Hurry up! Walk faster!* George drummed his fingers on the steering wheel, fighting his mounting impatience, then jerked into the space as the man finally pulled out. He and Cabot grabbed their bags and rushed to the elevator that led to the hotel lobby. The doors slid noiselessly open and George repeatedly smashed the lobby button, then punched the door close button. *C'mon, c'mon, c'mon…*

The elevator doors binged as the lobby light flashed overhead. George checked his watch—8:28 p.m. The doors opened, and he and

Cabot rushed out to look for the man they knew would be on time and waiting for them. Both men were breathing heavily; Cabot was bent over at the waist, his hands on his knees.

George scanned the lobby until his eyes stopped cold. No need to ask. George had found him.

Lima was standing against the wall. He faced the door, where he could easily survey the entire lobby. He had a wide, square stance. He wore an expensive blue suit with a white silk shirt, top button undone. His face was relaxed, his expression blank. He exuded a gravitas that said he was as comfortable in this five-star hotel as he was in the alley behind it. The lobby was crowded and bustling, except around Lima. No one was within ten feet of him.

George and Cabot crossed the lobby to greet him.

"George, you're *staring!*" Cabot whispered. He surreptitiously smacked George's side.

They reached Lima together. He casually folded the newspaper he was holding and placed it on the table beside him. He was just as Cabot described, but more.

"Henry, my friend, so good to see you again," Lima said with a Portuguese-tinged accent. He swallowed Cabot in a bear hug, and the two men then exchanged warm pleasantries. Lima made no effort to acknowledge George until after he'd finished with Cabot. He then gracefully turned his body, and his heavy-lidded light brown eyes blazed as he took George in. George drew a short breath that felt like a gasp.

"You must be George," Lima said, extending his hand. "You may call me Luiz. Henry has said some very nice things about you."

George clasped his hand. It was heavy, callused and rough. Not as big as George's, but equally strong. "Nice to meet you, Luiz."

"Very good," Lima said with a smile that did not reach his eyes. "We have much to do tonight. So let us begin. Follow me and do exactly as I say."

Cabot and George fell in behind Lima and did exactly as he said.

Lima started by walking them all over the hotel, looking for anything that seemed out of place. They then crossed California Street to the Fairmont, where Lima had reserved three rooms. He instructed George and Cabot to stay in their rooms until he came for them.

Lima returned for them three hours later. It was close to midnight. He led George and Cabot to a freight elevator that took them to a back entrance of the hotel, where a black Porsche Panamera Turbo was waiting. They got in, and Lima conducted SDRs throughout the city until he was satisfied they were alone. It was only then, now well past one in the morning, that he took them to their third and final hotel for the evening, the St. Regis San Francisco.

Lima booked the St. Regis Suite for himself, and put George and Cabot into the adjoining grand deluxe double guest rooms. Lima appeared more comfortable at the St. Regis. The executive staff all seemed to know him. He delivered George and Cabot to their rooms and bid them goodnight. They would all meet tomorrow in Lima's suite for further discussion.

George entered his room and walked right into a giant of a man who was standing at attention just inside the door. He was huge—six foot eight, three hundred pounds easy. JD proportions. But the man before him lacked any of JD's jocularity. This man looked as though he had never laughed a day in his life. He wore a dirty-blond buzz cut and appeared to be in his early thirties. George guessed he was Russian, or possibly Israeli.

"Who are you?" George asked, taking a half-step backward.

"I work for Mr. Lima."

"What're you doing in my room?"

"You sleep. I watch."

"You're going to watch me sleep?" George asked. "All night?"

"Ya."

"So… are you here to protect me or guard me?"

The man smiled, but only slightly. "On my watch you sleep. Nothing else. It's good."

"You're a big man. I've a friend about your size."

"Good for him. You sleep now."

George examined the man, who had taken up position with his back against the locked door. He had an arsenal of weaponry: handgun; extra magazines; commando knives; an assault rifle slung over his shoulder.

"You American FBI, yes?" the giant asked him.

"Yes," George responded. "Used to be."

"What do FBI carry?"

"Glock 19, nine mil."

"It's good gun… for little girl," the man said. "I have forty-five caliber. Big round, big hole. But I prefer the knife."

"Does my friend have a bodyguard too? Like you?"

"Ya."

"Does Luiz?"

"Mr. Lima?"

"Yes. I mean Mr. Lima."

The man laughed, a disturbing, deep, guttural growl. "No one guards Mr. Lima." He jerked his massive head to one side. "Who you think taught me to love the knife?"

George cleared his throat. "Well, it's been a long day. And it looks like I'm in good hands. So, good night… uhm, what's your name?"

"Call me Noam."

"Okay. Good night, Noam. You can call me George."

"Good night, Agent Moore."

CHAPTER 38

George was jolted awake by a large hand that jerked his entire body back and forth. His eyes shot open. Noam stood over him.

"Wake up, Agent Moore. Mr. Lima is expecting you at ten o'clock. He does not like to be kept waiting."

"What time is it?" George asked. He covered his face with his hands, then rubbed his eyes. He had slept hard.

"Time to get up," Noam answered. He whipped the top sheet off George.

"Were you standing at my bed all night?"

"Go!" Noam looked at his watch.

George rolled out of bed and shook himself. He did a couple of quick stretches to get the blood flowing. Noam stared through him.

"All right, all right! I'm going." George quickly showered, brushed, and threw on the clothes that had been neatly folded and set aside for him. Noam remained silent as he escorted George out into the hall and down to Lima's suite.

George entered the suite as Noam posted up outside the door. Lima was seated at the dining table. He sipped coffee, backlit by the sun streaming through the window shades. He sat erect, impeccably groomed and wearing another custom suit. He motioned for George to join him. Cabot was already seated to his right.

"Good morning, George," Lima said with a polite smile. "Please join us for brunch. You must be hungry."

"Morning, George," Cabot said.

"Henry."

Lima made a hand gesture, and three butlers instantly appeared. They showed Lima the utmost deference as they delivered tray after tray of gourmet food. No need to order; they brought one course of everything.

George and Cabot tucked into the bounty of food spread out before them. Neither one had eaten much during the past two days, and they eagerly remedied this deficiency now.

In between fork loads, George stole glances at Lima. He was clean-shaven, with wide sideburns squared to the bottoms of his ears. His raven hair had begun to streak gray. It was parted high on his head and pushed to one side; a single unruly tendril hung down over his forehead. Lima's eyebrows permanently arched downward to frame a perpetual squint, the left one bisected by a two-inch jagged scar. The left eye had a fleck of blood in it, which shone bright red against the clear white sclera.

One of Lima's men approached the table with his hands clasped in front of him.

"Excuse me, sir. May I speak with you for a moment?"

Lima apologized and excused himself from the table. He and the man talked in whispered tones a few feet away. George watched their exchange.

"Are you finished, George?" Lima asked, his back to George.

"Excuse me?"

"I asked if you were finished."

"Finished?"

"Finished staring, George. I'm certain Henry told you not to. And yet... here we are." Lima slowly turned around.

"But I..."

"Under the circumstances, I'll excuse your lapse of etiquette. It's your lapse of discipline that's more concerning. A minor and insignificant lapse, I grant you. But I have bested many worthy men with such lapses."

"Sorry." George felt his face flush.

"No worries, my friend," Lima said with a hand gesture. "We are just getting acquainted. But you will soon meet Mr. Flanagan, and he is not as forgiving as I."

"Got it."

"You see, George, most people sleepwalk through their lives. They are blind to the world around them." Lima covered his eyes with his hand for emphasis.

"Now you, with your FBI training—you walk around about here." Lima bent at the waist and placed his palm at knee height. "Me—I'm about here." He placed his hand at eye level. "But Mr. Flanagan." Lima shook his head and smiled. "He's here." His hand shot up as high above his head as it would go.

"Closer to the ceiling, actually," Cabot added.

"He is one hundred steps ahead of everyone. Always," Lima said. "You will see."

Lima sat back down at the table. They finished their meal in silence.

Once the meal ended, the butlers promptly bused the table, replaced the old tablecloth with a fresh one, and served coffee. Lima dismissed them with a nod of his head, then cleared the suite of his security team.

"Okay," Lima said. "We sit here alone. Three friends." He turned to face George. "George, I am a direct man. No bullshit, as is said. I have no time for lies or deceit. All I ask is that you respect this. If you waste my time, I withdraw. If you betray me, I kill you. Do we understand each other?"

George nodded.

Lima waited.

"Yes, we understand each other," George said.

"Good. We will not speak of such things again." Lima took a slow sip of coffee.

George and Cabot did the same.

"I did your background package last week. Myself. Pulled most of my team in to work on it. I personally wrote it and presented it to Mr. Flanagan. Only Mr. Flanagan and I know the most sensitive parts—TRENTON and related matters. We corroborated what we could in the time we had, and accepted Henry's word on the stuff we couldn't."

Cabot shook his head solemnly. He knew the consequences of a broken word or false fact.

"It was very close, George. If it were not for the man sitting next to you," Lima pointed at Cabot, "you would not be going to the island. Simple as that."

"I understand," George said.

"I have work to do to prepare for the next leg of our journey. We leave the hotel tonight, around midnight. You will both wait here in the suite until I return. Do not leave this room. As my guests, please make yourselves at home. The butlers will get you anything you need. My men will stay with you. Any questions?"

George and Cabot shook their heads.

"Very good," Lima said as he clapped his hands together. "Enjoy." Two behemoths, Noam and a man who looked like his twin, immediately entered the suite and posted up at the door. George assumed the second man to be Cabot's bodyguard.

George and Cabot poured themselves second cups of coffee and strolled over to the window. The suite had spectacular high-rise views of the Yerba Buena Gardens across Third Street and Market Street beyond.

Cabot found a book to read and settled into a chair. George took a seat in front of the window and stayed there, looking thoughtfully out at the view for a long time. After a while, he got up and approached Noam.

"Hey, Noam. How you doin'?" he asked.

The big man nodded.

"You coming with us tonight?"

"Ya."

"We taking the same car as last night?"

"Mr. Flanagan has only German cars in fleet. All modified with latest military-grade technology. All bulletproof, blast-proof. Advanced racing, communication, and computer technology."

"How many does he have?" George asked.

"Hundreds… too many to count."

"*Damn*," George said under his breath.

"Mr. Flanagan has many things. You lucky man to go to island. Very few go."

George smiled. "I could use a little luck right about now, Noam."

To George's surprise, Noam returned the smile. "Mr. Flanagan, he give you luck."

George and Cabot spent the remainder of the day as captives in the luxurious suite. They ate, read a little, and watched a movie. They both fell asleep before the movie ended, George in a chair, Cabot reclined on the sofa.

Noam shook George awake around eleven thirty p.m. Cabot was already up and rubbing the sleep out of his eyes. Five minutes later Lima re-entered the suite.

"All is set," he said. "We are ready. Just one more thing before we go. It is non-negotiable." He placed his hand gently on Cabot's shoulder. "Henry, I know you have heard this speech many times. I say it now for George's benefit, not yours. But everything applies to you as well. Like always."

"Certainly, Luiz. I understand."

Lima turned to face George. "I become your island sponsor the minute you leave this suite, and as such I am held personally accountable for everything you do. So you see, our lives are now in each other's hands. Do you understand this?"

"Yes," George replied.

"Starting now, you cannot leave my presence until we arrive safely at the island. Do you understand?"

"Yes."

"Good. Now you must both be cleaned before we leave."

"Cleaned?" George looked between Lima and Cabot.

"Yes," Lima said. "Strip and cavity search. It's the only way I will accept custody of you both. You must be clean."

"Henry—"

"It's standard island procedure, George," Cabot said. "I've done it for all my trips. It's mandatory, no exceptions."

"Henry, please follow Ivan to my bedroom," Lima said, pointing to Noam's companion. "And George, Noam will meet you in the bathroom to my left."

George and Noam exchanged glances. Noam started toward the bathroom. George felt Lima's eyes on him. *Better to submit to this like a man.* He rose and followed Noam into the bathroom.

Several minutes later, George joined Cabot back in the suite and studied the carpet intently, unable to meet his uncle's gaze. Noam's hands had been as big as they looked. George hoped this would be his last "cleaning."

The butlers arrived and swarmed the room like forensic examiners, removing all trace evidence of their stay.

The rest of the men left the suite together and took the freight elevator down to the underground parking garage, where another Porsche Panamera Turbo, white this time, was waiting for them. Noam and Ivan got into a gray BMW M5, with a small arsenal hidden behind the second row of seats. They would be the chase vehicle.

Lima drove his two clean men out of the garage and into the dark night.

CHAPTER 39

The muted interior lights glowed like the cabin of a red-eye flight. Cabot was asleep in the seat next to George, his chest rising and falling softly with each breath. His face was old and worn; in the soft light, he looked like the seventy-six-year-old man he was. Cabot had risked everything, as George had, to stop General Taylor. Their fates were now forever joined.

They glided north on the I-5 freeway, en route to Sea-Tac Airport. The rear seat monitor displayed the trip data: Sat 06/19/21; 3:35 a.m.; six hours three minutes (541 miles) to destination; average speed 82 m.p.h.

Lima's face replaced the map on George's monitor.

"Good morning, George," he said from the driver's seat.

"So we're headed to Sea-Tac?"

"Not exactly."

Cabot stirred next to George.

"Tell me, what do you make of General Taylor?" Lima asked. "You have both met this man, and I as yet have not had the pleasure."

George rubbed his eyes. "Well, he's smart. Cunning. Highly capable. Very ambitious. Most of America finds him charismatic, a real hero." George paused. "Oh yeah—he's a real asshole too."

"I will attest to that," Cabot said, yawning.

"Weaknesses?" Lima asked.

"I would say arrogance and ambition," George said. "You agree, Henry?"

"I do." Cabot leaned forward in his seat and spoke directly at Lima via his monitor. "Taylor espouses the 'Great Man' theory of history, that history is shaped by heroic 'great men' who make a decisive historical impact. He views himself as such a man. His historical heroes are the great military men of Ancient Rome: Marius, Sulla, Julius Caesar. But he holds one man—Augustus—above all others, for it was Augustus who ended the Roman Republic and installed himself as an autocratic dictator. This is why we must stop him."

Lima was silent; he drove for several more miles before he spoke again.

"America must never submit to dictatorship," he said. "Brazil suffered under such military dictators from '64 to '85. The worst was General Médici. Your General Taylor—he reminds me of Médici, only more gifted. Which makes him more dangerous."

"It is always the autocrat that fails the autocracy," Cabot said.

"It is so," Lima agreed. He stretched the fingers on each hand one by one against the steering wheel, popping his knuckles. "Mr. Flanagan ordered a background investigation of General Taylor as well. He approved the report three days before I met both of you in San Francisco."

For the next hour Lima briefed George and Cabot on the results of his investigation of Taylor. "This man, General Taylor, he is a worthy adversary," he concluded. "A dangerous man. It will be difficult, even with Mr. Flanagan. Next to impossible without. Do you agree, George?"

"I dunno."

"Do you intend to kill him?"

"I intend to see him dead, one way or another."

"I understand this," Lima said. "If I were you, I would feel likewise. But I must have your word that you will take no action until after Mr. Flanagan renders his decision in this matter. Do I have your word?"

George bit his lip. "Yes."

"Very good, then," Lima responded.

Cabot reached over and patted George's knee. "Thank you," he mouthed.

Lima turned his attention back to driving, and the car was silent once more. He maintained an average speed of over eighty miles per hour as he smoothly navigated around slower vehicles and decelerated through all the highway patrol speed traps. They sped toward the Washington State border.

"How does it feel? To *be* him—General Washington?" Lima asked at length, looking at George in the rear-view mirror. "Forgive my indiscretion," he said after a long pause. "I am a direct man, as I have said."

George was unsure how to answer. He was skeptical and wary of most people, but his gut told him he could trust Lima. And so he did. It turned out to be one of the best decisions of his life.

"Still coming to terms with it," he said honestly. "Well, I believe I am... *him*... but I'm not sure what that really means as yet. I mean, it's not a comic-book superpower or anything. I'm not sure yet if it's a blessing or a curse."

"I have had the same struggle," Cabot said. "For the past forty-plus years I have cursed TRENTON and my role in it. But since I told George the truth about who he is, and we have reconnected with Virginia, I now consider this a blessing. The timing was fated, I believe."

"What about you?" George directed his question to Lima.

"Luiz has had an unorthodox childhood as well, George," Cabot said. "Tell him, Luiz."

He did. Lima was a direct man.

He had been born in an impoverished rural Brazilian village in 1974. Four years later, his father had moved the family to Rio de Janeiro in search of work, but had found little success. In 1979, under the Brazilian military dictator João Figueiredo, Lima's family had been forcibly relocated to the infamous "City of God" favela, where they had endured grinding poverty and extreme violence for two years.

One night, as he slept, Lima's family had abandoned him and fled back to the Brazilian countryside. Lima's father could no longer feed or protect his entire family, and so with a prayer he had taken his wife and daughter and abandoned young Luiz to his fate on the violent streets of Rio de Janeiro. The boy had been just seven years old.

Lima had quickly adapted to the jungle law that ruled the favela. He became an accomplished thief who stole from local merchants to survive. Eventually, the paramilitary troops had come after him. They had almost killed him when he was eleven years old. He had vowed revenge, and thus the legend of "God's Assassin" was born.

Lima ended his story, then switched gears as smoothly as the Porsche.

"Do you believe in God, George?"

"Not as such, no."

"I thought of God often, after my family left." Lima took a long pause. "I asked Him many things. Questions a young boy would ask his father. I needed answers for the many things I saw… and did… in the favela. Brazil has more Catholics than any other country on earth. Did you know that?"

George shook his head.

"And Massachusetts is the most Catholic state in the U.S.," Cabot added.

"Indeed," Lima said. "Do you think He speaks to us, George? Through people or events? Is it possible to know His will in this way?"

"You mean like blind faith?"

"Must all faith be blind?"

George was unsure where Lima was heading with this, but he wanted out of this conversation. He elbowed Cabot for help.

"I'm looking forward to seeing Daniel again," Cabot said, changing the subject. "It's been about five years since my last island visit. How is he?"

"Very well," Lima responded. He kept one eye on George in the rear-view mirror. "He's been busy. Many interesting projects on the island since you visited last. You will see."

"The hardest part of visiting the island is leaving," Cabot said. "Every time I visit, I want to stay."

"Yes," Lima replied. "When I do operations off-island, I get anxious to return. Always."

They traveled in silence until they approached Sea-Tac Airport, at which point Lima informed George that he would be blindfolded for the remainder of their journey. With apology, Cabot placed a large black sleeping mask over George's eyes.

Darkness. George closed his eyes and tried to relax. Lima turned up the classical music. George could feel the lean of the car as it took the off-ramp. Long straightaways gave way to stops and turns. They were outside the city now. George felt the car gently rock and shake. A dirt road?

Another twenty minutes passed before the car came to a stop. Lima and Cabot each took an arm and helped George out of the back seat. It was quiet; George smelled the fresh tang of pine and felt the squelch of wet, mulched leaves underfoot. He heard another vehicle come to a stop, then the grunts of Noam and Ivan approaching.

They walked George about thirty paces and stopped. There was the metallic sound of a door opening, and he was guided up a handful of steps, turned, and then buckled into a seat. George felt Noam's bulk settle in next to him.

Lima wrapped George's hand around a small glass and instructed him to drink. George sniffed the liquid. It was odorless. Cabot assured George that everything was fine, and that this was standard procedure for one's first visit to the island. George exhaled and downed the glass in one big gulp. Spearmint with a touch of citrus.

The last thing George heard was the deep thrum of a large engine and the *whop-whop-whop* of rotor blades.

CHAPTER 40

George squinted against the brilliant light. His blindfold had been removed while he slept. The helicopter was over open water. He was in the back, on a large U-shaped bench seat, flanked by Noam and Ivan. His night mask was in front of him on a knee-high rectangular table. Cabot and Lima sat in swivel captains' chairs on the opposite side of the table.

"How long have I been out?"

"Several hours," Cabot responded. "How do you feel?"

"Okay," George said, rubbing his temples. The drink had knocked him out good. He knew better than to ask what it was.

"Welcome to Verity Island, George," Lima said. "Eighteen miles wide, ninety miles long. Ninth largest island in the United States, slightly bigger than Rhode Island. We land at the manor in ten minutes."

The island soon appeared as a dot on the horizon. It rapidly grew as the helicopter buzzed over the open water at nearly two hundred miles per hour. From the angle of the sun, George could see that they were approaching the southern end.

It had an irregularly shaped coast, which was ringed with a wide ribbon of white sand. Perpendicular cliffs rose five hundred feet straight up from the beach. The helicopter approached the island low to the water.

"It reminds me of the NaPali Coast, on the North Shore of Kauai," George said. "I had my honeymoon there…"

"Mr. Flanagan purchased Verity after his visit to a Japanese volcanic island named Aogashima."

The helicopter sped closer to the cliffs. The island approached rapidly now, filling the entire field of view. At the last moment the pilot executed a steep climb. George's stomach leapt into his throat. They crested the top of the cliff and leveled off. What George beheld rendered him speechless.

It was heaven on earth. Shangri-La.

A huge sunken volcanic crater, about eighteen miles square, lay hidden behind the cliffs. It formed a valley of Arcadian bliss, its floor three hundred feet below the clifftops. In the center of this valley was a magnificent manor house that resembled an English royal castle.

Beyond the manor house lay 2,500 acres of manicured estate grounds, including fenced fields, horse stables, and orchards. The estate grounds were surrounded by over two hundred thousand acres of virgin temperate rainforest.

The helicopter flew at treetop height, which prevented George from seeing the remainder of the island outside the valley bowl.

Flanagan had designed his manor house after Sutton Place, a seventy-two-room mansion built thirty-five miles outside of London in 1525 by Sir Richard Weston, a courtier of Henry VIII. The architecture was predominantly Tudor, with a trace of Italianate Renaissance. Sutton Place had once been owned by oil tycoon J. Paul Getty, the world's richest man in his day, and a man Flanagan greatly admired.

The two-story manor house was built of rosy brown brick and stone, its steep-pitched roof dotted with brick chimneys. The second wing of the house, attached but segregated, contained a twenty-vehicle motor court, servant quarters, and all the utility buildings necessary to maintain a manor house and estate grounds on this scale.

They touched down on the helipad that was connected by a walkway to the second wing of the house. George gawked at it all in stunned silence.

"I know," Cabot said, watching him. "I felt the same way the first time I saw this place. I get emotional every time I return."

They disembarked, and Lima led them along a gravel pathway to the manor house. He sequenced through the biometric security, then entered the daily password on the keypad. The solid front door unlocked with a thud, and they entered the towering two-story great hall. Sunlight streamed through the windows and illuminated the fine art and tapestries that hung on the walls. The bodyguards escorted George and Cabot to their guest quarters, while Lima left to check in with Flanagan.

Both guest rooms shared a common hallway. Noam opened the door to George's room and motioned him inside. George entered and was immediately greeted by his room butler. The man was in his early fifties, with graying temples and a perfectly pitched British accent. He was impeccably attired in a deep blue suit with a lavender striped tie. The guest room décor was equally impressive: a polished stone floor with dark oak paneled walls and authentic old world furniture.

The butler informed George he would dine with Mr. Flanagan at 6:00 p.m.—*sharp*. Apparently punctuality was a virtue on Verity Island. The room was fully stocked with all the clothes and toiletries George would need for the duration of his island visit. The butler laid out George's dinner attire on the bed and bid him adieu.

———————

The butler returned at 5:45 p.m. to collect George and escort him to dinner. It took most of fifteen minutes to reach the solid oak double doors of the dining hall. Cabot was waiting outside, accompanied by his own butler. George buzzed with anticipation. He was about to meet the all-powerful, all-knowing Wizard of Oz.

George's butler stacked the men in front of the door, then took his place at the head of this procession and studied his pocket watch. At exactly 6:00 p.m., he heaved the heavy doors open. The men marched in and stood as instructed.

"Sir, may I present your esteemed dinner guests for the evening, Messrs. Henry Codman Cabot and George Nelson Moore."

"Thank you, Oliver," the man said. "Bring them forward."

The dining hall was cavernous, about seventy-five feet in length, with thirty-foot ceilings. Massive chandeliers, equally spaced lengthwise down the center axis of the room, threw concentric light circles on the polished stone floor. A ruby-red rug runner bisected the room lengthwise and terminated at a three-foot-high platform on the other side of the hall, opposite the door. Long, rectangular wooden dining tables sat on either side of the ruby rug, by the windows. Smaller, less formal round tables flanked the raised platform.

Cabot and George walked along the ruby rug to the platform and stopped at the foot of the steps. George's eyes widened in disbelief. He surmised the older man in the middle was Flanagan. Lima sat to his left, and a shockingly beautiful woman was seated on his right. George recognized her instantly. It was Grace, the woman he and JD had met three weeks ago at the bar in DC. She returned his stare with a playful wink.

What the hell is she doing here? George shifted his gaze to the man in the middle—Daniel Freeman Flanagan. He was in his late sixties but looked younger. Black Irish by heritage, George guessed. He had a strong chin and the lean features of an endurance athlete. He kept his hair closely cropped, which minimized his balding pate. His eyes were chocolate brown; the eyes of a hawk, alert and alive. His ears were tapered and pinned back flush against the sides of his head.

"Henry!" Flanagan said, with a strong, clear voice and shining eyes. "Welcome back to Verity Island. So good to see you again, my friend."

"Thank you, Daniel."

Cabot appeared to be the only one who called this man by his first name. George would stick with 'Mr. Flanagan' until told otherwise.

Cabot and Flanagan spoke the pleasantries of two old friends reunited after a long separation. George listened in silence, like a soldier standing at ease.

"So, Henry," Mr. Flanagan said as his eyes flicked over to George. "Who have you brought with you today?"

"This is my nephew, George Moore," Cabot said, turning toward him with a graceful sweep of his hand. "George, it is my pleasure to introduce you to Mr. Daniel Flanagan."

"Pleased to meet you, Mr. Flanagan," George responded, without further banality.

"Welcome to Verity Island, George. I look forward to us getting acquainted during your stay. I believe you know my associates, Mr. Lima and Miss Davis?"

"Mr. Lima has been the perfect host," George replied. "And Grace... Miss Davis. Yes, we have, uhm, met."

Grace smiled. She looked stunning.

"Excellent," Flanagan said. "Please join us for dinner." He motioned to the circular dining table to his right, at the foot of the platform stairs. "You both must be hungry after such a long trip."

Flanagan rose to his feet, followed by Lima and Grace. He appeared to be about six foot, and moved with a regal bearing. They proceeded to the dining table, where Flanagan held out a chair for Grace, then seated himself. The others took their seats.

A small army of waitstaff served their meal, which was presented as a chef's tasting menu. Mr. Flanagan proudly explained that their meal was made from organic ingredients grown and raised solely on Verity Island. George marveled at the presentation: a fruit/nut/cheese plate; warm crusted bread; freshly picked greens and vegetables; entrees of duck, king salmon and crab, and a full dessert tray of ice cream, gelato, chocolate cake, bread pudding, and crème brûlée. The executive chef, a suave man with a thick European accent, visited the table discreetly several times during the entrée service to ensure the meal and service were all meeting Flanagan's expectations. A sommelier floated in and out with expert wine pairings. They finished the meal with a choice of spirits, dessert wines, tea, coffee, or espresso.

Flanagan kept the dinner conversation light. He reminisced with Cabot about the old days in Cambridge, then turned to George and questioned him about his childhood in Woburn and his FBI career. He asked about Kacey Anne and their divorce, a topic Grace seemed particularly interested in. There was a palpable avoidance of any discussion about the two elephants in the room: George's unique relationship to General Washington, and what to do about General Taylor. George read this, correctly, as an intentional omission.

The mood became more somber as they sipped their after-dinner drinks.

"George," Flanagan began. "The people at this table comprise the Verity Alliance. These are the only people on earth I fully trust. For us to work together, I need you to unconditionally trust everyone at this table. Will you do that?"

"Yes."

"Good. Then I have only two questions for you this evening." Flanagan sipped his espresso, then clinked the cup back onto its saucer.

"First question: Who are you?"

"I beg your pardon?"

"*Who are you?* Right now."

George pondered the question for a moment. Then it hit him. *I know what he means.* "I am George Moore," he said. "And George Washington."

Flanagan smiled at his answer.

"Second question: If I help you, will you to do everything I ask of you, without question or hesitation? Even if you can't appreciate what I'm doing or why I'm doing it?"

"Yes."

"Excellent." Flanagan clapped his hands together. The sound echoed through the dining hall like a gunshot. "We will talk at length soon. But now, you and Henry must be tired. Your butlers will escort you back to your rooms."

Everyone thanked Flanagan for the sumptuous meal and exchanged goodnights. The butlers entered the hall and walked down the ruby rug toward the table.

"I have an idea, George," Flanagan announced. "Why don't you accompany Grace on a walk around the estate grounds tomorrow? Meet her in the manor foyer at, say, nine a.m."

The invitation caught George off-guard. "Uhm… I—"

Grace kicked George's foot under the table. He turned to her. A few hours alone in the woods with this beautiful creature? A man didn't get an offer like this every day. More to the point, he believed it prudent not to refuse a "suggestion" from Flanagan. And besides, he had a few questions for Miss Davis.

"Certainly. Nine o'clock tomorrow is fine," George said.

"Splendid," said Flanagan, getting to his feet. "You two kids have fun. Grace knows the estate grounds better than anyone." He turned and set off toward the exit.

George and Cabot waited for Grace to rise, then stood and began to follow their respective butlers back to their guest rooms.

"Say, George," Flanagan called out from the other end of the room. George turned around to face him.

"Verity' means fundamental and inevitable truth. You would do well to remember that while on the island."

CHAPTER 41

Last night's rain had opened up the bouquet of the surrounding fields and gardens, as a decanter breathes a fine bottle of Bordeaux. George inhaled and held the crisp air in his lungs. He and Grace had hiked the manicured trails through kitchen gardens, fruit orchards, and the wine vineyard. Past the horse stables and falconry fields. She had exchanged waves with the groundskeepers, all diligently at work in their matching attire.

The width of the trail allowed them to hike side by side, and they had settled into an easy pace together.

"Sooo…" George began. "Three weeks ago in DC. What was that all about?"

"All business. Standard stuff, really," Grace responded. "Daniel asked me to do an initial workup on you after Henry had called asking for help. Just intel gathering." She turned to George. "No hard feelings?"

"Nah. Figured something was up. I felt like a fossil in that place. A beautiful woman like you—"

"Nonsense. You're an attractive man, George. Besides, I prefer older men. Obviously." She elbowed him playfully.

"May I ask…" George began, then hesitated. "What's the story with you and Mr. Flanagan?"

He caught her scent as she leaned in; her silky, dark hair brushed against him. "What would you like to know, George?"

"I dunno. How did you two meet?"

"I was doing some modeling to pay for my master's degree at Stanford. I didn't like it much. I found the runway work ridiculous. But I needed the money. A friend of mine told me she made ten thousand dollars a night at a high-end escort service in San Francisco. So I tried it. Daniel was my second client. We went exclusive, and he put me up in Pacific Heights. It took me three years to get here." She swept her arms wide. "I love it so."

"Do you love him?"

Grace slowed her pace, then stopped in the middle of the trail. She turned to George.

"Daniel is an amazing man. I love him dearly. But ours is not a romantic love, if that's what you're asking. If such a thing even exists."

She turned back to the trail and began walking again. George had to trot to keep up with her.

"What about you?" she asked him. "Were you in love with your wife?"

"I got married too young. Right outta law school. I thought I loved her. Maybe I did for a time. I never really liked her, though, as dumb as that sounds. I worked long hours at the FBI and we drifted apart. A relationship is kinda like a campfire: you've got to keep stoking it, adding firewood, or it burns out. We both just ran out of wood, I guess."

"So we have that in common," Grace said. "We're both still searching for our one true love." She tilted her head and gave George a coy smile. Her hazel-green eyes sparkled.

They hiked off the estate grounds and into the old-growth forest. Everything was a brilliant shade of green, except the boggy hiking trail, which was the color of dark taffy. The canopy of trees filtered most of the sunlight, which gave the woods a spooky feel. The ground was covered with ferns and mosses; it looked almost prehistoric; as if any minute a tyrannosaur would emerge from behind a tree to size them up for dinner. George recognized grizzly bear tracks in the muddy trail, as well as moose scat.

The temperature had dropped. George and Grace zipped up their jackets under their chins. The trail had narrowed to a single track, and Grace took the lead. George enjoyed his view as they made their way down the serpentine trail. They kept their chatter going, partly because they enjoyed talking with each other, and partly because noise was a good defense against a bear attack. They talked and laughed about all kinds of things, and discovered they had similar interests. Grace had a quick mind and biting wit. She also possessed a rather bawdy sense of humor, just like George.

They stopped about an hour into their hike to shed their backpacks and grab a drink from their water bottles.

"You know," Grace said in between gulps, "we have something else in common. We're both adopted."

George raised his eyebrows. "I'll bet you can't beat my adoption story," he declared.

"Probably not," Grace said with a laugh. She took one last sip of water, then slid her bottle back into her pack. "My momma was a sixteen-year-old crack addict. I never met my daddy. He ran the streets selling dope and whatever he could steal. Died in Corcoran Prison when I was ten. My grandma Mabel raised me in West Oakland. Back then, my name was Kai'Ann Ellis. You like that name?"

George nodded and smiled.

"Me too." Grace sighed heavily. "When I was eight, our house got shot up in a drive-by. Fools had the wrong house, which happened often. I almost died. Four bullets hit my headboard before I woke up and jumped under my bed. My grandma placed me with a wealthy couple in the suburbs. Said it was best for me. They changed my name to Tessa Davis. I never liked Tessa, so in the ninth grade I chose my middle name, Grace."

She stood, hoisted her pack off the ground, and lurched back into it. George followed her lead. They started back down the trail.

"They were good people, my adoptive parents," she went on. "Did a lot for me, and I love them for it. But my grandma," Grace patted her heart, "she's my real momma. I visited her in the old neighborhood until she died four years ago."

"I'm sorry," said George gently, and Grace smiled at him.

They hiked in silence for a while, enjoying the natural symphony of the forest. George loved the sound of Grace hiking; the soft exhales, the sweet way she cleared her throat occasionally. He found himself drawn to her, now even more than he had initially been at the bar. But she and Flanagan were a couple, of sorts, and George knew not to cross that line. Still, he wondered if she felt the same way about him. Or ever could. Maybe if he was younger, if he bore fewer of life's scars?

"Hey, old man," Grace said, turning around to face George, hands on hips, grinning. "You got a few more miles in you today? I want to show you something."

"Lead the way."

Two hours later, they stood atop a three-hundred-foot summit. To the north stretched the rest of Verity Island, all seventy miles of it. It was a sylvan paradise, spotted with small mountains and glacial lakes. A bald eagle soared overhead, as if on cue.

"Verity Island," Grace announced over George's shoulder. She tucked into him to shield herself from the wind. "Beautiful, isn't it?"

"Where are we?" George turned to face Grace. "Based on the climate, the plants and animals here, and the duration of my flight from Seattle, I figure we must be in—"

"I'll let Daniel explain all that to you."

George turned back to the view. Grace felt good behind him. He looked a long time before he saw something that made his heart skip a beat. "Is that..." George stammered. "Is it... It looks like white skyscrapers, in the distance, at the far end of the island." George lifted his hand to shield his eyes. "Yeah. It looks like four of 'em."

"Five, actually," Grace said. "Each one is fifty stories tall."

George spun around. "Does anyone else live here?"

"I really can't say, George."

George swallowed hard. This was much bigger than just another rich guy partying on his island.

Grace remained huddled close to George. She was shivering. He took off his jacket and gave it to her, then vigorously rubbed her shoulders until she stopped shaking.

"C'mon," George said. "Let's head back. There's a man I gotta see."

CHAPTER 42

The German shorthaired pointers rustled around in the forest undergrowth at the edge of an expansive field. Their glossy liver and white coats shone in the sun when it appeared from behind the clouds. The dogs' movement alerted the goshawk. Her keen orange-red eyes scanned the brush, seeking her opportunity.

It all happened in an instant. The pointers flushed a snowshoe hare from its hiding place. It lit out across the field, its hind legs pumping. The hare had shed most of its winter white, and it was camouflaged well against the clover and wild grasses.

The goshawk immediately came off Flanagan's fist and took to the air, stretching to her full four-foot wingspan. Her slate-gray wings were broad and pointed. Strips of kangaroo-leather jesses, tied to both legs, trailed behind her as she flew. Her bells jangled.

The goshawk swooped in on the terrified hare, her powerful wings propelling her forward at close to forty miles per hour. She maneuvered herself above her quarry, using her long tail as a rudder, then struck the hare feet first, her razor talons sinking into flesh and pinning her meal to the ground. Her dark head spun around, eyes burning, as if daring anyone to approach. She shielded her prey with her wings and began to feast. *Death from above.*

"Outstanding!" Flanagan exclaimed as he hustled across the field. George followed, as did the gaggle of excited dogs.

Falconry has been the "sport of kings" for over eight thousand years. It was practiced by the ancient Persians and Egyptians. By 1,000 BC, the Khans of Mongolia had advanced falconry to a point where they took down tigers with golden eagles.

Falconry was not practiced in America until the 1960s. Flanagan had become a devotee only after he arrived at Verity Island. He preferred to fly goshawks, which technically made him an *austringer,* not a falconer. Attila the Hun had also loved to fly these majestic birds, so much so that in 434 AD he included the image of a goshawk in the military insignia of his army.

Flanagan approached his goshawk, who was still pecking at her kill. He skillfully pulled her off the hare and hid it in his satchel. He wished to fly the goshawk some more this day, and she would not fly sated.

"This hare will make a fine dish," Flanagan said. "We shall dine on it tonight. With some luck we shall bag a pheasant as well."

He and George continued across the field to the opposite end of the clearing. Flanagan carried the goshawk on his fist, arm extended. The dogs resumed rustling around in the undergrowth. The two men strolled the perimeter of the large fenced field, awaiting the goshawk's next flight.

"So, what do you make of falconry?"

"Not sure. It's my first time." George could not stop staring at the goshawk. It paid him no heed.

"I love the primal truth in it," Flanagan said. "Predator and prey, stripped of all pretense. My goshawk has no animosity toward the hare, nor affection toward me. She is not my pet, nor I her master. No subtext."

George hesitated. "Mr. Flanagan, with all respect, sir, you didn't bring me here to introduce me to falconry. What *am* I doing here, exactly?"

Flanagan turned to face him squarely. "You're here because I had to see for myself," he said. "This Washington clone thing is remarkable. The implications are truly extraordinary."

"I didn't ask for any of it."

"Yes, but here we are, all the same," Flanagan said. They continued to walk. "Tell me, George, what do you think my goshawk here thinks of you being General Washington's clone, walking with me, in this field, in twenty-first-century America?"

Silence.

"Exactly," Flanagan said. "Nothing. She is unburdened by sentience or reason, free to be only what she is. A goshawk. We humans are not so lucky, George. We carry the burden of consciousness, and forever suffer in the quagmire between who we are and who we think we should be."

Flanagan petted the goshawk's sleek feathers. She allowed it.

"You're also here because I think you and I, together, can change the world. Does that interest you, George?"

"As long as it involves the death of General Taylor."

"Ah, yes. Your friend General Taylor. I understand your thirst for vengeance, George. But not your myopia. Our current situation is much bigger than you or General Taylor. Sure, Luiz and my men could assassinate the general, and, who knows, with some luck maybe you could too. They would survive the mission; you would not. You are a brave man who does not fear death. But Henry fears you will die in vain, regardless of General Taylor's fate."

"I have to do this."

"And you shall, George. You shall. But if you do it alone, you will fail. If you allow me to help you, we will succeed."

"What's the catch? What do you get out of all this?"

"You are right to ask me that. I did not bring you here to simply help you kill a man—a man who has, as yet, done me no personal harm or slight. But there is one thing I desperately want. And you can help me get this thing, George." Flanagan clapped his hands. "We will get to all that in due course. First I must ask you this: What do you think of the current state of your country and countrymen?"

"I think we're in trouble," George said.

"I'm afraid I agree with you, George. The human brain has outpaced its host. For the past two hundred and fifty years, Western civilization has pursued the proposition of individual over tribe, feelings over facts, personal desires over shared ideals. These enlightened individuals inevitably became narcissistic over time, demanding all manner of rights and privileges they did not earn. Modern systems as disparate as communism and democracy have failed to effectively address this."

"Now I really think we're in trouble," George said.

"Have you heard of Dunbar's Number?" Flanagan asked.

George shook his head no.

"A British anthropologist named Robin Dunbar established a correlation between primate brain size and social group size, and extrapolated that humans can comfortably maintain only one hundred and fifty stable relationships." Flanagan paused. "I have found the true number to be closer to one hundred, about the same size as primitive hunter-gatherer groups or the modern U.S. Army company."

George was confused. What did this have to do with killing Taylor? It must have shown on his face.

"Tribalism!" Flanagan exclaimed. "Tribalism, George. The inescapable fact of human neurology is that the human brain has not evolved to socialize effectively in large modern populations. We need to be true to who we are. Like the goshawk."

George wondered how long it had been since Flanagan had been off-island.

"Now let's talk about you and the other Founding Fathers."

"I'm a clone, not a time traveler," George responded, with a tinge of impatience.

Flanagan ignored the comment and continued. "The founders created their democratic republican government for a homogeneous population of three million, thirteen states proximately located along the eastern seaboard in predominantly small agrarian towns and villages—the functional equivalent of social tribes. Today, America has three hundred and fifty million citizens, a mostly urban population of all races and creeds, spread out over fifty states and three thousand miles. We cling to an antiquated system of government that is not scalable to address modern realities." Flanagan shook his head solemnly. "What would General Washington say if he could see what we have done to his beloved country?"

"He'd be pissed," George said. "I certainly am. Our current government is completely broken. Toxic. It can only be fixed from the outside."

"Perhaps you are that outside force, George?"

The dogs suddenly rooted out a pheasant, and it took wing over the field. The cacophony caused George to jump. The goshawk flew off Flanagan's fist in pursuit and chased the pheasant clear across the field and out of sight. Flanagan pulled out a gadget from his satchel and began to track the goshawk via the telemetry transmitter on its leg. Both men walked calmly in the direction of the audible pings.

"What would you do with six trillion dollars?" Flanagan asked.

"That's one problem I've never had to concern myself with."

"It has consumed me," Flanagan said. They walked in silence as they followed the pinging of the telemetry monitor toward the goshawk, who had grounded the pheasant in the distance.

"I saw something on my hike yesterday. At the other end of the island."

"And what did you see, George?"

George slowed to a stop. "Buildings. Big, tall white buildings."

Flanagan stopped abruptly, turned and paced back until he faced George at close distance.

"What is this place?" George asked.

"Would you like to see what I did with all my money?"

"Sure," George replied.

"I became a Founding Father, just like you."

CHAPTER 43

The underground bullet train accelerated away from the station and into the dark tunnel. It could accommodate up to one hundred passengers, but on this trip only two seats were occupied. The train's interior was entirely white. Its polished surfaces reflected the bright interior lights. The train ran silent and smooth at top speed. The surfaces of their black coffee barely moved in their mugs as they hurtled down the track.

"We'll be at Village Blue in about ten minutes," Lima said.

"Luiz, did Mr. Flanagan say anything to you about Taylor?"

"Patience, George, patience. Mr. Flanagan is a deliberate man. Believe me, he has a plan for General Taylor. It involves you and Verity Island."

"So he has decided to help me. That's great!" George exclaimed.

"He's still deliberating," Lima said. "But he likes you, George. If he didn't, you'd be off-island by now. And certainly not on this train to Village Blue. The islanders don't even know this underground train network exists. It covers the entire island. All the villages. Central City too."

"A city?"

"Yes," Lima responded. "The white towers you saw on your hike with Grace the other day. It's at the north end of the island, near the airport and nuclear power plant."

George's eyes widened. "This island has an airport? And a nuclear power plant?"

Lima chuckled. "Verity Island has many things. Best if I explain before we get to Village Blue." He drained the last of his coffee and gave George a short history of Verity Island as they sped through the dark tunnel.

Lima explained that Flanagan had become disenchanted with life in his thirty-second year. Too much corruption, hypocrisy and avarice. He wanted out. In 1984, he had hidden his trillion-dollar fortune and disappeared to Verity Island, located in the Alexander Archipelago of Southeast Alaska. It was the largest private island on earth.

A small army of construction contractors had worked around the clock for five years to complete the manor house and eighteen square miles of estate grounds. The concept was the medieval working estates of Europe. Upon completion, the staff had stayed to work and live on the estate.

Flanagan had grown more restless as years passed. He longed for a new challenge. It had come to him in 1992, in a flash: *He would create his own world.* A better world, master-planned from the ground up. An Arcadian utopia.

He had spent his fortune freely; no detail had escaped his notice. The project fascinated and consumed him. It had taken over ten years to complete, and pushed him to the brink of his considerable capabilities. The first Verity Islanders had arrived a few years after the Twin Towers fell.

Flanagan built his society to reflect the baojia system, which had flourished in the sixteenth century during the Ming dynasty in China. It was a base ten system. Ten families formed a tribe. Ten tribes formed a village. Each village was ruled by a village elder, who was held accountable for the actions of the entire village.

Verity was a meritocratic republic with a social capitalistic economy. Accountability, and the sublimation of individual needs for the greater good, permeated island culture. Verity ran on advanced algorithms created by Flanagan himself. He loved mathematics, and scribbled algorithms as others did crossword puzzles.

What had George walked into here? Was this some kind of cult or something? Henry, Flanagan, Lima—they all appeared to be perfectly rational men. But this was a little crazy, right? George's eyes ricocheted about the train, his mind racing. Lima maintained his usual calm countenance.

The bullet train decelerated into the station, which was covered in matte white tiles accented in azure blue. The doors whooshed open, and they walked across the station platform to a security kiosk. Lima entered a code, then completed a fingerprint and retinal scan. The flat panel validated his identity, and elevator doors opened five feet to their right. There was only one button on the elevator panel. Lima pushed it, and they began their ascent.

The elevator doors opened into the middle of a forest. They stepped out, and George watched in amazement as the elevator disappeared back into the forest floor.

"C'mon, this way," Lima said. "The village is not far."

Lima led George along a path under dense overhanging branches. They hiked half a mile before they reached a road made of azure bricks and headed north. George fought back a sense of bewilderment, feeling like a modern-day Dorothy in Oz. *Follow the azure brick road.*

Lima walked briskly, and George had to adjust his stride to keep pace. They reached the outer wall of Village Blue in less than ten minutes. The ten-foot stone perimeter wall extended a square mile around the village. A stout cast iron gate, which was open, crossed the road, and they passed through it. Inside the village wall, an allée of matching maples and oaks lined the road to the village itself, about a quarter-mile ahead. Well-tended gardens and orchards extended into the distance on either side of the road.

The village was a large circle, enclosed by a white three-rail fence.

The brick road entered the village at the six o'clock position. A residential gatehouse was perched on top of a twenty-foot arch that spanned the road. An ornate cupola was centered on top of the gatehouse, which lent the village the quaintness of a colonial town square.

They accessed the interior gatehouse stairwell and walked up two flights of stairs. A distinguished older gentleman greeted them in a small foyer. He was small-framed and stooped, with olive skin, a full head of unruly white hair, and bright almond eyes. He introduced himself as Aadarsh Laghari, the Village Blue Elder. He waved Lima and George into his office.

Laghari stood behind his desk, facing Lima. He thrust both his hands out, palms down, fingers spread. He then flipped his hands over to display empty palms. Lima did the same, and George saw that he and Laghari sported nearly identical tattoos in the webbing of their hands, between the right thumb and forefinger. Lima's tattoo was pure white, Laghari's azure blue. After this introductory ritual was complete, all three men then took their seats.

"Welcome back to Village Blue, Mr. Lima," Laghari said. "As village elder, and on behalf of every Blue Villager, I offer you all the hospitality at our disposal." He then turned to George. "Welcome, Mr. Moore." He had a faint accent that George could not discern. "I have been authorized to provide you with a tour of Village Blue, and to answer any questions you might have. Shall we begin?"

George nodded.

Laghari stood and motioned George to join him at the window behind his desk. It was magnificent—ten feet high and half as wide. Lima and George flanked Laghari as they looked out at the circular village center, which resembled a large clock face. This large circle was composed of azure gravel, with ten equidistant matching gravel footpaths disappearing into the woods all around its perimeter. The village center contained a lush open market, square in shape, with various shops and outdoor cafés. Blue Villagers sauntered about, greeting one another as they passed. They all looked perfectly normal. *And happy.*

"The tribe is the fundamental unit on Verity," Laghari said with solemnity. "Everything begins and ends with the tribe. You must remember this, Mr. Moore, if you are to understand our way of life."

The tribe, he explained, maintained on average one hundred members, comprising ten extended biological families. Each tribe was led by an elder, a patriarch or matriarch, selected by the tribe. All tribes were self-governed and policed by the elder, in accordance with the laws, ideals, and values common to all Verity Islanders.

Each tribe was a secular, mixed-race monoculture, with its own unique history and symbol. This symbol, combined with the village color and tribal number, functioned like a medieval coat of arms, and instantly identified each tribe member to all other islanders.

Laghari held out his right hand and pointed to the space between his thumb and forefinger. George studied the tattoo; it was a soaring eagle with the number 8 grasped in its talons. The entire tattoo was done in azure blue, and identified Laghari as Tribe 8 of Village Blue. He explained that new members earned their tribal tattoos in their eighteenth year. It was bestowed at a sacred ceremony attended by all tribal members, and was the linchpin of tribal life. The hand-flip greeting was required by Verity law: both hands palm down (to display the tribal tattoo), then both hands palm up (to show empty hands, symbolizing peace and truth).

George now understood the color of Lima's tattoo. In light, white was the sum of all colors. Lima's bright white ink provided him with the neutrality he needed as head of security for the entire island.

"Would you like to go down and walk around?" Laghari asked.

George said that he would. Laghari looked at Lima, who nodded his permission. They left the big window and descended the stairs back to the village road. George stood in the shade of the arch, looking into the brilliant sunshine.

"Shall we?" Laghari said as he motioned George forward. The three men entered the village.

Village Blue was a collection of ten tribes, which put the population at about one thousand villagers. Each tribe had its own residential building, connected to the village center by a wooded footpath. From above, the arrangement looked like the spokes of a wheel; these were the same footpaths George had seen from the elder's window. Laghari explained that the position of village elder rotated annually among the ten tribal elders, and that he would be rejoining Tribe 8 at the end of his term.

All communal village activities occurred in the open market area of the village center.

Blue children were home-schooled until age eight, and then attended primary and secondary schools in the village center. All young people were given a battery of aptitude tests at age eighteen, and an algorithm identified the most gifted students. The top 10 percent of Blue students joined their counterparts from the other nine villages for five years of advanced study at the island's university, which was located in Central City.

They stopped in front of an ornate building made of stone block, which stood in stark contrast to the rest of the village center's wooden colonial structures. Laghari identified this as the Fine Arts building. Blue Villagers took great pride in this structure, which hosted all manner of cultural and live entertainment events. Inter-tribal social and sporting events occurred on the elevated stage, which served to deepen village bonds. Medical treatment occurred at a state-of-the-art village clinic, while advanced and life-threatening conditions were addressed at University Hospital in Central City.

From there, they walked toward the market area; George saw dozens of contented-looking villagers strolling in and out of the various shops all along the perimeter of the market. Young and old talked and laughed together in the outdoor cafés. Groups of small children mingled about with no apparent parental supervision. The villagers came in a variety of shades and sizes, but all shared a common dress and demeanor. George noted how clean and shiny everything was; there was no litter or graffiti anywhere, the buildings all well designed and in good repair. Village Blue looked like any wealthy upscale American suburb, but felt somehow different. It was lighter, more relaxed. *Happier.*

The three men were greeted with smiles as they strolled about the center. Their eyes lingered on George. People sat in pairs on park benches, or in solitude with a book or personal electronic device. A few bold individuals approached the group and exchanged hand-flip greetings with Laghari and Lima. George, self-conscious, nodded his greeting and kept both hands buried deep in his pockets.

The three men did a few turns around the village center, with Laghari explaining various facets of village and island life. They made their way over to a café, where they took seats at an empty table. A smiling waitress delivered three cups of tea.

George sipped his drink and sat back to take in his surroundings. His eyes were drawn to a man in the distance. He moved with military precision as he swept the azure brick pavers and cleaned every surface to a high glossy shine. His pale blue work clothes were properly creased, his black boots polished. The man actually smiled as he worked, only stopping to converse briefly with the multitude of villagers that greeted him. After one such exchange with a middle-aged couple, the sweeper glanced over his shoulder directly at George. He smiled and waved. George waved back, and the sweeper set down his broom and began to walk across the courtyard toward him. George tapped Lima on the arm. Lima immediately registered the sweeper's approach and alerted the elder.

"That's the village sweeper, Bai Zhou," Laghari responded. "From Tribe 3. He does a wonderful job for the village. Got a wife and two children in secondary school. The son has a good chance at university."

Zhou approached the table. He was a short, stout raven-haired man, with heavy-lidded dark eyes and an open smile. He was missing one of his eyeteeth, and clearly did not care a whit. He made the traditional greeting with Laghari and Lima, then, without hesitation, extended his hand to George. George shook it, which pleased Zhou a great deal. He beamed a crooked gap-toothed grin. George liked him immediately.

They all chatted for a few minutes, and Zhou soon had everyone laughing, even Lima. Zhou then bowed and turned to leave.

"I have an idea." Laghari called after Zhou.

"George, how would you like to have dinner tonight with our sweeper and his family? No better way to learn about our village life. What do you say, Mr. Lima?"

"I say that is between George and the sweeper," Lima responded, to George's surprise.

"It'd be my honor to host our guest from away," Zhou exclaimed. "My son would love to meet you. He'll be on sabbatical soon, and has a million questions about the off-island world."

George looked at Lima, who nodded. "Sure. It'd be my pleasure to join you and your family for dinner this evening."

"I'll bring him by around six," Lima said.

Zhou grinned with delight, thanked everyone and returned to work with a bounce in his step.

And just like that, George had a dinner date. With Tribe 3. In Village Blue. On Verity Island.

CHAPTER 44

TUESDAY, JUNE 22, 2021; 5:55 P.M. (AKDT)
VERITY ISLAND; VILLAGE BLUE; TRIBE 3; ALEXANDER ARCHIPELAGO
SOUTHEASTERN ALASKA

At a few minutes before six, George and Lima walked the shady quarter-mile footpath toward the sweeper's house. The summer solstice had just passed, and George was enjoying the novelty of eighteen hours of daylight.

They saw their destination ahead, in the wooded clearing. The tribal building was five stories high and semicircular in shape, with the flat side facing the path. Like all other tribal domiciles, it was white with azure blue trim and had the same colonial Georgian architectural style of the buildings in the village center. The entry level was wrapped in glass, while the upper floors had two matching sets of windows on each side of the entry. The hipped roof had three equidistant chimneys of azure brick.

"I'll be back at ten o'clock sharp to pick you up. Right here, in front of this building," Lima told him.

"Got it, Luiz. Thanks."

George approached the glass double doors, which had the number 3 centered above it. He heaved the doors open and entered the lobby, where Zhou greeted him with the same gap-toothed smile. They shook hands and then walked to the elevators, where Zhou summoned the car. A muted ping signaled its arrival; the doors slid noiselessly open, and both men got in. The doors re-opened into the foyer of unit 103, where the sweeper's wife and two children stood awaiting their guest.

"This is my family," Zhou said as he gestured to them with pride. "Welcome to our home." The son was fifteen, the daughter thirteen. Neither bore the tribal tattoo of their parents. The group exchanged awkward pleasantries in the foyer for several minutes. The teenage children were poised beyond their years.

"How 'bout I give you a tour of the place?" Zhou suggested at last. George readily agreed, and they set off. The Zhou residence was one of three units on the second floor of the building. All second-floor units were one thousand square feet in size. The third- and fourth-floor units were the same size, while the entire fifth floor was a grand penthouse suite. The ground floor was dedicated to common tribal facilities, including a dining hall, laundry, group shower/spa area, and a nursery.

Each family member slept in their own stacked sleeping pod that retracted into the inside wall on either side of the elevator. A curved window wall opposite the elevator provided an unobstructed view of the common garden and orchard that surrounded the village. The furniture was grouped to promote family gatherings, and the window wall, open floor plan, and ten-foot ceilings gave the space a grand feel.

The sweeper explained that all village housing was assigned based on merit, meaning one's contribution to the tribe. The units on each floor were identical, and grew in opulence on each higher floor. The fifth-floor penthouse was spectacular, with long views of the island's interior. A doctor who worked at the village medical clinic currently occupied the Tribe 3 penthouse. It had previously been the residence of the village schoolmaster.

Zhou concluded the tour and led George to a seating area

opposite the arched window wall. The vegetables and fruit trees were in full bloom, and the heady fragrance wafted through the open windows and permeated the unit. The two men sat down opposite one another in cushy leather chairs, a low table between them. "The village gives us everything we need," Zhou said. "This apartment, food, clothing, health care, education for my kids, everything. I pay twenty-five percent tribute to the village, and we all work ten hours a week in the village garden."

As a social capitalist economy, the island had begun with strong regulation of key markets but had gradually transitioned to a free market and barter system. The island economy emphasized self-sufficiency, which kept imported mainland goods to a minimum.

"Not bad, huh?" Zhou beamed.

"Not bad at all," George said. "What's that?" he asked, pointing to a framed scroll prominently displayed on the wall.

"The Ten Laws of Verity Island," the sweeper responded. "All islanders have them in their homes." He explained that the tribal elder enforced these ten laws and was held accountable for all tribe transgressions. Misdemeanors were adjudicated and punished at the village level. First offenders were branded with a black "X" at the wrist, above their tribal tattoo. All felonies, and second offenses of any kind, were referred to Central City.

The accused was represented by his or her village elder, with the city leader presiding. A guilty verdict in City Court resulted in mandatory banishment. Banishment meant that the offender was shunned by the tribe and expelled from the island—the most severe punishment for any islander.

Zhou's face darkened. "About five years ago, a man from Tribe 3—my tribe—was banished for the crime of... well, let us just say certain indecencies with some children of our tribe." Zhou lowered his gaze momentarily, then again locked eyes with George. "We disowned this man and haven't seen or heard from him since."

"What happened to him?" George asked.

"He was banished from Verity. Forever."

George thought of Zhou's own two children. "I see."

"This man betrayed the trust of our tribe. He betrayed *my* trust. All Verity Islanders have voluntarily pledged to follow the ten laws. These laws are our fundamental truths. We believe in them and choose to live by them. Anyone who breaks these laws has violated their pledge and betrayed their family. Such a person no longer belongs in the tribe."

A charged silence filled the space between them. George shifted in his chair; the groan of the leather pierced the quiet. An uneasy smile pursed George's lips.

"You don't understand, Mr. Moore," Zhou said, straightening in his chair. "All tribe members are answerable to each other. Always. And those who harm their family and tribe must be punished."

"Banishment?"

"He'd already been "X'd" for a prior offense—theft from the village store," Zhou said with a scowl. "He got what he deserved. We in Tribe 3 were happy to be rid of him."

George noticed that the sweeper's son, Cheng Zhou, had crept close to the sofa where he and Zhou were sitting. He wondered how much he had overheard. George smiled at the boy, who blushed.

"Care to join us?" George asked him.

"May I, Father?" Cheng implored.

"If it pleases our guest," Zhou said.

George smiled and nodded at Cheng, who bounded over to shake George's hand and then plopped himself down on a cushioned chair across from the two men.

"Are you really from out there?" Cheng blurted out. "I mean, you know, from away?"

"Hush, Cheng," Zhou admonished. "There's no need to be so forward with our guest."

The boy reddened and stared at his lap.

"It's okay," George said. "Yes, I'm from away."

"I knew it!" Cheng exclaimed, slapping his hand against his thigh.

"Tell me about yourself," George said, deftly guiding the conversation into safer waters.

Cheng told George that he would do his yearlong sabbatical in three years, and that he was anxious to see the outside world. He boasted he would then return to Verity Island and receive his tribal tattoo.

"Do all the village youth do this sabbatical when they finish secondary school?" George asked Zhou.

"Yes," he replied. "All do the sabbatical in their eighteenth year. It's important for the youth to experience the outside world before they commit to their tribe and life on Verity."

"What's it like out there?" Cheng asked, unable to contain his curiosity any longer.

"It's big," George responded, unsure what to tell this impressionable boy of the world outside the blissful shores of Verity Island. "It's a paradox. Loving and hateful. Good and evil. Appalling and beautiful. Brilliant and ignorant. Merciful and cruel. It's everything... all at once... all the time." George trailed off.

Cheng stared at him, unblinking and wide-eyed. George recovered and cleared his throat.

"I mean... it's great. You'll be fine."

"What are the people like?" Cheng pressed. "Are they like me... us?"

"Yes, no different," George said. But he already knew this to be untrue. Blue villagers were different than their fellow Americans from away.

"I knew it!" Cheng again slapped his thigh. He had recently earned his Internet privileges at the Village Café and was enamored with Google and YouTube.

"Why is there so much anger out there? In your world?" Cheng asked.

"I don't know," George said. "Maybe it'll be better when you get out there."

"Have you ever met the vice president? Taylor?" Cheng asked. "Google says he's trying to take over the Internet. And that all the major tech companies are being threatened—"

"When did you read this?" George asked in a sharp tone.

"Yesterday, at the café," Cheng said. "You don't think they're gonna shut down the Internet, do you? I just got on!"

This was the first George had heard of this. He had been unplugged since he'd landed on Verity. This was not good. Clearly, Taylor had started to make his move: all dictatorships start by controlling the flow of information.

"No, no one can control the Internet." George tried to assure the boy, but he knew different.

Cheng nodded. His face relaxed.

"Have you ever met a Kardashian?"

"No I haven't," George responded, with a chuckle.

"Well I'm gonna… when I get out there."

"I'm sure you will."

"What do you think of our village?" Cheng asked, his eyebrows raised.

"It's very nice. I like it."

"Yeah… it's cool. Kinda boring, though. Can't wait till I do my sabbatical."

"Don't be in too much of a hurry," George said. "There are much worse places to be than here."

"Oh!" Cheng blurted out. "And I'm doing my passage next week!"

"What's that?" George asked him.

"Passage," Cheng explained, was an island ritual whereby all fifteen-year-old boys and girls were taken deep into the island's interior to endure a series of challenges to test their physical, mental, and moral toughness. Successful passage was a necessary precursor for sabbatical.

Zhou's wife approached the group. "That's enough, young man. Time for dinner. Go get dressed."

But, I—"

"Go," she repeated.

The boy did as he was told. Zhou excused himself as well, and George sat and chatted with his wife. The two males soon returned, with the young daughter alongside them, and the group took the elevator down one floor to the dining hall.

The hall occupied over half the ground floor. All tribal meals were served here. It was an elaborate cafeteria-style eatery offering unlimited servings of gourmet-quality food. The food lines snaked along the interior of the building; the dining tables were arranged along the windows overlooking the village garden. The sturdy wood tables were covered in thick azure tablecloths and fine silverware. Muted lighting and soft classical music set the mood. A fire crackled in a vast open fireplace in the center of the hall.

The group loaded their trays with food and headed toward the tables. A man motioned for them to join him, which they did. Zhou introduced the man to George as the Tribe 3 doctor—the penthouse dweller. Dr. Rich Kozlowski and his wife Claire warmly greeted the sweeper and his family. Cheng nudged his way into the seat next to George and continued to whisper questions to him in between return trips to the food line. The conversation between Dr. Kozlowski and Zhou was convivial, and focused as much on the sweeper's work as the doctor's. Dr. Kozlowski displayed no pretension, Zhou no envy. Each man had earned his seat at this tribal table.

George thought of Nesha and her own tribe at the Gardens.

CHAPTER 45

Tuesday, July 6, 2021; 6:10 p.m. (AKDT)
Verity Island; Manor House; Alexander Archipelago
Southeastern Alaska

"I'll have the pan-roasted breast of pheasant with vanilla and pears," George said.

"Very good, sir," the waiter responded. He collected the menus and departed.

"Well done, George," Flanagan said. "I bagged that pheasant just the other day. Bravura!"

The three men toasted the pheasant, and then the goshawk. Flanagan sat across from George, and next to Lima. The men had dined together for the past two weeks, every night since George had returned from his trip to Village Blue. They had also met daily in Flanagan's study, where they had discussed many topics; George had done most of the talking. It soon became apparent to George that this was his two-week interview and assessment. Flanagan was subtly probing George's heart and mind, and both he and Lima liked what they saw.

"I spoke with Henry today," Flanagan said. "He and I are still working on his situation." Last week Cabot had been abruptly notified that he had been fired from Harvard. He'd immediately left the island for Cambridge. When he arrived on campus, the administration had refused to speak with him. His office was boxed up and his belongings shipped to his Back Bay townhouse. Cabot had been at Harvard since 1962. He was a Harvard institution, a Pulitzer nominee who had taught Crimson students for over fifty years. Now he had been fired without explanation. Evicted like a delinquent tenant. Taylor was playing hardball.

It got worse. Flanagan had already developed a well-placed source close to Taylor. This source reported that Taylor had quietly replaced his Secret Service detail with his own military imperial guard force, fashioned after the Roman Praetorian Guard of his hero, Emperor Augustus. He had also created a domestic secret police force that answered only to him.

"Any good news?" Lima asked.

"Other than the pheasant?" Flanagan responded.

Lima's eyes narrowed, a faint smile curled his lips.

"Well, George, you've now visited several of our villages—Blue, Yellow, Red, and… Orange, I believe?" Flanagan asked.

George and Lima nodded.

"Even spent a half-day in Village Indigo all by yourself, isn't that right?"

"Yes," George said. "I particularly enjoyed that."

"So, George, tell me: What do you make of our island?"

"I love it!" George chuckled at his exuberance. "I mean, I really like it here. The whole island is gorgeous, of course. I love the village tribal structure. How everyone is different but valued; each accountable to the other. Like a big family. All the people I've met have been so accepting and kind." George sipped his water, the glass trembled in his hand. He began again, in a softer voice. "I dunno, when I walked around the villages, and spoke with everyone, I didn't feel a man from away, an outsider. I guess I feel like I belong here somehow."

"Wonderful, George. I am glad to hear that," Flanagan said,

holding his smile as he glanced at Lima. The smile soon faded, as did Lima's, and both men turned to face George.

"How is Grace?" Flanagan asked. "I haven't seen much of her lately, and you two seem to be spending a lot of time together."

George felt his face flush.

"I believe you're blushing," Flanagan said in a playful voice that belied his expression. Lima remained expressionless.

Shit. Do they know?

George had been spending a considerable amount of time with Grace the past two weeks. They had gone for runs and long hikes on the estate, and spoke candidly of their lives. They had joked and laughed, even shed some tears together—at Grace's stories of her grandma Mabel, and when George spoke of his reunion with Virginia. Time passed quickly when they were together. George felt good in her company, like the man he used to be. He liked the feeling. And he knew what this feeling was. He had somehow fallen in love with Grace. But Grace was with Flanagan. George knew that he could never act on his feelings; his loyalty to Flanagan and Verity Island forbade it. He made a commitment to himself to try to spend less time with Grace in the future, and to better hide his true feelings from everyone, including himself.

George tucked into his pheasant, eager to change the subject. "This is delicious. Very good," he said, chewing and nervously smiling. He was relieved neither man pressed the issue.

When they had finished their meals and laid their napkins aside, the table was cleared and after-dinner drinks brought in. Twilight cast long shadows across the dining hall. The three men sipped their cognac in silence, until George cleared his throat to speak.

"There's a question I need to ask you."

"Yes, George," Flanagan said. "You may speak freely."

George took a deep breath. "That day we hunted with your bird—"

"Goshawk, George. And it's called falconry."

"Yes." George frowned. "That day, you said there was something you desperately wanted. What is it?"

Flanagan rolled the cognac against the sides of his crystal glass for a long moment, then placed the glass on the table and folded his hands.

"First, Henry is a dear friend of mine, and he has asked for my help. Second, General Taylor poses a genuine threat to Verity Island, which I have painstakingly built for the past thirty years."

"What threat?" George asked.

"Are you familiar with Verity Sabbaticals?"

George nodded. "The sweeper's son spoke of them."

"Verity is an open society. I individually selected each of its original inhabitants. All were fully informed volunteers. Their offspring are the first generation of native islanders. This generation is approaching sabbatical age. Because of General Taylor, they will visit a United States in chaos. I am deeply concerned our eighteen-year-olds will be swallowed up by Taylor's America. The future success of Verity depends on this first sabbatical generation. My algorithms did not account for the overthrow of the United States by a military dictator. The risk posed by General Taylor is intolerable to me. Verity Island is my legacy. He must be stopped."

George thought of Cheng Zhou walking into Taylor's America three years hence. He shuddered.

"The thing I desperately want," Flanagan continued, "which you will help me obtain, George, will have to wait until after we address General Taylor."

"When will we do that?" George asked. "And how?"

"All in good time, George. You have done well on the island and are almost ready. There is a banishment ceremony in Central City in a couple of days. I would like you to attend this with Luiz. We will finish our discussion of General Taylor after this ceremony. Agreed?"

George nodded, and the men finished their cognac in silence.

The lights of the dining hall twinkled as twilight surrendered to night. Darkness had fallen on Verity Island.

CHAPTER 46

The man's screams filled the room. There was no anger or defiance in the sound, just the plaintive wail of a wounded animal. He stood with both hands shackled at the wrist to the tabletop. He bucked like a branded calf when the sulfuric acid was applied. The soapy water was withheld until the acid had eaten away the tribal tattoo and much of the skin around it.

George and Lima stood to one side of the banished man while an attendant dressed his hand. They were in a windowless bunker under Tower One in Central City, a mere eleven-minute ride from the manor house on the underground bullet train. The concrete bunker was underneath a gleaming subway station, one of several locked rooms located in an empty industrial warehouse as big as an airplane hangar.

The attendant released the young man from his shackles and walked him over to Lima, where he stood shaking, averting his gaze. He looked at his shoes as Lima read from a piece of paper.

"You are hereby banished from Verity Island, forever forsaken by Gold Tribe 6, for the felony crime of treasonable betrayal of a tribal elder, and the attempted usurping of same. A tribunal of village elders has found you guilty of the charged offenses, and the Mayor of Central City has sentenced you to banishment, to be carried out this day—Friday, 9 July 2021." Lima folded the paper and put it in his pocket. "Do you have any final words?"

The man raised his head. He looked at Lima and began to whimper. "I'm so sorry. I have disgraced my tribe. My family." He looked down at his bandaged right hand, which intensified his sobbing. "I don't know what I'm gonna do out there... without my tribe... without anything."

Lima watched impassively as the man wept. Minutes passed before he gathered himself.

"Please give this note to my tribe elder." The man's voice wavered as he handed a sealed envelope to Lima. "And tell my family I love them, and that I faced my sentence as a man." He dried his eyes on his sleeve and took a deep breath. "Okay, I'm ready."

Lima stood directly in front of the man. He initiated the Verity hand greeting, but did not do the palm flip. Instead, he shoved both of his hands into his pockets, then turned on his heel and gave the man his back. He walked three paces and turned around. The young man's lip quivered, but he held his emotion.

"Until we meet again, my friend," Lima said.

Two towering guards took the man by his arms and walked him out the door and across the cavernous warehouse. Lima and George followed. The guards' footfalls echoed off the concrete and steel. Lima and George watched the man being led away as they waited for the elevator. It arrived quickly, and both men entered. There was only one button—penthouse. Lima pressed it, and the elevator delivered them non-stop to the fiftieth floor of Tower One. They entered Lima's private residence via the only door off the lobby.

The unit was vast, with wraparound floor-to-ceiling windows of tinted privacy glass. The views were jaw-dropping. To the south was the entire island, to the north a bird's-eye view of Central City, with the airport and Pacific Ocean beyond. Natural light infused the unit, which accented its cool color palette and crisp Scandinavian décor. An odd collection of modern art covered the walls. The framed paintings resembled red Rorschach inkblots against pure white backgrounds. They looked to be by the same artist.

Lima and George took seats at a table by a window that overlooked the city courtyard, where all island banishment ceremonies were held. Lima handed George a pair of magnifying goggles to watch the ceremony about to begin five hundred feet below them. He then flipped a wall switch, and outside noise filled the room. They would hear as well as see the ceremony.

George saw the faces in the windows of the four city towers that surrounded him. Lima explained that every islander had their own assigned seat in the towers. Each tower comfortably accommodated two thousand islanders, or forty per floor. The seating assignments were randomly assigned by algorithm, and rotated annually to provide the proper mix of villages and tribes. Each tower floor had four viewing suites that overlooked the large raised stage in the city courtyard. The top penthouse floors, which were private residences, were assigned by Flanagan. The Central City Stage was also utilized for major live events and other all-island gatherings.

Far below, the two brawny guards led the banished man to the center of the stage. A man in formal attire read aloud the same statement Lima had read him earlier, and allowed the banished man his final words. The formally dressed man reminded George of a boxing announcer. The lack of crowd noise was eerie. The four men were dwarfed by the vast stage and surrounding city.

The banished man finished his final address without emotion. He remained in the center of the stage, standing at attention with a guard on each arm.

The announcer shouted, "Villagers of Verity, line up!" A drum and fife corps began to play.

All the islanders began to file out of the towers. They stood shoulder to shoulder and formed two lines that began at stage-side and extended north all along both sides of the city road toward the airport. The banished man's family was first in line, followed by the members of Gold Tribe 6, and then the remaining Gold Villagers. The Verity Islanders fell in line with order and precision to quickly create a line of humanity three miles long.

The two guards then led the banished man off the stage and down the steps. They marched him in slow cadence as they approached the front of the line. The banished man faced his aged parents, who stood erect and opposite one another across the road. He looked from side to side at each parent as he walked between them.

"Shame!" the mother shouted, loud enough to make George flinch. The mother then turned her back to her son. The father then did the same thing. The young man froze. The guards jerked him forward. He bowed his head and continued down the line.

George removed his goggles and rubbed his eyes. The procession became two parallel lines of falling dominoes, choreographed with military precision. These Verity Islanders were clearly no strangers to this ceremony.

The "Shame!" chants grew muffled as the banished man made his way outside the city walls and down the road. Lima excused himself and disappeared into his bedroom. He returned minutes later wearing black tactical pants and polished black boots. He carried a large caliber handgun holstered at his waist. But it was his shirt that really caught George's eye—a brilliant white mock turtleneck that appeared incongruous with the rest of his outfit.

"We going somewhere?" George asked.

"Soon," was all Lima said.

They watched the banished man make his way further down the line, getting smaller and smaller in the distance. Lima checked his watch.

"Time to go," he said.

George followed Lima to the elevator and down to the secret subway station below Tower One. They took a northbound train. In three minutes they arrived at their stop, found the station elevator, and took it up to ground level. They emerged beside the road, about six miles outside the city and three miles from the airport at the northern tip of the island.

Lima's security team was already there: ten large men, dressed all in black. They stood across the road, near several white Mercedes SUVs. George recognized Noam and Ivan, and exchanged a silent greeting with them. Lima joined his men. They clustered together, and he spoke with them for ten minutes. Lima then crossed the road to rejoin George.

"What's up?" George asked.

"We wait," Lima responded. His demeanor had changed. He was somber and serious, as were his men across the road.

The men fixed their gaze on the crest of a hill, about half a mile south on the road toward Central City. George followed their gazes, not knowing what they were looking for. He decided it was best to not ask any more questions. He would stay close to Lima and follow his lead.

Thirty minutes passed in silence. The men occasionally swatted at insects and muttered obscenities. Then the small silhouette of the banished man, flanked by the two guards, crested the hill. He was now handcuffed in the front. The waiting men maintained their silence as the banished man approached. He was walking faster now that he had cleared the gauntlet of islanders.

The guards jerked the man to a stop in front of Lima. His shoulders were slumped, his face pale. Lima and his men regarded him impassively. The banished man stood, fidgeting, until he could endure the silence no longer.

"Uhm, sir?" he croaked. "Is this where I leave the island? Am I going by boat or air?"

"Yes," Lima responded.

Flanagan emerged from the back seat of one of the SUVs and walked over to Lima and the banished man.

"Are you the one taking me off the island?" the man asked him.

"Yes, son," Flanagan said. "In a manner of speaking."

He stood in front of the young man and gave him a soliloquy on banishment, and why it was essential to Verity society. He explained how a society needed common ideals and values, and laws and rules that supported these ideals. These laws required strict enforcement, and, when violated, swift accountability. To do otherwise courted anarchy and chaos. The banished man had broken Verity law and dishonored his family and tribe. He would be held accountable today.

Flanagan attended all Verity banishments, and he informed the man that he was number nine. He spoke of his profound sadness and disappointment in having to carry out these sentences.

The banished man's eyes darted from Flanagan to Lima and his men, then back again. He started to rock back and forth.

"I'm ready. I'm ready," the banished man said in a rushed staccato. "We can go any way you want, mister. Boat or plane. Don't matter none to me."

"Goodbye, son." Flanagan approached the banished man and kissed him lightly on the forehead. He gave Lima a sideways glance as he crossed the road to join the security team.

Lima stepped up now and stood toe-to-toe with the banished man. He looked him in the eye for an extended moment, which caused the man to squirm. Lima crossed himself, then drew a Karambit fixed blade from a sheath at the small of his back. In one fluid motion, he raked the tiger's claw deep and hard across the man's carotid artery. An arterial geyser of pulsating blood spewed from the gill sliced into the man's neck. Lima dropped his knife, then threw his head back and arms wide, assuming a pose of the crucifixion. His white shirt was instantly drenched in blood. In seconds, the banished man lost consciousness and went limp in the grasp of the guards. They released their hold on him as he bled out and crumpled to the ground, dead.

Lima crossed himself again, then bowed his head in a moment of silence. The rest of the security team held their positions. Lima carefully removed his bloody shirt, folded it, and placed it in a paper bag. George saw the web of angry scars that covered the entirety of Lima's broad back before he pulled a fresh black t-shirt over his head.

The security team now sprang into action. Two team members moved in quickly to drag the banished man across the road, where they folded his corpse into a ventilated black body bag. The men heaved the bag into the back of an SUV, and sped toward the boat dock, spraying gravel in their wake. The other team members cleaned the scene with the efficiency of a race car pit crew. They removed and replaced all the bloody road gravel. In ten minutes all traces of what had happened were gone.

George stood frozen in place. The world around him swirled in slow motion. He saw Flanagan and Lima staring at him from across the road. His stomach dropped. They motioned for George to join them. He crossed the road slowly on rubbery legs.

"Come, let's take a walk," Flanagan said as he guided George up the road with a hand on his shoulder. Lima joined them.

"Do you know why that was necessary, George?" Flanagan asked softly.

George shook his head.

"*Accountability*," Flanagan said. "People must be held accountable for their actions. The tribe, not the individual, is paramount. Truth resides with the tribe."

"I don't know," George said, rubbing his neck. "I'm not sure that was necessary."

"You were an FBI agent, George. You know your crime recidivism statistics," Flanagan countered. "Half of all crime is committed by only five percent of the population, and this population re-offends half the time within a year of their release from incarceration."

"I meant the killing part."

Flanagan's eyes hardened. "I programed my algorithms with statistics and logic, to favor accountability over mercy or forgiveness. Verity law is true but unyielding. It must be so. The tribe cannot survive with such transgressors in its midst."

"Why not just kick him off the island?"

"Accountability, George. I am accountable for him. And he to me. To show mercy or forgiveness would be a violation of Gold Tribe 6."

George looked down at his boots as he walked. He felt numb.

"Do you judge me too harsh, George?" Flanagan asked. "Hasn't our own country done similarly? We executed Julius and Ethel Rosenberg in 1953, did we not? And what was their offense? Conspiracy to commit espionage by seditious and disloyal acts—in their case selling atomic secrets to the Russians. Our banished man here today conspired to overthrow the duly appointed elder of his tribe, no less seditious a crime than that for which the Rosenbergs were condemned. The difference is, the Rosenbergs' treasonous acts betrayed the state, and as such were a political betrayal. Our banished man's treason betrayed his tribe, which is a *personal* betrayal. The Rosenbergs betrayed one hundred fifty million faceless fellow citizens in support of a political ideology. Our man betrayed one hundred tribe members; all he knew intimately, as they knew him. Greed and envy guided his treachery. He looked deep into the eyes of all he betrayed. The tribe, and by extension Verity society itself, cannot survive if such a betrayal is not avenged."

George slowed to a stop, and the three men stood in the middle of the road. The tops of the Central City towers gleamed over the rise of the hill in front of them. George exchanged a look with Lima, exhaled deeply once, then again.

"The people—villagers, the tribes—they all support this?" George asked both men.

Lima nodded and held his silence.

Flanagan responded. "You saw today's ceremony, did you not? The entire island was in attendance. Did you see any reluctance or enmity on the faces of the islanders? Or his tribe or family?"

"No, I guess not," George conceded. He returned his gaze toward the towers of Central City. The day's events rushed through his mind. "I dunno..."

"The American people widely supported the Rosenberg executions. We are no different here on Verity Island."

Flanagan allowed his words to hang in the air before he continued.

"Tribes, villages, cities, islands, countries... they all need strong leadership. And strong leaders sometimes have to do bad things for the greater good. That is what you witnessed here today. Do you understand, George?"

George nodded.

"General Washington understood this. He hanged his own soldiers to enforce rules and maintain troop discipline. He sometimes did bad things for the greater good." Flanagan turned to face George. "I see him in you, George."

"So do I," Lima said. He placed a hand on George's shoulder.

"The best leaders are reluctant to assume command," Flanagan said. "They do so only when necessary, and at great personal sacrifice. These are the indispensable men. General Washington was such a man. I believe you are as well."

"Why did you invite me here?" George asked. "What do you want of me?"

"I have a plan to stop General Taylor. You play a prominent role in that plan. Taylor is a powerful and dangerous enemy. We will have to do bad things if we are to prevail. I need to know that you are with us. I need to know if you are prepared to do some bad things."

The men now stood atop the hill in the middle of the gravel road. The skyline of Central City glimmered two miles in the distance.

George's mind raced. This was his do-or-die moment. His personal Crossing of the Delaware.

"I need to know that, if I do this, both of you are all in, to the end," George said.

Both men said they were.

"Then I'm in," George said, hoping he had not just struck a Faustian bargain.

The three men shook hands, then walked in silence together back to the SUVs. Flanagan instructed Lima to take George back to his penthouse. George offered his hand, but Flanagan instead stepped in for a quick embrace. He told George he was glad to have him on board, and that they would begin their operation straight away. They agreed to meet in the manor house study tomorrow afternoon. Flanagan turned and headed toward the SUV.

"Mr. Flanagan," George shouted.

Flanagan turned around. "Yes, George?"

"The sweeper's son, Cheng Zhou, in Village Blue. He had his passage a week or two ago. Did he make it?" George asked, with a slight catch in his voice.

"He did," Flanagan said, his face brightening. "The sweeper has done a fine job with that boy. Wouldn't surprise me if he makes tribe elder someday."

CHAPTER 47

They returned to the Tower One penthouse drained. It had been a long day for both men. The first order of business was to take hot showers and scrub the banishment from their bodies. George stood under the hot water for a long time.

He emerged from the bathroom to soft classical music floating through the large open room. Lima was already seated in a high-backed upholstered chair at the window. George sank deep into the matching chair opposite him. A neat bourbon waited on a coaster next to him. Lima had already started on his Bordeaux. A plate of fine cheese and roasted nuts sat on the low table between them.

"Started without you," Lima said. "Hope you don't mind."

"No worries," George replied.

Both men quickly emptied and refilled their glasses. They talked and ate little.

"How well do you know Henry, George?"

"Quite well. I've known him since I was five." George chuckled. "We're nothing alike. Henry's a cautious man. He's such a gentle soul."

Lima smirked, then paused before speaking.

"Henry's got a lot more Verity in him than you imagine, George. Mr. Flanagan does not align himself with cautious or gentle men."

George gave Lima a dubious look, which he absorbed without further comment. George awaited the warm numbness of his second bourbon to ask further questions.

He started slowly. "How did he get caught? The banished guy today, I mean."

"My source in Village Gold reported that the banished man had failed in his bid for tribal elder. He really wanted that village penthouse. Greed led to envy. Tried to overthrow the elder. To take what he failed to earn. Such a betrayal violates the stability of the entire tribe. I knew he was done as soon as I read the report."

"The banishments. The young boy who failed his tribal ritual. Does it ever get to you?"

"Mr. Flanagan created Verity for the same reason I've dedicated my life to it. To solve the world's biggest mystery—the meaning of life." Lima reached for a handful of Brazil nuts. "Mr. Flanagan looks to science and mathematics for his answers. I look elsewhere."

Lima smiled, tight-lipped; the corners of his mouth turned up slightly. They shared a comfortable silence. Then George had another question.

"I saw your back, earlier today, by the road," George said. "What… happened?"

Lima wiped the corner of his mouth with a cloth napkin. A delicate gesture for such a hard man. The discordance was striking.

"I was orphaned to the favela as a young boy. I stole what I needed to survive. The shopkeepers whipped me. When they could no longer catch me, they tried to kill me." Lima pointed to the scar that split his eyebrow and lined his forehead. "I killed the man who did this. He was the first." Lima sipped his wine. "I was an angry young man when I got to Verity. My instructors tamed my temper with the lash. They were right to do so. A man must tend the fire in his heart, or be consumed by it. General Washington knew this well."

Lima looked at George, and George felt the great Washington stir inside him. He took a long sip of bourbon. The topic could wait no longer.

"Luiz," he said. "The white shirt."

"Yes," Lima said. He studied George closely. "I want to show you something."

Lima walked George around the penthouse, stopping to show his prized artwork that hung on the walls. The same red-on-white inkblots George had noticed earlier. Lima had many more of these framed portraits stored in closets, and still hundreds more stored digitally on his iPad.

"What do you think?" Lima asked at the end of the tour.

"I'm not much of an art guy," George said. "They all kinda look the same to me."

"Do you recognize the artist?"

"No. I don't know any modern painters."

"Look again, George."

George studied the red blots.

"Today. At the road. The white shirt."

George's eyes widened. Of course. All that red—it was blood. Each portrait was the blood spatter of one of Lima's victims. *And there were hundreds of portraits.*

"Oh my God," George said as he slowly backed away.

"I suffered greatly as a child in Brazil," Lima said. "I asked God for help every day, but he never listened. So I helped myself. My first kill in the favela was self-defense. The rest were justified, at least as I saw it. When I was sixteen, I killed a corrupt cop, and afterwards saw the bloody outline of his face on my shirt. It scared me, and I hid it in a garbage pile. But I kept going back to that shirt, until I realized that God was speaking to me—through the men I killed. The blood spatter on each of my shirts is the spirit as it leaves the body. God, through these spirits, is teaching me the meaning of life."

George stared at Lima. His face was relaxed, with the innocence of a child.

"I never killed anyone who didn't earn it," Lima said.

"Women and children?"

"I've killed women. And children. They all had it coming."

George felt lightheaded, and returned to his seat. Lima refilled their glasses and joined him.

"Taught myself to paint," Lima said. "I paint every shirt. Got a climate-controlled storage unit for them all. I rotate the paintings on the wall. Study them at night, when I can't sleep. I still see the faces."

George clutched his bourbon. It shook in his hands. He watched the ice melt, stared at the sheen of alcohol on the inside of the glass.

He had been a respected FBI agent a mere two months ago. Now, he was arguably an accomplice to murder. Or a witness, at least. What to do? His mind raced—twenty-four years of law enforcement dies hard. Should he call the Alaska Troopers? Tell them everything? Help them arrest Lima and Flanagan? Did the troopers even have jurisdiction over Verity Island?

He took a shaky sip of bourbon and pondered all that had happened in his life these past two months. The Gardens, the cloning, Virginia, Verity. All of it. He was not the same man he had been before. He saw things differently now. Same frames, different lenses.

George had never really stopped to seriously consider the gravity of his situation—plotting the assassination of a sitting vice president. It had all been so personal for him, and he had not focused on the wider ramifications. He now knew how serious this business was going to be. And it would take serious people like Flanagan and Lima to do it.

He set his glass on the table and looked at Luiz, who looked back at him expectantly. George had already crossed his line, and would continue to the end. He followed Verity law now. He would do bad things. For the greater good.

"Luiz, I think—"

"I know how this must sound. But only sinners taste my blade. God speaks to me in their blood."

"What has He told you?"

"Many things," Lima said. "He told me of your arrival. He told me to follow you, that you would lead me to the truth. He told me you would help me find the answer to my question."

CHAPTER 48

The men crouched in the sandy dirt, their senses acute. The night would be black, thanks to the new moon and cloud cover. Their night vision goggles cut through the setting darkness and lit the world around them in a ghostly green glow. They took concealment near a small cedar kiosk. This seasonal gift shop was strategically located by the wharf, where many of the million-plus annual visitors disembarked to pay their respects to the father of their country—and buy swag.

George hid directly behind the shuttered kiosk, while Lima and another man, a forensic anthropologist named Alastair Evans, squatted in the brush twenty feet away. Evans was a Brit, mid-thirties and gawky, who had been selected due to his key role in the 2012 excavation of King Richard III after his remains were discovered buried under a parking lot in England.

Directly behind them a path rose from the beach to the mansion, less than half a mile away. George scanned the Potomac River, awaiting the rest of their team. Lima watched the hiking path to ensure no one approached from the rear.

Tonight was Step One of the Flanagan Plan. Flanagan had contacted Cabot after George had passed his banishment test and laid it all out for him. Given Cabot's current state of mind, he had readily agreed.

It had been a tough month for Cabot since he had left Verity Island to try—unsuccessfully, as it turned out—to regain his job at Harvard. A faculty friend had confided that General Taylor was indeed behind Cabot's fall from grace. He had orchestrated a plot that falsely alleged various academic improprieties, then exerted incremental pressure on the board until the university buckled. Other prominent historians, men and women Cabot had known and respected for decades, now publicly attacked him in the media. His former colleagues refused to speak with him. It had shaken Cabot to his core.

Taylor had succeeded in destroying Cabot's reputation by his mastery of the media. As vice president he had launched his own Internet media network, then dismissed the traditional White House–Capitol Hill press corps. His network was slick and colloquial: style over substance, message over facts. This propaganda platform had gone live thirty days ago and operated 24/7. It was free to the public, a simple mouse-click away. The American people loved it. Not surprisingly, it was this network that had broken the "story" that led to Cabot's dismissal.

And Cabot had other problems. With Hale's assistance, Taylor had hidden his Domestic Secret Police Force within the FBI. This shadowy force now had Cabot and his wife under warrantless surveillance around the clock. Virginia was receiving similar treatment down in Kentucky. George would surely be subject to more extreme measures if they could find him.

The Flanagan Plan had started with Margaret Dandridge Warner, president general of the Daughters of the American Revolution—or DAR, as it was known. Warner had been Cabot's wife Helen's college roommate. The two women had remained dear friends in the preceding fifty years since their graduation from Radcliffe College,

Class of '70. Warner had been born and raised in Charleston, South
Carolina, and carried herself with the refined dignity of a southern
belle. She was a thin, spare woman to whom age had struck but a
glancing blow. Now a wealthy widow, she ran her various
philanthropic activities from her stately home in Georgetown. She
threw lavish charitable fundraisers that were attended by all the
Washington power brokers. Anyone in the Beltway who mattered
dropped everything to take a call from Margaret Warner. Taylor had
eagerly accepted her invitation to be the keynote speaker at tonight's
A-list event.

George focused on his breathing to calm himself. *In, hold, out.*
Repeat. The crowd murmured a half-mile away, on the east lawn of
the mansion. He checked his watch: 8:39 p.m. The rest of the team
would arrive at 9:00 p.m., to coincide with the beginning of Taylor's
keynote speech. A charismatic public speaker, Taylor would surely
hold the attention of his audience as the six operators emerged
unnoticed from the depths of the Potomac.

Boisterous applause echoed through the woods. Then that voice.
His voice. George's gut tightened. Taylor's sonorous tones brought a
renewed sense of urgency to the task at hand. *This is really happening.*

The keynote speech was part of Flanagan's masterful strategy.
First, the video footage of Taylor paying tribute to General
Washington at his beloved estate would pay political dividends in the
future. Second, the speech proved a grand distraction to the Mount
Vernon security team and prevented the hounds from roaming the
grounds as they typically did at night. It also gave Warner a say in
the security plan that evening. She had taken full advantage of this
access to secretly install a computer virus that would wreak havoc on
the estate's video surveillance and communication systems tonight.

The keynote speech also brought Taylor to Mount Vernon—and
to Lima's team. The team's primary objective was to slip in and out
of the estate undetected, but should Murphy crash the party, Lima

had the authority to pivot his team to hunt and kill Taylor before he left the grounds of Mount Vernon.

9:06 p.m. George stared anxiously at the Potomac. *Where are they?* These men were always on time. They needed to take care of their business and be back in the water by the end of Taylor's speech.

The six-man team arrived two minutes later. They slowly rose like ghosts from the water, barely causing a ripple in the black Potomac. The green glow of George's night vision goggles made their approach all the more surreal. They wore matte black wetsuits, full-face masks with integrated night vision/underwater goggles, and air rebreathers. They emerged from the Potomac in assault formation, rifles at low ready, muzzles suppressed. They crept toward the beach in unison, a lethal free-fire circle with one man in front, one behind, and two on each side. Noam was on point. George instantly recognized him by his size and gait.

Lima gave George a silent thumbs-up when his men reached the beach, and they joined him behind the kiosk. Lima and Evans left their position and joined the group. Lima conducted a final thirty-second ops check.

"You ready, George?" Noam whispered.

"He's good," Lima immediately replied.

George nodded at Noam. The entire team understood the significance of what they were about to do. They had just invaded Mount Vernon, General Washington's beloved five-hundred-acre estate. *As the general's clone, isn't this all now really mine? Aren't I now standing on my beach? Am I home, or trespassing, as the others?* He shook the thoughts away. *Focus.*

Lima stacked his men. Three operators, single file, in the front and rear, with George, Evans, and Lima in the middle of the stack. Noam was on point.

On Noam's hand signal, the team silently left the beach and began to ascend the path, under a canopy of towering pecan, poplar, and walnut trees planted by General Washington himself. George's heart boomed in his chest. He fought to slow his breathing and move as silently as the operators that surrounded him.

The team trotted down the quarter-mile path to arrive at their objective. Located in a clearing, the tomb was built in 1831 of red brick and marble and was enclosed within a modern six-foot-high black wrought iron fence. A high lancet gothic arch, guarded on each side by two aged white marble obelisks, provided access to the interior of the tomb. The arch had a locked gate, as did the perimeter fence. George gaped at the ornate marble sarcophagus inside the tomb, visible from the perimeter. There was another plain sarcophagus to the left, in which the team had no interest. They had come for the one on the right, which had sat undisturbed since 1837.

Four operators posted up, one at each corner of the perimeter fence. The rest of the team stood in silence in front of the first locked gate. Taylor's disembodied voice, amplified by the loudspeakers, echoed through the trees. The sentry operators scanned the forest, then gave the go-ahead signal. Warner's handiwork had blinded the security cameras at this sacred site. The clock was ticking.

The breach team easily defeated the perimeter gate and crossed the courtyard pavers to the brick tomb. The tomb's entry arch was twelve feet high by six feet wide, and guarded by the same black wrought iron as the perimeter fence. Centered above the arch was an inscribed stone tablet. George's knees buckled as he read it:

"Within this Enclosure Rest the remains of Gen.'l George Washington."

The operators cleared the interior of the tomb, then stood frozen at its entrance. One man crossed himself. The other mumbled something George didn't catch. Lima came in behind the men, clasped both on the shoulder. They spun around and took up positions outside the tomb's entrance.

George, Lima, and Evans passed through the arch and into the tomb. Two marble sarcophagi, one inscribed "Washington," the other "Martha, Consort of Washington," lay five feet apart. A simple ceremonial wreath sat between them.

"Get started," Lima said to the scientist. "We don't have much time."

Evans tugged on the lid of the Washington sarcophagus. "Worth a try," he said with a laugh.

Lima ended his attempt at levity with a hard stare.

The scientist then pulled off his pack and removed a cordless circular saw. He put on goggles and earplugs, then tested it. The saw sprang to life in his hands, and a high-pitched buzz reverberated off the walls of the small tomb. George and Lima fixed their own goggles and earplugs. Evans again revved the saw, then applied it to the marble. The din increased tenfold as the diamond blade fought the ancient stone. George pulled a long drinking hose from his ten-liter hydration pack and streamed water on the front tip of the blade to keep it from seizing.

Evans was making steady progress around the lid when suddenly the saw groaned to a stop. He repeatedly clicked the trigger switch. Nothing. He then jerked the saw out of the marble, held it up to his face, examined it closely, then shook it violently. He hit the trigger switch again. No use.

Lima looked at his watch. "Fix it."

"This never happened before," Evans said. "It's a new saw. Fresh batteries," he said, offering the saw toward Lima. "I don't know what's wrong." He shook it again, played with it, slapped at the trigger. Nothing.

"We green or red here?" Lima asked tersely. Evans shrugged his shoulders and stepped back.

Lima summoned one of the operators into the tomb. "Blow this lid off. Nice and pretty. Just a kiss."

"Uhm, I don't know, boss," the operator stammered. "That saw was loud enough. We blow this, and we bring the cavalry down on us."

Lima turned to Evans, who had taken refuge beside George. "Can you do it—fast?"

"I don't know. I guess so," Evans stammered. "But the blast may damage the bones, contaminate the sample."

"And no promises I don't scatter the general all over this tomb," the operator added.

Lima rubbed his hands over his face, then spoke. "Let's ask the man himself. George… this is your house. What should we do?"

George did not hesitate. "Blow it."

Lima grinned. "You heard the man. Blow it."

The operator set a small Semtex charge, using the partial cut Evans had made as his marker. They all rushed from the tomb to the perimeter fence, gave the "fire in the hole" signal to the rest of the team, and braced for the blast. It was loud. Too loud. Everyone on the estate must have heard it. George's mental clock activated, its sweeping second-hand mercilessly spinning. Lima waved George back into the tomb; Evans followed.

Just enough of the marble lid had blown off. Evans reached in and cleared the debris. The inner lead casket was intact. Evans fumbled with the sharp knife, slicing a finger as the blade fell from his hand to the ground. It took him almost a minute on hands and knees to find it among all the marble shards on the tomb's floor. Lima pulled him to his feet, shook him, then pointed to the casket. This served to focus Evans, who got to work cutting lead. He leaned into the shattered sarcophagus, bent at the waist. His knife easily sliced through the soft lead. At last, he lifted the severed top of the lead casket and gasped. George and Lima rushed in for a look.

The skeleton of General Washington lay on top of the jagged lead tray; it had survived the blast in rough anatomical order. A few fragments of linen lay among the dust and faded bones. The skeleton appeared to match the general's height and frame. George's eyes were drawn to the head of the casket, to the general's skull and a tuft of reddish-brown hair. *The same reddish-brown hair as my own.*

Evans eased George and Lima away from the casket and continued his work. He took some establishing photographs, then bagged a hair sample and placed it in his pack, which was perched on a broken block of marble on the floor. He then retrieved the cadaver femur from the pack and returned to the casket, where he stood silently for a moment. He exhaled hard and closed his eyes; George saw his lips move in silent prayer. Evans then reached back into the casket, removed the general's right femur bone, and placed it in a sealed bag. He initialed over the seal, then gently placed it in his pack. The false cadaver bone was then placed exactly where the general's femur had been. Evans pulled his hands out of the casket, staggered back a few steps and began to hyperventilate. He wiped his dripping bloody finger on his pant leg.

Lima listened to something outside, barked commands into his throat mic, and then turned to George and Evans. "We got company. Time to go. Now."

George grabbed his pack and ran from the tomb to join the rest of the team at the perimeter gate. Lima emerged last, pushing Evans in front of him.

"Okay, let's go," Lima shouted. "Back to the—"

George heard a commotion and spun his head to the right. A group of Taylor's men were rushing down the path toward him, suppressed handguns rising to target acquisition. As George drew his weapon, the men's heads exploded with a *thwack* into a pulpy crimson mist and the remains of their bodies thudded to the ground.

Lexington and Concord. The shots heard round the world.

The team re-stacked and sprinted down the path toward the beach. George was in the middle, Evans behind him. Lima ran behind Evans, pushing and jostling him like a rag doll. A second group of men now chased them, yelling and indiscriminately shooting from 150 feet to their rear. The path descended sharply as it approached the beach. Lima held Evans upright so he would not stumble and take them all down like dominoes.

The stack split up as it hit the beach. The six operators sprinted the length of the wharf and dove into the Potomac. They submerged and disappeared into the river. They would swim across to the Maryland side, to be extracted by another team. No one would be looking for them in Maryland.

George and Lima had an overland escape route, which was more dangerous. And they had Evans to contend with. The group took a hard right at the beach, toward Pioneer Farm, a four-acre clearing where General Washington had experimented with various new farming practices of his own design.

They reached the edge of the clearing just as their pursuers emerged from the wooded path on the opposite side. Muzzle flash lit up the night. George plunged into the woods, Lima guarding their rear. George bushwhacked through the dense forest to the extraction vehicle, which he hoped awaited their arrival a half-mile away at the far northwest point of the 500-acre estate.

Evans was slowing them down; he was out of shape and had not bargained on this race to safety. George and Lima ran with resolve. It was not the first time they had been shot at. But Evans was shutting down, his movements spasmodic. Lima had him by the scruff of the neck, driving him forward. More gunfire to their rear. Men shouting, cursing. Stray bullets zipped past them, splintering trees to his right and left. They kept running.

George threw up a closed fist as he approached the woods' edge. Lima jerked Evans to a dead stop. George was breathing hard, sweat-soaked in the July humidity. Evans was right behind him, doubled over and heaving for breath. Through the green glow of his night vision, George saw the silhouette of a vehicle parked off the estate exit road. It was directly in front of them and across a cut-grass field that resembled a landing strip. Lima said something into his mic, and the headlights flashed twice. He slapped George on the back, and George took off across the field with all the remaining strength he could muster. Lima followed, dragging Evans.

Another bullet whizzed by. More gunshots and muzzle flashes. Their pursuers were gaining ground.

The side door to the minivan slid wide. George sprinted toward the cavernous opening. Time lagged; his vision blurred to slow motion for the last twenty-five feet.

He dove head first into the minivan. Evans landed on top of him. Lima slammed the side door shut and jumped into the passenger seat. They took more fire as the van sped away. The three men immediately began to strip off their clothes and gear.

The van raced down the exit road, then went south for two miles on Route 235. They did the first of several planned vehicle swaps, ditching the van in favor of a nondescript sedan. They concealed their gear in a hidden compartment built into the back seat, then threw on fresh sets of clothes. The sedan headed south on the Richmond Highway. Just four guys heading home after a night on the town.

They were counting on out-racing the roadblocks that would come. They crossed I-95; no sirens or flashing lights in sight. A good omen. They would take back roads to Charlottesville, then Roanoke. With luck they would be in Charlotte, NC, by daybreak.

"Jesus… you killed them!" Evans screeched. "You *killed* them. You—"

Lima whirled to face him. His icy stare pushed Evans back into his seat like an invisible blow.

"I mean… I'm not gonna say anything," Evans pleaded, his palms up in surrender, his head bobbing from side to side. "I'm not."

"I know you're not," Lima responded with a tight smile. He shifted his gaze toward George and looked down at Evans's bloody hand. George's eyes widened in dismayed understanding, and Lima turned back around in his seat. And that was it. It was over for Evans. Just like that. He would not see Charlotte. He had cut his finger, left his blood on the floor of the tomb. They would identify him, but never find his body.

George turned his face to the darkness out his side window. The heavy bass beat of his heart filled his ears.

After a few moments, Evans nudged George, leaned in and whispered, "I'm not gonna tell. Really. You guys can trust me." He smiled weakly, then faced forward again. "Everything's gonna be all right," he said to himself. "Everything's gonna be all right."

The dead man's weak smile would come to haunt George.

In his first fifty years, George had never once broken the law— never even stolen a pack of gum. In the past month, since visiting Verity Island, he had taken part in the killing of six men, including Evans.

Bad things for the greater good.

CHAPTER 49

George sat erect, his fingers laced in his lap in a grip that turned his knuckles crimson. Grace and Cabot flanked him on the sofa, with Lima at the right hand of his boss, across the table that separated the two groups. Morning coffee sat untouched on leather coasters.

George and Lima had returned to Verity less than forty-eight hours ago. Their escape from Mount Vernon to Seattle had been grueling; neither man had slept on the cross-country flight from Charlotte, or during the seventeen-hour drive up the West Coast from Los Angeles. George had caught a catnap on the helicopter to Verity, but it had not been nearly enough. He was not blindfolded as before.

Flanagan excused himself to retrieve his reading glasses from his grand oak desk, then crossed the study to rejoin the group by the fireplace. He pulled a single document from a folder and handed it to George. It shook in his hand as he scanned its contents; he sharply released the document as if it had bitten him, and it fell to the floor like an autumn leaf.

"Congratulations, George... or should I say, General Washington?" he said, breaking into a wide smile George had not seen before. He held out his hand, which George shook robotically.

My God! It's true. I am George Washington.

The confiscated femur had yielded good mitochondrial DNA, but, unlike the fully sequenced nuclear DNA sample previously swabbed from George's cheek, General Washington's fragmented mtDNA had to be amplified and directly sequenced to create sufficient base pairs for conclusive comparison.

Verity Lab had compared the amplified mtDNA of General Washington to George's cheek swab, and using standard Bayesian analysis, had concluded to a 99.9999 percent scientific probability that the samples were an identical match. Additional radiocarbon and stable isotope testing had dated the femur to the American Revolution period.

George had first learned he was him from Cabot, on that bench in Boston over two months ago. He had tried to believe, but a part of him still thought this one big mistake. That there was still a chance he could return to who he always was. Cold facts and dispassionate laboratory analysis disabused him of this notion. *99.9999% scientific probability.* The words slammed George like a fist. He felt it now. Truly felt the weight of it.

Grace retrieved the document from the floor and handed it to Flanagan, who returned the document to its folder and placed it on the table. Flanagan removed his glasses, searched George's face for reaction.

George gripped his thighs to arrest his vertigo. He gulped air with the urgency of a drowning man. He felt the stares upon him. They waited. Time stopped.

"I didn't ask for any of this," George said, finally, in a voice barely above a whisper.

"I know," Cabot responded. He and Flanagan exchanged a furtive look.

"And I didn't ask for this either," George said, more loudly now, pointing at the folder on the table, his mouth twisted in a scowl.

Flanagan's face clouded. "Agreed. It was my decision."

"That femur killed five men, including one of our own—Evans, the scientist," George said.

"Yes, I know, George," Flanagan said. "Regrettable, but necessary."

"Necessary for who?" George shouted.

"In time you will understand," Flanagan responded. "I did this for both of us. I needed to be sure before we continued any further, and you needed to know to do the things I will require of you in the days ahead."

George felt chilled.

Lima cleared his throat and began his after-action report. No viable witnesses or evidence had been left behind. The drops of Evans's blood recovered in the tomb would not match any U.S. databases. Media coverage was extensive, but the next step in their plan would redirect attention to their advantage. They had only to stay on the offensive, maintain one step ahead of Taylor.

Lima ended his briefing.

George rose and walked to the fireplace, where he stood with his back to the group. "What's our next move?"

"Please sit down, George," Flanagan said. "We have much to discuss."

George gripped the top of the marble railing that enclosed the expansive patio deck directly outside the second floor of Flanagan's study. The morning sun had warmed the marble. George closed his eyes and absorbed its stored radiant heat. The crisp mountain air was a cold drink of water on the back of his parched throat. The view was sublime: 200,000 acres of verdant forest encircled by snow-capped mountains in the distance.

"Thanks a lot. How the hell am I ever going to look at a dollar bill again?"

George spun around. Grace wore a soft, off-white sundress that hugged her body. She flashed George a smile, the same smile that had sold millions of magazines. She approached. George forgot all about the view.

"I imagine a woman like you doesn't have much use for dollar bills," he said.

"Think of the damage I could do at Neiman's Washington's Day Sale when I roll in there with you on my arm."

George laughed, in spite of himself. "Think they call it Presidents' Day now." The fact that he would never have this exquisite woman in his life darkened his already somber mood.

They turned back to the view. Stood close, enjoying the silence. Together, at least for a moment.

CHAPTER 50

TUESDAY, JULY 27, 2021; 9:18 P.M. (EDT)
GEORGE WASHINGTON'S MOUNT VERNON; MANSION RESIDENCE
MOUNT VERNON, VIRGINIA

They sipped tea in the room that General Washington added to the mansion while he was away fighting the British. The general had remained immersed in the details of Mount Vernon throughout the war, and said of this room in a letter to his caretaker: *"I would have the whole executed in a masterly manner."* The general had got what he wanted.

He had called it his "New Room": a grand two-story salon, itself larger than most colonial homes of its time. It was here that the general had received distinguished visitors and large parties.

Tonight's guests sat at a long rectangular dining table, across from the large Palladian window that dominated the north wall. Two open exterior doors at each end of the room provided a cross-breeze that cut the evening humidity.

Lima had smuggled them onto Mount Vernon under cover of darkness. It was his second operation on the estate in less than a week. He hoped no one died this time. He and his men would provide a secure perimeter in the woods around the mansion, then extract the group when the event was over. The hardest part would be the eighteen sleepless hours in the woods, maintaining their hyper-vigilance among the swarms of buzzing insects.

Cabot introduced George and Virginia to Margaret Warner, the long-standing DAR president general who held the keys to Mount Vernon.

Warner was a WASP from the Bible Belt who had fled north to attend "that Yankee school," Radcliffe College. She had raised eyebrows within the Charleston cotillion clique when she had rejected a fine southern gentleman, matched to her by her father, and married a liberal New York City Harvard Jew she'd met during her sophomore year. Upon her husband's untimely death, she had inherited his immense fortune, as well as his liberal activism.

Thus Warner, in her late forties, had become one of the wealthiest women in the country. For the past twenty-five years she had worked tirelessly through her many philanthropic non-profits on behalf of the working middle-class poor still clinging to the American Dream. She had become an astute student of power—the coin of the realm in the nation's capital—and had also become quite adept at wielding it. Beneath Warner's polished deportment lurked a bare-knuckled brawler who relished a good fight. She despised those who abused the power entrusted to them, and over the years had prostrated many a Beltway bully who made the fatal mistake of misjudging her. She viewed the imperialistic General Taylor as one such bully.

"So good to see you again, Henry," Warner said. "I haven't felt like this since the Vietnam protests. Remember the time when we broke into the Harvard registrar's office and occupied it for almost a week?"

"Yes," Cabot responded with an impish grin. "That was a long time ago."

"Yeah, and you're still not backing down from a good fight," Warner said. "Seems every time we get together laws get broken, Henry," she said through a wide smile.

Cabot had told Warner enough to secure her cooperation, but nothing more. She was initially incredulous, then skeptical, then hesitant. It had taken a long telephone call with Cabot's wife Helen to bring her around. Three days ago, Cabot had shared the DNA results with her in order to secure Mount Vernon as the venue for Flanagan's next chess move, scheduled for tomorrow at 2:00 p.m. on the east lawn of the mansion.

"I have fallen in love with this place over the years," Warner said now, with a flourish of her hand. "The general's spirit still inhabits his beloved Mount Vernon. I stroll the estate grounds most days, before we open to the public. I feel his presence in the early morning silence. Hear the clip-clop of his horse echo in the distance." Her eyes moistened. "And now, to be seated across from him—you—in this moment... I just... just—"

"I know," Cabot responded. He reached out and lightly grasped Warner's arm. "I have lived with this secret for the past fifty years, and I still struggle with it. As a historian, and a friend."

Warner had hosted every living U.S. president, foreign heads of state, billionaires, and all manner of celebrities at this estate—and had done so with impeccable dignity and grace. This same woman now trembled in George's presence.

All major print and electronic media outlets would gather on the east lawn of the mansion tomorrow at 2:00 p.m., expecting an update on the tomb bombing, as it was being called. The entire estate would be closed, with the full estate security team concentrated on the east lawn and the estate's outer perimeter. Lima's team would already be in place, unbeknownst to Warner.

"Are you ready, George?" asked Cabot.

"Just need to make some final changes to the address."

"We all look forward to hearing it," Warner said.

George nodded. "I want to thank you for all your help, Ms. Warner."

"Margaret, please," she said. "And I am proud to stand with you. General Taylor is a menace to the people of this country, and he must be stopped. When Henry gave me your DNA results, I knew in my heart I had to act."

"I apologize about the tomb," George said. "We wouldn't have blown it unless we had to."

"We?" Warner said with raised eyebrows. "Now I've been around long enough to know what questions not to ask. So I will not press you for details." She sipped her tea. "I must say, however, that I am deeply conflicted about the loss of life. Those four men. They may have been Taylor's men, but their families were not," she said, shaking her head. "I've reached out and established funds for the widows and orphans of those men." She paused. "All anonymous and untraceable, of course."

"Ms. Warner," Virginia said. "Those men were trying to kill George. He acted in self-defense."

"Make no mistake," Warner said, looking in turn into the faces of everyone at the table. "What George is about to do tomorrow will result in his murder indictment for the killing of those men. They will push for the death penalty. Taylor will see to it."

"I guess I'll just have to put my faith in the American people," George said. "That they'll see the truth and do the right thing."

"Rest assured, Margaret, I will do all in my power to limit the further loss of life," Cabot said. It was a heartfelt pledge, but not his to make, as taking human life was Lima's domain.

They finished their discussion of the logistics for tomorrow's event. The white taper candles on the table had burned to nubs, wax dripping onto their pewter holders. It had been a long day. George was exhausted and needed a good night's sleep.

Everyone stood to say their goodnights.

"One more thing," Warner said. "I've changed this evening's room assignments." She stepped around the table to George, took his hands in hers. "I want you to feel his spirit when you are up at that podium tomorrow. I've moved you from the yellow room into the Washington Bedchamber." Her hands began to shake. "The general drew his final breath lying in the canopy bed in this room. After his death, Martha closed it, and it has remained so since 1799. Until tonight. Tonight, you will sleep in the general's bed."

Warner appeared smaller, more vulnerable, standing next to George in the withering candlelight. She stood chest-high to him, craning her head back to search his eyes.

"Oh my God..." Warner mumbled at last. She reached up and gently touched his hair, then traced his chin with a jittery finger. George felt something give way inside. He fought to contain his emotion, as General Washington had been a famously stoic man, and he did not want to disappoint her.

Cabot led the group across the mansion, through the general's private study to the back staircase, which was narrow. The aged wooden treads groaned under George's heft. As they were the identical height and build, George imagined the general navigating this tight space by candlelight—the first of many déjà vu flashes he would experience in the coming twenty-four hours.

The staircase led them to a small landing on the second floor. The general's bedchamber was located opposite the landing. Its door was open, without the barrier normally in place to keep the tourists out.

The three stood crammed on the landing in front of the door, gawking in silence, as if the threshold emitted a force field denying entry. The bedchamber was one of the larger rooms in the house, with a low ceiling and white walls and robin's-egg blue molding. Fine French mahogany furnishings filled the room. The canopy bed, dressed in sheer cloth and white ruffled bedding, stood perpendicular to the door. The oversized bed had been custom made in Philadelphia in the early 1790s, as the general stood head and shoulders above his peers and could not fit his frame into any standard bed of his time.

The faint tick of the mantel clock marked the time. But time and space had become slippery concepts to George. Was the door to the bedchamber a time portal? When he crossed this threshold, would he remain in 2021, or transport back to 1799?

Virginia clasped George's right hand and Cabot clasped his left. They stepped forward and crossed the threshold together. George ran his hand gently along the bedding. Virginia and Cabot both traced the bed frame with their fingertips. All three stood frozen in place, unsure of what to do next. Finally, Cabot broke the silence and hugged George goodnight. Virginia did likewise. Her embrace lingered; her eyes teared when she pulled away. Cabot took Virginia's hand and led her from the room.

———————————

George jerked awake. He was fully clothed, on his back on top of the bed. He had never considered crawling under the bed covers, out of respect.

He had survived the night. George did not believe in spooks or spirits, and never expected to arise inhabited by Washington's ghost. But sitting in silence on the edge of the bed, he did feel *something* in this room. He stood and walked about, exploring the whole of it. Sliding drawers open, picking up items for closer examination. He began to feel more comfortable in the room, and in his own skin.

———————————

George met Cabot and Virginia downstairs in the dining room for coffee and breakfast. His nervous stomach would not accept much food, but he downed four cups of coffee. The three then wandered the empty estate grounds.

They strolled the paths that laced the estate, taking in the upper and lower gardens and orchards. The temperature and humidity rose. George swiped perspiration from his eyes.

They walked to the general's tomb. The perimeter fence and gate had been fortified, and still bore the remnants of an FBI crime scene. Warner had called in high favors to get the FBI to officially release the tomb so she could re-open the estate to the public. Cabot and Virginia examined the defiled tomb, then the three returned to the mansion in somber silence.

"It be a fine day for an address, Your Excellency," Warner said in perfect eighteenth-century pitch. "May providence be with you."

George bowed. Warner returned a curtsy.

Warner said the estate security staff was all ready and taking their positions. George had spoken with Lima this morning; he and his team had spent an uneventful night hidden in the nearby woods.

George excused himself from the group. He would meet the media in less than two hours, and wanted to spend his remaining time reviewing his address in the general's study. He had written the address in one long night at Verity Island, and it had never left his custody. He was as ready as he ever would be. He rose from his chair and paced the study. As in the bedchamber this morning, George was calmed by examining and holding the general's personal possessions.

He washed and dressed right there in the study, just as the general had done. When finished, he checked his watch: 1:45 p.m. Time to go.

George paced the mansion's foyer. The buzzing of the media grew louder outside. He shook out his hands and rolled his neck. Warner arrived first, Cabot and Virginia together a few minutes later.

Warner reviewed how she would bring George out and get him to the podium. He nodded, as a fighter does when receiving pre-fight instructions from the referee. She wished him well, then disappeared through the door to face the media horde waiting on the east lawn. Cabot and Virginia embraced George in turn, then walked away. Virginia froze at the door, turned to George once more, and pounded her fist against her heart, two times, with force. The blows echoed in the small foyer. She spun and walked out the door.

George stood erect, eyes closed, clenching his fists and rhythmically rocking side to side. Awaiting the bell.

His eyes shot open when Warner called his name. George strode to the door and threw it open. The bright lights and crowd noise blinded him momentarily. He stepped out onto the piazza, a stunning two-story covered patio at the back of the mansion. The crowd sat in white folding chairs, laid out in matching rows, with a wide middle isle centered on the podium. The Potomac glistened in the background.

George greeted Warner at the podium. They shared a nervous smile, then she took the seat nearest him, next to Cabot and Virginia.

The crowd, all expectant but unknowing, murmured at the sight of him.

George gripped the sides of the podium. He took a deep breath, and began to speak.

CHAPTER 51

Cheng Zhou scurried over the azure pathway, just short of a trot. He had scheduled his weekly Internet hour at the Village Café for nine a.m. this morning, and he didn't want to waste a minute of it. He whisked past old man Thompson, who lived with his son's family two floors above him in Unit 302, Tribe 3, Village Blue. The elder frowned as the boy extended him the tribal greeting without breaking stride.

Cheng had been counting down the days since his last session. Last week, the Internet had been ablaze over the second coming of George Washington, or GW2 as he had been dubbed. An independent Harvard geneticist had performed the DNA match, largely muting critics and conspiracy theorists. GW2 had exploded overnight into a worldwide sensation that almost melted the Internet. All the polls showed him with a double-digit lead over a Parker/Taylor ticket should an auxiliary presidential election be held. The administration responded with a clumsy smear campaign that only boosted GW2's popularity. The country awaited their opportunity to go to the voting booth and select their new president.

All this political theater interested the boy, as a carnival would, but what pulled him to the café this morning was his realization that GW2 was none other than the outsider who had visited his family last month. He was the first outsider the boy had ever met, and now this man was the center of a global media hurricane. He couldn't wait to see what had happened this past week.

The boy arrived at the café a few minutes early. He slunk over to the coffee station, furtively glanced about, then poured himself a cup. He had just started to drink coffee and did not want anyone, particularly any girls, to see him fumbling with the coffee maker and assortment of condiments.

He focused on his mug as he walked to his assigned terminal, careful not to spill.

The terminal was empty! What luck. Village kids were always running over their allotted time. Getting them off the Internet was worse than getting toddlers to sleep.

Cheng jumped into the chair and logged on. The screen blinked off, delayed, then flickered on again to display a strange image. He frowned. This was not Google search, his usual default page, but something entirely different.

A large photograph of an unsmiling man, in uniform, centered on a dark background.

Cheng furrowed his brow, typed "www.google.com" into the search bar, and hit enter. The same unsmiling man appeared. He checked his saved browser bookmarks—gone. He then tried direct news searches, typing New York Times, CNN, Fox News, Buzzfeed. Nothing. Frantically he tried YouTube, but it was also gone. He logged out and back in several times to no avail. The Verity Island intranet was working fine, but the Internet appeared to be broken.

Cheng frantically rebooted the computer, but again found himself staring at the unsmiling man. He waited a full minute before clicking on the photo, which linked him to a video of the same unsmiling man, standing in front of an oversized American flag. Martial music blared from his computer. The boy whacked at the keyboard to lower the volume. The music rose to a crescendo, then faded away.

General Taylor then began to speak.

On the opposite end of Verity Island, about forty miles north as the crow flies, a man, completely unknown to Cheng, spoke on an encrypted satellite telephone.

Flanagan spoke to his deep cover source, a source with direct and current access to Taylor. This source had leaked him an advance copy of Taylor's First Citizen Proclamation. The same proclamation Cheng had just watched in disbelief at the Village Blue Café.

Provoking Taylor into military dictatorship had been easier than Flanagan had imagined, but it was always easier to nudge a man in the direction he longs to go. Flanagan had pressed his source on Taylor's intentions and current state of mind. Battlefield intelligence, as his source called it.

George's clone bombshell, and his call for an auxiliary presidential election, was an unexpected first strike that had unnerved and infuriated Taylor. The source explained that Taylor was on war footing now, and that things were about to get much worse.

But Flanagan's first strike had pushed Taylor off his game, making him impatient, more prone to error and impulsive action. Taylor was accustomed to imposing his will upon his enemy, not responding to their dictates. General Taylor had not been punched in the mouth in years. He was angry and hungry for revenge.

Flanagan ended the call and smiled. His plan was working perfectly.

PART III

The time is near at hand which must determine whether Americans are to be free men or slaves.

— George Washington

The die is cast.

— Julius Caesar

CHAPTER 52

Friday, August 6, 2021; 10:05 a.m. (EDT)
Pedestrian Mall; White House North Lawn
Washington, DC

"*We are voters—put up a fight! No fascist dictator can steal our rights!*"

The listless crowd stirred.

"Again! Louder!" Judith Unger shrieked into Gloria, the bedazzled bullhorn that was her trademark. Her thin voice cracked in exhortation, betraying her age. Unger had not been on the streets in years, preferring to pontificate in the posh studios of the New York and Los Angeles media she now considered colleagues.

Unger exhorted her crowd again, with similar results. The chant, which she had hastily crafted, appeared to tongue-tie her audience. Perhaps too many consonants? Or simply just too many words to spit out?

It had only been four days since General Taylor's First Citizen Proclamation. Unger had scrambled all her resources and media contacts to rush this protest on the Pedestrian Mall, just outside the North Lawn of the White House. She had to be first.

She dropped Gloria to her side and inspected the gray skies. She had not planned for rain, and worried it would ruin her hair and

RICK BOSWORTH

makeup. She knew she was an imposter, a fraud, and that this was nothing more than performance art for the cameras. No matter. She and Gloria beat them all to the punch. She would lead the national news—what was left of it—tonight.

Unger tried again. *"Hey hey, ho ho! General Taylor has got to go!"*

This chant was picked up with more vigor by the crowd. Unger looked over at the camera, pleased to see it capturing the growing swell. In the can. They would get together later and edit out the rest.

Unger had been a naive eighteen-year-old in '68 at the Chicago Democratic National Convention, but had become a staunch social rights activist at the many anti-war and women's rights protests that followed. She'd burned out after Watergate, however, and had failed to find a national audience during the Carter and Reagan administrations. But Bill Clinton and CNN had changed all that. Political correctness and a twenty-four-hour news cycle had revitalized her career. Unger cleaned up nice for the camera, spoke in sound bites, and could feign outrage on any given issue. Add savvy marketing and branding (people loved Gloria), and she had become America's favorite complainer.

As much as the past fifty years had extinguished her idealism, Unger maintained her reverence for the Bill of Rights and First Amendment, which she employed as both shield and sword. The freedoms of speech, press, and assembly had built her empire. They were living breathing allies to her, not abstract concepts inked with quill pens on crinkled parchment 230 years ago. These magical ten amendments were what kept the tyrants at bay, and what had put her children through Ivy League schools.

Unger had never imagined she would live to see the day her civil rights were taken away by a U.S. Army general turned military dictator. Today's America made '68 Chicago look like a Girl Scout picnic, Watergate mere folly. Today's protest against Taylor would secure her legacy. She'd choreographed it down to the finest detail.

She knew the dance. She would play her part, and expected others to do the same. Her staff had paid the hundred or so "outraged" protesters to gather at the appointed place and time. These paid protesters knew what to do, and the dusting of true hard-cores (Unger called them "the Guy Fawkes Gang") added a little spice to the crowd. Unger would lead this crowd in a few chants, they would wave signs, Unger would do her interview with the bottle-blonde reporter, and then White House security would shoo them away. All would be caught on film and edited down to a tight two minutes that could capture America's ever-shrinking attention span.

It should have been that easy.

The uniformed White House security officers arrived too soon. They wore riot helmets and tactical vests in place of their usual white shirt/black pants mall security uniforms. The helmets' tinted face shields hid their intentions. Fifty officers formed a skirmish line, backs against the ten-foot black iron fence that separated the North Lawn and the protesters. They stood erect, hands down at their sides, like Western gunslingers. They remained motionless and silent. A supervisor spoke into his shoulder mic but otherwise made no effort to engage the crowd. Unger had led numerous protests on this spot over the decades but had never observed this behavior from these officers.

Unger's blood chilled. Gloria dropped to her side. The paid protesters mustered a few more half-hearted chants, then went silent. Shouted obscenities from the Guy Fawkes Gang drew no response from the officers. Unger turned around to address the gang, and saw the rock sail above her in a slow-motion arc toward the officers. It flew well over their heads and bounced harmlessly onto the North Lawn. She exhaled deeply. The supervisor spoke into his shoulder mic again.

Unger heard them first. The rhythmic beat of their boots as they marched double time toward the crowd, banging their batons in time against the protective shields they carried in front of them, in modified Roman phalanx formation. The line of soldiers fanned out twenty feet in front of the crowd, shields up. The uniformed officers closed rank behind them. The soldiers announced their arrival with a crisp guttural yell that buckled Unger's knees.

The silence was eerie. The crowd, unsettled, now looked to Unger to do something. They would follow her lead. She would get them out of this somehow.

Unger began to sweat, running her makeup in the rising August humidity. She drew a few deep breaths to steady herself. She could do this. A few parting words to save face, and she would march her crowd the hell out of there.

She took a position at the front of the crowd. The soldiers were completely obscured behind their shields, only slices of helmets and goggles showing. She could hear their breathing, like a singular beast. She felt dizzy, and widened her stance for balance. Unger's hand quaked as she raised Gloria to speak. She never got the chance.

Soldiers on each side of the line fired into the crowd, killing several of the Guy Fawkes Gang with head shots. Some gang members threw off their masks in an attempt to blend in with the paid protesters. This did not work, and they were not spared. A few even took human shields, thinking the soldiers would not shoot through innocents. They were shot and killed like the others.

Unger froze as the soldiers and security officers charged into the crowd, swinging batons and thrusting glinting steel weapons that looked like small swords. One soldier struck Unger a glancing blow to the head; another clipped her left knee as he rushed past. She dropped like wet laundry. From the ground, dazed and semi-conscious, she observed the soldiers beating and stabbing the fleeing protesters. The security officers began systematically stripping people, both living and dead, of their smartphones and cameras and smashing them on Pennsylvania Avenue with the butts of their weapons.

Unger wiped blood from her eyes and struggled to sit up. To her left, a bearded young man in a hoodie was furiously back-pedaling as he filmed the soldiers on his phone.

"I got you motherfuckers on tape! Wait till the world sees what you've done!" the hoodie shouted, unaware of the second soldier behind him. With a two-handed thrust, the soldier drove his sword through the hoodie's back. Unger saw the steel tip protrude out of his chest, just above his heart. The sight of that steel sword tip, and the bewildered look on Hoodie's face as he fell dead, shocked her into motion.

Unger struggled to her feet, wobbling and fighting for equilibrium. She slipped in a puddle of blood—her own. Anyone who could had already fled the area. Soldiers and officers dragged dead bodies by the feet across Pennsylvania Avenue toward the White House. Blood trails from the bodies formed haphazard crimson lines that crisscrossed the pavement. Unger saw the bodies of the bottle-blonde and her cameraman, both shot dead. His camera was missing. She knew he had two small children, one the same age as Unger's granddaughter. He was a quiet man, but quick to smile. And good at his job. She had liked working with him.

Her head began to clear. She had to get out of there. Wait—Gloria! She scanned the ground around her, to no avail. Her glittered friend was gone. Another casualty on this day.

Unger heard moaning and turned to see a young woman crumpled on the ground behind her. Her auburn hair was matted with blood, one eye swollen shut.

"Can you walk?" Unger asked.

"I dunno," the woman said, then started to sob.

"Get up," Unger shouted, motioning with her hands. "If we stay here, we're dead."

Unger helped the young woman to her feet and threw an arm around her shoulder, and the two limped across Pennsylvania Ave and Lafayette Square to H Street. Unger hailed the first taxi she saw, stuffed the young woman into the back seat, and told the driver to rush her to the nearest hospital.

She shuffled another block north, wanting to put more distance between her and the White House. She frantically waved down a taxi for herself. The driver took one look at her bloody face and said he didn't want any problems. Unger offered him fifty dollars for the ten-minute ride to her Georgetown townhouse. He agreed to do it for one hundred. Unger sat back in the seat and closed her eyes. The enormity of what she had just witnessed washed over her. She began to shake and quietly sob.

Friday, August 6th, 2021. The day the First Amendment died in the United States of America.

CHAPTER 53

U nger fingered the curtains open a crack; the fabric fluttered in her trembling hands. She looked up and down the darkened street with her one good eye. A long row of European sedans and big SUVs rested tightly against the curb, their shiny skins gleaming in the streetlights. All appeared normal in her genteel Georgetown enclave. But Unger knew better. She studied the blackness, expecting General Taylor's men to spring from the shadows, ninja-like, and finish what they'd started. She longed for daybreak, for this night's end. Perhaps her nerves would settle down as the darkness receded.

It had been a long night. A prominent friend had arranged for a doctor to come to Unger's townhouse and treat her injuries. She dared not go to a hospital. The doctor had closed her head wound with sixteen stitches, shaving a patch of her hair down to the skull. Her right eye was blood-red and swollen, but would regain full sight in a week or so. A mild concussion and tinnitus toyed with her equilibrium and heightened her anxiety. Her left knee was swollen and wrapped tight. The doctor said she was lucky; most seventy-year-olds would not have done as well. He gave her painkillers and a handful of Xanax to help her sleep. Unger took neither, knowing she would need a clear mind for what she feared awaited her.

"C'mon, Mom, sit back down," Unger's daughter Jennifer Levin said. "You've been looking out the window all night. You're starting to scare the kids."

The front parlor lights were dimmed. Jennifer sat crossed-legged on a sofa adjacent to the fireplace, next to her two adopted children, a four-year-old girl from China and an older African American boy from the inner city. Unger's son-in-law, Adam Levin, an attorney at an environmental non-profit, sat in a wingback leather chair, tapping out a text on his iPhone. Jennifer had rushed over as soon as her mother told her what happened at the White House. No one, other than the children, had slept much in the past twenty-four hours.

Unger hobbled from the window and dropped into the sofa opposite the flat-screen television. She grabbed the remote and turned the television on, frowning as she frantically cycled up and down the channels. All the national news outlets were still off the air, having been replaced by a single government-run network called USG News. USG News featured stark graphics and short declarative sentences, delivered by a curt female news anchor with pale eyes, dark bobbed hair, and a finely cut blazer. This icy woman never seemed to blink, which gave her performance an ominous, somewhat hypnotic, quality. USG News had hit the airways less than two hours after Unger's bloody protest. Unger knew network news, knew that an entire network cannot be conjured that quickly. Taylor must have been planning its launch months in advance.

USG News's coverage of the protest was overt propaganda: the protest was illegal; the protesters were violent aggressors; the government had ably dispersed the protesters with no injuries. Stock footage accompanied the reporting. Despite its high production value, the coverage had the farcical quality of old Cold War indoctrination films. The Internet was no better now, Unger knew. The government controlled most of the servers. You had to go deep into the web to find any remaining free voices. The fourth estate had been toppled.

"Turn that off," Jennifer said, wincing. Unger muted the volume but kept the television on.

Jennifer turned then and whispered in her daughter's ear. The little girl squinted and shook her head. Her mother whispered a second time. Slowly, the girl got up and shuffled toward Unger, sliding her stockinged feet across the oak hardwood. She crawled up on the sofa and nestled herself against her grandmother. Unger wrapped an arm around the girl, who stared at her bloody eye and patch-shaved head.

"Grandma, what happened to your face?"

"I told you, sweetheart. Nana met some bad men yesterday."

"Grandma, is… is everything all right?" the little girl asked, twisting a strand of her hair.

How could she explain what had happened yesterday to a four-year-old? Tell her of the foundational significance of the Bill of Rights? How it grants her individual liberties by limiting governmental power? Tell her that she had lost her First Amendment rights—religion, speech, press, assembly, government petition—before ever knowing these freedoms? Unger hugged the child closer, uncertain how to answer. How does one enjoy the beach without the sun?

Unger feared for her country. No, she was terrified. Now was the time for a Thomas Paine, or another such revolutionary firebrand, to ignite the people to action. Or was it too late even for that?

"Of course, sweetheart," Unger said. "Everything is going to be fine." She stroked the child's dark hair and pasted on a smile. The girl giggled and tucked in closer. They sat together like this in silence, Unger stroking the girl's hair until she fell asleep. Soon sleep found Unger as well.

———————

The front door shattered; shards of wood and glass sprayed the parlor. A metal flash-bang exploded, spewing blinding white smoke as it skidded across the floor. Large men streamed into the room, pointing assault weapons and shouting commands in deep, low voices. A giant gloved hand gripped Unger's neck, pinning her to the back of the sofa. The little girl was scooped up and removed, screaming, from her side.

The smoke cleared. Two men dressed in black tactical gear hovered over Unger, while two more trained their weapons on the rest of the family. The men yanked Unger off the sofa and to her feet. One man stepped behind her, wrapped a strong arm across her chest, and pulled her tight to him. He and his team then dragged her from room to room, using her as a human shield to clear her townhouse of any threats. Satisfied, they returned her to the parlor and threw her back on the sofa.

Jennifer's daughter sobbed. The little girl had buried her head into her mother's side; the older boy sat slumped with his head down. Adam Levin's wide eyes darted around the room. Every time Levin started to speak, he was shouted down by the two armed men that stood over his family.

More men entered the townhouse now and began their search. Some things were taken; other things were intentionally broken. Unger heard breaking glass from the kitchen, followed by laughter. Moments later two men walked from her kitchen eating and drinking from the contents of her refrigerator. A carnival-like atmosphere prevailed among the marauding men.

"I'm a lawyer. I know my rights!" Levin shouted. "Where's your warrant?"

One of the armed men stepped toward him and grinned. "Warrant? Here's your warrant." The man split Levin's nose with a short, powerful jab of his rifle butt. Blood sprayed everywhere. Both children, blood-soaked, started to scream.

"Shut those fucking pound puppies up, or I'll duct-tape both of 'em," the man said. Jennifer grabbed hold of her children and hushed them quiet. Levin held his nose and whimpered.

Unger rose from the sofa in protest. The man in charge nodded toward the kitchen. Two men seized her by the arms, dragged her through the parlor, and slammed her into a chair at the kitchen table. The man in charge sauntered in. He took his time taking the seat across from her.

"Am I under arrest?" Unger asked.

Silence.

"Do you have a warrant?"

Nothing.

The man looked down and picked at his fingernails, feasting on the silence. He finally raised his head. Dark eyes lit his otherwise expressionless face.

"Do you know who I am?" the man asked calmly, biting off the end of each of his words.

"FBI?"

The man snorted. "I am a captain in the Domestic Secret Police. The FBI licks my boots."

"What? Why are you—"

"I ask the questions, Ms. Unger. Not you."

Unger sat back in her chair, away from the captain.

"We know you led the illegal protest yesterday at the White House—"

"I had the proper permit!" Unger blurted out. The man standing next to her wrapped his hand around the back of her neck, his leather glove squeaking as he squeezed. A sharp pain knifed through her.

"You will provide me with a list of names of everyone who was at your protest yesterday," the captain said. "You will tell me of all who conspire against our new leader, General Taylor. You will tell me all I need to know. Now, at your kitchen table, or later at our detention center. Fast or slow. Which will it be?"

Unger sat mute, stunned. She opened her mouth, but for the first time in her life, words failed her.

"Very well, then," the captain said. "We will do this your way. Nice and slow." He nodded to his two colleagues. They jerked Unger to her feet, then dragged her back through the parlor.

Levin stood, slid his bloodied hand from his nose. "False arrest! Where are you taking her?"

"The lawyer's found his tongue, I see," the captain said. "Why not ask about her speedy jury trial, or what cruel and unusual punishments she will face?" The captain pointed at Levin and laughed. "The lawyer who plays Bill of Rights Bingo."

The captain's men joined in the laughter. One man twisted his fists at the corners of his eyes in pantomime of a crying baby. Levin watched as the men dragged Unger, deflated and limp, out the front door of the townhouse she had owned for thirty years. She would never return.

Levin stepped toward Jennifer, terrified and sobbing on the sofa. She turned her head, unable to look at him. His two young children clung to her in shock.

It was the Second Amendment Levin thought of now. He had always been a strident advocate for gun control, convinced that it was the guns that caused the violence. He had never even held a gun, nor knew anyone in his social circle who had. But as he slouched back into his chair, nose split and dignity lost, all he wanted was a gun. For the first time in his life, Levin wanted a gun in his hand. No— *needed* a gun in his hand. And he knew he would have used it. To protect his family.

Aah, sweet irony.

CHAPTER 54

George emerged from the woods and stood by the roadside. His dark sunglasses had fogged up in the August humidity. It was not yet nine a.m., and it was already over eighty degrees with a dew point over seventy. The steady drizzle and cloud cover mercifully cut the heat a bit, but George was roasting like a baked potato in his hooded rain jacket. He popped off his hood and tilted his head back toward the gray sky. The damp spray felt good on his face. He wiped his glasses clear on the bottom hem of his sodden cotton t-shirt. A brisk nudge from behind caused him to shuffle his feet. George looked over his shoulder and received a silent head nod from Lima. He put his glasses and hood back in place. George had become quite the celebrity in the two weeks after his Mount Vernon address, and they could not risk detection.

They stood alone at the edge of Ellipse Meadow at the U.S. National Arboretum. In the distance, on the opposite side of the twenty-acre grassy field, stood the Capitol Columns; twenty-two sandstone Corinthian columns that had supported the East Portico of the U.S. Capitol Building from the Jefferson to Eisenhower administrations.

These columns, each over three stories high, had been placed in the Arboretum in the late 1980s as landscape art. Most visitors likened the Capitol Columns, when viewed at a distance, to the Roman Colosseum ruins. What George saw was the final scene in *Planet of the Apes,* when the cameras pulled back to reveal the Statue of Liberty buried in the sand. No matter, he thought grimly. Both images spoke to the demise of republican democracy at the hands of primates.

George was sure they had not been followed. They were traveling in pseudo, their false identities fully backstopped. They had arrived at the Arboretum at opening, then cleaned themselves on the rustic hiking trails that ran through the Azalea Garden and up and over Mount Hamilton.

Lima slapped George's shoulder and the two men moved across the open meadow toward the columns. George led the way, with Lima tight on his right shoulder. The drizzle turned to a soft rain; the skies darkened. The area was empty, except for a large solitary man sitting on the steps at the reflecting pool, the Capitol Columns at his back. George quickened his pace at the sight of his friend.

JD stood now, his full six-foot-six unfurling like a wave crashing on the beach. He stepped back into the amphitheater, among the stone columns. George approached his friend cautiously, not sure how JD would receive him now that his secret was out in the open.

"George!" JD exclaimed, striding toward George with outstretched arms. They embraced. "Good to see you, man. It's been a while."

"I know," George said. "A lot's happened in the past two months."

JD had received the coded letter George had mailed before going underground to Verity Island. It seemed a lifetime ago. They had spoken often on their safe phones since then, JD being George's eyes and ears at the Bureau and in DC at large. George never spoke of TRENTON or his cloning to JD, as Flanagan had sworn him to secrecy and he did not want to endanger his friend with this knowledge.

JD put both hands on George's shoulders, then leaned in to get a closer look. His head tilted to the side, eyes unblinking. *He's looking for George Washington.* George turned away, breaking his grasp.

"I saw your little Mount Vernon thing on TV. Shit, everyone did." JD shook his big bucket head and grinned. "Dude—what the fuck?"

George gave him a thin smile.

"Is it true?" JD lowered his voice to a whisper. "I mean… really true? You're him? No bullshit?"

George nodded.

"Damn," JD said. He went silent for a long moment. "Why didn't you tell me?"

Lima cleared his throat.

George turned toward him, grateful for the interruption. So JD now knew about his cloning issue, but how in hell was he going to explain Verity Island to his friend? Or Flanagan? Or the fact that he was an accomplice to multiple homicides since they'd last met for drinks at the bar? What would he make of all of it? JD was his best friend, so George hoped he would eventually come to terms with it, as he himself was trying to do. George knew without a doubt what he and Lima had planned would change everything—forever.

George introduced Lima to JD, and the two men took cautious appraisal of each other. JD's smile slowly faded, while Lima's face remained impassive.

"You're as big as George said," Lima said.

"Corn fed and country strong," JD responded.

Lima smirked.

"George tells me you're from Brazil. That right?"

Lima glanced at George, then back to JD. "Yes. Rio."

"I got into Brazilian jiu-jitsu my last two years at Purdue," JD said. "Studied at a Gracie Studio in Indiana. You know any of the Gracies?"

"I learned to fight in the streets," Lima said. "No belts." His eyes narrowed. He took a step toward JD, flipped off his sunglasses and looked up at the man towering half a foot above him. "Tell me about the last few weeks," Lima said. "What have you been doing? Who have you talked to?"

JD's face darkened, and his jaw clenched. "I'm good. Hale called me in for an interview after the Mount Vernon thing, but I didn't tell him shit. I'm being watched, no doubt. But my phone's still fresh, and I cleaned myself good before I got here."

"You sure about that?" Lima asked. "Would you bet your life on it?" Lima pointed at George. "*His* life?"

"Dude... You can trust me."

"I trust only myself," Lima said. "And the few who have earned my trust, like the man standing next to me. You I don't trust. You now know my face, my name. If you betray me, or George, or our mission, I will find you. Understand?"

"You want me, you know where to find me," JD said. He squared his shoulders back.

Both men stared at each other, unblinking. JD's neck and face reddened; his fists clenched at his sides. Lima remained as cool as a summer breeze, his tight lips upturned in a faint grin.

"Okay, guys," George said, stepping between them. "That's gonna have to be good enough for now."

Both men turned to George. JD rolled his neck and shook his hands out. The natural color returned to his face. He took a half-step back from Lima, jammed his hands into his pockets.

"Okay, whatever," he said, shrugging his giant shoulders. "What *can* you tell me?"

"People are anxious, suspicious," George said. "They're waiting to see what happens next. Taylor is rushing to consolidate his grip on the country. Many are starting to turn against him. But they don't see the big picture. The people will not rally until they *feel* the threat

387

posed by Taylor, and by then it will be too late."

"You still running... for president?" JD asked.

"We'll see," George said. "There's a lot I can't tell you right now, JD. Sorry."

"Tell him about the photo," Lima said.

"Oh, yeah. Earlier this morning, Luiz took a photo of me in front of the White House. We're gonna post it on my GW2 website. A nice poke in the eye to Taylor. Mad bulls only see red, right?"

"Sweet," JD said.

"Reminds me. You been checking in on Nesha like I asked?"

"Yeah," JD replied. "She's fine. Worried about you. Me too."

"I'm fine," George said.

"Did you kill Taylor's guys at Mount Vernon?" JD asked. He looked into George's eyes and knew the answer. "They got a murder warrant out on you. They'll kill you, both of you, on sight. You know that, right?" JD bit his lip. "Let me jump in with you guys. I can help."

"We got this," deadpanned Lima.

JD turned from Lima to George. "George?"

"Thanks, JD. Really. Best you stay on the street. Eyes and ears." He quickly changed the subject. "What's the latest with Hale?"

"He's been strutting around HQ since Taylor made him director. This Domestic Police Force's got their own division embedded at HQ. They're calling the shots now. The head of the DSP is a bad dude."

"The FBI? Cops?"

"The FBI's split," JD said. "Most are pissed at Hale, and nobody likes the DSP embedded in our ranks. The usual vultures are hanging back to see how this shakes out. And cops are cops, you know. Morale's pretty low across the board."

"What's the talk about me?"

JD laughed. "Dude, it's crazy. This shit's pretty hard to wrap your head around, you know? Surreal. Hale's forbidden any official comms on it, but everyone's talking. People liked your address; most of them believe the DNA. People I talk to are watching and waiting to see what GW2 will do next. You know that's what they're calling you, right?"

George rolled his eyes.

"I think most of law enforcement will follow you if you move on Taylor," JD said. "That's what you guys are gonna do, right?"

JD was much shrewder than people thought, which he used this to his advantage. They saw his cartoonish size, affable—albeit idiosyncratic—personality, and assumed he was a dumb jock, a no-neck dullard who could be easily manipulated or outmaneuvered. George knew different. He looked at Lima and saw a gleam of respect in the man's eyes.

"This guy we're meeting tonight," Lima said. "Tell me about him."

JD looked at George.

"Do you trust this man?" Lima asked.

"Well, I hit him up like George asked me to," JD said. "I've been working him for three weeks. He's ready. But he's a proud man. Conflicted. Highly stressed."

"I asked you—"

"Yes, I trust him," JD said. "I wouldn't have set up the meeting tonight if I didn't. You have to trust me. See how this trust thing works?" Lima's eyes narrowed. JD ignored him. "And tonight, don't push the tough guy act on him. He'll go sideways on you. Treat him professionally, with honor. That's big with him. Tell him he's doing the right thing."

"Got it. Great job, JD," George said.

"And don't be late," JD said. "Dude's punctual as a morning shit."

CHAPTER 55

"You look like shit, Shelton," the man said as he glided through the secretary's office. He was one of General Taylor's henchmen, a member of the new Presidential Personal Guard, the PPG. He wore black battle dress uniform pants tucked into polished boots, with a black shirt buttoned to the neck. The smugness came with the uniform.

"Piss off," Shelton said to the man's back as he entered the Oval Office without appointment.

The personal secretary to the president, a middle-aged hold-over from Acting President Parker's brief tenure, gave Shelton a knowing smile. Shelton knew Taylor would have her replaced soon, with a less competent but blindly loyal Pentagon blonde.

"Don't worry, Tim," the secretary said. "These guys come by all day long now—no appointments, just breeze into the Oval. I tried to stop it, but they have the boss's ear. They are so rude." She looked around her office. "They're such… assholes," she whispered.

Shelton chuckled. He had never heard this proper gray-haired woman cuss before.

"You do look tired, Tim," the secretary said. "You feeling okay?"
Shelton rubbed his cloudy red eyes. "Yeah. Late night, I guess."
His right eyelid began to twitch. He pressed it closed with his index
finger until the spasm stopped. He had picked up this stress tic about
two weeks ago, when Taylor had taken over the White House and
made him his chief of staff. Shelton hated the White House and
missed his military life at the Pentagon.

He checked his watch: 3:50 p.m. He conducted his daily briefing
with Taylor at 4:00 p.m., and it irritated him when anyone jumped
his meeting.

"How long's this guy going to be?"

"I don't know, Tim," the secretary said. "Sorry."

Shelton's nerve endings were frayed. He had worked sixteen
straight days since Taylor had called an emergency meeting of his
closest staff immediately following his First Citizen declaration. In
that meeting, Shelton had been tasked with devising a strategy for
"First Citizen" Taylor to consolidate his power as an autocratic
military dictator. Time was of the essence. Taylor had authorized
swift and extreme measures to establish his regime.

Shelton still cringed at the thought of those long first days, sitting
in his spare Pentagon office plotting how to end the world's oldest
existing democracy. How does one put a match to the Constitution?
How do you tell 350 million people that the past 245 years were no
more than a failed experiment, a blank check they'd failed to cash?

As he always did, Shelton looked to history for answers. He
studied all the infamous autocratic dictators: Hitler, Stalin, Mao,
Mussolini, Pol Pot, Saddam Hussein, Caesar, Castro, and Napoleon,
among others. It was much more difficult to hold and wield power
than it was to seize it. How did these men do it? He looked for
patterns and consistencies that could be qualified and quantified.

It took him three caffeine-filled days to devise a strategy, which he
named Project P5C2-90. The strategy had seven main components: five

began with the letter P, two with the letter C, and all were to be completed in 90 days or less. Shelton had ranked the components in order of priority, with all components working simultaneously to ensure the success of the whole.

Taylor had approved Project P5C2-90 as submitted on Monday, August 2, 2021 at 10:21 a.m. (EDT). Shelton kept a date- and time-stamped signed copy of this memorandum in a hidden safe at his residence. This document would do him little good if they failed, but he wanted history to get it right.

The executive summary section of the memorandum explained Project P5C2-90 as follows:

- PURGE: Purge all governmental institutions and individuals (military, politicians, activists) who oppose the regime.

- PROTECT: Establish the Presidential Personal Guard, an elite military and intelligence force responsible for the personal safety of First Citizen Taylor and for the security and preservation of the regime.

- POLICE: Establish the Domestic Secret Police, a law enforcement and intelligence force responsible for finding and resolving subversives and agitators within the United States who oppose the regime.

- PROPAGANDA: Establish a vigorous cross-platform, deep-penetration media messaging campaign to ensure all citizens recognize the sovereignty of First Citizen Taylor and the supremacy of regime dogma. Replace mass media outlets with a regime-controlled news network (USG News Network).

- PROFIT: Utilize the United States Treasury to establish and preserve financial security for First Citizen Taylor and the regime.

- **CENSORSHIP**: Control the flow of information to strengthen and preserve the authority of First Citizen Taylor and the regime. Control all Internet servers within the regime's purview.
- **CONSTITUTION**: Void existing U.S. Constitution and replace it with one that expressly grants First Citizen Taylor autocratic power.

Shelton fidgeted in his chair. He was looking down at his briefing materials when the PPG interloper burst out of the Oval Office. He made some comment that Shelton ignored. The bastard had taken fifteen minutes of his time and had no doubt put Taylor in a foul mood.

Taylor stood behind his desk, his back to Shelton as he entered. His posture was rigid as he looked out over the city he now owned. Shelton greeted Taylor with a crisp salute, then silently took his seat in the side chair next to the desk. Taylor failed to acknowledge Shelton's arrival. He no longer returned salutes or shook hands. He now merely nodded his assent. After a full minute of silence, Taylor turned around languidly and sat at his desk.

He continued to wear his military dress uniform in the White House, despite Shelton's urging that he dress in civilian attire.

Taylor locked eyes with Shelton. He *was* in a foul mood. Better save the bad news for last, Shelton decided. He would start with new/urgent matters, then reverse order, working from bottom to top, C2 to P1. He took a deep breath and began to brief from his notes.

New/Urgent Matters (past 24 hours): *Decision Needed*

Ex-President Parker remains in a secure black site in the Nevada desert. He has proven to be tougher than expected. He regrouped after his initial emotional breakdown and is beginning to cause problems. Several failed suicide attempts have resulted in him being bound and gagged, and placed on suicide watch. He now refuses food and water. Forced feedings have been initiated. Parker is to remain alive and camera ready until further notice.

<u>Decision Needed</u>: Continue forced feeding? (Yes/No)

Constitution:

Manipulation of key congressional members is ongoing to secure the necessary votes to pass a law for First Citizen Taylor to rule by unilateral decree, without legislative branch consultation or judicial review.

Censorship:

All national print and broadcast news media have been shut down and replaced with the national news network—USG News.

Control and censorship of the Internet continues to prove difficult, but the regime has purchased the cooperation of the major tech companies, which has exponentially increased monitoring and data collection on hundreds of millions of Americans. It is projected that the regime will control all major servers and mainframe architecture by Project conclusion, 31 October 2021.

Profit:

The Secretary of the Treasury has been replaced with a regime loyalist who has siphoned billions of dollars of taxpayer money to secret offshore accounts. This practice will continue as a primary funding source for the regime.

Propaganda:

Weekly meetings with the Secretary of Propaganda are ongoing. First Citizen branding is being pushed on all regime-controlled platforms. A massive Internet campaign has been launched to manipulate Internet opinion via fake blogs, bots, sock puppets, news sites, Facebook, and other prominent social media sites.

Police: *The Domestic Secret Police Force*

DSP has improved since their initial operation, the 6 August White House demonstration, and is now fully integrated within the structure of the FBI. DSP is rapidly gaining operational capacity and is anticipated to be fully operational by Project end. Intelligence and Operations Branches are working together to find and resolve enemies of the regime.

Protect: *The Presidential Personal Guard*

PPG has improved since their initial operation, the rendition of President Parker. There are currently no viable threats against First Citizen Taylor or the regime. Four assassination cases were closed last week; all four subjects resolved.

Shelton's cadence slowed as he prepared to brief Taylor on his last Project topic—Purge Opponents. He gritted his teeth and began.

"The DSP have identified and resolved 189 Enemies of the State this week, bringing the total to 317," Shelton advised. "Most were from the military, national law enforcement and intelligence agencies—Director Hale has been particularly helpful on this point—and congressional aides and staffers. We continue to—"

"What of Agent Moore?" Taylor cut in. "Did you see the photo of him standing outside the White House yesterday?"

Shelton sank into his chair. "Yes, sir. I—"

"Standing right outside the window directly behind me. Do you believe he is mocking me, Colonel Shelton?"

Shelton knew better than to step on that grenade.

"This man is the Number One Enemy of the State. A man you say you cannot find, despite me giving you all the resources at my disposal. And still this man stands outside my window, mocking me. How is this possible, Colonel Shelton?"

Taylor leaned forward in his chair, eyes burning, his face expressionless.

"Well, sir, we've been searching for him at his—"

Taylor slammed his fist down on the table. "I want this man resolved, Colonel! Now!"

Resolved. Taylor's ubiquitous euphemism for fixing, handling, or killing his problems away. Resolved by any means necessary. The word had come to chill Shelton's blood.

"You think I'm a fool?" Taylor spat. "I know what you're not telling me. I know the people are warming to Moore, ever since that Mount Vernon stunt. They think he's goddamned George Washington, for Christ's sake. He's the shiny object they can't stop staring at. I cannot lead this nation of idiots with Moore still around. He needs to be resolved. Today."

"What do you propose, sir?"

Taylor sighed, then stared a hole into Shelton.

"If you cannot find Moore, you'd better find someone he cares about to flush him out into the open."

"Cabot—the professor. We haven't been able to find him, either. We—"

"Then find someone else. Now!"

Taylor rose from his chair and turned once more to the window behind his desk, between the American flags draped in floor stands. He stood in silence with his back to Shelton. After a long minute, he spoke without turning.

"I want Agent Moore resolved. Immediately. If you cannot accomplish this, then I will replace you with someone who can. Do you understand, Colonel Shelton?"

"Yes, sir!" Shelton saluted Taylor's back and strode out of the Oval Office. He blew past the secretary, waving his goodbye as she tried to engage him in conversation. He burst out of the White House and rushed down Pennsylvania Avenue NW. He was beyond all superficial emotions—anger, fear, disgust, sadness, surprise. He just felt hollow, empty. He slowed his pace and wandered toward Fifteenth Street, a phantom of the man he once was. He stopped at Old Ebbitt Grill. A beer was just what he needed to silence the buzzing in his head.

Resolve and *Replace*. The words rang in his ears. Each had seven letters. Each was spelled and defined differently. But Shelton knew better. To Taylor, these words were exactly the same.

CHAPTER 56

S *nap.*
Virginia's eyes darted toward the door. The sound came from outside her trailer. Close. She muted the television and tilted her head, ear cocked. Nothing. Virginia rose from the sofa and crept to the side window by the door. She put her ear to the trailer's thin wall and listened, careful not to silhouette herself in front of the window by the dim light of the living room. She stood motionless for minutes, her breath measured. Nothing.

She inched the curtain open and peeked outside. The trailer perimeter was well lit by the motion-activated lighting she had installed after her return from her DC confrontation with General Taylor. Her eyes adjusted to the bright light, then scanned the area. Nothing.

Maybe it had been a raccoon, or a possum. Virginia slowly opened the front door and stepped out onto the deck. She gripped the railing with both hands, took long looks in both directions, then spit tobacco juice into the darkness beyond.

Back on the sofa, she watched through the sheer curtain until the security lights went dark. She turned toward the television and un-muted the TV. The clipped speech of the newswoman made her unsettled. Virginia had been watching USG News Network since it aired. She cringed every time they did feature stories on George, which were laughably biased. Each time, they mocked his Washington claim and brought in a parade of government experts to trash both him and the science behind cloning. The CIA denied the existence of TRENTON, or any other government cloning project, past or present.

All this pissed Virginia off. But what concerned her was the change in the tone of the coverage the past two weeks. Taylor had taken to addressing the American people directly, demanding any information regarding the whereabouts of George, whom he called the number one enemy of the state. This threat was accompanied by a fifty-million-dollar bounty on George's head—dead or alive. George had promised her he would stay underground, and that he had the support of powerful people. But she still worried. A mother always does.

Virginia poured herself a fat two fingers of bourbon, then slugged back a mouthful. She had abandoned her government almost fifty years ago, spent decades drinking away her ghosts, then finally made peace with it all.

Then Cabot had brought George back into her life. Old emotions, long dead and buried, resurrected. She wished Cabot had kept their secret, as ignorance had shielded George his whole life. Virginia had prepared to take her sin to the grave and stand in judgment for it. But now George was suffering for her youthful lapse of judgment. It tormented her. And she knew it was going to get worse.

George and Cabot had pleaded with her to leave her land, telling her she was not safe. They had offered to take her underground with them, assured her they would all be protected. They said they had a plan to stop Taylor—a real plan this time—and the resources and allies to do it. She knew she should have taken them up on the offer, but the hillbilly in her had won out. She would not be scared off her land by anyone. *The bastards haven't gotten me yet.* Virginia downed the last of her bourbon, then flicked the television off and rose to her feet. She had seen enough.

She went into the kitchen and returned with a nightcap. She placed it on the end table next to her favorite chair. She took her Martin Acoustic from its stand and began to fingerpick a new song she was working on. She whisper-sang the lyrics as she kept time with the steady beat of her foot. She paused from time to time to listen. Nothing.

It was during one of these pauses that she heard another noise outside. This noise was more of a rustling than a snap, and it came from the other side of her trailer. Virginia put down her guitar and listened intently. Whatever had made this noise had not tripped the security lights. She again peeked out the window, peering in the direction of the noise. It was a dark night, the heavy cloud cover obscuring the night sky. She saw nothing.

Growing annoyed with herself for being so easily spooked, and in her bourbon glow, Virginia threw open the door and bounded onto the front deck. Her presence did not activate the security lights. *Damn unreliable lights.* She would have to adjust them tomorrow. She retrieved a flashlight and a shotgun from her bedroom and returned to the front porch. The flashlight beam cut through the dark. She held the shotgun at her shoulder, safety off, finger just outside the trigger guard. She almost hoped she saw someone out there. But again, nothing.

Virginia stomped inside and called her neighbor. It was after ten, but old Percy was a night owl and didn't mind. He said he hadn't seen or heard anything unusual over at his place.

Those stories tonight on USG News about the dead-or-alive

reward on George's head had rattled her. Or maybe it was the footage of Taylor, seeing that face and hearing that voice. She convinced herself that those noises she'd heard belonged to the holler. She went to bed and was asleep in minutes.

———————

Virginia felt pressure on her face. Her eyes flew open. The dark bedroom was filled with moving shadows. A large gloved hand covered her nose and mouth, pressing her head down into the pillow. She couldn't breathe. Other gloved hands pinned her arms and legs to the bed. Panic rose within her. She jerked violently, but the gloved hands only tightened. She heard her own muffled scream. She tried to bite the hand over her mouth, but its force was too great. She thrashed around in the bed; the growl of a trapped animal swelled in her throat.

"Tranq that fuckin' bitch," shouted a male voice.

The shadow on top of her kept one gloved hand over her face, and, without looking, retrieved something from his pants side pocket. A glint of metal then the prick of a needle stab in her neck.

Virginia held eye contact with the shadow crouched over her. She always knew they would come for her in the end. And now they had. She would make them watch her die. Make them see that she did not fear them, or fear death. The shadow grew blurrier. Her vision telescoped. She stopped struggling. The room faded to black.

Foolish pride.

CHAPTER 57

The 100-inch television monitor sprang to life. An oversized head-and-shoulder image of General Taylor appeared on screen. Bile leapt from George's stomach and burned his throat. He shot off the sofa, banging against the low table and spilling the glasses of water. His own image appeared in a small box in the upper right-hand corner of the monitor, his image cropped in such a way as to hide the other four occupants in the room.

"Where is she, Taylor?"

"You're a hard man to find, Agent Moore. Had to reach you through that harpy at the DAR. Ms. Warner is a big fan of yours, by the way. She sends her regards."

"Where's Virginia?"

"You don't seem to grasp the situation here. You do not ask questions of me. I am in command here, not you. The sooner you understand this fact, the happier your life will become. All this clone nonsense. That stunt at Mount Vernon. You've become quite the thorn in my side, Agent Moore. I am trying to lead this country to its destiny, and it is only you that stands in my way." Taylor took a step toward the camera. "Let us end this now."

"If you harm her in any way, I'll kill you."

"Yes, of course," Taylor said with a smirk. "Now to business. This is how it works. Very simple. A straight hostage swap. You take Virginia's place. You surrender to me; I let her go unharmed. Do we have a deal?"

"Not before I see her," George said.

Taylor sighed, then motioned to someone off camera. The camera then zoomed out to reveal an empty metal chair to the left of Taylor. In a moment Virginia appeared, escorted by two large men, oversized goggles and helmets obscuring their faces. The men slammed Virginia down into the chair, then took up positions on either side of her.

Off camera Grace gasped, then raised both hands to her mouth.

Virginia's hair was pulled back in a tight ponytail, her face lit by the bare lightbulb hanging above her head. Her left eye was half shut, swollen red with traces of purple. Her upper lip had been split open and appeared to be sutured. A strip of white tape lay across the bridge of her nose; there were half-moon bruises under each eye. Virginia smiled when she saw George on camera, which caused her sutures to split, then bleed. She sputtered and coughed.

"I'm sorry, George. I'm so sorry. I—"

"Taylor, what the hell have you done to her?" George shouted.

"She is as obtuse and obstinate as you, Agent Moore. I would swear you and she were kin." Taylor paused. "But you are not related. Isn't that right, Agent Moore?"

"Don't listen to him, George," Virginia said. The man on her left shook her by the shoulder. She rolled in the chair like a rag doll.

"Okay, show's over," Taylor said. "You can clearly see that she is still alive. I have held up my end of the deal." He looked over his shoulder at Virginia. "Now, Virginia, do you have something you would like to tell George?"

Virginia closed her eyes and dropped her head. She took a few deep breaths, her shoulders rising and falling. When she looked back into the camera, tears began to run down her cheeks. She jutted out her chin and began to speak.

"George, I know you will do the noble thing and switch places with me, as these people ask. That you would give your life for mine. I know this."

Virginia gently patted her heart with her right hand. The guard on her left reached across her body and swatted her hand away. The guard on her right remained motionless. Virginia smiled wide. Blood dripped off her chin and onto her shirt.

"General Taylor is right about one thing," Virginia said. "We do not share blood." She choked up, then regained her composure. "But you need to know that I have always loved you, George. Always. During TRENTON, and through all those lost years after. And I know you love me, too."

"Tell him!" Taylor barked. "Like we agreed."

Virginia cleared her throat, then sat up tall in the chair.

"I never wanted it to end this way. You were right. I should've gone with you and Henry. I screwed up, and now I'm a hostage. There's no escape. They want me to plead for mercy. Ask you to take my place. For you to exchange your life for my own." Virginia's voice caught. "I don't want to die…" Her voice cracked as she broke down.

George's throat tightened; his eyes filled with tears. He heard Cabot weeping, but did not turn around.

"Go on," Taylor repeated impatiently.

Virginia closed her eyes, gathered herself. Time slowed down. George took a step toward the television screen. She opened her eyes and looked straight into the camera, her eyes now hardened and fierce. She leaned forward in the chair.

"George—finish what we started."

This was clearly not what Taylor had scripted Virginia to say. He shouted an expletive, then turned to her, his back to the camera. The guard on Virginia's right spun to face her; the other grasped at her as she shifted hard to her right to avoid him.

A brief scuffle ensued. In the middle of the commotion, Virginia looked into the camera and shouted "I love you." The words struck George like a blow.

Everything after this came to George in slow motion. He would forever remember it all, every moment.

In a blur, Virginia pulled at the waist of the guard on her right. She retrieved the handgun from his holster with a fluid, circular motion. She put it to her temple, then pulled the trigger. Her head bucked to the left, red blood and gray brain matter spraying the guard grasping for the gun, which fell from her hand and clanked on the concrete floor. She slumped onto the guard, her gaping head wound inches from his face. He recoiled backward. Virginia's lifeless body collapsed to the floor.

Cabot and Grace both shrieked. Lima, his voice a low growl, uttered a few expletives in Portuguese. Flanagan maintained his silence. A halo of dark red blood expanded on the floor around Virginia's head. She landed in a heap, facing the camera. George stared into her open, lifeless eyes. He could no longer hear anything, the cacophony around him silent to his ears. Virginia wore a relaxed death mask; she had found the peace that had eluded her in life. Her final plea a mantra, repeating louder and faster in George's head: *Finish what we started.*

The television screen faded to black.

Virginia had been dead for almost an hour now. George had fallen back onto the sofa, where he remained in a stupor. Grace had not left his side. Her eyes were puffy and red. She had a tight grip on George's hand. Cabot and Lima stood at a distance. Cabot was still in shock. Lima's expression was grim and resolute.

Flanagan was on the telephone. He was having an intense conversation, gesticulating emphatically. George locked eyes with him. Flanagan ended his call and walked across the study toward George.

"Did you do this?" George asked.

Flanagan started to speak, then stopped. He stood in silence. George waited him out.

"George, I understand you're upset—"

"Were you involved?" George shouted.

"Do not ask questions you do not want answered."

The air rushed out of George's lungs, causing him to gasp. Adrenaline surged through his body. His hands trembled. Grace tightened her grip.

"I'm sorry, George," Flanagan said.

George looked past him to Lima. "Luiz?"

Lima squinted. His jaw muscles rippled.

So it was true, then.

"George. You must understand that this was Virginia's idea," Flanagan said. "I tried to talk her out of it, I truly did, but Virginia was adamant. I wanted to negotiate, but she refused. She knew what I knew: that any rescue effort was futile, that you would insist on participating, and that it would likely result in your death. Virginia refused to be Taylor's pawn, to be the bait in his trap to capture you. She gave her life for yours, George. Don't you see?"

George leaned forward, pulled his hand from Grace's and began pounding his fists against his thighs.

"So I agreed to do it her way," Flanagan continued. "My source arranged it so that she could grab the weapon. He will be at risk now, so we must act fast." Flanagan knelt at George's side. "In the end, it was my decision. Luiz worked closely with me on this. Henry and

Grace knew nothing of it." Flanagan's face softened. "Virginia was a brave woman. She loved you very much, George. Her sacrifice will not be in vain."

George turned to Grace. Tears again began to cascade down her cheeks.

Flanagan took a seat on the chair next to George. Lima and Cabot remained standing. Cabot quivered and appeared shaken to his core.

Flanagan leaned over and placed his hand on George's shoulder. His countenance was different now, softer. His detachment had been replaced with compassion. His touch was gentle yet firm.

"Virginia was proud she could do this for you," he said. "For all of us." The study fell silent. "Do you trust me, George? I mean, really trust me?" Flanagan asked.

George stared past Flanagan for a long moment, then nodded imperceptibly.

"Good. Because General Taylor now has my undivided attention."

CHAPTER 58

A steady rain fell as they crossed the Potomac. It was a Monday night and traffic heading into DC on 66 East was relatively light. Just as they'd planned. George examined the dark, still water from the front passenger seat of a late-model white Chevy Equinox, an everyday vehicle selected to camouflage itself within the late evening commute.

The air in the SUV was leaden, the only sound the rhythmic swish of the wipers. They took the ramp to Constitution Avenue and were immediately stopped at a red light at 23rd Street. George's pulse quickened. The Washington Monument spiked out of the treetops ahead of them, the two red lights at its top following George's return to the District. Almost two months had passed since he'd last been here, since he and Lima had met with JD at the Arboretum, then later that night had their first meeting with Flanagan's source, the man in General Taylor's inner circle. The same man who now drove George back into the city he had once called home.

The light turned green. The driver turned left and headed north into Foggy Bottom.

"We should be there in about ten minutes."

George studied the man's body language, looking for a tell, any sign of betrayal. He saw none, but that didn't mean it wasn't there. Taylor became unhinged after Virginia's bravery had eliminated his leverage, so the recruitment of the driver had had to be rushed, placing him in the center of this operation before he was properly vetted. A calculated risk worth taking. If he betrayed them tonight, many people would die. No one on the team had hesitated. It had been thirty-one days since Virginia's self-sacrifice. Her death would be avenged this night.

"I want you to know that I did everything I could to prevent what happened to her," the driver said.

George held his silence.

The driver turned his head, waited for George to look his way.

"I'm sorry, George."

The man appeared genuinely remorseful. But that hardly mattered now. His true allegiance would be put to the test soon enough.

From the passenger seat, George looked out upon the fallen city, past the graffiti and urine-soaked alleys, home to twitchy junkies and beggars. The nation's capital had decayed rapidly since Taylor had anointed himself First Citizen. Two black Suburbans, bearing the DSP insignia, sped past in tandem, sirens blaring. To George's relief, they headed east, in the opposite direction of the condo that was their destination. Automatic gunfire soon rang out. It felt apocalyptic.

In the wake of Virginia's death, Taylor had accelerated his stronghold on the country. Prominent military and political leaders suddenly disappeared, as did any activists, academics, or business leaders that dared oppose him. The DSP had eclipsed the FBI and answered to no one but Taylor and his loyal minions at the White House. A cowering Congress had voided the Constitution and replaced it with a new one that expressly granted Taylor, as First Citizen, autocratic power. Censorship and propaganda efforts increased one-hundred-fold. All dissenting voices were silenced. The American people fell into a stupor, too afraid or apathetic to act.

George thought of the dodos, flightless birds living happily in isolation on the island of Mauritius in the Indian Ocean. They had never seen humans before and had allowed the first visitors to walk right up and bludgeon them to death. This went on for sixty-five years, until their extinction in 1662. In much the same way, the American people had never seen a military dictator in all its 245 years. They, too, would go the way of the dodo if George failed tonight, and it would take Taylor much less than sixty-five years to bring the country to extinction.

George missed Verity Island, which he now considered his home. He longed to return to its isolated shores, to turn his back on his country and allow America to crash and burn. Early on, the people had cheered Taylor, then had stood idle as he'd revealed his true colors. Should George act to save the country, or let the American people get what they deserved? In his heart George wanted to stay on Verity, make a new life on the island. He *belonged* there. Flanagan and Lima could help him select a tribe, and he'd settle into village life. Or maybe he'd work security with Lima and live in a swank penthouse condo in Central City. It all sounded so perfect.

But George chose to leave Verity Island. Cabot had spurred him to action, appealed to his sense of duty and country. George had acquiesced, but not for this reason. Revenge drove him into the streets this evening. It burned within him. He was willing to risk all for it, including his life. But he had his Verity family to think about now. Grace was in his heart, had given him the gift of hope. And he hoped that someday—somehow—he and Grace could have a life together on Verity. It was this hope that keep him alive. He could no longer martyr himself in the name of vengeance. He wanted to live.

They arrived at the condo and walked around to the side door entrance. George glanced around. No gunshots, no swarm of

DSP/PPG men descending upon them. A good sign. The driver entered the four-digit code into the keypad, and the door buzzed open. They entered and George shut the door silently behind him. The driver had passed his first test.

The elderly condo owners couldn't believe their luck when they won a sweepstakes (that they couldn't recall entering) for a luxury vacation to Hawaii, all expenses paid. A well-worn but effective ruse to get residents to vacate a target property. It was George's idea; Flanagan had put up the funds. Money well spent, he said.

George and Lima sat shoulder to shoulder on the worn velour sofa facing the common wall to Taylor's condo, which he had kept for his private trysts. A fifteen-inch laptop computer sat between them on the coffee table. Both men had earbuds jammed in their ears. Lima's four-man entry team was stacked at the door. All operated in complete silence.

Lima and George watched Taylor on the laptop and waited.

Taylor wore only a baby-blue silk bathrobe, the Japanese kimono type with an embroidered dragon pattern. He sat at a small kitchen table off the open galley kitchen, legs crossed at the knee. Relaxed, with a cup of tea and a newspaper spread out before him.

The condo was spartan, decorated in divorced single dad melancholy. Taylor had gone to great lengths to soundproof the unit. He hid his ownership through an impenetrable maze of front companies.

Taylor answered his cellphone and spoke to the driver briefly. His tone was curt. Lima hit a key that allowed them to hear both sides of the conversation, courtesy of the tap on the driver's phone.

The call ended. Taylor placed his phone down on the table, then folded the newspaper. He placed his teacup and saucer in the kitchen sink, the newspaper in the trash. He remained standing in the kitchen, in perfect view of the hidden cameras Lima's men had placed in the condo the day before. He wore black socks and house slippers. The robe fell to the knee, revealing stark white legs. His right hand slipped under the robe and between his legs. He hummed as he masturbated, a children's song George could not place. He closed his eyes. His hand moved slowly, in rhythm with his humming, which grew louder and more high-pitched. The show continued until an erection tented the front of his robe. He smiled, then opened his eyes and looked into the camera, as if he knew it was there.

Click, click, click. The signal. Their perimeter man had keyed his radio three times fast. The driver had entered the building. George focused on the laptop monitor and began his countdown.

Two long minutes passed. Taylor remained in the kitchen. His creepy humming had mercifully ceased, as had his masturbating. A sharp knock at his door split the silence. Taylor looked up. Two quick knocks, pause, two more quick knocks, long pause, one knock. Taylor tightened the sash on his robe and straightened himself to greet his guests.

"Please come in," Taylor called.

The driver unlocked the door and entered alone. Taylor appeared puzzled.

"Where is she?"

"In the car. She's afraid to come up."

"Goddammit!" Taylor shouted irritably. "Get her up here right now. I don't care if you have to drag her by the hair. Now!"

The driver left. George heard Taylor's door lock click. The driver slid to the next door to unit 1103 and threw up a hand signal. Lima motioned to unlock the door. The driver hurried inside, handed the key to unit 1101 to Noam, then took a seat on the sofa next to George.

Lima and George shared a hard look, then Lima turned and gave

Noam the thumbs-up signal. The team rushed out the door.

George watched it all unfold on the laptop. It was over in seconds. The team surged into the room, silent, guns in ready position. Taylor's eyes opened wide to the threat, like the antelope surprised by the lion at the watering hole. He recovered quickly and lunged across the room for a gun. Noam surged after him, tackling him. The collision shook the common wall and caused the laptop to hop once on the table. Other operators piled on top.

In a moment, Taylor lay zip-tied on the floor, a rag jammed in his mouth to prevent him from screaming.

The driver then flashed across the screen and knelt down next to Taylor. George had been so fixated on the laptop that he had not even noticed him leave the room.

The driver pushed his face up against his mentor's.

"It was me, you bastard," Colonel Timothy Raymond Shelton said through gritted teeth. "I wanted you to know. It was *me*."

Taylor wailed. He thrashed against his zip ties. Noam jabbed a needle into his neck, and the general's body immediately went slack. Noam jammed a black hood over Taylor's head, and he and another team member carried him out of the condo.

"We got him," Lima whispered to George. "Let's clean up and bug out before the cops get here."

Eighteen years before, these same words had been uttered by the head of U.S. Occupation in Iraq at a press conference to announce that Saddam Hussein had been pulled out of his spider hole. George had worked on leads on this case as a young FBI agent at WFO. He had celebrated that capture then. He exulted in this one now.

"We got him!"

CHAPTER 59

TUESDAY, OCTOBER 5, 2021; 11:55 P.M. (AKDT)
VERITY ISLAND; MANOR HOUSE; ALEXANDER ARCHIPELAGO
SOUTHEASTERN ALASKA

"Your decision, General Taylor?" Flanagan asked.

Taylor sat in a straight-backed steel chair. Worn leather restraint cuffs were affixed to its arms and legs, but he remained unshackled. George, Lima, and Flanagan stood in a semicircle in front of him, while Lima's men stood behind in the shadows. They were in a windowless concrete and steel bunker under the manor house.

Taylor was in no hurry to answer. His good eye slowly rolled between the three men; the other eye lay dead and fixed in its socket from the blow struck by Noam. A sneer crept over his face as the bloody eye fixed on George.

Taylor drew in a labored breath and tried to shout. "Where the hell am I?" The effort caused him to cough violently. He swallowed hard, winced, then began again. "Flanagan, is it? Who are you? What do you want?"

"We spoke of this upon your arrival last night," Flanagan said in his neutral tone. "You know who I am, and what I propose. What is your answer, General?"

"You are a man of obvious means," Taylor said. "An intelligent man. We have more in common than you think. I am sure we can work something out, together, without these two." Taylor motioned to George and Lima.

"And you are a pragmatic man, General," Flanagan responded. "Join us in our plan and live, or fail to do so and die. I will entertain no counter-offers."

"But surely you and I can—"

"Do not test my patience, General Taylor, lest your evasiveness become your answer."

Taylor's bloody eye opened wide. The eyelid fluttered.

"Who the hell do you think you are?" he roared. "All of you! You don't dictate to me!" He slowly raised a finger and pointed it at George. "You want me to help *him*? Our country is on the verge of collapse, and you think this guileless fool a better leader than I? The people need to be ruled with an iron fist. I alone can do this. Not you, not that fraud standing next to you. Only I can save this country from itself. I was born to lead. Caesar. Augustus. Napoleon. All military men who seized power and led their people to greatness. I shall do the same. My time has arrived. History shines upon me."

Taylor gasped for breath. He hacked up something, turned his head, and spat. "I demand you release me at once!"

"I'm afraid our democratic experiment has run its course, General. On that you and I agree. The wisdom of crowds is not scalable in such a heterogeneous populace." Flanagan stepped forward. "I see you adhere to the Great Man theory of history—with you being that great man, of course. I reject your premise on two grounds. First, leaders are not born, but rather are products of their environment. And second, the great man inevitably becomes a self-selected megalomaniac psychopath, such as yourself. Would you not agree?"

Taylor snorted.

"The sanctification of subjective feelings over objective truths is no basis for governance, and is contrary to recorded history," Flanagan said. "Authority must spring from a small, cohesive band of people committed to the same ideology."

"Pretty words, Flanagan. Why don't you and I go back to Washington and discuss this further? I'll make you a White House whatever-you-want. Pick your title. Anything. What d'you say?"

Flanagan waited until the smile dissolved from Taylor's face. Taylor shifted in his chair, as if trying to rise, and one of Lima's men clamped a hand on his shoulder and pushed him down hard. He grunted in pain. Flanagan waited for his attention, then continued.

"You see the people you rule as pawns, whereas I see the people we govern on Verity Island as partners. Verity Islanders feel authentic, competent, and connected to their fellow islanders. If you create a society where these three fundamental needs are met, then the people you govern will function optimally."

Flanagan drew another half-step closer to the seated general. In response Lima's men also drew closer. Taylor shot each man a furtive glance, then looked back at Flanagan, who was now almost within arm's reach.

"I tell you all this," Flanagan went on, "to show you that you have another option. A better option than this First Citizen fiction you have created. Military dictatorship is not the answer. I created Verity Island over twenty-five years ago. We are now into our second generation, and we thrive. Ours is the system that must replace our fallen democracy, not yours. It is George who must now lead our country, not you. You help us in this aim, and you will be spared."

Silence settled over the group. Flanagan had said his piece.

George had opposed this part of the plan from the start. He had argued that they should kill Taylor at the condo. Taylor would never submit to abdication, he'd reasoned, especially if that meant being replaced by George. Better to just kill Taylor outright, even though his cooperation would make the remainder of their plan much easier. Taylor's hands began to shake. He gripped the armrests of his chair, then dropped his head. George watched in puzzlement. Maybe he had been wrong. Maybe, in the depths of his soul, Taylor was a coward and would choose dishonor over death. Or maybe he was stalling for time until he devised a scheme to end-run Flanagan, however inconceivable that might be.

Taylor raised his head gradually. He sat firm against the back of the chair, shoulders square. A sardonic smile curled his lip. He gave George a piercing look; his bloody eye blazed.

"Fuck you," Taylor said triumphantly, then roared with a mocking laughter that shook his entire body.

"I see we have our answer," Flanagan said. "You have forced my hand. It's a pity that so many innocent lives must now be sacrificed, but I put their souls on you, not me." He took a deep breath, then released it. "So be it." He nodded to Lima.

Lima motioned to his men, who raised Taylor to his feet. The men held him from behind, arms pinned at his sides. They knew this position well. Taylor did not struggle; instead, he leaned toward Lima as he approached. Lima removed his jacket to reveal a brilliant white t-shirt.

George placed his hand on Lima's arm. He turned and looked at George quizzically. George threw off his jacket and shirt, stripped down to his sleeveless undershirt. *A white cotton undershirt.* Lima's face brightened in recognition. He drew the Karambit fixed blade from the small of his back, handed it ceremoniously to George, then stepped aside.

George stepped up and stood toe-to-toe with Taylor. He removed the knife from its sheath and brought the curved steel blade up to eye level, affording both he and Taylor a better look. The black blade resembled a tiger's claw. It glistened in the light. George dropped the blade to his side. He closed his eyes and thought back to three months ago, to the banishment ceremony in Central City. Saw the flowing motion, the fountain of blood. His entire body relaxed.

His arm went into motion; his eyes fixed on the left side of Taylor's neck. George willed the blade to its destination. His aim was true. The tiger's claw sliced the carotid artery wide open. George stepped into the fountain of arterial blood. Bathed in it. It cleansed him.

It took twelve seconds for Taylor to bleed out. Lima's men released their hold, and he fell dead to the floor.

George had left his body, was now looking down upon himself. Time slowed. His vision blurred. Voices mumbled around him. Lima stepped up to him. George watched himself take off his blood-soaked undershirt and hand it to Lima, who carefully placed it in a paper bag. George toweled off, put his shirt and coat back on. Lima's men loaded Taylor's body into a heavy burlap bag. He would be at the bottom of the Gulf of Alaska by morning.

"Are you going to be okay, George?" Flanagan asked.

The two men sat alone, opposite each other, in soft leather chairs by the fireplace. Lima and his men were busy preparing for the next operation.

"Was that your first?" Flanagan paused. "I mean, the first man you've killed?"

George nodded. "I've seen men die before," he said. "More since I've met you."

Both men smiled weakly at George's attempt at levity.

"But this was the first by my own hand. I suspect my last, too." George stroked the stubble on his chin. "I'm glad the bastard's dead."

Both men sipped their drinks, deep in their own thoughts.

Flanagan drained his glass and placed it on the round cocktail table between them.

"Well, as our recently departed friend might say, we have crossed the Rubicon. No turning back now."

George chuckled. "Guess not."

"In many ways, killing Taylor was the easy part," Flanagan said. "It is always easier to seize power than hold it. Make no mistake: what comes next will be very difficult, George. We may have severed its head, but the snake remains quite venomous. We must strike quickly. What we do in the next seven days will determine our fate, and the fate of our country."

Flanagan stood. "The final sentence of the Declaration of Independence is a promise among the signers, to 'mutually pledge to each other our Lives, our Fortunes, and our Sacred Honor.' General Washington took this pledge in 1776. I now ask you, George, will you take this same pledge once more in 2021?"

George rose, and in a clear voice said one simple word.

"Yes."

CHAPTER 60

The handcrafted V8 biturbo engine rumbled to a stop, spraying gravel in its wake. This Mercedes AMG G63 SUV was obsidian black and loaded with options, like the other twenty-five in Flanagan's fleet. It effortlessly navigated the labyrinth of gravel roads that crisscrossed the 324 square miles of the manor estate grounds at the far south end of Verity Island.

Grace pushed the ignition button and the G63 fell silent. The door opened and closed with a confident metallic thud as she stepped out. She stood at the base of a mountain with a vertical rise of almost 400 feet. Shielding her eyes from the glare of the midday sun, she set off, following the winding switchback trail to the summit.

She was a strong hiker, and she reached the top quickly. A rolling glade, surrounded by towering spruce, maple and birch trees, stood before her. Beyond the glade, the slate-blue Gulf of Alaska sparkled to the horizon. Grace walked under an arched bronze sign that read "Verity Island Memorial Cemetery" in old English script. The cemetery was small, enclosed by an aged red brick wall that hugged the edge of a sheer 500-foot cliff.

Four plain white headstones were evenly spaced at the back of the cemetery, near the cliff line. Flanagan's stone was in the center, with Lima's to his right and Grace's to his left. The newest stone, laid just eight days ago on a brisk Sunday afternoon, belonged to Virginia Dare.

It had been a beautiful ceremony, conducted by Flanagan and attended by George, Grace, Cabot, Lima, and several of Lima's men. Flanagan spoke eloquently and with reverence of the proud woman who had willingly given her life for their cause. He posthumously made Virginia the first honorary citizen of Verity Island. Her selfless act had deeply moved him, and with George and Cabot's blessing, he had arranged for her estate to be settled as they imagined she would have wanted. The state-of-the-art Virginia Dare Elementary School was built in Booneville, Kentucky, and her beloved forty acres in Oneida had been deeded to her neighbor Percy, with the covenant that it would forever remain uninhabited. At George's insistence, Virginia's trailer was destroyed, a mighty red oak tree planted in its place.

Grace knelt at Virginia's headstone. *Virginia Eleanor Dare: Born August 18, 1951; Died September 3, 2021.* The word *"Veritas,"* in old English script, was the only epitaph.

She said a silent prayer, then reached into her bag and retrieved Curious George, the floppy old stuffed monkey that Virginia had recently returned to George. Last night, George had made Grace promise him she would place it at Virginia's grave, said it made him feel better knowing it was there. She leaned the stuffed monkey against the headstone. His wide grin and lopsided black felt eyes brought a rush of tears to Grace's eyes.

She thought of George now, her George. They had both laid their souls bare last night. Through tears, George had confessed his love for her. Grace had held him, had said she loved him too. She'd known it since he'd arrived on the island. George had told her they couldn't be together, that he wouldn't betray Flanagan or Verity Island. Said he had to go back to America and finish what he had started. He had made his sacrifice with the saddest eyes. Grace had tried to talk him out of it, had said that they would somehow find a way, but he was resolute in his decision. She knew how hard it was for George to leave her and Verity, to go back to being an outsider in a world where he had never truly belonged. He suffered with his decision, and it pained her to watch this honorable man's heart break. She had not felt such anguish since she was pulled screaming from her grandmother Mabel's arms.

They embraced, George kissed her tenderly, then walked out her door and out of her life. Grace had watched him go, uncertain if she would ever see him again, then lingered by the window of her bedroom at the manor and awaited the sunrise.

No unit of measure had yet been invented to gauge the relative absurdity of her situation. A man she had known less than four months had just professed his undying love, and then told her that they could have no life together. This edict had come on the heels of his confession to killing the leader of the free world, the same man who had ruined his career and caused the death of his surrogate mother. And this man of her dreams was a human clone. Of General George Washington. And, if that wasn't enough, this same man had partnered with her current boyfriend Daniel, the world's only trillionaire, to undertake an audacious plan to start the Second American Revolution.

Grace knew George's next mission with Lima could well prove fatal for both men. Taylor might be dead, but the despotic deep state he had created during his six-week reign as First Citizen was entrenched and well-funded. And then there was the control of the U.S. military, almost two million under arms with access to unlimited quantities of the most destructive weapons on earth. And the generals were not going to just lay down these weapons, as the palace guards had done with the broom of the wicked witch. No, it would not be that easy. As the wise Scarecrow had said to Dorothy, "I think it will get darker before it gets lighter."

And what of the American people? How would they greet George, their rebooted Founding Father? Were they ready for the Second Revolution? How could anyone manage a diverse population of 335 million people spread over 3,000 miles? A free and fractious population, entranced by technology and fearful of the future. It was a near impossible task.

Grace shook her head ruefully as she acknowledged the absurdity of her circumstances. She should accept George's decision and keep her beloved Verity life. Maybe if she stayed secluded on the island, safely under Daniel's wing, she could survive this thing, even if it all did go to hell. Daniel was a master at working the angles, bending the world to his will. True, their current situation was unprecedented, but Daniel's algorithms had never failed him. Or her, for that matter. Why not just stick with Daniel and play the odds?

Passion, wailed a voice from deep within her. Passion. Love's capricious cousin. Passion ignores the odds, plays by its own rules. She had felt sensations last night with George unknown to her in all her twenty-nine years. Their souls two missing pieces, reunited. It felt familiar. It felt true. This passion was a dangerous thing. Left unattended, it threatened to burn down her world. Grace had not had this with Daniel. They were physical, and loved each other, but that was not this. Last night with George had shaken Grace to her core. With Daniel, love was a noun, a word used to identify something. It was cerebral, a pleasant breeze. This love with George was a verb, a word used to describe action. It was visceral, a roaring tempest.

Her choice was binary, then: Daniel or George? Head or heart? Noun or verb? Familiar or new? Safe or risk?

And what about love? She and Daniel had a companionable love, a steadfast bond that gave her stability and inner peace. This passionate love with George aroused extreme feelings of elation Grace could only compare to—well, nothing. It was incomparable.

Wasn't romantic love, based in emotions like passion and desire, nothing but a myth that grew from the chivalric code of medieval knights? Or was romantic love real? By the end of the eighteenth century, the Age of Enlightenment—with its emphasis on the individual—had convinced Western culture that romantic love was real, that people should pair up and mate based simply on their feelings toward one another. *The heart wants what it wants.*

Grace was not so sure. She had no doubt about the powerful emotions George had awakened in her. But what were emotions, after all? Inputs from the five senses that generated neural electrical impulses in the brain? Mere reptilian impulses? And why should her superior judgment and reason yield to such capriciousness? Grace faced the biggest decision of her life. Why leave it to such whimsy? She had advanced degrees from Stanford, and the grit and pragmatism of a child raised on the streets of West Oakland. Shouldn't she think, not feel, this question to resolution? Hadn't cost-benefit and risk-reward analytical models always worked for her in the past?

But hadn't judgment and reason also separated her from her dear grandmother Mabel when she was just eight years old? Hadn't Mabel ignored her own emotion, and used judgment and reason to let her go? Over the years, Grace had seen how this decision had aged her grandmother, had stolen the light from her eyes. Only later had she understood Mabel's sacrifice, why she had done what she'd done. But every time she went back to the old neighborhood and visited Mabel, a big part of her wished Mabel had followed her heart and never let her go.

So maybe reason was predominant, but emotion was always lurking, like ants at a picnic. And Grace was hungry. Hungry to sprint, not jog. Hungry to shout, not whisper. She felt an abiding loyalty to Daniel. But it was time she paid a higher loyalty to herself. She would not surrender her passion, nor permit her intellect to talk her out of what she knew she must do.

In the end, it came down to Mabel. How she had become a mere shadow of herself after Grace left. Grace decided she would not live her life that way, a desiccated version of herself. It was the first time a man had spoken to her through her soul. She would listen.

She would go to him. Leave everything behind to be by his side. That would be her sacrifice. She could not imagine leaving her life on Verity behind, but also couldn't see a future for herself on the island without George. An old song wafted through her mind, a song she and Mabel loved to dance to when she was a child. Like her, Gladys Knight had taken her *Midnight Train to Georgia*, because, as Gladys and her Pips sing, *"I'd rather live in his world, than live without him in mine."*

Grace walked through the glade and back down the mountain to the G63. She barely remembered the descent.

She drove back to the manor to tell Daniel her decision.

CHAPTER 61

"These men, with their shiny medals," Lima said. "They know nothing of honor, and have earned no sympathy. Fate has come for them today."

Shelton shook his head. "There are some good men out there. I know many of them. What you're doing—it isn't right."

"These men must pay for what they did," Lima said. "Accountability is the foundation of Verity law. All these men. They either did wrong, or stood by and did nothing. All are equally guilty in my eyes. And all will be punished."

George rubbed his temples. He and Lima had been in DC for less than forty-eight hours, and had been up all night with Shelton planning today's operation. Shelton had not liked the plan from the start, but until now had been deferential to George and Lima. George had shared Shelton's apprehension, and had to be convinced by Flanagan and Lima that this was the only way. Cabot had also staunchly supported the operation, with a hardened conviction that had surprised George. Shelton had become steadily more agitated as the start of the operation approached. Perhaps it was because they were now on his turf—in the wings of the Pentagon Auditorium, Room BH650.

Martial music was playing from the loudspeakers on stage. The crowd noise rose as hundreds of generals greeted each another and took their places. The meeting was set to start in five minutes. Shelton turned to George. "It's not too late. We can still make the switch if we hurry. I can stall for a few minutes, I can—"

George lightly gripped Shelton's arm. "I know this is very difficult for you. It is for me too." Shelton searched George's eyes. "But this is Luiz's operation. It's his call, Tim."

Shelton would have to watch his house burn down with his family inside.

"Let me remind you, Mr. Shelton, that you swore us your loyalty, and I expect your fidelity today. If you betray us, I will kill you, of course. But I suspect, like me, you are not afraid to die for what you believe in." Lima stepped toward Shelton. "So I took the added precaution of detaining your family. Your parents. Your wife and kids. Your dog. They are unharmed and safe with my men. If they do not receive a call from me directly after this operation, they have their instructions. Are we clear, Mr. Shelton?"

Shelton gasped, then stiffened. The two men stared each other down, like boxers at center ring before a title fight. Shelton disengaged first. He turned his back to Lima and mumbled something. Lima's eyes danced. George would have to watch these two.

Shelton walked onstage to the rostrum located at the side of the broad auditorium, decorated with deep blue carpet and ornamental drapes on each flank. Five flags, one for each armed service branch, hung limply on their stands at back of center stage. An enormous DoD Seal was centered on a gray background that spanned the entire back wall. Shelton squinted into the lights as he looked out over his audience.

George checked his watch: 9:01 a.m.

The audience quieted. They represented the entire general officer staff of the U.S. Armed Forces: Army, Marine Corps, Navy, Air Force, and Coast Guard, which Taylor had transferred under DoD control. All generals were in attendance, except for the combatant commanders, who remained at their overseas billets and attended via secure video teleconference. Such a gathering was unprecedented, but these were volatile times, and no one had the courage to question an order from General Taylor.

To anyone paying attention, this meeting was different in other, more subtle ways.

They had dispensed with the ADA sign language interpreter at the lip of the stage; he had been replaced by a line of colonels that snaked around the entire auditorium. This Cadre of Colonels stood at attention, shoulder to shoulder, in full dress uniform. All wore sidearms and grim countenances.

All the seats in the auditorium had been removed, forcing the generals to stand. Shelton explained that in Taylor's new military, its leaders would stand like men, not sit like schoolchildren. But this was a lie, one of many Shelton had spun in the three days since Taylor's death. In truth, Lima had dictated the generals not sit but stand. Shelton looked out at their faces, so many familiar to him, and shuddered at the realization of what he was about to do. He glanced at George and Lima, standing no more than ten feet to his right in the shadows of the stage wing.

Shelton wiped the sweat from his face, then cleared his throat into the microphone. The audience quieted.

"Sirs, may I have your attention. On behalf of General Taylor, First Citizen of these United States, I welcome you to the inaugural bi-annual gathering of the General Officers of the U.S. Armed Forces."

Shelton told the generals that Taylor was running late, and that he had authorized him to begin the meeting in his stead. He lied through introductory comments and fabricated administrative matters. He said how this meeting would mark a new day for all of them, and that the drastic changes it would bring were necessary for the survival of the military they all loved. This part was true. Shelton believed it to his core. It was the reason he now stood at the rostrum.

Shelton signaled the colonels. The auditorium doors swung open. Wheeled carts entered.

"We start a new tradition this morning," Shelton said. "Whiskey and cider are being served. Please take one, face the flag, and join me and General Taylor in a toast to our country, our flag, and our beloved military. Combatant Commanders, please join us in this toast."

Shelton paused as the drinks were distributed. All took a glass, as no general in his right mind would refuse such a toast to flag and country, particularly when doing so would mark one an enemy of the state. Thousands of such enemies had already disappeared from government ranks at the hand of Taylor.

Shelton had hidden his glass behind the rostrum before the start of the meeting. He now raised this glass toward the American flag. "To new beginnings," he said, then downed the contents in one big gulp. He grimaced, then spun toward George and Lima, eyes wide with fear.

Lima leaned into George. "I put bitters in his cider," he whispered.

"Luiz!"

George mouthed "It's okay," smiled sheepishly, and gave Shelton the double thumbs-up.

Shelton eyed Lima. He mouthed a protracted "Fuck you" as the initial notes of the national anthem swelled throughout the auditorium, then turned away and joined his audience in saluting the flag.

"Choose a job you love, and you'll never have to work a day in your life," Lima whispered.

George gawked at him. What type of man could joke at a time

like this? Lima was serene, ready for the game to start. It had been his idea from the beginning. He had convinced George as to its necessity, then strong-armed Shelton into compliance. And now it was done. No turning back.

All three men set their watches as the anthem ended.

As choreographed, Shelton looked off stage for a beat, then back to his audience.

"The general's staff has just informed me that he will be another fifteen minutes," Shelton announced. "Something unexpected has arisen, a matter to which only General Taylor can attend. He sends his apology."

Now came the hard part. For the next fifteen minutes Shelton must stall. Only then would it begin. He needed to dull the senses of the audience, hypnotize them into a trance. Shelton grabbed the remote and began the PowerPoint.

Time dragged. George's eyes remained locked on the audience. The PowerPoint was doing its job. The generals shuffled and yawned. Some engaged in sidebar conversations, many sporadically checked their watches. All looked bored; most looked annoyed. But George detected no alarm or fear, which was good.

The Cadre of Colonels that lined the auditorium were a different story, however. As the minutes ticked by, they grew more fidgety. Some trembled, some looked around wildly, but most just stared straight ahead. That empty thousand-yard stare.

Shelton droned on, his voice a mumble in George's head.

George glanced down at this watch: *14:06, 14:07, 14:08...*

Shelton turned to George with pleading eyes. George nodded grimly. Shelton's face fell.

"I have just been told that General Taylor has arrived," Shelton announced in a soft, wavering voice. He paused, eyes downcast. An awkward silence ensued, punctuated by coughing and other crowd noises.

Shelton steadied himself, and in a strong voice said, "Generals, it is my honor to introduce to you the First Citizen of these United States."

Boisterous applause sputtered to dead air as George took the stage.

The command "Double time, MARCH!" rang out. A group of colonels broke away from their positions and jogged down the side wall of the auditorium. Synchronized boot stomps resounded. They formed a picket line in front of the stage, their sidearms held in ready gun position. The remaining colonels around the auditorium took a step toward the generals and likewise raised their weapons as George adjusted the microphone.

"My name is George Nelson Moore. A generation ago, generals such as you created me. You created me to wins wars. To keep our nation safe. Or so you told yourselves. Bold, vainglorious men. Blinded by ego and ambition. Men with fluid ethics, weathervane men who allowed their compass to be set by the blowing wind. The crowd I see before me today is filled with such men. False men, who abandon their oaths and duty as it suits them."

The generals grumbled; isolated shouts lifted above the crowd.

"Silence!" George shouted, like the crack of a whip. He continued in a conversational tone. "Now, a generation after you created me, you have tried to destroy me. Perhaps it was envy, perhaps expediency. Perhaps you were simply following orders from General Taylor. No matter. It was you who created me, and it was your failure to destroy me that will be your undoing."

A general rushed the stage, his face contorted with anger. One of the colonels at the lip of the stage shot him dead. The crowd gasped; a handful of the generals fell to the floor and started to convulse.

"I see it is time," George said, "so I will be brief. Two days ago, I killed General Taylor. And fifteen minutes ago, I killed all of you. You die as traitors. To your country, your fellow citizens, and yourselves. Actor or witness, it matters not. You are equally culpable, and you will all meet the same fate."

More generals were now on the floor convulsing. The shrieking started.

"Everyone has their dare-to-be-great moment, that one opportunity to validate their existence in the world," George said. "I myself had such a moment recently, and my decision ultimately led me to you and this auditorium this morning. All of you had your opportunity when General Taylor declared himself First Citizen, but, unlike me, you all failed your test. I have struggled with this..." George's voice cracked with emotion. He paused, then began anew. "But a wise man has shown me that sometimes bad things must be done for the greater good." George looked upward, away from the macabre spectacle that was playing out in front of him. "May history and the American people forgive me for my role in what is about to happen."

George turned to the men that lined the auditorium. "Colonels— dismissed!" Into the camera he said, "Shoot and kill all combatant commanders now."

George then turned and walked off stage. Lima brushed past him, close enough for their shoulders to touch. Lima did not acknowledge him, but kept his eyes on his audience.

"George Moore, everybody!" Lima exclaimed into the microphone. "Let's all give George a hand for those truly inspiring words." Lima did a protracted slow clap, smiling as he scanned the audience. "Beautiful words. I've got goosebumps," he said with an exaggerated shudder and shrug of his shoulders.

The smile now slowly waned from Lima's face. In silence he stepped to the lip of the stage, drew his weapon, and started shooting.

Lima took his time; he was slow and laconic in his movements, moving with cold efficiency. As one does at a carnival shooting game. He reloaded several times; his empty magazines thudded on the carpet as he ejected them. Any general still standing got two—one to the body, one to the head. Some stood frozen in horror. Some ran for the exits, frantically pulling on locked doors. Some charged the stage in fury. Lima killed them all. One to the body, one to the head.

Once all the non-toasters were dispatched, Lima stepped back to the rostrum and began to speak into the microphone.

"I see that some of your colleagues refused my hospitality. And they have died for this transgression. But I can see the rest of you have drunk, and for that I thank you."

The colonels marched back into the auditorium, again took up their positions along the auditorium wall. Many more generals were now writhing on the floor. Screams of pain punctuated the moaning. Lima surveyed the growing pandemonium and smiled broadly.

"Vengeance is mine, and recompense, for the time when their foot shall slip; for the day of their calamity is at hand, and their doom comes swiftly," Lima said. "Old Testament. Deuteronomy, chapter thirty-two, verse thirty-five."

Shelton, in the wings next to George, turned away from the unfolding drama.

"How did you like your drinks?" Lima asked, as the comedian warms up his crowd. "A little bitter, yes? Strychnine is bitter, especially at ten times the lethal dose. And how fitting it is that you died toasting the flag of the country you betrayed. But let me not speak of poetry and paradox. Let me speak of what matters most to all of you at this moment."

The wailing and screaming grew louder now. George watched Shelton cover his ears and step deeper into the shadows. Lima shouted into the microphone over the din. His deadpan delivery remained unchanged.

"Strychnine turns off the 'off switches' to your muscles, causing severe muscle spasms throughout the body," he continued. "There is no antidote. You will all be dead in fifteen minutes. Sooner if you're lucky. You'll die of asphyxiation. Or your brain will tap out, or maybe you will simply die from exhaustion from all the convulsions. It's like the worst muscle cramp imaginable, times a million, in every muscle in your body, all at once."

George had thought he was prepared for this, but what he now witnessed could never be unseen. A giant mosh pit, with hundreds of generals in full dress uniform, all twitching and convulsing on the floor; a pile of screaming humanity. Bulging eyes, blue discolored faces, panting and gasping for air through locked jaws. Many were in the throes of horrific whole-body convulsions, as their nervous systems careened out of control. They arched upward, their arms clenched at their sides, with only their heels and the backs of their heads touching the hard cement of the auditorium floor.

Lima stood triumphant at center stage, the apex predator surveying his domain. A few of the colonels began weeping and shaking uncontrollably, abandoning their posts to wander among the convulsing generals, trying in vain to offer help. They did not escape Lima's scrutiny. One to the body, one to the head.

Shelton sat on the floor backstage, back against the wall, elbows on knees and head in hands. George considered going to his side, but did not. About two-thirds of the generals had stopped moving or making noise of any kind. George checked his watch: *27:42, 27:43, 27:44…*

Lima shielded his eyes with his hand. "We still have a few die-hards left in the crowd." He chuckled mirthlessly at his own joke. "I see you all smiling out there."

Strychnine poisoning caused the facial muscles to spasm into a ghoulish smile, known as *risus sardonicus,* or "sardonic grin."

"Now, my colleague, Mr. Shelton, has accused me of being excessively cruel. But he reads me wrong. Sure, potassium cyanide is quicker and more humane. But where's the fun in that? I've given you smiles! See how you dance on the floor?"

Shelton pulled his head out of his hands at the mention of his name. He stood up, fists balled up at his sides.

"But I am also a merciful man, and I have saved the best for last," Lima said. "I could let you all linger and die at my will, but under the circumstances that would be needlessly cruel. So—let's get this party started!"

Lima danced a pantomimed jig.

"The sooner you start dancing, the sooner your suffering will end in death's sweet embrace. I have the perfect song to kick us off. You guys are gonna to love this," he said, pointing at the remaining generals still writhing and moaning on the floor.

He surveyed the line colonels along the walls. "Feel free to join in. Today we all dance!"

Lima remained motionless, looking down at his feet. His left arm slowly rose, extended to ninety degrees. He pointed off stage, to the wing opposite George and Shelton.

This was not part of the plan. *What the hell is he doing?*

Lima stood bone still at middle stage, spotlit by the overhead lights. His head remained bowed. Both arms were now at his sides. A song began to play on the loudspeakers, at ear-ringing volume. First the melodic vocals, then the piano came in.

Lima snapped his head up, his hand holding an imaginary microphone to his lips. He beamed as the first verse of the song kicked in. He began to dance and lip-synch. George watched, dumbfounded. The most feared assassin on earth was doing his karaoke version of ABBA's "Dancing Queen."

It was a surreal sight. Lima danced rhythmically, his fluid movements in time with the melody. He moved with ethereal grace, surprising for a man of his size. He was utterly uninhibited, his face rapturous. His body was consumed by dance—all except the eyes, which remained dark and cold as they swept the auditorium from side to side.

The loud music caused intense convulsions in the remaining

generals still clinging to life. They would all be dead in minutes.

Shelton stood and tried to rush the stage. George wrestled him still.

"You don't want to do that," George said. "Let him be."

Shelton spit expletives.

"We didn't have to do it this way!" Shelton yelled. "Didn't have to kill them all." Shelton shook with anger. "This is a fucking massacre." He grimaced and gnashed his teeth.

"More people died on America's highways last week than did in this auditorium today," George said in a plaintive voice. "I deeply regret the suffering I have inflicted on the families of the men and woman who died here today. It sickens me and will haunt me for the rest of my life. But we had no other choice, Tim. All the generals sided with Taylor. If we hadn't done this operation, a cabal of generals loyal to Taylor would have surely formed and betrayed us."

"How do you know these colonels here today won't betray us?"

"That's your problem, Tim," George said. "You're head of the U.S. military now. I know you'll figure it out."

Shelton blew out a long breath.

"Tim, it's done. Time for you to get to work. Contact the colonels and make sure they have taken control of all the combatant commands. Then report back to me. Okay?"

Shelton nodded and left. George turned back to the stage.

The song ended. Lima stood silent and still in the middle of the stage. The twisted pile of bodies on the floor no longer moved. Lima closed his eyes, crossed and blessed himself. He walked off stage toward George, with a look of utter serenity on his face.

The two men stood together, then walked out of the auditorium and into the future.

Together.

CHAPTER 62

George and Lima walked single file down the long dark hallway. They were surrounded by large armed men. Two in the front, two behind. Different men than last time. Small children scurried behind locked doors as they approached.

Lima leaned over George's shoulder, whispered into his ear. "You sure about this?"

A beacon of light loomed before them in the distance. George felt its warmth, just as before. He smiled.

"No worries. We're good."

The four men posted up at the doorway and gestured them inside.

A flood of emotion stopped George in his tracks. It was just as he remembered it.

"Mr. George!" Nesha exclaimed. "Ooo-h, child. Look at you. It be good to see you again. Come here and give Nesha a kiss now."

George crossed the room and did as he was told. She grabbed his hand and wouldn't let go.

"Brought you two packs of Newports. Menthol Gold 100s, soft pack," George said.

"Thank you, baby. Just put them on the table over there. Come sit down with me." Nesha looked past George. "Who's this you bring with you?"

Grace emerged from behind George, stood next to him at Nesha's bedside. She arrived in DC just after the Pentagon operation, and had joined George and Lima just hours ago. George had been astonished to see her and had wept when she told him of her decision to leave Verity to join him. Flanagan had accepted her decision, she said, but George was uncertain. Flanagan had said nothing of this to George when he reported the results of the Pentagon operation to him, but George did sense a curtness in Flanagan's tone as they spoke. Lima took the big news surprisingly well, as if it was inevitable. But George could not focus on these things. Grace was by his side now. Forever. His heart soared.

George clasped Grace's hand and held it tight. She squeezed back.

"Nesha, this is Grace," George said, beaming. "We're... Well, we're together now."

Nesha snorted, which caused her to cough, a raspy, hacking sound. She lit a cigarette and took a deep pull as she gave Grace a long look up and down.

"Damn, you beautiful, girl. I had it goin' on back in the day myself, but shit..."

Grace smiled.

Nesha studied her. "Where you from?"

"I was raised by my grandma Mabel in West Oakland."

"I thought I saw a little street in you. When'd ya leave the hood?"

"I was eight."

"That's enough, then." Nesha drew deep on her Newport, turned her head and blew the smoke away from her guests. "I was raised by my G-Mama too. Right here in the Highlands. Been in the Gardens my whole life. Looks like you got out. Good for you, girl."

"I was lucky. But I'll always be Mabel's little girl from West Side."

Nesha smiled. "I like this girl, George. You betta lock this one down. Don't let her get away now."

Lima slid in next to Grace. George introduced him to Nesha. Lima extended his hand. She shook it.

"Luiz and I have been working closely together since I left the Gardens," George told her.

Nesha silently appraised Lima, then spoke. "You be keeping a good eye on Mr. George for Nesha?"

"Yes ma'am."

"You be messin' with JD?"

"We've worked together a little, yes," Lima replied.

"Me and JD are good. That's my big sexy man right there. He's the one came and got George up outta here. Never tells me shit, but lets me know George be all right."

Nesha stubbed out her Newport, lit another.

"So you three on the down low, need a place to shade?" Nesha asked. "What the hell you be doin', George?"

"I'm sorry. I wish I could tell you, Nesha, I really do. But I can't. Not right now."

"You been gone for months, and not a word from your ass. And then, outta nowhere, I see you all over the Internet, talking about being a clone and some shit."

There it was. Out in the open.

Nesha adjusted her huge thighs, rolled her hips so she faced George. "Is what you said true? Are you really George Washington?"

"Yeah, I'm afraid so."

"Fa-ril? Damn." Nesha laid her lit cigarette in the ashtray on the nightstand by the bed. The rising smoke spire twisted in the sunlight streaming through the window behind her. "I don't understand this shit, George. First you disappear, then you be some kinda clone, then this crazy-ass Taylor puts a death warrant on you, then the country falls out—"

"I know," George said. "I'm doing the best I can with it. I've got some really good people behind me on this; two are with me in this room right now. There are others. JD's with us. And we have a plan. It just might work. We'll know tomorrow. But tonight, we need a place to stay. I'm sorry to put you in this, Nesha. They're watching JD, and I had no one else here I could trust."

"You don't worry, baby. Ain't nobody gonna mess with you in the Gardens. They come up in here looking for you, they gonna get some. Mmmm-hhhhmmm."

George squeezed Nesha's hand.

"I always knew you be different, George, from the first time I set eyes on you," Nesha said. "I ain't never gonna understand any of this clone shit, but if you tell me you be George Washington, I believe you. Whether you are or not, ain't no matter. You always be Mr. George to me."

There was a loud knock on the door. Lima spun around as a little man with a full gold grill bounded past him into the room. He went straight for George.

"Dwayne!"

"White boy George!" Dwayne went in for a hug. "Man, good to see you again. How ya been, man?"

"Pretty good. You?"

"Still keepin' these hall rats correct. Right hand to the queen, ya know? Got my shit locked down tight."

"How's my old room?"

"Same as you left it," Dwayne said. "Shitty. At least it smells better now that your raggedy ass outta there. Maybe now we'll turn it into a museum or some shit." He turned to Grace. "Hey… hey! Who is this *fine* woman?"

George made the introduction. Grace leaned over and kissed Dwayne on the cheek. His eyes widened.

"Thank you for taking such good care of George while he was here," Grace said.

"You be with him?" Dwayne squealed, jerking a thumb at George. "Damn! I can tell you some stories about him. What you see in this white boy, anyhow? Now that you got this beautiful four-eleven block of black granite standing right in front of you? You know I'm full size all over, right? I can take care of business now."

Grace laughed. "Well, if this don't work out, I'll give you a call, Dwayne."

Dwayne winked at George. "Who's the scary dude?"

"Luiz," Lima said, extending his hand.

Dwayne shook it. "Bodyguard, right?"

"Something like that."

Dwayne nodded.

"What's all this Father of Our Country bullshit, George?" Dwayne asked. "This country's a motherfuckin' orphan right now. You better get on out there and fix this shit."

"I'll see what I can do, Dwayne. If I need a hand, I'll look you up."

"I got mad skills; you know that. Sneaky as fuck, too. My ass gets away with everything. Nobody ever suspects the dwarf. Remember that, George."

Nesha called Dwayne to her bedside and whispered something in his ear. He harrumphed as he looked around the room at the three guests, then bid them adieu and left the room.

Nesha motioned for Lima to close the door, which he did. All three stood gathered around her bed. Her face was serious now.

"What's the matter, George? What kinda trouble are you in, baby?"

George struggled to answer. What to say? Much to his relief, Grace had told him they still held Flanagan's loyalty. But who else? Shelton and the military? He was counting on this, but that alliance was just hours old. If it held, law enforcement would follow the military. Congress and the courts had been rendered impotent under Taylor, so posed no threat. The American people were the last remaining puzzle piece. If George could gain their support tomorrow, they would survive. If not, they would all perish.

"Check the Internet tomorrow," George said.

"I be on the Internet every day, all day—you know that," Nesha said.

"Just Google my name, about noon or so. You'll see."

Nesha gave him a hard look.

"I need you to watch what happens tomorrow."

"Okay, child. I'll be watchin'."

CHAPTER 63

"ETA in five minutes, Mr. Lima," the pilot said over the noise of the Bell 525's rotor blades. It was the same model, different version, of the helicopter that had brought George blindfolded to Verity Island almost four months earlier. Flanagan had a flying armada of five such helicopters.

The helicopter had picked them up before dawn at the Gardens. It had touched down inside the abandoned water fountain that fronted the building, a Great Society ghost now cracked and empty. Lima had wanted them out before sunrise, while the building and neighborhood still slept. They had said their goodbyes to Nesha the night before.

From the Gardens, they went to a nearby secluded area, where they had watched the sunrise to this historic day. There they waited for several hours until departure time: 8:45 a.m. (EDT). George had spent the time going over his notes and trying to relax. Lima was in perpetual motion, talking to Verity Command Center, conferring with the pilots and his on-site team, and keeping George in sight. JD stayed by George's side, while Grace and Cabot kept each other distracted.

They had been in the air now for about ten minutes, heading due east toward the National Mall, where it had all started.

"Think anyone will show up?" George asked.

"Mr. Flanagan has personally seen to all the details," Lima said. "Our little party will be well attended."

"And Shelton. Does he have the military—"

"Yes, George. This is my operation. You're the guest of honor. Sit back and relax."

George looked out the window and tried to slow his breathing. Getting closer now.

"ETA two minutes, Mr. Lima. We are cleared for touchdown."

George tilted his head back. His knees began to bounce up and down. A large hand clamped down on his thigh.

"You got this, dude," JD said. "All you gotta do is not fuck it up."

A deep rumble sounded off in the distance. It grew louder. George felt it as much as heard it, even over the din of the rotor blades.

"Game time, people!" Lima announced.

The helicopter descended to 500 feet, then accelerated laterally. They buzzed the U.S. Supreme Court building, then passed just north of the rebuilt U.S. Capitol Dome, which loomed large in the windows. Past the dome they saw—*millions of people… everywhere.* All along the full two-mile length of the National Mall, from the U.S. Capitol Reflecting Pool all the way to the Lincoln Memorial. Crammed into the Tidal Basin. They surrounded the White House, stood shoulder to shoulder in the Ellipse and Presidential Park. The same for the war memorials.

At the sight of the helicopter, all two million people roared as one.

"Oh my God," Grace whispered.

The helicopter did three circles around the Washington Monument. The crowd went wild, began to surge forward against the troops guarding the stone circle at the base of the monument. The troops stood shoulder to shoulder facing the crowd. Lima's men stood at their backs, facing inward toward the monument itself. From the air, the stone circle looked like a small island in a sea of humanity. Huge flat-screen monitors and loudspeakers had been placed all over the area. A long ten-foot-high dais was tucked up against the west side of the monument. By George's order, the fifty flags that lined the circumference of the stone circle flew inverted, union down.

As the pilot finished the third pass, he swooped down and landed in the stone circle, directly next to the monument, on the south side facing west. George's stomach dropped as the landing skids set down with a thump. He swallowed hard and wiped the sweat from his forehead, glad he had followed Grace's advice to shed the tie.

Lima slid open the side door. He pointed at George. "You stay with me," he ordered, then pointed to the others. "Go! Go! Go!"

Cabot was the first to leave. As he drew closer George saw strength, not fear, on his face. His eyes gleamed with firm resolve. He embraced George tightly. Lima slapped Cabot on the back. He stepped off the helicopter, and one of Lima's men escorted him to his place on the dais. JD reminded George not to fuck up, gave him a bracing hug, and bounded out the door.

Grace approached last, her expression loving and unflinching. She took George's face in her hands; her eyes searched his.

"Enjoy this." Grace kissed him tenderly. Then she turned and was gone.

Lima and George were now alone. Lima shouted instructions over the boom of the rotor blades. He would follow George to the dais; one of his men would lead the way.

Lima asked if he was ready. George gave him the double thumbs-up.

"You got this." For the first time, Lima embraced George, a tender hug filled with genuine emotion. George drew strength from it.

Lima stacked behind George at the door. When his man took point position, Lima slapped George on the back and shouted "Go!" George jumped from the helicopter onto the stone circle. He watched the helicopter take off and quickly gain altitude, up and over the Washington Monument, which loomed much larger now that he was standing at its base. George felt the sheer force of the crowd's energy as he walked slowly toward the dais.

George mounted the steps, steadying himself on the handrail. A tall rostrum stood in the center, flanked by a table on both sides. Lima, Grace, and Cabot sat to George's right, JD and Shelton at his left. Shelton, resplendent in his dress uniform and four new stars, stood and saluted George as he approached. George returned it as best he knew. It was something he was going to have to get used to.

George grabbed each side of the rostrum and held on; the Lincoln Memorial was clearly visible straight ahead, one mile distant. The crowd, still clapping and cheering, extended as far as he could see. The cacophony enveloped him from all sides.

Boom! George jumped at the explosion, awaited the impact that never came. *Boom!* Another, then another. Twenty-one in all. He saw smoke rising from a cannon in the distance and chuckled. Shelton had surprised them all by honoring George with a twenty-one-gun salute. George watched the color slowly return to Lima's face. Shelton gestured to Lima, a smirk on his face. *Dancing Queen payback.*

The twenty-one cannon shots were followed by a rendition of "Hail to the Chief" by the military band and honor guard. As the final notes were played, a tight formation of fighter jets roared in from the west. They came in low, over the Lincoln Memorial and straight at George. The noise was deafening. George's insides clenched. They passed overhead, down the National Mall, and over the U.S. Capitol. Just a ceremonial military fly-over, George told himself. He hadn't been vaporized. Perhaps his alliance with Shelton would work out after all.

George called for quiet from the crowd. It was like taming a bucking bronco, but after several minutes he had their attention. He took a deep breath, and in a strong, steady voice, began to speak.

The speech came to be known as the "Second Revolution Address." It was compared to the Gettysburg Address, as if anything could ever equal the eloquence of those 272 words.

Unlike Lincoln, who spoke of preservation, George spoke of independence, of starting anew. The founders' "Grand Experiment" had run its course. George had no intention of resuscitating it. It was time for another approach.

As with Pearl Harbor, JFK's assassination, and Allen's bombing, future generations of Americans would regale their grandchildren with stories of where they were and what they did this day—October 9, 2021, the day the Second Revolution was born. A couple of million lucky Americans could say they were there to bear witness to the rebirth of America.

As he looked out over the cheering crowd at the end of his address, George thought of Josh Allen. The patriot who had started it all. Not with words, but with action. George wished he were here to see all this.

But his last thought before he left the rostrum was of what Grace had said to him.

Enjoy this.

CHAPTER 64

Friday, January 20, 2023, 9:00 p.m. (EST)
State of the Union Address; House Chamber/Joint Session
Washington, DC

It was the one-year anniversary of George swearing his oath of office as the 46th President of the United States. Tonight, per tradition, he was delivering the State of the Union Address to both chambers of Congress.

He had abandoned many more traditions than he had kept in his year as president. George had been true to his word, and had held a general election within ninety days of his now hallowed Second Revolution Address. The people had rewarded him with a landslide victory, with over 70 percent of the popular vote.

In office, George had leveraged Verity technology to directly connect to the citizens he governed. He had established personal relationships, albeit digital ones, with hundreds of millions of people. FDR fireside video chats for the twenty-first century. No media or other special interest between him and the people; no one to skew or falsify his message. He spoke unfettered and unfiltered. The American people loved it, and they loved their new president. George's approval ratings consistently hovered around 80 percent, but he had no need for polls or pundits. He had an ongoing dialogue with the American people. He already knew what they thought and felt.

George stood at the lectern and waited out the nervous applause. He had reinstated Congress and the courts, after General Taylor had eviscerated both, but each institution cast a wary eye on the new president. George owned the hearts of the people. And the people could no longer be manipulated or pandered into victimhood. Elections would no longer be won at the shallow end of the voting pool.

George started by thanking the American people, then his audience. He then began to introduce his special guests, to more nervous applause.

Grace stood, looking stunning in red. She acknowledged the crowd with a wave of her hand and a tight smile. She and George had been married on Verity, with Flanagan's blessing, four months after the Second Revolution Address. She was an active First Lady, particularly as an advocate for the inner-city poor. She often joined George in his video chats with the American people. Her approval ratings matched his.

Cabot, wearing the Presidential Medal of Freedom he had received earlier that day, beamed next to his wife Helen. General Shelton stood next. He wore his four stars well. JD wore a robin's-egg blue Vicuna wool suit that cost more than the car he drove, a gift from Flanagan. JD found the television cameras, and they loved him.

Lima and Flanagan remained anonymous, the former hidden among the Secret Service detail, the latter ensconced on Verity Island.

There were, however, two Verity Islanders in the crowd: the sweeper Bai Zhou and his son, Cheng. Flanagan had broken protocol and approved their attendance. They stood wide-eyed as the applause washed over them, the father's smile tinged with fear, the son's with wonder.

George then called for a moment of silence for the two patriots who were not there on this night—Josh Allen and Virginia Dare. George had had Allen exhumed and buried with full military honors at Arlington National Cemetery, not far from JFK's burial site. Allen's posthumous Medal of Honor was buried with him, and George visited his gravesite often. George had tasked Lima to attend to Orlando Rodriguez, the cowardly cop who suffocated Allen while he lay restrained in his hospital bed. Lima killed Rodriguez on the same day Allen was interned at Arlington. Made him watch the whole thing as he died.

George spoke with emotion about Virginia. Her courage and sacrifice. Her role in TRENTON, and later the Second Revolution. Her new star on the CIA Memorial Wall. Her place in his heart.

With these introductions complete, George launched into the substance of his address.

First up were national security and control of the military. Two volatile topics, as he was now addressing a Congress that had failed to curb the military dictatorship impulses of General Taylor. The apostates Taylor and Parker were dead. So was the entire general officer staff of the U.S. military, a draconian but altogether necessary measure to regain civilian control of the armed forces. George spoke with humility and emotion. He asked for the forgiveness of the American people, and they gave it to him. He gave himself a presidential pardon, then informed Congress after the fact. They grumbled, some grandstanded, but in the end, there was nothing they could do.

General Shelton had grown into his role quickly, and he and George enjoyed a productive relationship, bordering on friendship. Shelton had had to weed out a few remaining Taylor hardliners from the ranks, but the past year had been stable. The military again answered to civilian leadership, and the world had the good sense not to challenge this commander-in-chief.

George had dramatically reshaped the government in his first year as president. He had replaced the old congressional leadership, via petition and recall voting, and the people had put in new leaders who were committed to their Second Revolution. Activist judges were replaced. Constitutional amendments were ratified to add term limits and prohibit special-interest lobbying. Corruption became a capital offense. The country converted to the metric system.

The Internal Revenue Code, with its bloated eight thousand pages of insidious and needless complexity, was eliminated, replaced by a flat tax of 10 percent collected electronically each January 1st. George broke out his red pen and balanced the budget in six months by ruthlessly slashing pork, graft, and inefficiencies in entitlements and military spending. He handled the nation's budget as the average American did their checkbook, and relied on his Cabinet advisors (Flanagan recommendations all) for economic and financial nuance. Government was shrunk to its proper size. The nation again became a meritocracy. Some took advantage and got rich for all the wrong reasons. Others refused to participate at all, and expressed themselves with violence. The law addressed both ends of this bell curve with equal vigor. Most Americans bought in and thrived. The economy recovered, then soared. Foreign markets responded. America again sat at the head of the global economy table.

George also called out the nation's continued dependence on fossil fuel for the national disgrace it was. On this night, and with all the flair of Willy Wonka, he announced a government-funded super-contest. He challenged every American to create the new sustainable energy source that would power America into the future. This contest would end five years from the date of announcement. The first person to perfect a new energy source meeting or exceeding all stated requirements would be awarded a prize of fifty billion dollars, tax exempt, and have a national holiday named after them. This super-contest created the frenzy George had anticipated: incentivized American ingenuity was a powerful thing. He expected he'd have to pay out, and looked forward to it.

He finished his first State of the Union Address with a controversial topic, one that had captivated the minds of most Americans: the Wyoming Project. With help from Grace, Cabot, and Lima, George had convinced Flanagan to do the one thing he desperately wanted—scale Verity in the modern world. George had given him the State of Wyoming as his blank canvas. Once convinced, Flanagan had thrown himself and all his resources into the Project. From there, it had moved apace.

Wyoming had been carefully selected. It was the least populated of the fifty states, and the nation's tenth largest, with vast amounts of federal land that could be easily converted. All told, about 600,000 people were relocated to their state of choice and paid a tax-exempt relocation stipend. All private businesses and land were nationalized, with owners cashed out at market rate. Surprisingly few residents resisted, and the few who did were forcibly removed. The military established a secure perimeter around the entire state once it was empty.

Wyoming scaled nicely with Verity, at a factor of 60x; that is, it was sixty times larger than what Flanagan had accomplished on Verity Island. The base-ten baojia societal system remained unchanged: ten central cities on Verity became sixty in Wyoming; ten villages became six hundred; and the number of individual tribes increased from one hundred on Verity to six thousand in Wyoming. In the end, Wyoming would still have 600,000 citizens, but they would live under Verity law.

The American people followed the Wyoming Project online with rapt attention. It became a grand reality show of sorts. The Project had its vocal critics, most shrill slippery-slopers forecasting end times. But in the Second Revolution, these charlatans were marginalized.

Because in the Second Revolution, the tail no longer wagged the dog.

CHAPTER 65

George slouched in his chair in the Oval Office, his tie and first button undone, long legs jutted out in repose. To his right sat Grace, her red dress displaying a hint of thigh over perfectly crossed legs. Two plush taupe sofas were separated by a low table, forming a casual seating area by the marble fireplace. Lima and JD sat on the sofa to George's right; Cabot was alone on the left sofa closest to Grace. All still wore their State of the Union attire, and all were glad the address was over.

The objectively ludicrous had become George's new normal since that fateful day when Cabot had sat him down on that Boston Garden bench and dropped his bombshell. He'd carried it around like a second shadow ever since. He straightened up in his chair.

"You know," he said, "it's been two years since Josh Allen blew up the Capitol. We all wouldn't be here without him." George raised his glass. "So—here's to Josh."

They clinked glasses and drank.

"We are our country's two greatest terrorists, he and I," George said. "He took out the political leadership, I the military. He started the Second Revolution; I finished it."

"One man's terrorist is another man's freedom fighter," JD said. "Someone smarter than me said that once. Henry, a little help?"

Cabot shook his head. "So many innocent lives lost."

"Innocence is a tricky thing, Henry," Lima said. "Most evil men think themselves innocent of their offenses, do they not?"

"I suppose they do, Luiz." Cabot sighed. "I've just grown weary of all the death." He stood and shuffled away from the group.

"George, pay it no attention," Lima said. "Let the politicians and philosophers talk. History is made by real men. Men of action. You and Josh Allen are such men."

A surge of nervous energy brought George to his feet. He stretched and stepped behind his chair to face the fireplace and the portrait of Washington over the mantel. The general wore his blue and pale yellow coat, his full martial bearing on display in half-profile. George studied it. The same deep-set grayish blue eyes, thick flat nose, and strong jaw. Not quite a mirror, but enough to send a shiver down George's spine.

Cabot stood at the French door that opened to the Rose Garden, looking out at the soft falling snow. George crossed the room to join him.

"You all right, Henry?" he asked.

"Just thinking." Cabot looked over his shoulder, paused, then turned back. "Daniel has no issue with you and Grace being together. He—"

"I know. He told me."

"Daniel is… different from most men. He loved Grace dearly, but in his own way. Still does."

Cabot's eye wandered to the artwork on the wall, to the right of the French door. He drew forward to examine it more closely. It was modern and minimalistic, red blotches thrown against a white canvas. It contrasted starkly with the rest of the décor in the Oval Office.

"Grace says it clashes with the room, but I like it in here."

"Luiz is a talented artist."

George's eyes widened. "You know?"

"Luiz and I are quite close, and more alike than you imagine."

Cabot adjusted his glasses. "George, I have something important I need to speak with you about." He guided George further away from the rest of the group and dropped his voice to a whisper. "What if I told you that TRENTON was a ruse? That you are not General Washington? That you are not a clone at all?"

George's knees buckled and he gasped for breath. "What the hell are you saying, Henry?"

Cabot paused to gather himself, then continued in a rushed, breathy voice. "The scientists could never get it to work right. So the Pentagon located you, as a newborn infant, and TRENTON continued. They matched you to General Washington as best we could. Pretty good job too, I must say. Only a few of us knew. All dead now, except me. The rest believed you to be Washington. Virginia most of all. It turned out it was a lot easier to convince people of cloning than it was to accomplish the actual cloning itself."

George spun away from Cabot, who grabbed hold of his arm with surprising strength.

"Oh, you should have seen the effect you had on people then, George. I never forgot it. I intended to take this secret to my grave, but then General Taylor emerged, and—"

"And you got your precious republic back... and Flanagan got Wyoming... and I got screwed!"

"You got what you wanted all along, George—Taylor's blood on your hands."

George's breathing became ragged, and he steadied himself on the edge of the presidential desk.

"Why now, Henry? Goddamn it! Why tell me now?"

"I am an old man, George." Cabot's voice wavered. "I have not forgiven myself for Virginia's death. I simply cannot have this secret on my conscience too." He sniffed, then swiped brusquely at his nose. "I'm sorry, George. Sorry I got you involved in all this. You were my indispensable man. I felt it was the only way."

George choked up. "And Virginia? She knew about—"

"No! She knew nothing. She birthed a baby as any surrogate would. She did not know anything about the DNA of the fetus she carried in her womb. She thought what we wanted her to think— that she'd birthed the world's first human clone. We swapped you for the baby she birthed. A cheap magician's trick. She never knew. To her death, she believed she gave birth to George Washington. You."

"Do they know?" George motioned to the group across the room.

"No. Just Daniel and I. And now you."

"Grace?"

"No."

"But she came to the bar before you even told me about Flanagan."

"I went to Daniel when General Taylor threw the president out of the White House."

"You went behind my back to Flanagan? Without telling me?"

"It was the only way."

"Then why did we pitch Taylor? Why not have Flanagan's men kill him from the start?"

"Daniel is a calculating man. He would not be rushed into this. He insisted on due diligence. That's why he sent Grace to the bar. Why he allowed me to approach Taylor. I tried to avoid all this bloodshed. I really did."

George looked across the room to the group for a long moment. Grace smiled back and gave him a quizzical look.

"And Mount Vernon?"

"Dr. Bruce Morgan, the world-renowned Harvard scientist who

publicly validated your DNA test results, is a dear friend of mine. And you met Margaret Warner. They both loathed Taylor and were eager to help. Neither knew anything about TRENTON. And of course, between the two, only Bruce knew the DNA test results were false."

"Taylor's men? The dead British scientist?"

"We had to make you believe, George."

"What the hell am I supposed to do now?" George clenched his jaw, his eyes narrowed. "I'm the goddamned president. What am I supposed to tell the American people?"

"Let them believe. As I let you believe, George. Belief led to the overthrow of a tyrant and the restoration of our republic. The truth is of no use to them now."

"You lied to me, Henry! I trusted you, and you betrayed me."

"I had to lie; don't you see? When I came for you, you were destitute. You didn't believe in yourself. You'd lost your faith. So I lied. This lie is what got you here—got all of us here. This lie made you believe you were him—General Washington. At this point, can you honestly claim that it matters that you are not? This is the lesson we learned from TRENTON. It was the *belief*, not the science, that proved most powerful."

Cabot followed George's eyes back to the group. Lima was watching them intently, while the others blithely chatted, oblivious.

Cabot stepped closer to George. "Luiz is a spiritual man," he said. "He believes God speaks to him through his art, and that God led him to you. I believe he will find what he seeks, for any belief, staunchly held, becomes one's truth." Cabot smiled as he looked deep into George's eyes. "And I staunchly believe what I did was right."

Cabot straightened, then cocked his chin high. "I guess Daniel was right," he said. "'*Sometimes bad things must be done for the greater good.*'"

The old man strode back to the sofa to sit with the others, with a spring in his step that had been missing for years.

Government is not reason, it is not eloquence, it is force; like fire, a troublesome servant and a fearful master. Never for a moment should it be left to irresponsible action.

— George Washington

AFTERWORD

I hope you enjoyed my first novel, *First Citizen*. The book that took five years to write and a lifetime to conceive.

Let's stay in touch. Click here (https://rickbosworth.link/verityguide) to sign up for my newsletter and receive my exclusive *Author's Guide to Verity Island*, a slick twenty-nine page handbook of everything you want to know about Verity Island—with pictures!

Visit my website (https://www.rickbosworth.com) to see all things me, including updates and exclusives on my next novel titled *Talion Justice*, the first book in my new Frank Luce series scheduled for publication in the first quarter of 2020.

And lastly, if you enjoyed this book, please consider leaving a review on my Amazon book page. It would help other readers find the book, and would also really make my day.

Enjoy.

ACKNOWLEDGEMENTS

Writing and self-publishing a first novel—particularly one the breadth and depth of *First Citizen*—is like climbing Mt. Everest. Wearing a bathing suit. In a blizzard. Blind. Luckily I had the help of a few good sherpas on my way to the summit.

First, to my family and friends who were kind enough to serve as my beta-readers: Mary Bosworth; Tracy Downey; Laurie Bosworth; Annette Gregory; Leslie Pickard; George Dobberstein; Kim Currie. You all unselfishly gave me your time and effort in reading through my rough first draft, and your feedback made this book better. I am forever grateful.

Next, to my line and copy editor, Jennifer McIntyre, who gave me a great edit and was a delight to work with. Being a newbie author can be overwhelming at times, and Jennifer's kindness and encouragement was just what I needed to keep climbing.

And to my proofreader, Lisa Gilliam, whose sharp eyes added necessary polish to this book and prevented numerous author miscues from slipping through to the reader.

To my cover artist, Hillary Pickard, who graciously worked me into her crazy schedule and brought her keen artistic sense to my book cover design.

Any and all errors in the published version of this book are mine and mine alone.

The view from the summit is everything I thought it would be. And more.

Thank you all.

ABOUT THE AUTHOR

Rick Bosworth is an attorney and retired FBI agent who worked and supervised street gang, drug, terrorism, and intelligence cases in six different offices during his 25-year bureau career. He survived the L.A. Riots, South Central, and the Northridge Earthquake as a street agent, and paper cuts, endless meetings, and vexation as a squad supervisor and program manager. Rick has walked dark alleys and Beltway power corridors, arrested killer gang members and briefed Cabinet members, all the while asking himself the same two questions: Why? What if? His answers became the basis for his first novel, *First Citizen*, an entertaining philosophical political thriller that touches both heart and mind.

Rick lives with his wife on the shore of Lake Superior in Michigan's Upper Peninsula. When he is not writing, Rick enjoys hiking in the woods, good bourbon, and slapping at his acoustic guitar. See what he's up to at his website, https://www.rickbosworth.com.

Made in the USA
Monee, IL
20 November 2020